HIDDEN TRUTHS

NEW YORK TIMES BESTSELLING AUTHOR

TESS GERRITSEN

Previously published as *Whistleblower*
and *The Missing Twin*

Recycling programs for this product may not exist in your area.

ISBN-13: 978-1-335-40642-2

Hidden Truths
First published as Whistleblower in 1992.
This edition published in 2021.
Copyright © 1992 by Terry Gerritsen

The Missing Twin
First published in 2011. This edition published in 2021.
Copyright © 2011 by Rita B. Herron

This edition published by arrangement with Harlequin Books S.A.

For questions and comments about the quality of this book, please contact us at CustomerService@Harlequin.com.

Harlequin Enterprises ULC
22 Adelaide St. West, 40th Floor
Toronto, Ontario M5H 4E3, Canada
www.Harlequin.com

Printed in U.S.A.

CONTENTS

Internationally bestselling author **Tess Gerritsen** is a graduate of Stanford University and went on to medical school at the University of California, San Francisco, where she was awarded her MD. Since 1987, her books have been translated into thirty-seven languages, and more than twenty-five million copies have been sold around the world. She has received the Nero Wolfe Award and the RITA® Award, and she was a finalist for the Edgar Award. Now retired from medicine, she writes full-time. She lives in Maine.

Books by Tess Gerritsen

Call After Midnight
Under the Knife
Never Say Die
Whistleblower
Presumed Guilty
In Their Footsteps
Thief of Hearts
Keeper of the Bride

Visit the Author Profile page at
Harlequin.com for more titles.

WHISTLEBLOWER

Tess Gerritsen

Prologue

Branches whipped his face, and his heart was pounding so hard he thought his chest would explode, but he couldn't stop running. Already, he could hear the man gaining on him, could almost imagine the bullet slicing through the night and slamming into his back. Maybe it already had. Maybe he was trailing a river of blood; he was too numb with terror to feel anything now, except the desperate hunger to live. The rain was pouring down his face, icy, blinding sheets of it, rattling on the dead leaves of winter. He stumbled through a pool of darkness and found himself sprawled flat on his belly in the mud. The sound of his fall was deafening. His pursuer, alerted by the sharp crack of branches, altered course and was now headed straight for him. The thud of a silencer, the zing of a bullet past his cheek, told him he'd been spotted. He forced himself to his feet and made a sharp right, zigzagging back toward the highway. Here in the woods, he was a dead man. But if he could flag down a car, if he could draw someone's attention, he might have a chance.

A crash of branches, a coarse oath, told him his pursuer had stumbled. He'd gained a few precious seconds. He kept running, moving only by an instinctive sense of direction. There was no light to guide his way, nothing except the dim glow of the clouds in the night sky. The road had to be just ahead. Any second now, his feet would hit pavement.

And then what? What if there's no car to flag down, no one to help me?

Then, through the trees ahead, he saw a faint flickering, two watery beams of light.

With a desperate burst of speed, he sprinted toward the car. His lungs were on fire, his eyes blinded by the lash of branches and rain. Another bullet whipped past him and thudded into a tree trunk, but the gunman behind him had suddenly lost all importance. All that mattered was those lights, beckoning him through the darkness, taunting him with the promise of salvation.

When his feet suddenly hit the pavement, he was shocked. The lights were still ahead, bobbing somewhere beyond the trees. Had he missed the car? Was it already moving away, around a curve? No, there it was, brighter now. It was coming this way. He ran to meet it, following the bend of the road and knowing all the time that here in the open, he was an easy target. The sound of his shoes slapping the wet road filled his ears. The lights twisted toward him. At that instant, he heard the gun fire a third time. The force of the impact made him stumble to his knees, and he was vaguely aware of the bullet tearing through his shoulder, of the warmth of his own blood dribbling down his arm, but he was oblivious to pain. He could focus only on staying alive. He struggled back to his feet, took a stumbling step forward...

And was blinded by the onrush of headlights. There was no time to throw himself out of the way, no time even to register panic. Tires screamed across the pavement, throwing up a spray of water.

He didn't feel the impact. All he knew was that he was suddenly lying on the ground and the rain was pouring into his mouth and he was very, very cold.

And that he had something to do, something important.

Feebly, he reached into the pocket of his windbreaker, and his fingers curled around the small plastic cylinder. He couldn't quite remember why it mattered so much, but it was still there and he was relieved. He clutched it tightly in his palm.

Someone was calling to him. A woman. He couldn't see her face through the rain, but he could hear her voice, hoarse with panic, floating through the buzz in his head. He tried to speak, tried to warn her that they had to get away, that death was waiting in the woods. But all that came out was a groan.

Chapter 1

Three miles out of Redwood Valley, a tree had fallen across the road, and with the heavy rains and backed-up cars, it took Catherine Weaver nearly three hours to get past the town of Willits. By then it was already ten o'clock and she knew she wouldn't reach Garberville till midnight. She hoped Sarah wouldn't sit up all night waiting for her. But knowing Sarah, there'd be a supper still warm in the oven and a fire blazing in the hearth. She wondered how pregnancy suited her friend. Wonderfully, of course. Sarah had talked about this baby for years, had chosen its name—Sam or Emma—long before it was conceived. The fact she no longer had a husband was a minor point. "You can only wait around so long for the right father," Sarah had said. "Then you have to take matters into your own hands."

And she had. With her biological clock furiously

ticking its last years away, Sarah had driven down to visit Cathy in San Francisco and had calmly selected a fertility clinic from the yellow pages. A liberal-minded one, of course. One that would understand the desperate longings of a thirty-nine-year-old single woman. The insemination itself had been a coolly clinical affair, she'd said later. Hop on the table, slip your feet into the stirrups, and five minutes later, you were pregnant. Well, almost. But it was a simple procedure, the donors were certifiably healthy, and best of all, a woman could fulfill her maternal instincts without all that foolishness about marriage.

Yes, the old marriage game. They'd both suffered through it. And after their divorces, they'd both carried on, albeit with battle scars.

Brave Sarah, thought Cathy. *At least she has the courage to go through with this on her own.*

The old anger washed through her, still potent enough to make her mouth tighten. She could forgive her ex-husband Jack for a lot of things. For his selfishness. His demands. His infidelity. But she could never forgive him for denying her the chance to have a child. Oh, she could have gone against his wishes and had a baby anyway, but she'd wanted him to want one as well. So she'd waited for the time to be right. But during their ten years of marriage, he'd never been "ready," never felt it was the "right time."

What he should have told her was the truth: that he was too self-centered to be bothered with a baby.

I'm thirty-seven years old, she thought. *I no longer have a husband. I don't even have a steady boyfriend. But I could be content, if only I could hold my own child in my arms.*

At least Sarah would soon be blessed.

Four months to go and then the baby was due. Sarah's baby. Cathy had to smile at that thought, despite the rain now pouring over her windshield. It was coming down harder now; even with the wipers thrashing at full speed, she could barely make out the road. She glanced at her watch and saw it was already eleven-thirty; there were no other cars in sight. If she had engine trouble out here, she'd probably have to spend the night huddled in the backseat, waiting for help to arrive.

Peering ahead, she tried to make out the road's dividing line and saw nothing but a solid wall of rain. This was ridiculous. She really should have stopped at that motel in Willits, but she hated the thought of being only fifty miles from her goal, especially when she'd already driven so far.

She spotted a sign ahead: Garberville, 10 Miles. So she was closer than she'd thought. Twenty-five miles more, then there'd be a turnoff and a five-mile drive through dense woods to Sarah's cedar house. The thought of being so close fueled her impatience. She fed the old Datsun some gas and sped up to forty-five miles an hour. It was a reckless thing to do, especially in these conditions, but the thought of a warm house and hot chocolate was just too tempting.

The road curved unexpectedly; startled, she jerked the wheel to the right and the car slid sideways, tobogganing wildly across the rain-slicked pavement. She knew enough not to slam on the brakes. Instead, she clutched the wheel, fighting to regain control. The tires skidded a few feet, a heart-stopping ride that took her to the very edge of the road. Just as she thought she'd clip the trees, the tires gripped the pavement. The car was still moving twenty miles an hour, but at least it was headed in a straight line. With clammy hands, she managed to negotiate the rest of the curve.

What happened next caught her completely by surprise. One instant she was congratulating herself for averting disaster, the next, she was staring ahead in disbelief.

The man had appeared out of nowhere. He was crouched in the road, captured like a wild animal in the glare of her headlights. Reflexes took over. She slammed on the brakes, but it was already too late. The screech of her tires was punctuated by the thud of the man's body against the hood of her car.

For what seemed like eternity, she sat frozen and unable to do anything but clutch the steering wheel and stare at the windshield wipers skating back and forth. Then, as the reality of what she'd just done sank in, she shoved the door open and dashed out into the rain.

At first she could see nothing through the downpour, only a glistening strip of blacktop lit by the dim glow of her taillights. *Where is he?* she thought frantically. With water streaming past her eyes, she traced the road backward, struggling to see in the darkness. Then, through the pounding rain, she heard a low moan. It came from somewhere off to the side, near the trees.

Shifting direction, she plunged into the shadows and sank ankle-deep in mud and pine needles. Again she heard the moan, closer now, almost within reach.

"Where are you?" she screamed. "Help me find you!"

"Here…" The answer was so weak she barely heard it, but it was all she needed. Turning, she took a few steps and practically stumbled over his crumpled body in the darkness. At first, he seemed to be only a con-

fusing jumble of soaked clothes, then she managed to
locate his hand and feel for his pulse. It was fast but
steady, probably steadier than her own pulse, which was
skipping wildly. His fingers suddenly closed over hers
in a desperate grip. He rolled against her and struggled
to sit up.

"Please! Don't move!" she said.

"Can't—can't stay here—"

"Where are you hurt?"

"No time. Help me. Hurry—"

"Not till you tell me where you're hurt!"

He reached out and grabbed her shoulder in a clumsy
attempt to rise to his feet. To her amazement, he managed to pull himself halfway up. For an instant they
wobbled against each other, then his strength seemed
to collapse and they both slid to their knees in the mud.
His breathing had turned harsh and irregular and she
wondered about his injuries. If he was bleeding inter-
nally he could die within minutes. She had to get him
to a hospital now, even if it meant dragging him back
to the car.

"Okay. Let's try again," she said, grabbing his left
arm and draping it around her neck. She was startled by
his gasp of agony. Immediately she released him. His
arm left a sticky trail of warmth around her neck. *Blood.*

"My other side's okay," he grunted. "Try again."

She shifted to his right side and pulled his arm over
her neck. If she weren't so frantic, it would have struck
her as a comical scene, the two of them struggling like
drunkards to stand up. When at last he was on his feet
and they stood swaying together in the mud, she wondered if he even had the strength to put one foot in front
of the other. She certainly couldn't move them both.

Though he was slender, he was also a great deal taller than she'd expected, and much more than her five-foot-five frame could support.

But something seemed to compel him forward, a kindling of some hidden reserves. Even through their soaked clothes, she could feel the heat of his body and could sense the urgency driving him onward. A dozen questions formed in her head, but she was breathing too hard to voice them. Her every effort had to be concentrated on getting him to the car, and then to a hospital.

Gripping him around the waist, she latched her fingers through his belt. Painfully they made their way to the road, struggling step by step. His arm felt taut as wire over her neck. It seemed everything about him was wound up tight. There was something desperate about the way his muscles strained to move forward. His urgency penetrated right through to her skin. It was a panic as palpable as the warmth of his body, and she was suddenly infected with his need to flee, a need made more desperate by the fact they could move no faster than they already were. Every few feet she had to stop and shove back her dripping hair just to see where she was going. And all around them, the rain and darkness closed off all view of whatever danger pursued.

The taillights of her car glowed ahead like ruby eyes winking in the night. With every step the man grew heavier and her legs felt so rubbery she thought they'd both topple in the road. If they did, she wouldn't have the strength to haul him back up again. Already, his head was sagging against her cheek and water trickled from his rain-matted hair down her neck. The simple act of putting one foot in front of the other was so automatic that she never even considered dropping him on the road and backing the car to him instead. And the taillights were already so close, just beyond the next veil of rain.

By the time she'd guided him to the passenger side, her arm felt ready to fall off. With the man on the verge of sliding from her grasp, she barely managed to wrench the door open. She had no strength left to be gentle; she simply shoved him inside.

He flopped onto the front seat with his legs still hanging out. She bent down, grabbed his ankles, and heaved them one by one into the car, noting with a sense of detachment that no man with feet this big could possibly be graceful.

As she slid into the driver's seat, he made a feeble attempt to raise his head, then let it sink back again. "Hurry," he whispered.

At the first turn of the key in the ignition, the engine sputtered and died. Dear God, she pleaded. Start. *Start!* She switched the key off, counted slowly to three, and tried again. This time the engine caught. Almost shouting with relief, she jammed it into gear and made a tire-screeching takeoff toward Garberville. Even a town that small must have a hospital or, at the very least, an emergency clinic. The question was: could she find it in this downpour? And what if she was wrong? What if the nearest medical help was in Willits, the other direction? She might be wasting precious minutes on the road while the man bled to death.

Suddenly panicked by that thought, she glanced at her passenger. By the glow of the dashboard, she saw that his head was still flopped back against the seat. He wasn't moving.

"Hey! Are you all right?" she cried.

The answer came back in a whisper. "I'm still here."

"Dear God. For a minute I thought…" She looked back at the road, her heart pounding. "There's got to be a clinic somewhere—"

"Near Garberville—there's a hospital—"

"Do you know how to find it?"

"I drove past it—fifteen miles…"

If he drove here, where's his car? she thought. "What happened?" she asked. "Did you have an accident?"

He started to speak but his answer was cut off by a sudden flicker of light. Struggling to sit up, he turned and stared at the headlights of another car far behind them. His whispered oath made her look sideways in alarm.

"What is it?"

"That car."

She glanced in the rearview mirror. "What about it?"

"How long's it been following us?"

"I don't know. A few miles. Why?"

The effort of keeping his head up suddenly seemed too much for him, and he let it sink back down with a groan. "Can't think," he whispered. "Christ, I can't think…"

He's lost too much blood, she thought. In a panic, she shoved hard on the gas pedal. The car seemed to leap through the rain, the steering wheel vibrating wildly as sheets of spray flew up from the tires. Darkness flew at dizzying speed against their windshield. *Slow down, slow down! Or I'll get us both killed.*

Easing back on the gas, she let the speedometer fall to a more manageable forty-five miles per hour. The man was struggling to sit up again.

"Please, keep your head down!" she pleaded.

"That car—"

"It's not there anymore."

"Are you sure?"

She looked at the rearview mirror. Through the rain, she saw only a faint twinkling of light, but nothing as definite as headlights. "I'm sure," she lied and was relieved to see him slowly settle back again. *How much farther?* she thought. *Five miles? Ten?* And then the next thought forced its way into her mind: *He might die before we get there.*

His silence terrified her. She needed to hear his voice, needed to be reassured that he hadn't slipped into oblivion. "Talk to me," she urged. "Please."

"I'm tired…"

"Don't stop. Keep talking. What—what's your name?"

The answer was a mere whisper: "Victor."

"Victor. That's a great name. I like that name. What do you do, Victor?"

His silence told her he was too weak to carry on any conversation. She couldn't let him lose consciousness! For some reason it suddenly seemed crucial to keep him awake, to keep him in touch with a living voice. If that fragile connection was broken, she feared he might slip away entirely.

"All right," she said, forcing her voice to remain low and steady. "Then *I'll* talk. You don't have to say a thing. Just listen. Keep listening. My name is Catherine. Cathy Weaver. I live in San Francisco, the Richmond district. Do you know the city?" There was no answer, but she sensed some movement in his head, a silent acknowledgement of her words. "Okay," she went on, mindlessly filling the silence. "Maybe you don't know the city. It really doesn't matter. I work with an independent film company. Actually, it's Jack's company. My ex-husband. We make horror films. Grade B, really, but they turn a profit. Our last one was *Reptilian*. I did the special-effects makeup. Really gruesome stuff. Lots of green scales and slime…" She laughed—it was a strange, panicked sound. It had an unmistakable note of hysteria.

She had to fight to regain control.

A wink of light made her glance up sharply at the rearview mirror. A pair of headlights was barely discernible through the rain. For a few seconds she watched them, debating whether to say anything to Victor. Then, like phantoms, the lights flickered off and vanished.

"Victor?" she called softly. He responded with an unintelligible grunt, but it was all she needed to be reassured that he was still alive. That he was listening. *I've got to keep him awake,* she thought, her mind scrambling for some new topic of conversation. She'd never been good at the glib sort of chitchat so highly valued at filmmakers' cocktail parties. What she needed was a joke, however stupid, as long as it was vaguely funny. *Laughter heals.* Hadn't she read it somewhere? That a steady barrage of comedy could shrink tumors? *Oh sure,* she chided herself. *Just make him laugh and the bleeding will miraculously stop…*

But she couldn't think of a joke, anyway, not a single damn one. So she returned to the topic that had first come to mind: her work.

"Our next project's slated for January. *Ghouls.* We'll be filming in Mexico, which I hate, because the damn heat always melts the makeup…"

She looked at Victor but saw no response, not even a flicker of movement. Terrified that she was losing him, she reached out to feel for his pulse and discovered that his hand was buried deep in the pocket of his windbreaker. She tried to tug it free, and to her amazement he reacted to her invasion with immediate and savage resistance. Lurching awake, he blindly lashed at her, trying to force her away.

"Victor, it's all right!" she cried, fighting to steer the car and protect herself at the same time. "It's all right! It's me, Cathy. I'm only trying to help!"

At the sound of her voice, his struggles weakened. As the tension eased from his body, she felt his head settle slowly against her shoulder. "Cathy," he whispered. It was a sound of wonder, of relief. "Cathy…"

"That's right. It's only me." Gently, she reached up and brushed back the tendrils of his wet hair. She wondered what color it was, a concern that struck her as totally irrelevant but nonetheless compelling. He reached for her hand. His fingers closed around hers in a grip that was surprisingly strong and steadying. *I'm still here,* it said. *I'm warm and alive and breathing.* He pressed her palm to his lips. So tender was the gesture, she was startled by the roughness of his unshaven jaw against her skin. It was a caress between strangers, and it left her shaken and trembling.

She returned her grip to the steering wheel and shifted her full attention back to the road. He had fallen silent again, but she couldn't ignore the weight of his head on her shoulder or the heat of his breath in her hair.

The torrent eased to a slow but steady rain, and she coaxed the car to fifty. The Sunnyside Up cafe whipped past, a drab little box beneath a single streetlight, and she caught a glimpse of Victor's face in the brief glow of light. She saw him only in profile: a high forehead, sharp nose, a jutting chin, and then the light was gone and he was only a shadow breathing softly against her. But she'd seen enough to know she'd never forget that face. Even as she peered through the darkness, his profile floated before her like an image burned into her memory.

"We have to be getting close," she said, as much to reassure herself as him. "Where a cafe appears, a town is sure to follow." There was no response. "Victor?" Still no response. Swallowing her panic, she sped up to fifty-five.

Though they'd passed the Sunnyside Up over a mile ago, she could still make out the streetlight winking on and off in her mirror. It took her a few seconds to realize it wasn't just one light she was watching but two, and that they were moving—a pair of headlights, winding along the highway. Was it the same car she'd spotted earlier?

Mesmerized, she watched the lights dance like twin wraiths among the trees, then, suddenly, they vanished and she saw only darkness. A ghost? she wondered irrationally. Any instant she expected the lights to rematerialize, to resume their phantom twinkling in the woods. She was watching the mirror so intently that she almost missed the road sign:

Garberville, Pop, 5,750
Gas—Food—Lodging

A half mile later streetlights appeared, glowing a hazy yellow in the drizzle; a flatbed truck splashed by, headed in the other direction. Though the speed limit had dropped to thirty-five, she kept her foot firmly on the gas pedal and for once in her life prayed for a police car to give chase.

The *Hospital* road sign seemed to leap out at her from nowhere. She braked and swerved onto the turn-off. A quarter mile away, a red *Emergency* sign directed her up a driveway to a side entrance. Leaving Victor in the front seat, she ran inside, through a deserted waiting room, and cried to a nurse sitting at her desk: "Please, help me! I've got a man in my car..."

The nurse responded instantly. She followed Cathy outside, took one look at the man slumped in the front seat, and yelled for assistance.

Even with the help of a burly ER physician, they had difficulty pulling Victor out of the car. He had slid sideways, and his arm was wedged under the emergency hand brake.

"Hey, Miss!" the doctor barked at Cathy. "Climb in the other side and free up his arm!"

Cathy scrambled to the driver's seat. There she hesitated. She would have to manipulate his injured arm. She took his elbow and tried to unhook it from around the brake, but discovered his wristwatch was snagged in the pocket of his windbreaker. After unsnapping the watchband, she took hold of his arm and lifted it over the brake. He responded with a groan of pure agony. The arm slid limply toward the floor.

"Okay!" said the doctor. "Arm's free! Now, just ease him toward me and we'll take it from there."

Gingerly, she guided Victor's head and shoulders safely past the emergency brake. Then she scrambled back outside to help load him onto the wheeled stretcher. Three straps were buckled into place. Everything became a blur of noise and motion as the stretcher was wheeled through the open double doors into the building.

"What happened?" the doctor barked over his shoulder at Cathy.

"I hit him—on the road—"

"When?"

"Fifteen—twenty minutes ago."

"How fast were you driving?"

"About thirty-five."

"Was he conscious when you found him?"

"For about ten minutes—then he sort of faded—"

A nurse said: "Shirt's soaked with blood. He's got broken glass in his shoulder."

In that mad dash beneath harsh fluorescent lights, Cathy had her first clear look at Victor, and she saw a lean, mud-streaked face, a jaw tightly squared in pain, a broad forehead matted damply with light brown hair. He reached out to her, grasping for her hand.

"Cathy—"

"I'm here, Victor."

He held on tightly, refusing to break contact. The pressure of his fingers in her flesh was almost painful. Squinting through the pain, he focused on her face. "I have to—have to tell you—"

"Later!" snapped the doctor.

"No, wait!" Victor was fighting to keep her in view, to hold her beside him. He struggled to speak, agony etching lines on his face.

Cathy bent close, drawn by the desperation of his gaze. "Yes, Victor," she whispered, stroking his hair, longing to ease his pain. This link between their hands, their gazes, felt forged in timeless steel. "Tell me."

"We can't delay!" barked the doctor. "Get him in the room."

All at once, Victor's hand was wrenched away from her as they whisked him into the trauma suite, a nightmarish room of stainless steel and blindingly bright lights. He was lifted onto the surgical table.

"Pulse 110," said a nurse. "Blood pressure eight-five over fifty!"

The doctor ordered, "Let's get two IVs in. Type and cross six units of blood. And get hold of a surgeon. We're going to need help…"

The machine-gun fire of voices, the metallic clang of cabinets and IV poles and instruments was deafening. No one seemed to notice Cathy standing in the doorway, watching in horrified fascination as a nurse pulled out a knife and began to tear off Victor's bloody clothing. With each rip, more and more flesh was exposed, until the shirt and windbreaker were shredded off, revealing a broad chest thickly matted with tawny hair. To the doctors and nurses, this was just another body to labor over, another patient to be saved. To Cathy, this was a living, breathing man, a man she cared about, if only because they had shared those last harrowing moments. The nurse shifted her attention to his belt, which she quickly unbuckled. With a few firm tugs, she peeled off his trousers and shorts and threw them into a pile with the other soiled clothing. Cathy scarcely noticed the man's nakedness, or the nurses and technicians shoving past her into the room. Her shocked gaze had focused on Victor's left shoulder, which was oozing fresh blood onto the table. She remembered how his whole body had resonated with pain when she'd grabbed that shoulder; only now did she understand how much he must have suffered.

A sour taste flooded her throat. She was going to be sick.

Struggling against the nausea, she somehow managed to stumble away and sink into a nearby chair. There she sat for a few minutes, oblivious to the chaos whirling around her. Looking down, she noted with instinctive horror the blood on her hands.

"There you are," someone said. A nurse had just emerged from the trauma room, carrying a bundle of the patient's belongings. She motioned Cathy over to a desk. "We'll need your name and address in case the doctors have any more questions. And the police will have to be notified. Have you called them?"

Cathy shook her head numbly. "I—I guess I should…"

"You can use this phone."

"Thank you."

It rang eight times before anyone answered. The voice that greeted her was raspy with sleep. Obviously, Garberville provided little late-night stimulation, even for the local police. The desk officer took down Cathy's report and told her he'd be in touch with her later, after they'd checked the accident scene.

The nurse had opened Victor's wallet and was flipping through the various ID cards for information. Cathy watched her fill in the blanks on a patient admission form: *Name: Victor Holland. Age: 41. Occupation: Biochemist. Next of kin: Unknown.*

So that was his full name. Victor Holland. Cathy stared down at the stack of ID cards and focused on what appeared to be a security pass for some company called Viratek. A color photograph showed Victor's quietly sober face, its green eyes gazing straight into the camera. Even if she had never seen his face, this was exactly how she would have pictured him, his expression unyielding, his gaze unflinchingly direct. She touched her palm, where he had kissed her. She could still recall how his beard had stung her flesh.

Softly, she asked, "Is he going to be all right?"

The nurse continued writing. "He's lost a lot of blood. But he looks like a pretty tough guy…"

Cathy nodded, remembering how, even in his agony, Victor had somehow dredged up the strength to keep moving through the rain. Yes, she knew just how tough a man he was.

The nurse handed her a pen and the information sheet. "If you could write your name and address at the bottom. In case the doctor has any more questions."

Cathy fished out Sarah's address and phone number from her purse and copied them onto the form. "My name's Cathy Weaver. You can get hold of me at this number."

"You're staying in Garberville?"

"For three weeks. I'm just visiting."

"Oh. Terrific way to start a vacation, huh?"

Cathy sighed as she rose to leave. "Yeah. Terrific."

She paused outside the trauma room, wondering what was happening inside, knowing that Victor was fighting for his life. She wondered if he was still conscious, if he would remember her. It seemed important that he *did* remember her.

Cathy turned to the nurse. "You will call me, won't you? I mean, you'll let me know if he…"

The nurse nodded. "We'll keep you informed."

Outside, the rain had finally stopped and a belt of stars twinkled through a parting in the clouds. To Cathy's weary eyes, it was an exhilarating sight, that first glimpse of the storm's end. As she drove out of the hospital parking lot, she was shaking from fatigue. She never noticed the car parked across the street or the brief glow of the cigarette before it was snuffed out.

Chapter 2

Barely a minute after Cathy left the hospital, a man walked into the emergency room, sweeping the smells of a stormy night in with him through the double doors. The nurse on duty was busy with the new patient's admission papers. At the sudden rush of cold air, she looked up to see a man approach her desk. He was about thirty-five, gaunt-faced, silent, his dark hair lightly feathered by gray. Droplets of water sparkled on his tan Burberry raincoat.

"Can I help you, sir?" she asked, focusing on his eyes, which were as black and polished as pebbles in a pond.

Nodding, he said quietly, "Was there a man brought in a short time ago? Victor Holland?"

The nurse glanced down at the papers on her desk. That was the name. Victor Holland. "Yes," she said. "Are you a relative?"

"I'm his brother. How is he?"

"He just arrived, sir. They're working on him now. If you'll wait, I can check on how he's doing—" She stopped to answer the ringing telephone. It was a technician calling with the new patient's laboratory results. As she jotted down the numbers, she noticed out of the corner of her eye that the man had turned and was gazing at the closed door to the trauma room. It suddenly swung open as an orderly emerged carrying a bulging plastic bag streaked with blood. The clamor of voices spilled from the room:

"Pressure up to 110 over 70!"

"OR says they're ready to go."

"Where's that surgeon?"

"On his way. He had car trouble."

"Ready for X-rays! Everyone back!"

Slowly the door closed, muffling the voices. The nurse hung up just as the orderly deposited the plastic bag on her desk. "What's this?" she asked.

"Patient's clothes. They're a mess. Should I just toss 'em?"

"I'll take them home," the man in the raincoat cut in. "Is everything here?"

The orderly flashed the nurse an uncomfortable glance. "I'm not sure he'd want to… I mean, they're kind of…uh, dirty…"

The nurse said quickly, "Mr. Holland, why don't you let us dispose of the clothes for you? There's nothing worth keeping in there. I've already collected his valuables." She unlocked a drawer and pulled out a sealed manila envelope labeled: Holland, Victor. Contents: Wallet, Wristwatch. "You can take these home. Just sign this receipt."

The man nodded and signed his name: David Holland. "Tell me," he said, sliding the envelope in his pocket. "Is Victor awake? Has he said anything?"

"I'm afraid not. He was semiconscious when he arrived."

The man took this information in silence, a silence that the nurse found suddenly and profoundly disturbing. "Excuse me, Mr. Holland?" she asked. "How did you hear your brother was hurt? I didn't get a chance to contact any relatives…"

"The police called me. Victor was driving my car. They found it smashed up at the side of the road."

"Oh. What an awful way to be notified."

"Yes. The stuff of nightmares."

"At least someone was able to get in touch with you." She sifted through the sheaf of papers on her desk. "Can we get your address and phone number? In case we need to reach you?"

"Of course." The man took the ER papers, which he quickly scanned before scrawling his name and phone number on the blank marked Next of Kin. "Who's this Catherine Weaver?" he asked, pointing to the name and address at the bottom of the page.

"She's the woman who brought him in."

"I'll have to thank her." He handed back the papers.

"Nurse?"

She looked around and saw that the doctor was calling to her from the trauma room doorway. "Yes?"

"I want you to call the police. Tell them to get in here as soon as possible."

"They've been called, Doctor. They know about the accident—"

"Call them again. This is no accident."

"What?"

"We just got the X-rays. The man's got a bullet in his shoulder."

"A *bullet?*" A chill went through the nurse's body, like a cold wind sweeping in from the night. Slowly, she turned toward the man in the raincoat, the man who'd claimed to be Victor Holland's brother. To her amazement, no one was there. She felt only a cold puff of night air, and then she saw the double doors quietly slide shut.

"Where the hell did he go?" the orderly whispered.

For a few seconds she could only stare at the closed doors. Then her gaze dropped and she focused on the empty spot on her desk. The bag containing Victor Holland's clothes had vanished.

"Why did the police call again?"

Cathy slowly replaced the telephone receiver. Even though she was bundled in a warm terry-cloth robe, she was shivering. She turned and stared across the kitchen at Sarah. "That man on the road—they found a bullet in his shoulder."

In the midst of pouring tea, Sarah glanced up in surprise. "You mean—someone *shot* him?"

Cathy sank down at the kitchen table and gazed numbly at the cup of cinnamon tea that Sarah had just slid in front of her. A hot bath and a soothing hour of sitting by the fireplace had made the night's events seem like nothing more than a bad dream. Here in Sarah's kitchen, with its chintz curtains and its cinnamon and spice smells, the violence of the real world seemed a million miles away.

Sarah leaned toward her. "Do they know what happened? Has he said anything?"

"He just got out of surgery." She turned and glanced at the telephone. "I should call the hospital again—"

"No. You shouldn't. You've done everything you possibly can." Sarah gently touched her arm. "And your tea's getting cold."

With a shaking hand, Cathy brushed back a strand of damp hair and settled uneasily in her chair. A bullet in his shoulder, she thought. Why? Had it been a random attack, a highway gunslinger blasting out the car window at a total stranger? She'd read about it in the newspapers, the stories of freeway arguments settled by the pulling of a trigger.

Or had it been a deliberate attack? Had Victor Holland been targeted for death?

Outside, something rattled and clanged against the house. Cathy sat up sharply. "What was that?"

"Believe me, it's not the bogeyman," said Sarah, laughing. She went to the kitchen door and reached for the bolt.

"Sarah!" Cathy called in panic as the bolt slid open. "Wait!"

"Take a look for yourself." Sarah opened the door. The kitchen light swung across a cluster of trash cans sitting in the carport. A shadow slid to the ground and scurried away, trailing food wrappers across the driveway. "Raccoons," said Sarah. "If I don't tie the lids down, those pests'll scatter trash all over the yard." Another shadow popped its head out of a can and stared at her, its eyes glowing in the darkness. Sarah clapped her hands and yelled, "Go on, get lost!" The raccoon didn't budge. "Don't you have a home to go to?" At last, the raccoon dropped to the ground and ambled off into the trees. "They get bolder every year," Sarah sighed, closing the door. She turned and winked at Cathy. "So take it easy. This isn't the big city."

"Keep reminding me." Cathy took a slice of banana bread and began to spread it with sweet butter. "You know, Sarah, I think it'll be a lot nicer spending Christmas with you than it ever was with old Jack."

"Uh-oh. Since we're now speaking of ex-husbands—" Sarah shuffled over to a cabinet "—we might as well get in the right frame of mind. And tea just won't cut it." She grinned and waved a bottle of brandy.

"Sarah, you're not drinking alcohol, are you?"

"It's not for *me*." Sarah set the bottle and a single wine glass in front of Cathy. "But I think *you* could use a nip. After all, it's been a cold, traumatic night. And here we are, talking about turkeys of the male variety."

"Well, since you put it that way..." Cathy poured out a generous shot of brandy. "To the turkeys of the world," she declared and took a sip. It felt just right going down.

"So how *is* old Jack?" asked Sarah.

"Same as always."

"Blondes?"

"He's moved on to brunettes."

"It took him only a year to go through the world's supply of blondes?"

Cathy shrugged. "He might have missed a few."

They both laughed then, light and easy laughter that told them their wounds were well on the way to healing, that men were now creatures to be discussed without pain, without sorrow.

Cathy regarded her glass of brandy. "Do you think there *are* any good men left in the world? I mean, shouldn't there be *one* floating around somewhere?

Maybe a mutation or something? One measly decent guy?"

"Sure. Somewhere in Siberia. But he's a hundred-and-twenty years old."

"I've always liked older men."

They laughed again, but this time the sound wasn't as lighthearted. So many years had passed since their college days together, the days when they had *known,* had never doubted, that Prince Charmings abounded in the world.

Cathy drained her glass of brandy and set it down. "What a lousy friend I am. Keeping a pregnant lady up all night! What time is it, anyway?"

"Only two-thirty in the morning."

"Oh, Sarah! Go to bed!" Cathy went to the sink and began wetting a handful of paper towels.

"And what are you going to do?" Sarah asked.

"I just want to clean up the car. I didn't get all the blood off the seat."

"I already did it."

"What? When?"

"While you were taking a bath."

"Sarah, you idiot."

"Hey, I didn't have a miscarriage or anything. Oh, I almost forgot." Sarah pointed to a tiny film canister on the counter. "I found that on the floor of your car."

Cathy shook her head and sighed. "It's Hickey's."

"Hickey! Now *there's* a waste of a man."

"He's also a good friend of mine."

"That's all Hickey will ever be to a woman. A *friend.* So what's on the roll of film? Naked women, as usual?"

"I don't even want to know. When I dropped him off at the airport, he handed me a half-dozen rolls and

told me he'd pick them up when he got back. Guess he
didn't want to lug 'em all the way to Nairobi."

"Is that where he went? Nairobi?"

"He's shooting 'gorgeous ladies of Africa' or something." Cathy slipped the film canister into her bathrobe
pocket. "This must've dropped out of the glove compartment. Gee. I hope it's not pornographic."

"Knowing Hickey, it probably is."

They both laughed at the irony of it all. Hickman Von
Trapp, whose only job it was to photograph naked fe-
males in erotic poses, had absolutely no interest in the
opposite sex, with the possible exception of his mother.

"A guy like Hickey only goes to prove my point,"
Sarah said over her shoulder as she headed up the hall
to bed.

"What point is that?"

"There really *are* no good men left in the world!"

It was the light that dragged Victor up from the
depths of unconsciousness, a light brighter than a dozen
suns, beating against his closed eyelids. He didn't want
to wake up; he knew, in some dim, scarcely function-
ing part of his brain, that if he continued to struggle
against this blessed oblivion he would feel pain and nausea and something else, something much, much worse:
terror. Of what, he couldn't remember. Of death? No,
no, this was death, or as close as one could come to
it, and it was warm and black and comfortable. But
he had something important to do, something that he
couldn't allow himself to forget. He tried to think, but
all he could remember was a hand, gentle but somehow
strong, brushing his forehead, and a voice, reaching to
him softly in the darkness.

My name is Catherine...

As her touch, her voice, flooded his memory, so too did the fear. Not for himself (he was dead, wasn't he?) but for her. Strong, gentle Catherine. He'd seen her face only briefly, could scarcely remember it, but somehow he knew she was beautiful, the way a blind man knows, without benefit of vision, that a rainbow or the sky or his own dear child's face is beautiful. And now he was afraid for her.

Where are you? he wanted to cry out.

"He's coming around," said a female voice (not Catherine's, it was too hard, too crisp) followed by a confusing rush of other voices.

"Watch that IV!"

"Mr. Holland, hold still. Everything's going to be all right—"

"I said, watch the IV!"

"Hand me that second unit of blood—"

"Don't move, Mr. Holland—"

Where are you, Catherine? The shout exploded in his head. Fighting the temptation to sink back into unconsciousness, he struggled to lift his eyelids. At first, there was only a blur of light and color, so harsh he felt it stab through his sockets straight to his brain. Gradually the blur took the shape of faces, strangers in blue, frowning down at him. He tried to focus but the effort made his stomach rebel.

"Mr. Holland, take it easy," said a quietly gruff voice. "You're in the hospital—the recovery room. They've just operated on your shoulder. You just rest and go back to sleep..."

No. No, I can't, he tried to say.

"Five milligrams of morphine going in," someone

said, and Victor felt a warm flush creep up his arm and spread across his chest.

"That should help," he heard. "Now, sleep. Everything went just fine..."

You don't understand, he wanted to scream. *I have to warn her*—It was the last conscious thought he had before the lights once again were swallowed by the gentle darkness.

Alone in her husbandless bed, Sarah lay smiling. No, laughing! Her whole body seemed filled with laughter tonight. She wanted to sing, to dance. To stand at the open window and shout out her joy! It was all hormonal, she'd been told, this chemical pandemonium of pregnancy, dragging her body on a roller coaster of emotions. She knew she should rest, she should work toward serenity, but tonight she wasn't tired at all. Poor exhausted Cathy had dragged herself up the attic steps to bed. But here was Sarah, still wide awake.

She closed her eyes and focused her thoughts on the child resting in her belly. *How are you, my love? Are you asleep? Or are you listening, hearing my thoughts even now?*

The baby wiggled in her belly, then fell silent. It was a reply, secret words shared only between them. Sarah was almost glad there was no husband to distract her from this silent conversation, to lie here in jealousy, an outsider. There was only mother and child, the ancient bond, the mystical link.

Poor Cathy, she thought, riding those roller coaster emotions from joy to sadness for her friend. She knew Cathy yearned just as deeply for a child, but eventually time would snatch the chance away from her. Cathy was too much of a romantic to realize that the man, the circumstances, might never be right. Hadn't it taken Cathy ten long years to finally acknowledge that her marriage was a miserable failure? Not that Cathy hadn't tried to make it work. She had tried to the point of developing a monumental blind spot to Jack's faults, primarily his selfishness. It was surprising how a woman so bright, so intuitive, could have let things drag on as long as she did. But that was Cathy. Even at thirty-seven she was open and trusting and loyal to the point of idiocy.

The clatter of gravel outside on the driveway pricked Sarah's awareness. Lying perfectly still, she listened and for a moment heard only the familiar creak of the trees, the rustle of branches against the shake roof. Then—there it was again. Stones skittering across the road, and then the faint squeal of metal. Those raccoons again. If she didn't shoo them off now, they'd litter garbage all over the driveway.

Sighing, she sat up and hunted in the darkness for her slippers. Shuffling quietly out of her bedroom, she navigated instinctively down the hallway and into the kitchen. Her eyes found the night too comfortable; she didn't want to assault them with light. Instead of flipping on the carport switch, she grabbed the flashlight from its usual spot on the kitchen shelf and unlocked the door.

Outside, moonlight glowed dimly through the clouds. She pointed the flashlight at the trash cans, but her beam caught no raccoon eyes, no telltale scattering of garbage, only the dull reflection of stainless steel. Puzzled, she crossed the carport and paused next to the Datsun that Cathy had parked in the driveway.

That was when she noticed the light glowing faintly

inside the car. Glancing through the window, she saw that the glove compartment was open. Her first thought was that it had somehow fallen open by itself or that she or Cathy had forgotten to close it. Then she spotted the road maps strewn haphazardly across the front seat.

With fear suddenly hissing in her ear, she backed away, but terror made her legs slow and stiff. Only then did she sense that someone was nearby, waiting in the darkness; she could feel his presence, like a chill wind in the night.

She wheeled around for the house. As she turned, the beam of her flashlight swung around in a wild arc, only to freeze on the face of a man. The eyes that stared down at her were as slick and as black as pebbles. She scarcely focused on the rest of his face: the hawk nose, the thin, bloodless lips. It was only the eyes she saw. They were the eyes of a man without a soul.

"Hello, Catherine," he whispered, and she heard, in his voice, the greeting of death.

Please, she wanted to cry out as she felt him wrench her hair backward, exposing her neck. *Let me live!*

But no sound escaped. The words, like his blade, were buried in her throat.

Cathy woke up to the quarreling of blue jays outside her window, a sound that brought a smile to her lips for it struck her as somehow whimsical, this flap and flutter of wings across the panes, this maniacal crackling of feathered enemies. So unlike the morning roar of buses and cars she was accustomed to. The blue jays' quarrel moved to the rooftop, and she heard their claws scratching across the shakes in a dance of combat. She trailed their progress across the ceiling, up one side of the roof and down the other. Then, tired of the battle, she focused on the window.

Morning sunlight cascaded in, bathing the attic room in a soft haze. Such a perfect room for a nursery! She could see all the changes Sarah had already made here—the Jack-and-Jill curtains, the watercolor animal portraits. The very prospect of a baby sleeping in this room filled her with such joy that she sat up, grinning, and hugged the covers to her knees. Then she glanced at her watch on the nightstand and saw it was already nine-thirty—half the morning gone!

Reluctantly, she left the warmth of her bed and poked around in her suitcase for a sweater and jeans. She dressed to the thrashing of blue jays in the branches, the battle having moved from the roof to the treetops. From the window, she watched them dart from twig to twig until one finally hoisted up the feathered version of a white flag and took off, defeated. The victor, his authority no longer in question, gave one last screech and settled back to preen his feathers.

Only then did Cathy notice the silence of the house, a stillness that magnified her every heartbeat, her every breath.

Leaving the room, she descended the attic steps and confronted the empty living room. Ashes from last night's fire mounded the grate. A silver garland drooped from the Christmas tree. A cardboard angel with glittery wings winked on the mantelpiece. She followed the hallway to Sarah's room and frowned at the rumpled bed, the coverlet flung aside. "Sarah?"

Her voice was swallowed up in the stillness. How could a cottage seem so immense? She wandered back through the living room and into the kitchen. Last night's teacups still sat in the sink. On the windowsill, an asparagus fern trembled, stirred by a breeze through the open door.

Cathy stepped out into the carport where Sarah's old Dodge was parked. "Sarah?" she called.

Something skittered across the roof. Startled, Cathy looked up and suddenly laughed as she heard the blue jay chattering in the tree above—a victory speech, no doubt. Even the animal kingdom had its conceits.

She started to head back into the house when her gaze swept past a stain on the gravel near the car's rear tire. For a few seconds she stared at the blot of rust-brown, unable to comprehend its meaning. Slowly, she moved alongside the car, her gaze tracing the stain backward along its meandering course.

As she rounded the rear of the car, the driveway came into full view. The dried rivulet of brown became a crimson lake in which a single swimmer lay open-eyed and still.

The blue jay's chatter abruptly ceased as another sound rose up and filled the trees. It was Cathy, screaming.

"Hey, mister. Hey, mister."

Victor tried to brush off the sound but it kept buzzing in his ear, like a fly that can't be shooed away.

"Hey, mister. You awake?"

Victor opened his eyes and focused painfully on a wry little face stubbled with gray whiskers. The apparition grinned, and darkness gaped where teeth should have been. Victor stared into that foul black hole of a mouth and thought: *I've died and gone to hell.*

"Hey, mister, you got a cigarette?"

Victor shook his head and barely managed to whisper: "I don't think so."

"Well, you got a dollar I could borrow?"

"Go away," groaned Victor, shutting his eyes against the daylight. He tried to think, tried to remember where he was, but his head ached and the little man's voice kept distracting him.

"Can't get no cigarettes in this place. Like a jail in here. Don't know why I don't just get up and walk out. But y'know, streets are cold this time of year. Been rainin' all night long. Least in here it's warm…"

Raining all night long… Suddenly Victor remembered. The rain. Running and running through the rain.

Victor's eyes shot open. "Where am I?"

"Three East. Land o' the bitches."

He struggled to sit up and almost gasped from the pain. Dizzily, he focused on the metal pole with its bag of fluid dripping slowly into the plastic intravenous tube, then stared at the bandages on his left shoulder. Through the window, he saw that the day was already drenched in sunshine. "What time is it?"

"Dunno. Nine o'clock, I guess. You missed breakfast."

"I've got to get out of here." Victor swung his legs out of bed and discovered that, except for a flimsy hospital gown, he was stark naked. "Where's my clothes? My wallet?"

The old man shrugged. "Nurse'd know. Ask her."

Victor found the call button buried among the bedsheets. He stabbed it a few times, then turned his attention to peeling off the tape affixing the IV tube to his arm.

The door hissed open and a woman's voice barked, *"Mr. Holland! What do you think you're doing?"*

"I'm getting out of here, that's what I'm doing," said Victor as he stripped off the last piece of tape. Before he could pull the IV out, the nurse rushed across the room as fast as her stout legs could carry her and slapped a piece of gauze over the catheter.

"Don't blame me, Miss Redfern!" screeched the little man.

"Lenny, go back to your own bed this instant! And as for you, Mr. Holland," she said, turning her steel-blue eyes on Victor, "you've lost too much blood." Trapping his arm against her massive biceps, she began to retape the catheter firmly in place.

"Just get me my clothes."

"Don't argue, Mr. Holland. You have to stay."

"Why?"

"Because you've got an IV, that's why!" she snapped, as if the plastic tube itself was some sort of irreversible condition.

"I want my clothes."

"I'd have to check with the ER. Nothing of yours came up to the floor."

"Then call the ER, damn you!" At Miss Redfern's disapproving scowl, he added with strained politeness, *"If* you don't mind."

It was another half hour before a woman showed up from the business office to explain what had happened to Victor's belongings.

"I'm afraid we—well, we seem to have…lost your clothes, Mr. Holland," she said, fidgeting under his astonished gaze.

"What do you mean, *lost?*"

"They were—" she cleared her throat "—er, stolen. From the emergency room. Believe me, this has never happened before. We're really very sorry about this, Mr. Holland, and I'm sure we'll be able to arrange a purchase of replacement clothing…"

She was too busy trying to make excuses to notice that Victor's face had frozen in alarm. That his mind was racing as he tried to remember, through the blur of last night's events, just what had happened to the film canister. He knew he'd had it in his pocket during the endless drive to the hospital. He remembered clutching it there, remembered flailing senselessly at the woman when she'd tried to pull his hand from his pocket. After that, nothing was clear, nothing was certain. *Have I lost it?* he thought. *Have I lost my only evidence?*

"…While the money's missing, your credit cards seem to be all there, so I guess that's something to be thankful for."

He looked at her blankly. "What?"

"Your valuables, Mr. Holland." She pointed to the wallet and watch she'd just placed on the bedside table. "The security guard found them in the trash bin outside the hospital. Looks like the thief only wanted your cash."

"And my clothes. Right."

The instant the woman left, Victor pressed the button for Miss Redfern. She walked in carrying a breakfast tray. "Eat, Mr. Holland," she said. "Maybe your behavior's all due to hypoglycemia."

"A woman brought me to the ER," he said. "Her first name was Catherine. I have to get hold of her."

"Oh, look! Eggs and Rice Krispies! Here's your fork—"

"Miss Redfern, will you forget the damned Rice Krispies!"

Miss Redfern slapped down the cereal box. "There is no need for profanity!"

"I have to find that woman!"

Without a word, Miss Redfern spun around and marched out of the room. A few minutes later she returned and brusquely handed him a slip of paper. On it was written the name Catherine Weaver followed by a local address.

"You'd better eat fast," she said. "There's a policeman coming over to talk to you."

"Fine," he grunted, stuffing a forkful of cold, rubbery egg in his mouth.

"And some man from the FBI called. He's on his way, too."

Victor's head jerked up in alarm. "The FBI? What was his name?"

"Oh, for heaven's sake, how should I know? Something Polish, I think."

Staring at her, Victor slowly put down his fork. "Polowski," he said softly.

"That sounds like it. Polowski." She turned and headed out of the room. "The FBI indeed," she muttered. "Wonder what he did to get *their* attention…"

Before the door had even swung shut behind her, Victor was out of bed and tearing at his IV. He scarcely felt the sting of the tape wrenching the hair off his arm; he had to concentrate on getting the hell out of this hospital before Polowski showed up. He was certain the FBI agent had set him up for that ambush last night, and he wasn't about to wait around for another attack.

He turned and snapped at his roommate, "Lenny, where are your clothes?"

Lenny's gaze traveled reluctantly to a cabinet near the sink. "Don't got no other clothes. Besides, they wouldn't fit you, mister..."

Victor yanked open the cabinet door and pulled out a frayed cotton shirt and a pair of baggy polyester pants. The pants were too short and about six inches of Victor's hairy legs stuck out below the cuffs, but he had no trouble fastening the belt. The real trouble was going to be finding a pair of size twelve shoes. To his relief, he discovered that the cabinet also contained a pair of Lenny's thongs. His heels hung at least an inch over the back edge, but at least he wouldn't be barefoot.

"Those are mine!" protested Lenny.

"Here. You can have this." Victor tossed his wristwatch to the old man. "You should be able to hock that for a whole new outfit."

Suspicious, Lenny put the watch up against his ear. "Piece of junk. It's not ticking."

"It's quartz."

"Oh. Yeah. I knew that."

Victor pocketed his wallet and went to the door. Opening it just a crack, he peered down the hall toward the nurses' station. The coast was clear. He glanced back at Lenny. "So long, buddy. Give my regards to Miss Redfern."

Slipping out of the room, Victor headed quietly down the hall, away from the nurses' station. The emergency stairwell door was at the far end, marked by the warning painted in red: Alarm Will Sound If Opened. He walked steadily towards it, willing himself not to run, not to attract attention. But just as he neared the door, a familiar voice echoed in the hall.

"Mr. Holland! You come back here this instant!"

Victor lunged for the door, slammed against the closing bar, and dashed into the stairwell.

His footsteps echoed against the concrete as he pounded down the stairs. By the time he heard Miss Redfern scramble after him into the stairwell, he'd already reached the first floor and was pushing through the last door to freedom.

"Mr. Holland!" yelled Miss Redfern.

Even as he dashed across the parking lot, he could still hear Miss Redfern's outraged voice echoing in his ears.

Eight blocks away he turned into a K Mart, and within ten minutes had bought a shirt, blue jeans, underwear, socks and a pair of size-twelve tennis shoes, all of which he paid for with his credit card. He tossed Lenny's old clothes into a trash can.

Before emerging back outside, he peered through the store window at the street. It seemed like a perfectly normal mid-December morning in a small town, shoppers strolling beneath a tacky garland of Christmas decorations, a half-dozen cars waiting patiently at a red light. He was just about to step out the door when he spotted the police car creeping down the road. Immediately he ducked behind an undressed mannequin and watched through the nude plastic limbs as the police car made its way slowly past the K Mart and continued in the direction of the hospital. They were obviously searching for someone. Was he the one they wanted?

He couldn't afford to risk a stroll down Main Street.

There was no way of knowing who else besides Polowski was involved in the double cross.

It took him at least an hour on foot to reach the outskirts of town, and by then he was so weak and wobbly he could barely stand. The surge of adrenaline that had sent him dashing from the hospital was at last petering out. Too tired to take another step, he sank onto a boulder at the side of the highway and halfheartedly held out his thumb. To his immense relief, the next vehicle to come along—a pickup truck loaded with firewood— pulled over. Victor climbed in and collapsed gratefully on the seat.

The driver spat out the window, then squinted at Victor from beneath an Agway Seeds cap. "Goin' far?"

"Just a few miles. Oak Hill Road."

"Yep. I go right past it." The driver pulled back onto the road. The truck spewed black exhaust as they roared down the highway, country music blaring from the radio.

Through the plucked strains of guitar music, Victor heard a sound that made him sit up sharply. A siren. Whipping his head around, he saw a patrol car zooming up fast behind them. *That's it,* thought Victor. *They've found me. They're going to stop this truck and arrest me...*

But for what? For walking away from the hospital? For insulting Miss Redfern? Or had Polowski fabricated some charge against him?

With a sense of impending doom, he waited for the patrol car to overtake them and start flashing its signal to pull over. In fact, he was so certain they *would* be pulled over that when the police car sped right past them and roared off down the highway, he could only stare ahead in amazement.

"Must be some kinda trouble," his companion said blandly, nodding at the rapidly vanishing police car.

Victor managed to clear his throat. "Trouble?"

"Yep. Don't get much of a chance to use that siren of theirs but when they do, boy oh boy, do they go to town with it."

With his heart hammering against his ribs, Victor sat back and forced himself to calm down. He had nothing to worry about. The police weren't after him, they were busy with some other concern. He wondered what sort of small-town catastrophe could warrant blaring sirens. Probably nothing more exciting than a few kids out on a joyride.

By the time they reached the turnoff to Oak Hill Road, Victor's pulse had settled back to normal. He thanked the driver, climbed out, and began the trek to Catherine Weaver's house. It was a long walk, and the road wound through a forest of pines. Every so often he'd pass a mailbox along the road and, peering through the trees, would spot a house. Catherine's address was coming up fast.

What on earth should he say to her? Up till now he'd concentrated only on reaching her house. Now that he was almost there, he had to come up with some reasonable explanation for why he'd dragged himself out of a hospital bed and trudged all this way to see her. A simple *thanks for saving my life* just wouldn't do it. He had to find out if she had the film canister. But she, of course, would want to know why the damn thing was so important.

You could tell her the truth.

No, forget that. He could imagine her reaction if he were to launch into his wild tale about viruses and dead scientists and double-crossing FBI agents. *The FBI is out to get you? I see. And who else is after you, Mr. Holland?* It was so absurdly paranoid he almost felt like laughing. No, he couldn't tell her any of it or he'd end up right back in a hospital, and this time in a ward that would make Miss Redfern's Three East look like paradise.

She didn't need to know any of it. In fact, she was better off ignorant. The woman had saved his life, and the last thing he wanted to do was put her in any danger. The film was all he wanted from her. After today, she'd never see him again.

He was so busy debating what to tell her that he didn't notice the police cars until well after he'd rounded the road's bend. Suddenly he froze, confronted by three squad cars—probably the entire police fleet of Garberville—parked in front of a rustic cedar house. A half-dozen neighbors lingered in the gravel driveway, shaking their heads in disbelief. Good God, had something happened to Catherine?

Swallowing the urge to turn and flee, Victor propelled himself forward, past the squad cars and through the loose gathering of onlookers, only to be stopped by a uniformed officer.

"I'm sorry, sir. No one's allowed past this point."

Dazed, Victor stared down and saw that the police had strung out a perimeter of red tape. Slowly, his gaze moved beyond the tape, to the old Datsun parked near the carport. Was that Catherine's car? He tried desperately to remember if she'd driven a Datsun, but last night it had been so dark and he'd been in so much pain that he hadn't bothered to pay attention. All he could remember was that it was a compact model, with scarcely enough room for his legs. Then he noticed the faded parking sticker on the rear bumper: Parking Permit, Studio Lot A.

I work for an independent film company, she'd told him last night.

It was Catherine's car.

Unwillingly, he focused on the stained gravel just beside the Datsun, and even though the rational part of him knew that that peculiar brick red could only be dried blood, he wanted to deny it. He wanted to believe there was some other explanation for that stain, for this ominous gathering of police.

He tried to speak, but his voice sounded like something dragged up through gravel.

"What did you say, sir?" the police officer asked.

"What—what happened?"

The officer shook his head sadly. "Woman was killed here last night. Our first murder in ten years."

"Murder?" Victor's gaze was still fixed in horror on the bloodstained gravel. "But—*why?*"

The officer shrugged. "Don't know yet. Maybe robbery, though I don't think he got much." He nodded at the Datsun. "Car was the only thing broken into."

If Victor said anything at that point, he never remembered what it was. He was vaguely aware of his legs carrying him back through the onlookers, past the three police cars, toward the road. The sunshine was so brilliant it hurt his eyes and he could barely see where he was going.

I killed her, he thought. *She saved my life and I killed her...*

Guilt slashed its way to his throat and he could scarcely breathe, could barely take another step for the pain. For a long time he stood there at the side of the road, his head bent in the sunshine, his ears filled with the sound of blue jays, and mourned a woman he'd never known.

When at last he was able to raise his head again, rage fueled the rest of his walk back to the highway, rage against Catherine's murderer. Rage at himself for having put her in such danger. It was the film the killer had been searching for, and he'd probably found it in the Datsun. If he hadn't, the house would have been ransacked, as well.

Now what? thought Victor. He dismissed the possibility that his briefcase—with most of the evidence— might still be in his wrecked car. That was the first place the killer would have searched. Without the film, Victor was left with no evidence at all. It would all come down to his word against Viratek's. The newspapers would dismiss him as nothing more than a disgruntled ex-employee. And after Polowski's double cross, he couldn't trust the FBI.

At that last thought, he quickened his pace. The sooner he got out of Garberville, the better. When he got back to the highway, he'd hitch another ride. Once safely out of town, he could take the time to plan his next move.

He decided to head south, to San Francisco.

Chapter 3

From the window of his office at Viratek, Archibald Black watched the limousine glide up the tree-lined driveway and pull to a stop at the front entrance. Black snorted derisively. The cowboy was back in town, damn him. And after all the man's fussing about the importance of secrecy, about keeping his little visit discreet, the idiot had the gall to show up in a limousine—with a uniformed driver, no less.

Black turned from the window and paced over to his desk. Despite his contempt for the visitor, he had to acknowledge the man made him uneasy, the way all so-called men of action made him uneasy. Not enough brains behind all that muscle. Too much power in the hands of imbeciles, he thought. Is this an example of who we have running the country?

The intercom buzzed. "Mr. Black?" said his secretary. "A Mr. Tyrone is here to see you."

"Send him in, please," said Black, smoothing the scorn from his expression. He was wearing a look of polite deference when the door opened and Matthew Tyrone walked into the office.

They shook hands. Tyrone's grip was unreasonably firm, as though he was trying to remind Black of their relative positions of power. His bearing had all the spit and polish of an ex-marine, which Tyrone was. Only the thickening waist betrayed the fact that Tyrone's marine days had been left far behind.

"How was the flight from Washington?" inquired Black as they sat down.

"Terrible service. I tell you, commercial flights aren't what they used to be. To think the average American pays good money for the privilege."

"I imagine it can't compare with Air Force One."

Tyrone smiled. "Let's get down to business. Tell me where things stand with this little crisis of yours."

Black noted Tyrone's use of the word *yours. So now it's my problem,* he thought. Naturally. That's what they meant by deniability: When things go wrong, the other guy gets the blame. If any of this leaked out, Black's head would be the one to fall. But then, that's why this contract was so lucrative—because he—meaning Viratek—was willing to take that risk.

"We've recovered the documents," said Black. "And the film canisters. The negatives are being developed now."

"And your two employees?"

Black cleared his throat. "There's no need to take this any further."

"They're a risk to national security."

"You can't just kill them off!"

"Can't we?" Tyrone's eyes were a cold, gunmetal gray. An appropriate color for someone who called himself "the Cowboy." You didn't argue with anyone who had eyes like that. Not if you had an instinct for self-preservation.

Black dipped his head deferentially. "I'm not accustomed to this sort of…business. And I don't like dealing with your man Savitch."

"Mr. Savitch has performed well for us before."

"He killed one of my senior scientists!"

"I assume it was necessary."

Black looked down unhappily at his desk. Just the thought of that monster Savitch made him shudder.

"Why, exactly, did Martinique go bad?"

Because he had a conscience, thought Black. He looked at Tyrone. "There was no way to predict it. He'd worked in commercial R and D for ten years. He'd never presented a security problem before. We only found out last week that he'd taken classified documents. And then Victor Holland got involved…"

"How much does Holland know?"

"Holland wasn't involved with the project. But he's clever. If he looked over those papers, he might have pieced it together."

Now Tyrone was agitated, his fingers drumming the desktop. "Tell me about Holland. What do you know about him?"

"I've gone over his personnel file. He's forty-one years old, born and raised in San Diego. Entered the seminary but dropped out after a year. Went on to Stanford, then MIT. Doctorate in biochemistry. He was with Viratek for four years. One of our most promising researchers."

"What about his personal life?"

"His wife died three years ago of leukemia. Keeps pretty much to himself these days. Quiet kind of guy, likes classical jazz. Plays the saxophone in some amateur group."

Tyrone laughed. "Your typical nerd scientist." It was just the sort of moronic comment an ex-marine like Tyrone would make. It was an insult that grated on Black. Years ago, before he created Viratek Industries, Black too had been a research biochemist.

"He should be a simple matter to dispose of," said Tyrone. "Inexperienced. And probably scared." He reached for his briefcase. "Mr. Savitch is an expert on these matters. I suggest you let him take care of the problem."

"Of course." In truth, Black didn't think he had any choice. Nicholas Savitch was like some evil, frightening force that, once unleashed, could not be controlled.

The intercom buzzed. "Mr. Gregorian's here from the photo lab," said the secretary.

"Send him in." Black glanced at Tyrone. "The film's been developed. Let's see just what Martinique managed to photograph."

Gregorian walked in carrying a bulky envelope. "Here are those contact prints you requested," he said, handing the bundle across the desk to Black. Then he cupped his hand over his mouth, muffling a sound suspiciously like laughter.

"Yes, Mr. Gregorian?" inquired Black.

"Nothing, sir."

Tyrone cut in, "Well, let's see them!"

Black removed the five contact sheets and lay them out on the desk for everyone to see. The men stared.

For a long time, no one spoke. Then Tyrone said, "Is this some sort of joke?"

Gregorian burst out laughing.

Black said, "What the hell is this?"

"Those are the negatives you gave me, sir," Gregorian insisted. "I processed them myself."

"These are the photos you got back from Victor Holland?" Tyrone's voice started soft and rose slowly to a roar. "Five rolls of *naked women?*"

"There's been a mistake," said Black. "It's the wrong film—"

Gregorian laughed harder.

"Shut up!" yelled Black. He looked at Tyrone. "I don't know how this happened."

"Then the roll we want is still out there?"

Black nodded wearily.

Tyrone reached for the phone. "We need to clean things up. Fast."

"Who are you calling?" asked Black.

"The man who can do the job," said Tyrone as he punched in the numbers. "Savitch."

In his motel room on Lombard Street, Victor paced the avocado-green carpet, wracking his brain for a plan. Any plan. His well-organized scientist's mind had already distilled the situation into the elements of a research project. Identify the problem: someone is out to kill me. State your hypothesis: Jerry Martinique uncovered something dangerous and he was killed for it. Now they think I have the information—and the evidence. Which I don't. Goal: Stay alive. Method: *Any damn way I can!*

For the last two days, his only strategy had consisted

of holing up in various cheap motel rooms and pacing the carpets. He couldn't hide out forever. If the feds were involved, and he had reason to believe they were, they'd soon have his credit card charges traced, would know exactly where to find him.

I need a plan of attack.

Going to the FBI was definitely out. Sam Polowski was the agent Victor had contacted, the one who'd arranged to meet him in Garberville. No one else should have known about that meeting. Sam Polowski had never shown up.

But someone else had. Victor's aching shoulder was a constant reminder of that near-disastrous rendezvous.

I could go to the newspapers. But how would he convince some skeptical reporter? Who would believe his stories of a project so dangerous it could kill millions? They would think his tale was some fabrication of a paranoid mind.

And I am not paranoid.

He paced over to the TV and switched it on to the five o'clock news. A perfectly coiffed anchorwoman smiled from the screen as she read a piece of fluff about the last day of school, happy children, Christmas vacation. Then her expression sobered. Transition. Victor found himself staring at the TV as the next story came on.

"And in Garberville, California, there have been no new leads in the murder investigation of a woman found slain Wednesday morning. A houseguest found Sarah Boylan, 39, lying in the driveway, dead of stab wounds to the neck. The victim was five months pregnant. Police say they are puzzled by the lack of motive in this terrible tragedy, and at the present time there are no suspects. Moving on to national news…"

No, no, no! Victor thought. She wasn't pregnant. Her name wasn't Sarah. It's a mistake…

Or was it?

My name is Catherine, she had told him.

Catherine Weaver. Yes, he was sure of the name. He'd remember it till the day he died.

He sat on the bed, the facts spinning around in his brain. Sarah. Cathy. A murder in Garberville.

When at last he rose to his feet, it was with a swelling sense of urgency, even panic. He grabbed the hotel room phone book and flipped to the *W*s. He understood now. The killer had made a mistake. If Cathy Weaver was still alive, she might have that roll of film—or know where to find it. Victor had to reach her.

Before someone else did.

Nothing could have prepared Cathy for the indescribable sense of gloom she felt upon returning to her flat in San Francisco. She had thought she'd cried out all her tears that night in the Garberville motel, the night after Sarah's death. But here she was, still bursting into tears, then sinking into deep, dark meditations. The drive to the city had been temporarily numbing. But as soon as she'd climbed the steps to her door and confronted the deathly silence of her second-story flat, she felt overwhelmed once again by grief. And bewilderment. Of all the people in the world to die, why Sarah?

She made a feeble attempt at unpacking. Then, forcing herself to stay busy, she surveyed the refrigerator and saw that her shelves were practically empty. It was all the excuse she needed to flee her apartment. She pulled a sweater over her jeans and, with a sense of escape, walked the four blocks to the neighborhood grocery store. She bought only the essentials, bread and eggs and fruit. Enough to tide her over for a few days, until she was back on her feet and could think clearly about any sort of menu.

Carrying a sack of groceries in each arm, she walked through the gathering darkness back to her apartment building. The night was chilly, and she regretted not wearing a coat. Through an open window, a woman called, "Time for dinner!" and two children playing kickball in the street turned and scampered for home.

By the time Cathy reached her building, she was shivering and her arms were aching from the weight of the groceries. She trudged up the steps and, balancing one sack on her hip, managed to pull out her keys and unlock the security door. Just as she swung through, she heard footsteps, then glimpsed a blur of movement rushing toward her from the side. She was swept through the doorway, into the building. A grocery bag tumbled from her arms, spilling apples across the floor. She stumbled forward, catching herself on the wood banister. The door slammed shut behind her.

She spun around, ready to fight off her attacker.

It was Victor Holland.

"You!" she whispered in amazement.

He didn't seem so sure of *her* identity. He was frantically searching her face, as though trying to confirm he had the right woman. "Cathy Weaver?"

"What do you think you're—"

"Where's your apartment?" he cut in.

"What?"

"We can't stand around out here."

"It's—it's upstairs—"

"Let's go." He reached for her arm but she pulled away.

"My groceries," she said, glancing down at the scattered apples.

He quickly scooped up the fruit, tossed it in one of the bags, and nudged her toward the stairs. "We don't have a lot of time."

Cathy allowed herself to be herded up the stairs and halfway down the hall before she stopped dead in her tracks. "Wait a minute. You tell me what this is all about, Mr. Holland, and you tell me right now or I don't move another step!"

"Give me your keys."

"You can't just—"

"Give me your keys!"

She stared at him, shocked by the command. Suddenly she realized that what she saw in his eyes was panic. They were the eyes of a hunted man.

Automatically she handed him her keys.

"Wait here," he said. "Let me check the apartment first."

She watched in bewilderment as he unlocked her door and cautiously eased his way inside. For a few moments she heard nothing. She pictured him moving through the flat, tried to estimate how many seconds each room would require for inspection. It was a small flat, so why was he taking so long?

Slowly she moved toward the doorway. Just as she reached it, his head popped out. She let out a little squeak of surprise. He barely caught the bag of groceries as it slipped from her grasp.

"It's okay," he said. "Come on inside."

The instant she stepped over the threshold, he had the door locked and bolted behind her. Then he quickly circled the living room, closing the drapes, locking windows.

"Are you going to tell me what's going on?" she asked, following him around the room.

"We're in trouble."

"You mean *you're* in trouble."

"No. I mean *we*. Both of us." He turned to her, his gaze clear and steady. "Do you have the film?"

"What are you talking about?" she asked, utterly confused by the sudden shift of conversation.

"A roll of film. Thirty-five millimeter. In a black plastic container. Do you have it?"

She didn't answer. But an image from that last night with Sarah had already taken shape in her mind: a roll of film on the kitchen counter. Film she'd thought belonged to her friend Hickey. Film she'd slipped into her bathrobe pocket and later into her purse. But she wasn't about to reveal any of this, not until she found out why he wanted it. The gaze she returned to him was purposefully blank and unrevealing.

Frustrated, he forced himself to take a deep breath, and started over. "That night you found me—on the highway—I had it in my pocket. It wasn't with me when I woke up in the hospital. I might have dropped it in your car."

"Why do you want this roll of film?"

"I need it. As evidence—"

"For what?"

"It would take too long to explain."

She shrugged. "I've got nothing better to do at the moment—"

"Damn it!" He stalked over to her. Taking her by
the shoulders, he forced her to look at him. "Don't you
understand? That's why your friend was killed! The
night they broke into your car, they were looking for
that film!"

She stared at him, a look of sudden comprehension
and horror. "Sarah..."

"Was in the wrong place at the wrong time. The
killer must have thought she was *you*."

Cathy felt trapped by his unrelenting gaze. And by
the inescapable threat of his revelation. Her knees wobbled, gave way. She sank into the nearest chair and sat
there in numb silence.

"You have to get out of here," he said. "Before
they find you. Before they figure out you're the Cathy
Weaver they're looking for."

She didn't move. She couldn't move.

"Come on, Cathy. There isn't much time!"

"What was on that roll of film?" she asked softly.

"I told you. Evidence. Against a company called Viratek."

She frowned. "Isn't—isn't that the company you
work for?"

"Used to work for."

"What did they do?"

"They're involved in some sort of illegal research
project. I can't tell you the particulars."

"Why not?"

"Because I don't know them. I'm not the one who
gathered the evidence. A colleague—a friend—passed
it to me, just before he was killed."

"What do you mean by killed?"

"The police called it an accident. I think otherwise."

"You're saying he was murdered over a research project?" She shook her head. "Must have been dangerous stuff he was working on."

"I know this much. It involves biological weapons. Which makes the research illegal. And incredibly dangerous."

"Weapons? For what government?"

"Ours."

"I don't understand. If this is a federal project, that makes it all legal, right?"

"Not by a long shot. People in high places have been known to break the rules."

"How high are we talking about?"

"I don't know. I can't be sure of anyone. Not the police, not the Justice Department. Not the FBI."

Her eyes narrowed. The words she was hearing sounded like paranoid ravings. But the voice—and the eyes—were perfectly sane. They were sea-green, those eyes. They held an honesty, a steadiness that should have been all the assurance she needed.

It wasn't. Not by a long shot.

Quietly she said, "So you're telling me the FBI is after you. Is that correct?"

Sudden anger flared in his eyes, then just as quickly, it was gone. Groaning, he sank onto the couch and ran his hands through his hair. "I don't blame you for thinking I'm nuts. Sometimes I wonder if I'm all there. I thought if I could trust anyone, it'd be you…"

"Why me?"

He looked at her. "Because you're the one who saved my life. You're the one they'll try to kill next."

She froze. No, no, this was insane. Now he was pulling her into his delusion, making her believe in his nightmare world of murder and conspiracy. She wouldn't let him! She stood up and started to walk away, but his voice made her stop again.

"Cathy, think about it. Why was your friend Sarah killed? Because they thought she was *you*. By now they've figured out they killed the wrong woman. They'll have to come back and do the job right. Just in case you know something. In case you have evidence—"

"This is crazy!" she cried, clapping her hands over her ears. "No one's going to—"

"They already have!" He whipped out a scrap of newspaper from his shirt pocket. "On my way over here, I happened to pass a newsstand. This was on the front page." He handed her the piece of paper.

She stared in bewilderment at the photograph of a middle-aged woman, a total stranger. "San Francisco woman shot to death on front doorstep," read the accompanying headline.

"This has nothing to do with me," she said.

"Look at her name."

Cathy's gaze slid to the third paragraph, which identified the victim.

Her name was Catherine Weaver.

The scrap of newsprint slipped from her grasp and fluttered to the floor.

"There are three Catherine Weavers in the San Francisco phone book," he said. "That one was shot to death at nine o'clock this morning. I don't know what's happened to the second. She might already be dead. Which makes you next on the list. They've had enough time to locate you."

"I've been out of town—I only got back an hour ago—"

"Which explains why you're still alive. Maybe they came here earlier. Maybe they decided to check out the other two women first."

She shot to her feet, suddenly frantic with the need to flee. "I have to pack my things—"

"No. Let's just get the hell out of here."

Yes, do what he says! an inner voice screamed at her.

She nodded. Turning, she headed blindly for the door. Halfway there, she halted. "My purse—"

"Where is it?"

She headed back, past a curtained window. "I think I left it by the—"

Her next words were cut off by an explosion of shattering glass. Only the closed curtains kept the shards from piercing her flesh. Pure reflex sent Cathy diving to the floor just as the second gun blast went off. An instant later she found Victor Holland sprawled on top of her, covering her body with his as the third bullet slammed into the far wall, splintering wood and plaster.

The curtains shuddered, then hung still.

For a few seconds Cathy was paralyzed by terror, by the weight of Victor's body on hers. Then panic took hold. She squirmed free, intent on fleeing the apartment.

"Stay down!" Victor snapped.

"They're trying to kill us!"

"Don't make it easy for them!" He dragged her back to the floor. "We're getting out. But not through the front door."

"How—"

"Where's your fire escape?"

"My bedroom window."

"Does it go to the roof?"

"I'm not sure—I think so—"

"Then let's move it."

On hands and knees they crawled down the hall, into Cathy's unlit bedroom. Beneath the window they paused, listening. Outside, in the darkness, there was no sound. Then, from downstairs in the lobby, came the tinkle of breaking glass.

"He's already in the building!" hissed Victor. He yanked open the window. "Out, out!"

Cathy didn't need to be prodded. Hands shaking, she scrambled out and lowered herself onto the fire escape. Victor was right behind her.

"Up," he whispered. "To the roof."

And then what? she wondered, climbing the ladder to the third floor, past Mrs. Chang's flat. Mrs. Chang was out of town this week, visiting her son in New Jersey. The apartment was dark, the windows locked tight. No way in there.

"Keep going," said Victor, nudging her forward.

Only a few more rungs to go.

At last, she pulled herself up and over the edge and onto the asphalt roof. A second later, Victor dropped down beside her. Potted plants shuddered in the darkness. It was Mrs. Chang's rooftop garden, a fragrant mélange of Chinese herbs and vegetables.

Together, Victor and Cathy weaved their way through the plants and crossed to the opposite edge of the roof, where the next building abutted theirs.

"All the way?" said Cathy.

"All the way."

They hopped onto the adjoining roof and ran across

to the other side, where three feet of emptiness separated them from the next building. She didn't pause to think of the perils of that leap, she simply flung herself across the gap and kept running, aware that every step took her farther and farther from danger.

On the roof of the fourth building, Cathy finally halted and stared over the edge at the street below. End of the line. It suddenly occurred to her that it was a very long drop to the ground below. The fire escape looked as sturdy as a Tinkertoy.

She swallowed. "This probably isn't a good time to tell you this, but—"

"Tell me what?"

"I'm afraid of heights."

He clambered over the edge. "Then don't look down."

Right, she thought, slithering onto the fire escape. *Don't look down.* Her palms were so slick with sweat she could barely grip the rungs. Suddenly seized by an attack of vertigo, she froze there, clinging desperately to that flimsy steel skeleton.

"Don't stop now!" Victor whispered up to her. "Just keep moving!"

Still she didn't move. She pressed her face against the rung, so hard she felt the rough edge bite into her flesh.

"You're okay, Cathy!" he said. "Come on."

The pain became all-encompassing, blocking out the dizziness, even the fear. When she opened her eyes again, the world had steadied. On rubbery legs, she descended the ladder, pausing on the third floor landing to wipe her sweaty palms on her jeans. She continued downward, to the second-floor landing. It was still a good fifteen-foot drop to the ground. She unlatched the extension ladder and started to slide it down, but it let out such a screech that Victor immediately stopped her.

"Too noisy. We have to jump!"

"But—"

To her astonishment, he scrambled over the railing and dropped to the ground. "Come on!" he hissed from below. "It's not that far. I'll catch you."

Murmuring a prayer, she lowered herself over the side and let go.

To her surprise he did catch her—but held on only for a second. The bullet wound had left his injured shoulder too weak to hold on. They both tumbled to the ground. She landed smack on top of him, her legs astride his hips, their faces inches apart. They stared at each other, so stunned they could scarcely breathe.

Upstairs, a window slid open and someone yelled, "Hey, you bums! If you don't clear out this instant, I'm calling the cops!"

Instantly Cathy rolled off Victor, only to stagger into a trash can. The lid fell off and slammed like a cymbal against the sidewalk.

"That's it for rest stops," Victor grunted and scrambled to his feet. *"Move it."*

They took off at a wild dash down the street, turned up an alley, and kept running. It was a good five blocks before they finally stopped to catch their breath. They glanced back.

The street was deserted.

They were safe!

Nicholas Savitch stood beside the neatly made bed and surveyed the room. It was every inch a woman's room, from the closet hung with a half-dozen simple but elegant dresses, to the sweetly scented powders and lotions lined up on the vanity table. It took only a single circuit around the room to tell him about the woman whose bedroom this was. She was slim, a size seven dress, size six-and-a-half shoe. The hairs on the brush were brown and shoulder-length. She owned only a few pieces of jewelry, and she favored natural scents, rose-water and lavender. Her favorite color was green.

Back in the living room, he continued to gather information. The woman subscribed to the Hollywood trade journals. Her taste in music, like her taste in books, was eclectic. He noticed a scrap of newspaper lying on the floor. He picked it up and glanced at the article. Now this was interesting. The death of Catherine Weaver I had not gone unnoticed by Catherine Weaver III.

He pocketed the article. Then he saw the purse, lying on the floor near the shattered window.

Bingo.

He emptied the contents on the coffee table. Out tumbled a wallet, checkbook, pens, loose change, and...an address book. He opened it to the *B*s. There he found the name he was looking for: Sarah Boylan.

He now knew this was the Catherine Weaver he'd been seeking. What a shame he'd wasted his time hunting down the other two.

He flipped through the address book and spotted a half dozen or so San Francisco listings. The woman may have been clever enough to slip away from him this time. But staying out of sight was a more difficult matter. And this little book, with its names of friends and relatives and colleagues, could lead him straight to her.

Somewhere in the distance, a police siren was wailing.

It was time to leave.

Savitch took the address book and the woman's wallet and headed out the door. Outside, his breath misted in the cold air as he walked at a leisurely pace down the street,

He could afford to take his time.

But for Catherine Weaver and Victor Holland, time was running out.

Chapter 4

There was no time to rest. They jogged for the next six blocks, miles and miles, it seemed to Cathy. Victor moved tirelessly, leading her down side streets, avoiding busy intersections. She let him do the thinking and navigating. Her terror slowly gave way to numbness and a disorienting sense of unreality. The city itself seemed little more than a dreamscape, asphalt and streetlights and endless twists and turns of concrete. The only reality was the man striding close beside her, his gaze alert, his movements swift and sure. She knew he too must be afraid, but she couldn't see his fear.

He took her hand; the warmth of that grasp, the strength of those fingers, seemed to flow into her cold, exhausted limbs.

She quickened her pace. "I think there's a police substation down that street," she said. "If we go a block or two further—"

"We're not going to the police."

"What?" She stopped dead, staring at him.

"Not yet. Not until I've had a chance to think this through."

"Victor," she said slowly. "Someone is trying to kill us. Trying to kill *me*. What do you mean, you need time to *think this through?*"

"Look, we can't stand around talking about it. We have to get off the streets." He grabbed her hand again. "Come on."

"Where?"

"I have a room. It's only a few blocks away."

She let him drag her only a few yards before she mustered the will to pull free. "Wait a minute. Just *wait*."

He turned, his face a mask of frustration, and confronted her. "Wait for what? For that maniac to catch up? For the bullets to start flying again?"

"For an explanation!"

"I'll explain it all. When we're safe."

She backed away. "Why are you afraid of the police?"

"I can't be sure of them."

"Do you have a reason to be afraid? What have you done?"

With two steps he closed the gap between them and grabbed her hard by the shoulders. "I just pulled you out of a death trap, remember? The bullets were going through your window, not mine!"

"Maybe they were aimed at you!"

"Okay!" He let her go, let her back away from him. "You want to try it on your own? Do it. Maybe the police'll be a help. Maybe not. But I can't risk it. Not until I know all the players behind this."

"You—you're letting me go?"

"You were never my prisoner."

"No." She took a breath—it misted in the cold air. She glanced down the street, toward the police substation. "It's...the reasonable thing to do," she muttered, almost to reassure herself. "That's what they're there for."

"Right."

She frowned, anticipating what lay ahead. "They'll ask a lot of questions."

"What are you going to tell them?"

She looked at him, her gaze unflinchingly meeting his. "The truth."

"Which'll be at best, incomplete. And at worst, unbelievable."

"I have broken glass all over my apartment to prove it."

"A drive-by shooting. Purely random."

"It's their job to protect me."

"What if they don't think you need protection?"

"I'll tell them about you! About Sarah."

"They may or may not take you seriously."

"They have to take me seriously! Someone's trying to kill me!" Her voice, shrill with desperation, seemed to echo endlessly through the maze of streets.

Quietly he said, "I know."

She glanced back toward the substation. "I'm going."

He said nothing.

"Where will you be?" she asked.

"On my own. For now."

She took two steps away, then stopped. "Victor?"

"I'm still here."

"You did save my life. Thank you."

He didn't respond. She heard his footsteps slowly

walk away. She stood there thinking, wondering if she was doing the right thing. Of course she was. A man afraid of the police—with a story as paranoid as his was—had to be dangerous.

But he saved my life.

And once, on a rainy night in Garberville, she had saved his.

She replayed all the events of the last week. Sarah's murder, never explained. The other Catherine Weaver, shot to death on her front doorstep. The film canister that Sarah had retrieved from the car, the one Cathy had slipped into her bathrobe pocket...

Victor's footsteps had faded.

In that instant she realized she'd lost the only man who could help her find the answers to all those questions, the one man who'd stood by her in her darkest moment of terror. The one man she knew, by some strange intuition, she could trust. Facing that deserted street, she felt abandoned and utterly friendless. In sudden panic, she whirled around and called out: "Victor!"

At the far end of the block, a silhouette stopped and turned. He seemed an island of refuge in that crazy, dangerous world. She started toward him, her legs moving her faster and faster, until she was running, yearning for the safety of his arms, the arms of a man she scarcely knew. Yet it didn't feel like a stranger's arms gathering her to his chest, welcoming her into his protective embrace. She felt the pounding of his heart, the grip of his fingers against her back, and something told her that this was a man she could depend upon, a man who wouldn't fold when she needed him most.

"I'm right here," he murmured. "Right here." He stroked through her windblown hair, his fingers burying deep in the tangled strands. She felt the heat of his breath against her face, felt her own quick and shuddering response. And then, all at once, his mouth hungrily sought hers and he was kissing her. She responded with a kiss just as desperate, just as needy. Stranger though he was, he had been there for her and he was still here, his arms sheltering her from the terrors of the night.

She burrowed her face against his chest, longing to press ever deeper, ever closer. "I don't know what to do! I'm so afraid, Victor, and I don't know what to do..."

"We'll work this out together. Okay?" He cupped her face in his hands and tilted it up to his. "You and I, we'll beat this thing."

She nodded. Searching his eyes, connecting with that rock-solid gaze, she found all the assurance she needed.

A wind gusted down the street. She shivered in its wake. "What do we do first?" she whispered.

"First," he said, pulling off his windbreaker and draping it over her shoulders, "We get you warmed up. And inside." He took her hand. "Come on. A hot bath, a good supper, and you'll be operating on all cylinders again."

It was another five blocks to the Kon-Tiki Motel. Though not exactly a five-star establishment, the Kon-Tiki was comfortingly drab and anonymous, one of a dozen on motel row. They climbed the steps to Room 214, overlooking the half-empty parking lot. He unlocked the door and motioned her inside.

The rush of warmth against her cheeks was delicious. She stood in the center of that utterly charmless space and marveled at how good it felt to be safely surrounded by four walls. The furnishings were spare: a double bed, a dresser, two nightstands with lamps, and a single chair. On the wall was a framed print of some nameless South Pacific island. The only luggage she saw was a cheap nylon bag on the floor. The bedcovers were rumpled, recently napped in, the pillows punched up against the headboard.

"Not much," he said. "But it's warm. And it's paid for." He turned on the TV. "We'd better keep an eye on the news. Maybe they'll have something on the Weaver woman."

The Weaver woman, she thought. *It could have been me.* She was shivering again, but now it wasn't from the cold. Settling onto the bed she stared numbly at the TV, not really seeing what was on the screen. She was more aware of *him.* He was circling the room, checking the windows, fiddling with the lock on the door. He moved quietly, efficiently, his silence a testimony to the dangers of their situation. Most men she knew began to babble nonsense when they were scared; Victor Holland simply turned quiet. His mere presence was overwhelming. He seemed to fill the room.

He moved to her side. She flinched as he took her hands and gently inspected them, palm side up. Looking down, she saw the bloodied scratches, the flakes of rust from the fire escape embedded in her skin.

"I guess I'm a mess," she murmured.

He smiled and stroked her face. "You could use some washing up. Go ahead. I'll get us something to eat."

She retreated into the bathroom. Through the door she could hear the drone of the TV, the sound of Victor's voice ordering a pizza over the phone. She ran hot water over her cold, numb hands. In the mirror over the sink she caught an unflattering glimpse of herself, her hair a tangled mess, her chin smudged with dirt.

She washed her face, rubbing new life, new circulation into those frigid cheeks. Glancing down, she noticed Victor's razor on the counter. The sight of that blade cast her situation into a new focus—a frightening one. She picked up the razor, thinking how lethal that blade looked, how vulnerable she would be tonight. Victor was a large man, at least six foot two, with powerful arms. She was scarcely five foot five, a comparative weakling. There was only one bed in the next room. She had come here voluntarily. What would he assume about her? That she was a willing victim? She thought of all the ways a man could hurt her, kill her. It wouldn't take a razor to finish the job. Victor could use his bare hands. *What am I doing here?* she wondered. *Spending the night with a man I scarcely know?*

This was not the time to have doubts. She'd made the decision. She had to go by her instincts, and her instincts told her Victor Holland would never hurt her.

Deliberately she set down the razor. She would have to trust him. She was afraid not to.

In the other room, a door slammed shut. Had he left?

Opening the door a crack, she peered out. The TV was still on. There was no sign of Victor. Slowly she emerged, to find she was alone. She began to circle the room, searching for clues, anything that would tell her more about the man. The bureau drawers were empty, and so was the closet. Obviously he had not moved into this room for a long stay. He'd planned only one night, maybe two. She went to the nylon bag and glanced inside. She saw a clean pair of socks, an unopened package of underwear, and a day-old edition of the *San Francisco Chronicle*. All it told her was that the man kept himself informed and he traveled light.

Like a man on the run.

She dug deeper and came up with a receipt from an automatic teller machine. Yesterday he'd tried to withdraw cash. The machine had printed out the message: *Transaction cannot be completed. Please contact your bank.* Why had it refused him the cash? she wondered. Was he overdrawn? Had the machine been out of order?

The sound of a key grating in the lock caught her by surprise. She glanced up as the door swung open.

The look he gave her made her cheeks flush with guilt. Slowly she rose to her feet, unable to answer that look of accusation in his eyes.

The door swung shut behind him.

"I suppose it's a reasonable thing for you to do," he said. "Search my things."

"I'm sorry. I was just…" She swallowed. "I had to know more about you."

"And what terrible things have you dug up?"

"Nothing!"

"No deep dark secrets? Don't be afraid. Tell me, Cathy."

"Only…only that you had trouble getting cash out of your account."

He nodded. "A frustrating state of affairs. Since by my estimate I have a balance of six thousand dollars. And now I can't seem to touch it." He sat down in the chair, his gaze still on her face. "What else did you learn?"

"You—you read the newspaper."

"So do a lot of people. What else?"

She shrugged. "You wear boxer shorts."

Amusement flickered in his eyes. "Now we're getting personal."

"You…" She took a deep breath. "You're on the run."

He looked at her a long time without saying a word.

"That's why you won't go to the police," she said. "Isn't it?"

He turned away, gazing not at her but at the far wall. "There are reasons."

"Give me one, Victor. One good reason is all I need and then I'll shut up."

He sighed. "I doubt it."

"Try me. I have every reason to believe you."

"You have every reason to think I'm paranoid." Leaning forward, he ran his hands over his face. "Lord, sometimes *I* think I must be."

Quietly she went to him and knelt down beside his chair. "Victor, these people who are trying to kill me—who are they?"

"I don't know."

"You said it might involve people in high places."

"It's just a guess. It's a case of federal money going to illegal research. Deadly research."

"And federal money has to be doled out by someone in authority."

He nodded. "This is someone who's bent the rules. Someone who could be hurt by a political scandal. He just might try to protect himself by manipulating the Bureau. Or even your local police. That's why I won't go to them. That's why I left the room to make my call."

"When?"

"While you were in the bathroom. I went to a pay phone and called the police. I didn't want it traced."

"You just said you don't want them involved."

"This call I had to make. There's a third Catherine Weaver in that phone book. Remember?"

A third victim on the list. Suddenly weak, she sat down on the bed. "What did you say?" she asked softly.

"That I had reason to think she might be in danger. That she wasn't answering her phone."

"You tried it?"

"Twice."

"Did they listen to you?"

"Not only did they listen, they demanded to know my name. That's when I picked up the cue that something must already have happened to her. At that point I hung up and hightailed it out of the booth. A call can be traced in seconds. They could've had me surrounded."

"That makes three," she whispered. "Those two other women. And me."

"They have no way of finding you. Not as long as you stay away from your apartment. Stay out of—"

They both froze in panic.

Someone was knocking on the door.

They stared at each other, fear mirrored in their eyes. Then, after a moment's hesitation, Victor said, "Who is it?"

"Domino's," called a thin voice.

Cautiously, Victor eased open the door. A teenage boy stood outside, wielding a bag and a flat cardboard box.

"Hi!" chirped the boy. "A large combo with the works, two Cokes and extra napkins. Right?"

"Right." Victor handed the boy a few bills. "Keep the change," he said and closed the door. Turning, he gave Cathy a sheepish look. "Well," he admitted. "Just goes to show you. Sometimes a knock at the door really is just the pizza man."

They both laughed, a sound not of humor but of

frayed nerves. The release of tension seemed to trans-
form his face, melted his wariness to warmth. Erase
those haggard lines, she thought, and he could almost
be called a handsome man.

"I tell you what," he said. "Let's not think about this
mess right now. Why don't we just get right down to the
really important issue of the day. Food."

Nodding, she reached out for the box. "Better hand
it over. Before I eat the damn bedspread."

While the ten o'clock news droned from the television set, they tore into the pizza like two ravenous
animals. It was a greasy and utterly satisfying banquet
on a motel bed. They scarcely bothered with conversation—their mouths were too busy devouring cheese and
pepperoni. On the TV, a dapper anchorman announced
a shakeup in the mayor's office, the resignation of the
city manager, news that, given their current situation,
seemed ridiculously trivial. Scarcely thirty seconds
were devoted to that morning's killing of Catherine
Weaver I; as yet, no suspects were in custody. No mention was made of any second victim by the same name.

Victor frowned. "Looks like the other woman didn't
make it to the news."

"Or nothing's happened to her." She glanced at him
questioningly. "What if the second Cathy Weaver is all
right? When you called the police, they might've been
asking you routine questions. When you're on edge,
it's easy to—"

"Imagine things?" The look he gave her almost made
her bite her tongue.

"No," she said quietly. "Misinterpret. The police
can't respond to every anonymous call. It's natural
they'd ask for your name."

"It was more than a request, Cathy. They were champing at the bit to interrogate me."

"I'm not doubting your word. I'm just playing devil's advocate. Trying to keep things level and sane in a crazy situation."

He looked at her long and hard. At last he nodded. "The voice of a rational woman," he sighed. "Exactly what I need right now. To keep me from jumping at my own shadow."

"And remind you to eat." She held out another slice of pizza. "You ordered this giant thing. You'd better help me finish it."

The tension between them instantly evaporated. He settled onto the bed and accepted the proferred slice. "That maternal look becomes you," he noted wryly. "So does the pizza sauce."

"What?" She swiped at her chin.

"You look like a two-year-old who's decided to fingerpaint her face."

"Good grief, can you hand me the napkins?"

"Let me do it." Leaning forward, he gently dabbed away the sauce. As he did, she studied his face, saw the laugh lines creasing the corners of his eyes, the strands of silver intertwined with the brown hair. She remembered the photo of that very face, pasted on a Viratek badge. How somber he'd looked, the unsmiling portrait of a scientist. Now he appeared young and alive and almost happy.

Suddenly aware that she was watching him, he looked up and met her gaze. Slowly his smile faded. They both went very still, as though seeing, in each other's eyes, something they had not noticed before. The voices on the television seemed to fade into a far-off dimension. She felt his fingers trace lightly down her cheek. It was only a touch, but it left her shivering.

She asked, softly, "What happens now, Victor? Where do we go from here?"

"We have several choices."

"Such as?"

"I have friends in Palo Alto. We could turn to them."

"Or?"

"Or we could stay right where we are. For a while."

Right where we are. In this room, on this bed. She wouldn't mind that. Not at all.

She felt herself leaning toward him, drawn by a force against which she could offer no resistance. Both his hands came up to cradle her face, such large hands, but so infinitely gentle. She closed her eyes, knowing that this kiss, too, would be a gentle one.

And it was. This wasn't a kiss driven by fear or desperation. This was a quiet melting together of warmth, of souls. She swayed against him, felt his arms circle behind her to pull her inescapably close. It was a dangerous moment. She could feel herself tottering on the edge of total surrender to this man she scarcely knew. Already, her arms had found their way around his neck and her hands were roaming through the silver-streaked thickness of his hair.

His kisses dropped to her neck, exploring all the tender rises and hollows of her throat. All the needs that had lain dormant these past few years, all the hungers and desires, seemed to stir inside her, awakening at his touch.

And then, in an instant, the magic slipped away. At first she didn't understand why he suddenly pulled back. He sat bolt upright. The expression on his face was one of frozen astonishment. Bewildered, she followed his gaze and saw that he was focused on the television set behind her. She turned to see what had captured his attention.

A disturbingly familiar face stared back from the screen. She recognized the Viratek logo at the top, the straight-ahead gaze of the man in the photo. Why on earth would they be broadcasting Victor Holland's ID badge?

"...Sought on charges of industrial espionage. Evidence now links Dr. Holland to the death of a fellow Viratek researcher, Dr. Gerald Martinique. Investigators fear the suspect has already sold extensive research data to a European competitor..."

Neither one of them seemed able to move from the bed. They could only stare in disbelief at the newscaster with the Ken doll haircut. The station switched to a commercial break, raisins dancing crazily on a field, proclaiming the wonders of California sunshine. The lilting music was unbearable.

Victor rose to his feet and flicked off the television.

Slowly he turned to look at her. The silence between them grew agonizing.

"It's not true," he said quietly. "None of it."

She tried to read those unfathomable green eyes, wanting desperately to believe him. The taste of his kisses were still warm on her lips. The kisses of a con artist? *Is this just another lie? Has everything you've told me been nothing but lies? Who and what are you, Victor Holland?*

She glanced sideways, at the telephone on the bedside stand. It was so close. One call to the police, that's all it would take to end this nightmare.

"It's a frame-up," he said. "Viratek's releasing false information."

"Why?"

"To corner me. What easier way to find me than to have the police help them?"

She edged toward the phone.

"Don't, Cathy."

She froze, startled by the threat in his voice.

He saw the instant fear in her eyes. Gently he said, "Please. Don't call. I won't hurt you. I promise you can walk right out that door if you want. But first listen to me. Let me tell you what happened. Give me a chance."

His gaze was steady and absolutely believable. And he was right beside her, ready to stop her from making a move. Or to break her arm, if need be. She had no other choice. Nodding, she settled back down on the bed.

He began to pace, his feet tracing a path in the dull green carpet.

"It's all some—some incredible lie," he said. "It's crazy to think I'd kill him. Jerry Martinique and I were the best of friends. We both worked at Viratek. I was in vaccine development, he was a microbiologist. His specialty was viral studies. Genome research."

"You mean—like chromosomes?"

"The viral equivalent. Anyway, Jerry and I, we helped each other through some bad times. He'd gone through a painful divorce and I…" He paused, his voice dropping. "I lost my wife three years ago. To leukemia."

So he'd been married. Somehow it surprised her. He seemed like the sort of man who was far too independent to have ever said, "I do."

"About two months ago," he continued, "Jerry was transferred to a new research department. Viratek had been awarded a grant for some defense project. It was top security—Jerry couldn't talk about it. But I could see he was bothered by something that was going on in that lab. All he'd say to me was, 'They don't understand the danger. They don't know what they're getting into.' Jerry's field was the alteration of viral genes. So I assume the project had something to do with viruses as weapons. Jerry was fully aware that those weapons are outlawed by international agreement."

"If he knew it was illegal, why did he take part in it?"

"Maybe he didn't realize at first what the project was aiming for. Maybe they sold it to him as purely defensive research. In any event, he got upset enough to resign from the project. He went right to the top— the founder of Viratek. Walked into Archibald Black's office and threatened to go public if the project wasn't terminated. Four days later he had an accident." Anger flashed in Victor's eyes. It wasn't directed at her, but the fury in that gaze was frightening all the same.

"What happened to him?" she asked.

"His wrecked car was found at the side of the road. Jerry was still inside. Dead, of course." Suddenly, the anger was gone, replaced by overwhelming weariness. He sank onto the bed. "I thought the accident investigation would blow everything into the open. It was a farce. The local cops did their best, but then some federal transportation 'expert' showed up on the scene and took over. He said Jerry must've fallen asleep at the wheel. Case closed. That's when I realized just how deep this went. I didn't know who to go to, so I called the FBI in San Francisco. Told them I had evidence."

"You mean the film?" asked Cathy.

Victor nodded. "Just before he was killed, Jerry told

me about some duplicate papers he'd stashed away in his garden shed. After the…accident, I went over to his house. Found the place ransacked. But they never bothered to search the shed. That's how I got hold of the evidence, a single file and a roll of film. I arranged a meeting with one of the San Francisco agents, a guy named Sam Polowski. I'd already talked to him a few times on the phone. He offered to meet me in Garberville. We wanted to keep it private, so we agreed to a spot just outside of town. I drove down, fully expecting him to show. Well, someone showed up, all right. Someone who ran me off the road." He paused and looked straight at her. "That's the night you found me."

The night my whole life changed, she thought.

"You have to believe me," he said.

She studied him, her instincts battling against logic. The story was just barely plausible, halfway between truth and fantasy. But the man looked solid as stone.

Wearily she nodded. "I do believe you, Victor. Maybe I'm crazy. Or just gullible. But I do."

The bed shifted as he sat down beside her. They didn't touch, yet she could almost feel the warmth radiating between them.

"That's all that matters to me right now," he said. "That you know, in your heart, I'm telling the truth."

"In my heart?" She shook her head and laughed. "My heart's always been a lousy judge of character. No, I'm guessing. I'm going by the fact you kept me alive. By the fact there's another Cathy Weaver who's now dead…"

Remembering the face of that other woman, the face in the newspaper, she suddenly began to shake. It all added up to the terrible truth. The gun blasts into her apartment, the other dead Cathy. And Sarah, poor Sarah.

She was gulping in shaky breaths, hovering on the verge of tears.

She let him take her in his arms, let him pull her down on the bed beside him. He murmured into her hair, gentle words of comfort and reassurance. He turned off the lamp. In darkness they held each other, two frightened souls joined against a terrifying world. She felt safe there, tucked away against his chest. This was a place where no one could hurt her. It was a stranger's arms, but from the smell of his shirt to the beat of his heart, it all seemed somehow familiar. She never wanted to leave that spot, ever.

She trembled as his lips brushed her forehead. He was stroking her face now, her neck, warming her with his touch. When his hand slipped beneath her blouse, she didn't protest. Somehow it seemed so natural, that that hand would come to lie at her breast. It wasn't the touch of a marauder, it was simply a gentle reminder that she was in safekeeping.

And yet, she found herself responding…

Her nipple tingled and grew taut beneath his cupping hand. The tingling spread, a warmth that crept to her face and flushed her cheeks. She reached for his shirt and began to unbutton it. In the darkness she was slow and clumsy. By the time she finally slid her hand under the fabric, they were both breathing hard and fast with anticipation.

She brushed through the coarse mat of hair, stroking her way across that broad chest. He took in a sharp breath as her fingers skimmed a delicate circle around his nipple.

If playing with fire had been her intention, then she had just struck the match.

His mouth was suddenly on hers, seeking, devouring. The force of his kiss pressed her onto her back, trapping her head against the pillows. For a dizzy eternity she was swimming in sensations, the scent of male heat, the unyielding grip of his hands imprisoning her face. Only when he at last drew away did they both come up for air.

He stared down at her, as though hovering on the edge of temptation.

"This is crazy," he whispered.

"Yes. Yes, it is—"

"I never meant to do this—"

"Neither did I."

"It's just that you're scared. We're both scared. And we don't know what the hell we're doing."

"No." She closed her eyes, felt the unexpected bite of tears. "We don't. But I *am* scared. And I just want to be held. Please, Victor. Hold me, that's all. Just hold me."

He pulled her close, murmuring her name. This time the embrace was gentle, without the fever of desire. His shirt was still unbuttoned, his chest bared. And that's where she lay her head, against that curling nest of hair. Yes, he was right, so wise. They were crazy to be making love when they both knew it was fear, nothing else, that had driven their desire. And now the fever had broken.

A sense of peace fell over her. She curled up against him. Exhaustion robbed them both of speech. Her muscles gradually fell limp as sleep tugged her into its shadow. Even if she tried to, she could not move her arms or legs. Instead she was drifting free, like a wraith in the darkness, floating somewhere in a warm and inky sea.

Vaguely she was aware of light sliding past her eyelids.

The warmth encircling her body seemed to melt away. No, she wanted it back, wanted *him* back! An instant later she felt him shaking her.

"Cathy. Come on, wake up!"

Through drowsy eyes she peered at him. "Victor?"

"Something's going on outside."

She tumbled out of bed and followed him to the window. Through a slit in the curtains she spotted what had alarmed him: a patrol car, its radio crackling faintly, parked by the motel registration door. At once she snapped wide awake, her mind going over the exits from their room. There was only one.

"Out, now!" he ordered. "Before we're trapped."

He eased open the door. They scrambled out onto the walkway. The frigid night air was like a slap in the face. She was already shivering, more from fear than from the cold. Running at a crouch, they moved along the walkway, away from the stairs, and ducked past the ice machine.

Below, they heard the lobby door open and the voice of the motel manager: "Yeah, that'll be right upstairs. Gee, he sure seemed like a nice-enough guy…"

Tires screeched as another patrol car pulled up, lights flashing.

Victor gave her a push. *"Go!"*

They slipped into a breezeway and scurried through, to the other side of the building. No stairways there! They climbed over the walkway railing and dropped into the parking lot.

Faintly they heard a banging, then the command: "Open up! This is the police."

At once they were sprinting instinctively for the shadows. No one spotted them, no one gave chase. Still they kept running, until they'd left the Kon-Tiki Motel blocks and blocks behind them, until they were so tired they were stumbling.

At last Cathy slowed to a halt and leaned back against a doorway, her breath coming out in clouds of cold mist. "How did they find you?" she said between gasps.

"It couldn't have been the call..." Suddenly he groaned. "My credit card! I had to use it to pay the bill."

"Where now? Should we try another motel?"

He shook his head. "I'm down to my last forty bucks. I can't risk a credit card again."

"And I left my purse at the apartment. I—I'm not sure I want to—"

"We're not going back for it. They'll be watching the place."

They. Meaning the killers.

"So we're broke," she said weakly.

He didn't answer. He stood with his hands in his pockets, his whole body a study in frustration. "You have friends you can go to?"

"I think so. Uh, no. She's out of town till Friday. And what would I tell her? How would I explain you?"

"You can't. And we can't handle any questions right now."

That leaves out most of my friends, she thought. Nowhere to go, no one to turn to. Unless...

No, she'd promised herself never to sink that low, never to beg for *that* particular source of help.

Victor glanced up the street. "There's a bus stop over

there." He reached in his pocket and took out a handful of money. "Here," he said. "Take it and get out of the city. Go visit some friends on your own."

"What about you?"

"I'll be okay."

"Broke? With everyone after you?" She shook her head.

"I'll only make things more dangerous for you." He pressed the money into her hand.

She stared down at the wad of bills, thinking: *This is all he has. And he's giving it to me.* "I can't," she said.

"You have to."

"But—"

"Don't argue with me." The look in his eyes left no alternative.

Reluctantly she closed her fingers around the money.

"I'll wait till you get on the bus. It should take you right past the station."

"Victor?"

He silenced her with a single look. Placing both hands on her shoulders, he stood her before him. "You'll be fine," he said. Then he pressed a kiss to her forehead. For a moment his lips lingered, and the warmth of his breath in her hair left her trembling. "I wouldn't leave you if I thought otherwise."

The roar of a bus down the block made them both turn.

"There's your limousine," he whispered. "Go." He gave her a nudge. "Take care of yourself, Cathy."

She started toward the bus stop. Three steps, four. She slowed and came to a halt. Turning, she saw that he had already edged away into the shadows.

"Get on it!" he called.

She looked at the bus. *I won't do it,* she thought.

She turned back to Victor. "I know a place! A place we can both stay!"

"What?"

"I didn't want to use it but—"

Her words were drowned out as the bus wheezed to the stop, then roared away.

"It's a bit of a walk," she said. "But we'd have beds and a meal. And I can guarantee no one would call the police."

He came out of the shadows. "Why didn't you think of this earlier?"

"I did think of it. But up till now, things weren't, well...desperate enough."

"Not desperate enough," he repeated slowly. He moved toward her, his face taut with incredulity. "Not *desperate* enough? Hell, lady. I'd like to know exactly what kind of crisis would qualify!"

"You have to understand, this is a last resort. It's not an easy place for me to turn to."

His eyes narrowed in suspicion. "This place is beginning to sound worse and worse. What are we talking about? A flophouse?"

"No, it's in Pacific Heights. You could even call the place a mansion."

"Who lives there? A friend?"

"Quite the opposite."

His eyebrow shot up. "An enemy?"

"Close." She let out a sigh of resignation. "My ex-husband."

Chapter 5

"Jack, open up! Jack!" Cathy banged again and again on the door of the formidable Pacific Heights home. There was no answer. Through the windows they saw only darkness.

"Damn you, Jack!" She gave the door a slap of frustration. "Why aren't you *ever* home when I need you?"

Victor glanced around at the neighborhood of elegant homes and neatly trimmed shrubbery. "We can't stand around out here all night."

"We're not going to," she muttered. Crouching on her knees, she began to dig around in a red-brick planter.

"What are you doing?"

"Something I swore I'd never do." Her fingers raked the loamy soil, searching for the key Jack kept buried under the geraniums. Sure enough, there it was, right where it had always been. She rose to her feet, clapping the dirt off her hands. "But there are limits to my pride. Threat of death being one of them." She inserted the key and felt a momentary dart of panic when it didn't turn. But with a little jiggling, the lock at last gave way. The door swung open to the faint gleam of a polished wood floor, a massive bannister.

She motioned Victor inside. The solid thunk of the door closing behind them seemed to shut out all the dangers of the night. Cloaked in the darkness, they both let out a sigh of relief.

"Just what kind of terms are you on with your ex-husband?" Victor asked, following her blindly through the unlit foyer.

"Speaking. Barely."

"He doesn't mind you wandering around his house?"

"Why not?" She snorted. "Jack lets half the human race wander through his bedroom. The only prerequisite being XX chromosomes."

She felt her way into the pitch-dark living room and flipped on the light switch. There she froze in astonishment and stared at the two naked bodies intertwined on the polar bear rug.

"Jack!" she blurted out.

The larger of the two bodies extricated himself and sat up. "Hello, Cathy!" He raked his hand through his dark hair and grinned. "Seems like old times."

The woman lying next to him spat out a shocking obscenity, scrambled to her feet, and stormed off in a blur of wild red hair and bare bottom toward the bedroom.

"That's Lulu," yawned Jack, by way of introduction.

Cathy sighed. "I see your taste in women hasn't improved."

"No, sweetheart, my taste in women hit a high point

when I married you." Unmindful of his state of nudity, Jack rose to his feet and regarded Victor. The contrast between the two men was instantly apparent. Though both were tall and lean, it was Jack who possessed the striking good looks, and he knew it. He'd always known it. Vanity wasn't a label one could ever pin on Victor Holland.

"I see you brought a fourth," said Jack, giving Victor the once-over. "So, what'll it be, folks? Bridge or poker?"

"Neither," said Cathy.

"That opens up all *sorts* of possibilities."

"Jack, I need your help."

He turned and looked at her with mock incredulity. *"No!"*

"You know damn well I wouldn't be here if I could avoid it!"

He winked at Victor. "Don't believe her. She's still madly in love with me."

"Can we get serious?"

"Darling, you never did have a sense of humor."

"Damn you, Jack!" Everyone had a breaking point and Cathy had reached hers. She couldn't help it; without warning she burst into tears. "For once in your life will you *listen* to me?"

That's when Victor's patience finally snapped. He didn't need a degree in psychology to know this Jack character was a first-class jerk. Couldn't he see that Cathy was exhausted and terrified? Up till this moment, Victor had admired her for her strength. Now he ached at the sight of her vulnerability.

It was only natural to pull her into his arms, to ease her tear-streaked face against his chest. Over her shoulder, he growled out an oath that impugned not only Jack's name but that of Jack's mother as well.

The other man didn't seem to take offense, probably because he'd been called far worse names, and on a regular basis. He simply crossed his arms and regarded Victor with a raised eyebrow. "Being protective, are we?"

"She needs protection."

"From what, pray tell?"

"Maybe you haven't heard. Three days ago, someone murdered her friend Sarah."

"Sarah…Boylan?"

Victor nodded. "Tonight, someone tried to kill Cathy."

Jack stared at him. He looked at his ex-wife. "Is this true? What he's saying?"

Cathy, wiping away tears, nodded.

"Why didn't you tell me this to begin with?"

"Because you were acting like an ass to begin with!" she shot back.

Down the hall came the *click-click* of high-heeled shoes. "She's absolutely right!" yelled a female voice from the foyer. "You *are* an ass, Jack Zuckerman!" The front door opened and slammed shut again. The thud seemed to echo endlessly through the mansion.

There was a long silence.

Suddenly, through her tears, Cathy laughed. "You know what, Jack? I *like* that woman."

Jack crossed his arms and gave his ex-wife the critical once-over. "Either I'm going senile or you forgot to tell me something. Why haven't you gone to the police? Why bother old Jack about this?"

Cathy and Victor glanced at each other.

"We can't go to the police," Cathy said.

"I assume this has to do with *him?*" He cocked a thumb at Victor.

Cathy let out a breath. "It's a complicated story…"

"It must be. If you're afraid to go to the police."

"I can explain it," said Victor.

"Mm-hm. Well." Jack reached for the bathrobe lying in a heap by the polar bear rug. "Well," he said again, calmly tying the sash. "I've always enjoyed watching creativity at work. So let's have it." He sat down on the leather couch and smiled at Victor. "I'm waiting. It's showtime."

Special Agent Sam Polowski lay shivering in his bed, watching the eleven o'clock news. Every muscle in his body ached, his head pounded, and the thermometer at his bedside read an irrefutable 101 degrees. So much for changing flat tires in the pouring rain. He wished he could get his hands on the joker who'd punched that nail in his tire while he was grabbing a quick bite at that roadside cafe. Not only had the culprit managed to keep Sam from his appointment in Garberville, thereby shredding the Viratek case into confetti, Sam had also lost track of his only contact in the affair: Victor Holland. And now, the flu.

Sam reached over for the bottle of aspirin. To hell with the ulcer. His head hurt. And when it came to headaches, there was nothing like Mom's time-tested remedy.

He was in the midst of gulping down three tablets when the news about Victor Holland flashed on the screen.

"…New evidence links the suspect to the murder of fellow Viratek researcher, Dr. Gerald Martinique…"

Sam sat up straight in bed. "What the hell?" he growled at the TV.

Then he grabbed the telephone.

It took six rings for his supervisor to answer. "Dafoe?" Sam said. "This is Polowski."

"Do you know what time it is?"

"Have you seen the late-night news?"

"I happen to be in bed."

"There's a story on Viratek."

A pause. "Yeah, I know. I cleared it."

"What's with this crap about industrial espionage? They're making Holland out to be a—"

"Polowski, drop it."

"Since when did he become a murder suspect?"

"Look, just consider it a cover story. I want him brought in. For his own good."

"So you sic him with a bunch of trigger-happy cops?"

"I said drop it."

"But—"

"You're off the case." Dafoe hung up.

Sam stared in disbelief at the receiver, then at the television, then back at the receiver.

Pull me off the case? He slammed the receiver down so hard the bottle of aspirin tumbled off the nightstand.

That's what you think.

"I think I've heard about enough," said Jack, rising to his feet. "I want this man out of my house. And I want him out now."

"Jack, please!" said Cathy. "Give him a chance—"

"You're buying this ridiculous tale?"

"I believe him."

"Why?"

She looked at Victor and saw the clear fire of honesty burning in his eyes. "Because he saved my life."

"You're a fool, babycakes." Jack reached for the phone. "You yourself saw the TV. He's wanted for murder. If you don't call the police, I will."

But as Jack picked up the receiver, Victor grabbed his arm. "No," he said. Though his voice was quiet, it held the unmistakable note of authority.

The two men stared at each other, neither willing to back down.

"This is more than just a case of murder," said Victor. "This is deadly research. The manufacture of illegal weapons. This could reach all the way to Washington."

"Who in Washington?"

"Someone in control. Someone with the federal funds to authorize that research."

"I see. Some lofty public servant is out knocking off scientists. With the help of the FBI."

"Jerry wasn't just any scientist. He had a conscience. He was a whistleblower who would've taken this to the press to stop that research. The political fallout would've been disastrous, for the whole administration."

"Wait. Are we talking Pennsylvania Avenue?"

"Maybe."

Jack snorted. "Holland, I *make* Grade B horror films. I don't live them."

"This isn't a film. This is real. Real bullets, real bodies."

"Then that's all the more reason I want nothing to do with it." Jack turned to Cathy. "Sorry, sweetcakes. It's nothing personal, but I detest the company you keep."

"Jack," she said. "You have to help us!"

"You, I'll help. Him—no way. I draw the line at lunatics and felons."

"You heard what he said! It's a frame-up!"

"You are so gullible."

"Only about you."

"Cathy, it's all right," said Victor. He was standing very still, very calm. "I'll leave."

"No, you won't." Cathy shot to her feet and stalked over to her ex-husband. She stared him straight in the eye, a gaze so direct, so accusing, he seemed to wilt right down into a chair. "You owe it to me, Jack. You owe me for all the years we were married. All the years I put into *your* career, *your* company, *your* idiotic flicks. I haven't asked for anything. You have the house. The Jaguar. The bank account. I never asked because I didn't want to take a damn thing from this marriage except my own soul. But now I'm asking. This man saved my life tonight. If you ever cared about me, if you ever loved me, even a little, then you'll do me this favor."

"Harbor a criminal?"

"Only until we figure out what to do next."

"And how long might that take? Weeks? Months?"

"I don't know."

"Just the kind of definite answer I like."

Victor said, "I need time to find out what Jerry was trying to prove. What it is Viratek's working on—"

"You had one of his files," said Jack. "Why didn't you read the blasted thing?"

"I'm not a virologist. I couldn't interpret the data. It was some sort of RNA sequence, probably a viral genome. A lot of the data was coded. All I can be sure of is the name: Project Cerberus."

"Where is all this vital evidence now?"

"I lost the file. It was in my car the night I was shot. I'm sure they have it back."

"And the film?"

Victor sank into a chair, his face suddenly lined by weariness. "I don't have it. I was hoping that Cathy..." Sighing, he ran his hands through his hair. "I've lost that, too."

"Well," said Jack. "Give or take a few miracles, I'd say this puts your chances at just about zero. And I'm known as an optimist."

"I know where the film is," said Cathy.

There was a long silence. Victor raised his head and stared at her. "What?"

"I wasn't sure about you—not at first. I didn't want to tell you until I could be certain—"

Victor shot to his feet. *"Where is it?"*

She flinched at the sharpness of his voice. He must have noticed how startled she was—his next words were quiet but urgent. "I need that film, Cathy. Before they find it. Where is it?"

"Sarah found it in my car. I didn't know it was yours! I thought it was Hickey's."

"Who's Hickey?"

"A photographer—a friend of mine—"

Jack snorted. "Hickey. Now *there's* a ladies' man."

"He was in a rush to get to the airport," she continued. "At the last minute he left me with some rolls of film. Asked me to take care of them till he got back from Nairobi. But all his film was stolen from my car."

"And my roll?" asked Victor.

"It was in my bathrobe pocket the night Sarah—the night she—" She paused, swallowing at the mention of her friend. "When I got back here, to the city, I mailed it to Hickey's studio."

"Where's the studio?"

"Over on Union Street. I mailed it this afternoon—"

"So it should be there sometime tomorrow." He began to pace the room. "All we have to do is wait for the mail to arrive."

"I don't have a key."

"We'll find a way in."

"Terrific," sighed Jack. "Now he's turning my ex-wife into a burglar."

"We're only after the film!" said Cathy.

"It's still breaking and entering, sweetie."

"You don't have to get involved."

"But you're asking me to harbor the breakers and enterers."

"Just one night, Jack. That's all I'm asking."

"That sounds like one of *my* lines."

"And your lines always work, don't they?"

"Not this time."

"Then here's another line to chew on: 1988. Your federal tax return. Or lack of one."

Jack froze. He glowered at Victor, then at Cathy. "That's below the belt."

"Your most vulnerable spot."

"I'll get around to filing—"

"More words to chew on. Audit. IRS. Jail."

"Okay, okay!" Jack threw his arms up in surrender. "God, I *hate* that word."

"What, *jail?*"

"Don't laugh, babycakes. The word could soon apply to all of us." He turned and headed for the stairs.

"Where are you going?" Cathy demanded.

"To make up the spare beds. Seems I have house-guests for the night…"

"Can we trust him?" Victor asked after Jack had vanished upstairs.

Cathy sank back on the couch, all the energy suddenly drained from her body, and closed her eyes. "We have to. I can't think of anywhere else to go…"

She was suddenly aware of his approach, and then he was sitting beside her, so close she could feel the overwhelming strength of his presence. He didn't say a word, yet she knew he was watching her.

She opened her eyes and met his gaze. So steady, so intense, it seemed to infuse her with new strength.

"I know it wasn't easy for you," he said. "Asking Jack for favors."

She smiled. "I've always wanted to talk tough with Jack." Ruefully she added, "Until tonight, I've never quite been able to pull it off."

"My guess is, talking tough isn't in your repertoire."

"No, it isn't. When it comes to confrontation, I'm a gutless wonder."

"For a gutless wonder, you did pretty well. In fact, you were magnificent."

"That's because I wasn't fighting for me. I was fighting for you."

"You don't consider yourself worth fighting for?"

She shrugged. "It's the way I was raised. I was always told that sticking up for yourself was unladylike. Whereas sticking up for other people was okay."

He nodded gravely. "Self-sacrifice. A fine feminine tradition."

That made her laugh. "Spoken like a man who knows women well."

"Only two women. My mother and my wife."

At the mention of his dead wife, she fell silent. She wondered what the woman's name was, what she'd looked like, how much he'd loved her. He must have loved her a great deal—she'd heard the pain in his voice earlier that evening when he'd mentioned her death. She felt an unexpected stab of envy that this unnamed wife had been so loved. What Cathy would give to be as dearly loved by a man! Just as quickly she suppressed the thought, appalled that she could be jealous of a dead woman.

She turned away, her face tinged with guilt. "I think Jack will go along," she said. "Tonight, at least."

"That was blackmail, wasn't it? That stuff about the tax return?"

"He's a careless man. I just reminded him of his oversight."

Victor shook his head. "You are amazing. Jumping along rooftops one minute, blackmailing ex-husbands the next."

"You're so right," said Jack, who'd reappeared at the bottom of the stairs. "She is an amazing woman. I can't wait to see what she'll do next."

Cathy rose wearily to her feet. "At this point I'll do anything." She slipped past Jack and headed up the stairs. "Anything I have to to stay alive."

The two men listened to her footsteps recede along the hall. Then they regarded each other in silence.

"Well," said Jack with forced cheerfulness. "What's next on the agenda? Scrabble?"

"Try solitaire," said Victor, hauling himself off the couch. He was in no mood to share pleasantries with Jack Zuckerman. The man was slick and self-centered and he obviously went through women the way most men went through socks. Victor had a hard time imagining what Cathy had ever seen in the man. That is, aside from Jack's good looks and obvious wealth. There was no denying the fact he was a classic hunk, with the added attraction of money thrown in. Maybe it was that combination that had dazzled her.

A combination I'll certainly never possess, he thought.

He crossed the room, then stopped and turned. "Zuckerman?" he asked. "Do you still love your wife?"

Jack looked faintly startled by the question. "Do I still love her? Well, let me see. No, not exactly. But I suppose I have a sentimental attachment, based on ten years of marriage. And I respect her."

"Respect her? You?"

"Yes. Her talents. Her technical skill. After all, she's my number-one makeup artist."

That's what she meant to him. An asset he could use. *Thinking of himself, the jerk.* If there was anyone else Victor could turn to, he would. But the one man he would've trusted—Jerry—was dead. His other friends might already be under observation. Plus, they weren't in the sort of tax brackets that allowed private little hideaways in the woods. Jack, on the other hand, had the resources to spirit Cathy away to a safe place. Victor could only hope the man's sentimental attachment was strong enough to make him watch out for her.

"I have a proposition," said Victor.

Jack instantly looked suspicious. "What might that be?"

"I'm the one they're really after. Not Cathy. I don't want to make things any more dangerous for her than I already have."

"Big of you."

"It's better if I go off on my own. If I leave her with you, will you keep her safe?"

Jack shifted, looked down at his feet. "Well, sure. I guess so."

"Don't guess. Can you?"

"Look, we start shooting a film in Mexico next month. Jungle scenes, black lagoons, that sort of stuff. Should be a safe-enough place."

"That's next month. What about now?"

"I'll think of something. But first you get yourself out of the picture. Since you're the reason she's in danger in the first place."

Victor couldn't disagree with that last point. *Since the night I met her I've caused her nothing but trouble.*

He nodded. "I'm out of here tomorrow."

"Good."

"Take care of Cathy. Get her out of the city. Out of the country. Don't wait."

"Yeah. Sure."

Something about the way Jack said it, his hasty, whatever-you-say tone, made Victor wonder if the man gave a damn about anyone but himself. But at this point Victor had no choice. He had to trust Jack Zuckerman.

As he climbed the stairs to the guest rooms, it occurred to him that, come morning, it would be good-bye. A quiet little bond had formed between them. He owed his life to her and she to him. That was the sort of link one could never break.

Even if we never see each other again.

In the upstairs hall, he paused outside her closed door. He could hear her moving around the room, opening and closing drawers, squeaking bedsprings.

He knocked on the door. "Cathy?"

There was a pause. Then, "Come in."

One dim lamp lit the room. She was sitting on the bed, dressed in a ridiculously huge man's shirt. Her hair hung in damp waves to her shoulders. The scent of soap and shampoo permeated the shadows. It reminded him of his wife, of the shower smells and feminine sweetness. He stood there, pierced by a sense of longing he hadn't felt in over a year, longing for the warmth, the love, of a woman. Not just any woman. He wasn't like Jack, to whom a soft body with the right equipment would be sufficient. What Victor wanted was the heart and soul; the package they came wrapped in was only of minor importance.

His own wife Lily hadn't been beautiful; neither had she been unattractive. Even at the end, when the ravages of illness had left her shrunken and bruised, there had been a light in her eyes, a gentle spirit's glow.

The same glow he'd seen in Catherine Weaver's eyes the night she'd saved his life. The same glow he saw now.

She sat with her back propped up on pillows. Her gaze was silently expectant, maybe a little fearful. She was clutching a handful of tissues. *Why were you crying?* he wondered.

He didn't approach; he stood just inside the doorway. Their gazes locked together in the gloom. "I've just talked with Jack," he said.

She nodded but said nothing.

"We both agree. It's better that I leave as soon as possible. So I'll be taking off in the morning."

"What about the film?"

"I'll get it. All I need is Hickey's address."

"Yes. Of course." She looked down at the tissues in her fist.

He could tell she wanted to say something. He went to the bed and sat down. Those sweet woman smells grew intoxicating. The neckline of her oversized shirt sagged low enough to reveal a tempting glimpse of shadow. He forced himself to focus on her face.

"Cathy, you'll be fine. Jack said he'd watch out for you. Get you out of the city."

"Jack?" What sounded like a laugh escaped her throat.

"You'll be safer with him. I don't even know where I'll be going. I don't want to drag you into this—"

"But you already have. You've dragged me in over my head, Victor. What am I supposed to do now? I can't just—just sit around and wait for you to fix things. I owe it to Sarah—"

"And I owe it to you not to let you get hurt."

"You think you can hand me over to Jack and make everything be fine again? Well, it won't be fine. Sarah's dead. Her baby's dead. And somehow it's not just your fault. It's mine as well."

"No, it's not. Cathy—"

"It is my fault! Did you know she was lying there in the driveway all night? In the rain. In the cold. There she was, dying, and I slept through the whole damn thing…" She dropped her face in her hands. The guilt that had been tormenting her since Sarah's death at last burst through. She began to cry, silently, ashamedly, unable to hold back the tears any longer.

Victor's response was automatic and instinctively male. He pulled her against him and gave her a warm, safe place to cry. As soon as he felt her settle into his arms, he knew it was a mistake. It was too perfect a fit.

She felt as if she belonged there, against his heart, felt that if she ever pulled away there would be left a hole so gaping it could never be filled. He pressed his lips to her damp hair and inhaled her heady scent of soap and warm skin. That gentle fragrance was enough to drown a man with need. So was the softness of her face, the silken luster of that shoulder peeking out from beneath the shirt. And all the time he was stroking her hair, murmuring inane words of comfort, he was thinking: *I have to leave her. For her sake I have to abandon this woman. Or I'll get us both killed.*

"Cathy," he said. It took all the willpower he could muster to pull away. He placed his hands on her shoulders, made her look at him. Her gaze was confused and brimming with tears. "We have to talk about tomorrow."

She nodded and swiped at the tears on her cheeks.

"I want you out of the city, first thing in the morning. Go to Mexico with Jack. Anywhere. Just keep out of sight."

"What will you do?"

"I'm going to take a look at that roll of film, see what kind of evidence it has."

"And then?"

"I don't know yet. Maybe I'll take it to the newspapers. The FBI is definitely out."

"How will I know you're all right? How do I reach you?"

He thought hard, fighting the distraction of her scent, her hair. He found himself stroking the bare skin of her shoulder, marveling at how smooth it felt beneath his fingers.

He focused on her face, on the look of worry in her eyes. "Every other Sunday I'll put an ad in the Personals.

Los Angeles Times. It'll be addressed to, let's say, Cora. Anything I need to tell you will be there."

"Cora." She nodded. "I'll remember."

They looked at each other, a silent acknowledgment that this parting had to be. He cupped her face and pressed a kiss to her mouth. She barely responded; already, it seemed, she had said her goodbyes.

He rose from the bed and started for the door. There he couldn't resist asking, one more time: "You'll be all right?"

She nodded, but it was too automatic. The sort of nod one gave to dismiss an unimportant question. "I'll be fine. After all, I'll have Jack to watch over me."

He didn't miss the faint note of irony in her reply. Jack, it seemed, didn't inspire confidence in either of them. *What's my alternative? Drag her along with me as a moving target?*

He gripped the doorknob. No, it was better this way. He'd already ripped her life apart; he wasn't going to scatter the pieces as well.

As he was leaving, he took one last backward glance. She was still huddled on the bed, her knees drawn up to her chest. The oversized shirt had slid off one bare shoulder. For a moment he thought she was crying. Then she raised her head and met his gaze. What he saw in her eyes wasn't tears. It was something far more moving, something pure and bright and beautiful.

Courage.

In the pale light of dawn, Savitch stood outside Jack Zuckerman's house. Through the fingers of morning mist, Savitch studied the curtained windows, trying to picture the inhabitants within. He wondered who they were, in which room they slept, and whether Catherine Weaver was among them.

He'd find out soon.

He pocketed the black address book he'd taken from the woman's apartment. The name C. Zuckerman and this Pacific Heights address had been written on the inside front cover. Then the Zuckerman had been crossed out and replaced with Weaver. She was a divorcée, he concluded. Under *Z*, he'd found a prominent listing for a man named Jack, with various phone numbers and addresses, both foreign and domestic. Her ex-husband, he'd confirmed, after a brief chat with another name listed in the book. Pumping strangers for information was a simple matter. All it took was an air of authority and a cop's ID. The same ID he was planning to use now.

He gave the house one final perusal, taking in the manicured lawns and shrubbery, the trellis with its vines of winter-dormant wisteria. A successful man, this Jack Zuckerman. Savitch had always admired men of wealth. He gave his jacket a final tug to assure himself that the shoulder holster was concealed. Then he crossed the street to the front porch and rang the doorbell.

Chapter 6

At first light, Cathy awakened. It wasn't a gentle return but a startling jerk back to consciousness. She was instantly aware that she was not in her own bed and that something was terribly wrong. It took her a few seconds to remember exactly what it was. And when she did remember, the sense of urgency was so compelling she rose at once from bed and began to dress in the semi-darkness. *Have to be ready to run...*

The creak of floorboards in the next room told her that Victor was awake as well, probably planning his moves for the day. She rummaged through the closet, searching for things he might need in his flight. All she came up with was a zippered nylon bag and a raincoat. She searched the dresser next and found a few men's socks. She also found a collection of women's underwear. *Damn Jack and all his women,* she thought with sudden irritation and slammed the drawer shut. The thud was still resonating in the room when another sound echoed through the house.

The doorbell was ringing.

It was only seven o'clock, too early for visitors or deliverymen. Suddenly her door swung open. She turned to see Victor, his face etched with tension.

"What should we do?" she asked.

"Get ready to leave. Fast."

"There's a back door—"

"Let's go."

They hurried along the hall and had almost reached the top of the stairs when they heard Jack's sleepy voice below, grumbling: "I'm coming, dammit! Stop that racket, I'm coming!"

The doorbell rang again.

"Don't answer it!" hissed Cathy. "Not yet—"

Jack had already opened the door. Instantly Victor snatched Cathy back up the hall, out of sight. They froze with their backs against the wall, listening to the voices below.

"Yeah," they heard Jack say. "I'm Jack Zuckerman. And who are you?"

The visitor's voice was soft. They could tell only that it was a man.

"Is that so?" said Jack, his voice suddenly edged with panic. "You're with the *FBI,* you say? And what on earth would the *FBI* want with my *ex-wife?*"

Cathy's gaze flew to Victor. She read the frantic message in his eyes: *Which way out?*

She pointed toward the bedroom at the end of the hall. He nodded. Together they tiptoed along the carpet, all the time aware that one misstep, one loud creak, might be enough to alert the agent downstairs.

"Where's your warrant?" they heard Jack demand of the visitor. "Hey, wait a minute! You can't just barge in here without a court order or something!"

No time left! thought Cathy in panic as she slipped into the last room. They closed the door behind them.

"The window!" she whispered.

"You mean jump?"

"No." She hurried across the room and gingerly eased the window open. "There's a trellis!"

He glanced down dubiously at the tangled vines of wisteria. "Are you sure it'll hold us?"

"I know it will," she said, swinging her leg over the sill. "I caught one of Jack's blondes hanging off it one night. And believe me, she was a *big* girl." She glanced down at the ground far below and felt a sudden wave of nausea as the old fear of heights washed through her. "God," she muttered. "Why do we always seem to be hanging out of windows?"

From somewhere in the house came Jack's outraged shout: "You can't go up there! You haven't shown me your warrant!"

"Move!" snapped Victor.

Cathy lowered herself onto the trellis. Branches clawed her face as she scrambled down the vine. An instant after she landed on the dew-soaked grass, Victor dropped beside her.

At once they were on their feet and sprinting for the cover of shrubbery. Just as they rolled behind the azalea bushes, they heard a second-floor window slide open, and then Jack's voice complaining loudly: "I know my rights! This is an illegal search! I'm going to call my lawyer!"

Don't let him see us! prayed Cathy, burrowing frantically into the bush. She felt Victor's body curl around her back, his arms pulling her tightly to him, his breath hot and ragged against her neck. For an eternity they lay shivering in the grass as mist swirled around them.

"You see?" they heard Jack say. "There's no one here but me. Or would you like to check the garage?"

The window slid shut.

Victor gave Cathy a little push. "Go," he whispered. "The end of the hedge. We'll run from there."

On hands and knees she crawled along the row of azalea bushes. Her soaked jeans were icy and her palms scratched and bleeding, but she was too numbed by terror to feel any pain. All her attention was focused on moving forward. Victor was crawling close behind her. When she felt him bump up against her hip, it occurred to her what a ridiculous view he had, her rump swaying practically under his nose.

She reached the last bush and stopped to shove a handful of tangled hair off her face. "That house next?" she asked.

"Go for it!"

They both took off like scared rabbits, dashing across the twenty yards of lawn between houses. Once they reached the cover of the next house, they didn't stop. They kept running, past parked cars and early-morning pedestrians. Five blocks later, they ducked into a coffee shop. Through the front window, they glanced out at the street, watching for signs of pursuit. All they saw was the typical Monday morning bustle: the stop-

and-go traffic, the passersby bundled up in scarves and overcoats.

From the grill behind them came the hiss and sizzle of bacon. The smell of freshly brewed coffee wafted from the counter burner. The aromas were almost painful; they reminded Cathy that she and Victor probably had a total of forty dollars between them. Damn it, why hadn't she begged, borrowed or stolen some cash from Jack?

"What now?" she asked, half hoping he'd suggest blowing the rest of their cash on breakfast.

He scanned the street. "Let's go on."

"Where?"

"Hickey's studio."

"Oh." She sighed. Another long walk, and all on an empty stomach.

Outside, a car passed by bearing the bumper sticker: Today is the First Day of the Rest of Your Life.

Lord, I hope it gets better than this, she thought. Then she followed Victor out the door and into the morning chill.

Field Supervisor Larry Dafoe was sitting at his desk, pumping away at his executive power chair. Upper body strength, he always said, was the key to success as a man. Bulk out those muscles *pull!*, fill out that size forty-four jacket *pull!*, and what you got was a pair of shoulders that'd impress any woman, intimidate any rival. And with this snazzy 700-buck model, you didn't even have to get out of your chair.

Sam Polowski watched his superior strain at the system of wires and pulleys and thought the device looked more like an exotic instrument of torture.

"What you gotta understand," gasped Dafoe, "is that there are other *pull!* issues at work here. Things you know nothing about."

"Like what?" asked Polowski.

Dafoe released the handles and looked up, his face sheened with a healthy sweat. "If I was at liberty to tell you, don't you think I already would've?"

Polowski looked at the gleaming black exercise handles, wondering whether he'd benefit from an executive power chair. Maybe a souped-up set of biceps was what he needed to get a little respect around this office.

"I still don't see what the point is," he said. "Putting Victor Holland in the hot seat."

"The point," said Dafoe, "is that you don't call the shots."

"I gave Holland my word he'd be left out of this mess."

"He's *part* of the mess! First he claims he has evidence, then he pulls a vanishing act."

"That's partly my fault. I never made it to the rendezvous."

"Why hasn't he tried to contact you?"

"I don't know." Polowski sighed and shook his head. "Maybe he's dead."

"Maybe we just need to find him." Dafoe reached for the exercise handles. "Maybe you need to get to work on the Lanzano file. Or maybe you should just go home. You look terrible."

"Yeah. Sure." Polowski turned. As he left the office, he could hear Dafoe once again huffing and puffing. He went to his desk, sat down and contemplated his collection of cold capsules, aspirin and cough syrup. He took a double dose of each. Then he reached in his briefcase and pulled out the Viratek file.

It was his own private collection of scrambled notes and phone numbers and news clippings. He sifted through them, stopping to ponder once again the link between Holland and the woman Catherine Weaver. He'd first seen her name on the hospital admission sheet, and had later been startled to hear of her connection to the murdered Garberville woman. Too many coincidences, too many twists and turns. Was there something obvious here he was missing? Might the woman have an answer or two?

He reached for the telephone and dialed the Garberville police department. They would know how to reach their witness. And maybe she would know how to find Victor Holland. It was a long shot but Sam Polowski was an inveterate horseplayer. He had a penchant for long shots.

The man ringing his doorbell looked like a tree stump dressed in a brown polyester suit. Jack opened the door and said, "Sorry, I'm not buying today."

"I'm not selling anything, Mr. Zuckerman," said the man. "I'm with the FBI."

Jack sighed. "Not again."

"I'm Special Agent Sam Polowski. I'm trying to locate a woman named Catherine Weaver, formerly Zuckerman. I believe she—"

"Don't you guys ever know when to quit?"

"Quit what?"

"One of your agents was here this morning. Talk to him!"

The man frowned. "One of *our* agents?"

"Yeah. And I just might register a complaint against him. Barged right in here without a warrant and started tramping all over my house."

"What did he look like?"

"Oh, I don't know! Dark hair, terrific build. But he could've used a course in charm school."

"Was he about my height?"

"Taller. Skinnier. Lots more hair."

"Did he give you his name? It wasn't Mac Braden, was it?"

"Naw, he didn't give me any name."

Polowski pulled out his badge. Jack squinted at the words: Federal Bureau of Investigation. "Did he show you one of these?" asked Polowski.

"No. He just asked about Cathy and some guy named Victor Holland. Whether I knew how to find them."

"Did you tell him?"

"That jerk?" Jack laughed. "I wouldn't bother to give him the time of day. I sure as hell wasn't going to tell him about—" Jack paused and cleared his throat. "I wasn't going to tell him anything. Even if I knew. Which I don't."

Polowski slipped his badge into his pocket, all the time gazing steadily at Jack. "I think we should talk, Mr. Zuckerman."

"What about?"

"About your ex-wife. About the fact she's in big trouble."

"That," sighed Jack, "I already know."

"She's going to get hurt. I can't fill you in on all the details because I'm still in the dark myself. But I do know one woman's already been hit. Your wife—"

"My ex-wife."

"Your ex-wife could be next."

Jack, unconvinced, merely looked at him.

"It's your duty as a citizen to tell me what you know," Polowski reminded him.

"My duty. Right."

"Look, cooperate, and you and me, we'll get along just fine. Give me grief, and I'll give *you* grief." Polowski smiled. Jack didn't. "Now, Mr. Zuckerman. Hey, can I call you Jack? Jack, why don't you tell me where she is? Before it's too late. For both of you."

Jack scowled at him. He drummed his fingers against the door frame. He debated. At last he stepped aside. "As a law-abiding citizen, I suppose it is my duty." Grudgingly, he waved the man in. "Oh, just come in, Polowski. I'll tell you what I know."

The window shattered, raining slivers into the gloomy space beyond.

Cathy winced at the sound. "Sorry, Hickey," she said under her breath.

"We'll make it up to him," said Victor, knocking off the remaining shards. "We'll send him a nice fat check. You see anyone?"

She glanced up and down the alley. Except for a crumpled newspaper tumbling past the trash cans, nothing moved. A few blocks away, car horns blared, the sounds of another Union Street traffic jam.

"All clear," she whispered.

"Okay." Victor draped his windbreaker over the sill. "Up you go."

He gave her a lift to the window. She clambered through and landed among the glass shards. Seconds later, Victor dropped down beside her.

They were standing in the studio dressing room. Against one wall hung a rack of women's lingerie; against the other were makeup tables and a long mirror.

Victor frowned at a cloud of peach silk flung over one of the chairs. "What kind of photos does your friend take, anyway?"

"Hickey specializes in what's politely known as 'boudoir portraits.'"

Victor's startled gaze turned to a black lace negligee hanging from a wall hook. "Does that mean what I think it means?"

"What do you think it means?"

"You know."

She headed into the next room. "Hickey insists it's not pornography. It's tasteful erotic art…" She stopped in her tracks as she came face-to-face with a photo blowup on the wall. Naked limbs—eight, maybe more—were entwined in a sort of human octopus. Nothing was left to the imagination. Nothing at all.

"Tasteful," Victor said dryly.

"That must be one of his, uh, commercial assignments."

"I wonder what product they were selling."

She turned and found herself staring at another photograph. This time it was two women, drop-dead gorgeous and wearing not a stitch.

"Another commercial assignment?" Victor inquired politely over her shoulder.

She shook her head. "Don't ask."

In the front room they found a week's worth of mail piled up beneath the door slot, darkroom catalogues and advertising flyers. The roll of film Cathy had mailed the day before was not yet in the mound.

"I guess we just sit around and wait for the post-man," she said.

He nodded. "Seems like a safe-enough place. Any chance your friend keeps food around?"

"I seem to remember a refrigerator in the other room."

She led Victor into what Hickey had dubbed his "shooting gallery." Cathy flipped the wall switch and the vast room was instantly illuminated by a dazzling array of spotlights.

"So this is where he does it," said Victor, blinking in the sudden glare. He stepped over a jumble of electrical cords and slowly circled the room, regarding with humorous disbelief the various props. It was a strange collection of objects: a genuine English phone booth, a street bench, an exercise bicycle. In a place of honor sat a four-poster bed. The ruffled coverlet was Victorian; the handcuffs dangling from the bedposts were not.

Victor picked up one of the cuffs and let it fall again. "Just how good a friend *is* this Hickey guy, anyway?"

"None of this stuff was here when he shot me a month ago."

"He photographed *you?*" Victor turned and stared at her.

She flushed, imagining the images that must be flashing through his mind. She could feel his gaze un-dressing her, posing her in a sprawl across that ridiculous four-poster bed. With the handcuffs, no less.

"It wasn't like—like these other photos," she protested. "I mean, I just did it as a favor…"

"A favor?"

"It was a purely *commercial* shot!"

"Oh."

"I was fully dressed. In overalls, as a matter of fact. I was supposed to be a plumber."

"A lady plumber?"

"I was an emergency stand-in. One of his models didn't show up that day, and he needed someone with an ordinary face. I guess that's me. Ordinary. And it really was just my face."

"And your overalls."

"Right."

They looked at each other and burst out laughing.

"I can guess what you were thinking," she said.

"I don't even want to *tell* you what I was thinking." He turned and glanced around the room. "Didn't you say there was some food around here?"

She crossed the room to the refrigerator. Inside she found a shelf of film plus a jar of sweet pickles, some rubbery carrots and half a salami. In the freezer they discovered real treasures: ground Sumatran coffee and a loaf of sourdough bread.

Grinning, she turned to him. "A feast!"

They sat together on the four-poster bed and gnawed on salami and half-frozen sourdough, all washed down with cups of coffee. It was a bizarre little picnic, paper plates with pickles and carrots resting in their laps, the spotlights glaring down like a dozen hot suns from the ceiling.

"Why did you say that about yourself?" he asked, watching her munch a carrot.

"Say what?"

"That you're ordinary. So ordinary that you get cast as the lady plumber?"

"Because I am ordinary."

"I don't think so. And I happen to be a pretty good judge of character."

She looked up at a wall poster featuring one of Hickey's super models. The woman stared back with a look of glossy confidence. "Well, I certainly don't measure up to *that.*"

"That," he said, "is pure fantasy. *That* isn't a real woman, but an amalgam of makeup, hairspray and fake eyelashes."

"Oh, I know that. That's my job, turning actors into some moviegoer's fantasy. Or nightmare, as the case may be." She reached into the jar and fished out the last pickle. "No, I really meant *underneath* it all. Deep inside, I *feel* ordinary."

"I think you're quite extraordinary. And after last night, I should know."

She gazed down, at the limp carrot stretched out like a little corpse across the paper plate. "There was a time—I suppose there's always that time, for everyone, when we're still young, when we feel special. When we feel the world's meant just for us. The last time I felt that way was when I married Jack." She sighed. "It didn't last long."

"Why did you marry him?"

"I don't know. Dazzle? I was only twenty-three, a mere apprentice on the set. He was the director." She paused. "He was *God.*"

"He impressed you, did he?"

"Jack can be very impressive. He can turn on the power, the charisma, and just overwhelm a gal. Then there was the champagne, the suppers, the flowers. I think what attracted him to me was that I didn't immediately fall for him. That I wasn't swooning at his every look. He thought of me as a challenge, the one he finally conquered." She gave him a rueful look. "That accomplished, he moved onto bigger and better things. That's when I realized that I wasn't particularly special. That I'm really just a perfectly ordinary woman. It's not a bad feeling. It's not as if I go through life longing to be someone different, someone special."

"Then who do you consider special?"

"Well, my grandmother. But she's dead."

"Venerable grandmothers always make the list."

"Okay, then. Mother Teresa."

"She's on everyone's list."

"Kate Hepburn. Gloria Steinem. My friend Sarah…" Her voice faded. Looking down, she added softly: "But she's dead, too."

Gently he took her hand. With a strange sense of wonder she watched his long fingers close over hers and thought about how the strength she felt in that grasp reflected the strength of the man himself. Jack, for all his dazzle and polish, had never inspired a fraction of the confidence she now felt in Victor. No man ever had.

He was watching her with quiet sympathy. "Tell me about Sarah," he said.

Cathy swallowed, trying to stem the tears. "She was absolutely lovely. I don't mean in *that* way." She nodded at the photo of Hickey's picture-perfect model. "I mean, in an inner sort of way. It was this look in her eyes. A perfect calmness. As though she'd found exactly what she wanted while all the rest of us were still grubbing around for lost treasure. I don't think she was born like that. She came to it, all by herself. In college, we were both pretty unsure of ourselves. Marriage certainly didn't help either of us. My divorce—it was nothing short of devastating. But Sarah's divorce only seemed to make her stronger. Better able to take care of herself. When she finally got pregnant, it was exactly as she planned it. There wasn't a father, you see, just a test tube. An anonymous donor. Sarah used to say that the primeval family unit wasn't man, woman and child. It was just woman and child. I thought she was brave, to take that step. She was a lot braver than I could ever be…" She cleared her throat. "Anyway, Sarah *was* special. Some people simply are."

"Yes," he said. "Some people are."

She looked up at him. He was staring off at the far wall, his gaze infinitely sad. What had etched those lines of pain in his face? She wondered if lines so deep could ever be erased. There were some losses one never got over, never accepted.

Softly she asked, "What was your wife like?"

He didn't answer at first. She thought: *Why did I ask that? Why did I have to bring up such terrible memories?*

He said, "She was a kind woman. That's what I'll always remember about her. Her kindness." He looked at Cathy and she sensed it wasn't sadness she saw in those eyes, but acceptance.

"What was her name?"

"Lily. Lillian Dorinda Cassidy. A mouthful for such a tiny woman." He smiled. "She was about five foot one, maybe ninety pounds sopping wet. It used to scare me, how small she always seemed. Almost breakable. Especially toward the end, when she'd lost all that weight. It seemed as if she'd shrunk down to nothing but a pair of big brown eyes."

"She must have been young when she died."

"Only thirty-eight. It seemed so unfair. All her life, she'd done everything right. Never smoked, hardly ever touched a glass of wine. She even refused to eat meat. After she was diagnosed, we kept trying to figure out how it could've happened. Then it occurred to us what might have caused it. She grew up in a small town in Massachusetts. Directly downwind from a nuclear power plant."

"You think that was it?"

"One can never be sure. But we asked around. And we learned that, just in her neighborhood, at least twenty families had someone with leukemia. It took four years and a class-action suit to force an investigation. What they found was a history of safety violations going back all the way to the plant's opening."

Cathy shook her head in disbelief. "And all those years they allowed it to operate?"

"No one knew about it. The violations were hushed up so well even the federal regulators were kept in the dark."

"They shut it down, didn't they?"

He nodded. "I can't say I got much satisfaction, seeing the plant finally close. By that time Lily was gone. And all the families, well, we were exhausted by the fight. Even though it sometimes felt as though we were banging our heads against a wall, we knew it was something we had to do. *Somebody* had to do it, for all the Lilys of the world." He looked up, at the spotlights shining above. "And here I am again, still banging my head against walls. Only this time, it feels like the Great Wall of China. And the lives at stake are yours and mine."

Their gazes met. She sat absolutely still as he lightly stroked down the curve of her cheek. She took his hand, pressed it to her lips. His fingers closed over hers, refusing to release her hand. Gently he tugged her close. Their lips met, a tentative kiss that left her longing for more.

"I'm sorry you were pulled into this," he murmured. "You and Sarah and those other Cathy Weavers. None of you asked to be part of it. And somehow I've managed to hurt you all."

"Not you, Victor. You're not the one to blame. It's this windmill you're tilting at. This giant, dangerous windmill. Anyone else would have dropped his lance and fled. You're still going at it."

"I didn't have much of a choice."

"But you did. You could have walked away from your friend's death. Turned a blind eye to whatever's going on at Viratek. That's what Jack would have done."

"But I'm not Jack. There are things I can't walk away from. I'd always be thinking of the Lilys. All the thousands of people who might get hurt."

At the mention once again of his dead wife, Cathy felt some unbreachable barrier form between them—the shadow of Lily, the wife she'd never met. Cathy drew back, at once aching from the loss of his touch.

"You think that many people could die?" she asked.

"Jerry must have thought so. There's no way to predict the outcome. The world's never seen the effects of all-out biological warfare. I like to think it's because we're too smart to play with our own self-destruction. Then I think of all the crazy things people have done over the years and it scares me..."

"Are viral weapons that dangerous?"

"If you alter a few genes, make it just a little more contagious, raise the kill ratio, you'd end up with a devastating strain. The research alone is hazardous. A single slip-up in lab security and you could have millions of people accidentally infected. And no means of treatment. It's the kind of worldwide disaster a scientist doesn't want to think about."

"Armageddon."

He nodded, his gaze frighteningly sane. "If you believe in such a thing. That's exactly what it'd be."

She shook her head. "I don't understand why these things are allowed."

"They aren't. By international agreement, they're outlawed. But there's always some madman lurking in the shadows who wants that extra bit of leverage, that weapon no one else has."

A madman. That's what one would have to be, to even think of unleashing such a weapon on the world. She thought of a novel she'd read, about just such a plague, how the cities had lain dead and decaying, how the very air had turned poisonous. But those were only the nightmares of science fiction. This was real.

From somewhere in the building came the sound of whistling.

Cathy and Victor both sat up straight. The melody traveled along the hall, closer and closer, until it stopped right outside Hickey's door. They heard a rustling, then the slap of magazines hitting the floor.

"It's here!" said Cathy, leaping to her feet.

Victor was right behind her as she hurried into the front room. She spotted it immediately, sitting atop the pile: a padded envelope, addressed in her handwriting. She scooped it up and ripped the envelope open. Out slid the roll of film. The note she'd scribbled to Hickey fluttered to the floor. Grinning in triumph, she held up the canister. "Here's your evidence!"

"We hope. Let's see what we've got on the roll. Where's the darkroom?"

"Next to the dressing room." She handed him the film. "Do you know how to process it?"

"I've done some amateur photography. As long as I've got the chemicals I can—" He stopped and glanced over at the desk.

The phone was ringing.

Victor shook his head. "Ignore it," he said and turned for the darkroom.

As they left the reception room, they heard the answering machine click on. Hickey's voice, smooth as silk, spoke on the recording. "This is the studio of Hickman Von Trapp, specializing in tasteful and artistic images of the female form..."

Victor laughed. "Tasteful?"

"It depends on your taste," said Cathy as she followed him up the hall.

They had just reached the darkroom when the recording ended and was followed by the message beep. An agitated voice rattled from the speaker. "Hello? Hello, Cathy? If you're there, answer me, will you? There's an FBI agent looking for you—some guy named Polowski—"

Cathy stopped dead. "It's Jack!" she said, turning to retrace her steps toward the front room.

The voice on the speaker had taken on a note of panic. "I couldn't help it—he made me tell him about Hickey. Get out of there now!"

The message clicked off just as Cathy grabbed the receiver. "Hello? *Jack?*"

She heard only the dial tone. He'd already hung up. Hands shaking, she began to punch in Jack's phone number.

"There's no time!" said Victor.

"I have to talk to him—"

He grabbed the receiver and slammed it down. "Later! We have to get out of here!"

She nodded numbly and started for the door. There she halted. "Wait. We need money!" She turned back to the reception desk and searched the drawers until she found the petty cash box. Twenty-two dollars was all it contained. "Always keep just enough for decent coffee beans," Hickey used to say. She pocketed the money. Then she reached up and yanked one of Hickey's old raincoats from the door hook. He wouldn't miss it. And she might need it for concealment. "Okay," she said, slipping on the coat. "Let's go."

They paused only a second to check the corridor. From another suite came the faint echo of laughter. Somewhere above, high heels clicked across a wooden floor. With Victor in the lead, they darted down the hall and out the front door.

The midday sun seemed to glare down on them like an accusing eye. Quickly they fell into step with the rest of the lunch crowd, the businessmen and artists, the Union Street chic. No one glanced their way. But even with people all around her, Cathy felt conspicuous. As though, in this bright cityscape of crowds and concrete, she was the focus of the painter's eye.

She huddled deeper into the raincoat, wishing it were a mantle of invisibility. Victor had quickened his pace, and she had to run to keep up.

"Where do we go now?" she whispered.

"We've got the film. Now I say we head for the bus station."

"And then?"

"Anywhere." He kept his gaze straight ahead. "As long as it's out of this city."

Chapter 7

That pesky FBI agent was ringing his doorbell again.

Sighing, Jack opened the front door. "Back already?"

"Damn right I'm back." Polowski stamped in and shoved the door closed behind him. "I want to know where to find 'em next."

"I told you, Mr. Polowski. Over on Union Street there's a studio owned by Mr. Hickman—"

"I've been to Von Whats-his-name's studio."

Jack swallowed. "You didn't find them?"

"You knew I wouldn't. You warned 'em, didn't you?"

"Really, I don't know why you're harrassing me. I've tried to be—"

"They left in a hurry. The door was wide open. Food was still lying around. They left the empty cash box just sitting on the desk."

Jack drew himself up in outrage. "Are you calling my ex-wife a petty thief?"

"I'm calling her a desperate woman. And I'm calling you an imbecile for screwing things up. Now where is she?"

"I don't know."

"Who would she turn to?"

"No one I know."

"Think harder."

Jack stared down at Polowski's turgid face and marveled that any human being could be so unattractive. Surely the process of natural selection would have dictated against such unacceptable genes?

Jack shook his head. "I honestly don't know."

It was the truth, and Polowski must have sensed it. After a moment of silent confrontation, he backed off. "Then maybe you can tell me this. Why did you warn them?"

"It—it was—" Jack shrugged helplessly. "Oh, I don't know! After you left, I wasn't sure I'd done the right thing. I wasn't sure whether to trust you. *He* doesn't trust you."

"Who?"

"Victor Holland. He thinks you're in on some conspiracy. Frankly, the man struck me as just the slightest bit paranoid."

"He has a right to be. Considering what's happened to him so far." Polowski turned for the door.

"Now what happens?"

"I keep looking for them."

"Where?"

"You think I'd tell *you?*" He stalked out. "Don't leave town, Zuckerman," he snapped over his shoulder. "I'll be back to see you later."

"I don't think so," Jack muttered softly as he watched

the other man lumber back to his car. He looked up and saw there wasn't a cloud in the sky. Smiling to himself, he shut the door.

It would be sunny in Mexico, as well.

Someone had left in a hurry.

Savitch strolled through the rooms of the photo studio, which had been left unlocked. He noted the scraps of a meal on the four-poster bed: crumbs of sourdough bread, part of a salami, an empty pickle jar. He also took note of the coffee cups: there were two of them. Interesting, since Savitch had spotted only one person leaving the studio, a squat little man in a polyester suit. The man hadn't been there long. Savitch had observed him climb into a dark green Ford parked at a fifteen-minute meter. The meter still had three minutes remaining.

Savitch continued his tour of the studio, eyeing the tawdry photos, wondering if this wasn't another waste of his time. After all, every other address he'd pulled from the woman's black book had turned up no sign of her. Why should Hickman Von Trapp's address be any different?

Still, he couldn't shake the instinct that he was getting close. Clues were everywhere. He read them, put them together. Today, this studio had been visited by two hungry people. They'd entered through a broken window in the dressing room. They'd eaten scraps taken from the refrigerator. They (or the man in the polyester suit) had emptied the petty cash box.

Savitch completed his tour and returned to the front room. That's when he noticed the telephone message machine blinking on and off.

He pressed the play button. The string of messages

seemed endless. The calls were for someone named Hickey—no doubt the Hickman Von Trapp of the address book. Savitch lazily circled the room, half listening to the succession of voices. Business calls for the most part, inquiring about appointments, asking when proofs would be ready and would he like to do the shoot for *Snoop* magazine? Near the door, Savitch halted and stooped down to sift through the pile of mail. It was boring stuff, all addressed to Von Trapp. Then he noticed, off to the side, a loose slip of paper. It was a note, addressed to Hickey.

"Feel awful about this, but someone stole all those rolls of film from my car. This was the only one left. Thought I'd get it to you before it's lost, as well. Hope it's enough to save your shoot from being a complete waste—"

It was signed "Cathy."

He stood up straight. Catherine Weaver? It had to be! The roll of film—where the hell was the roll of film?

He rifled through the mail, searching, searching. He turned up only a torn envelope with Cathy Weaver's return address. The film was gone. In frustration, he began to fling magazines across the room. Then, in mid-toss, he froze.

A new message was playing on the recorder.

"Hello? Hello, Cathy? If you're there, answer me, will you? There's an FBI agent looking for you—some guy named Polowski. I couldn't help it—he made me tell him about Hickey. Get out of there now!"

Savitch stalked over to the answering machine and stared down as the mechanism automatically whirred back to the beginning. He replayed it.

Get out of there now!

There was now no doubt. Catherine Weaver had been here, and Victor Holland was with her. But who was this agent Polowski and why was he searching for Holland? Savitch had been assured that the Bureau was off the case. He would have to check into the matter.

He crossed over to the window and stared out at the bright sunshine, the crowded sidewalks. So many faces, so many strangers. Where, in this city, would two terrified fugitives hide? Finding them would be difficult, but not impossible.

He left the suite and went outside to a pay phone. There he dialed a Washington, D.C., number. He wasn't fond of asking the Cowboy for help, but now he had no choice. Victor Holland had his hands on the evidence, and the stakes had shot sky-high.

It was time to step up the pursuit.

The clerk yelled, "Next window, please!" and closed the grate.

"Wait!" cried Cathy, tapping at the pane. "My bus is leaving right now!"

"Which one?"

"Number 23 to Palo Alto—"

"There's another at seven o'clock."

"But—"

"I'm on my dinner break."

Cathy stared helplessly as the clerk walked away. Over the PA system came the last call for the Palo Alto express. Cathy glanced around just in time to see the Number 23 roar away from the curb.

"Service just ain't what it used to be," an old man muttered behind her. "Get there faster usin' yer damn thumb."

Sighing, Cathy shifted to the next line, which was eight-deep and slow as molasses. The woman at the front was trying to convince the clerk that her social security card was an acceptable ID for a check.

Okay, Cathy thought. *So we leave at seven o'clock. That puts us in Palo Alto at eight. Then what? Camp in a park? Beg a few scraps from a restaurant? What does Victor have in mind...?*

She glanced around and spotted his broad back hunched inside one of the phone booths. Whom could he possibly be calling? She saw him hang up and run his hand wearily through his hair. Then he picked up the receiver and dialed another number.

"Next!" Someone tapped Cathy on the shoulder. "Go ahead, Miss."

Cathy turned and saw that the ticket clerk was waiting. She stepped to the window.

"Where to?" asked the clerk.

"I need two tickets to..." Cathy's voice suddenly faded.

"Where?"

Cathy didn't speak. Her gaze had frozen on a poster tacked right beside the ticket window. The words Have You seen This Man? appeared above an unsmiling photo of Victor Holland. And at the bottom were listed the charges: Industrial espionage and murder. If you have any information about this man, please contact your local police or the FBI.

"Lady, you wanna go somewhere or not?"

"What?" Cathy's gaze jerked back to the clerk, who was watching her with obvious annoyance. "Oh. Yes, I'm—I'd like two tickets. To Palo Alto." Numbly she handed over a fistful of cash. "One way."

"Two to Palo Alto. That bus will depart at 7:00, Gate 11."

"Yes. Thank you…" Cathy took the tickets and turned to leave the line. That's when she spotted the two policemen, standing just inside the front entrance. They seemed to be scanning the terminal, searching— for what?

In a panic, her gaze shot to the phone booth. It was empty. She stared at it with a sense of abandonment. *You left me! You left me with two tickets to Palo Alto and five bucks in my pocket!*

Where are you, Victor?

She couldn't stand here like an idiot. She had to do something, had to move. She pulled the raincoat tightly around her shoulders and forced herself to stroll across the terminal. *Don't let them notice me,* she prayed. *Please. I'm nobody. Nothing.* She paused at a chair and picked up a discarded *San Francisco Chronicle.* Then, thumbing through the Want Ads, she sauntered right past the two policemen. They didn't even glance at her as she went out the front entrance.

Now what? she wondered, pausing amidst the confusion of a busy sidewalk. Automatically she started to walk and had taken only half a dozen steps down the street when she was wrenched sideways, into an alley.

She reeled back against the trash cans and almost sobbed with relief. "Victor!"

"Did they see you?"

"No. I mean, yes, but they didn't seem to care—"

"Are you sure?" She nodded. He turned and slapped the wall in frustration. "What the hell do we do now?"

"I have the tickets."

"We can't use them."

"How are we going to get out of town? Hitchhike? Victor, we're down to our last five dollars!"

"They'll be watching every bus that leaves. And they've got my face plastered all over the damn terminal!" He slumped back against the wall and groaned. "*Have you seen this man?* God, I looked like some two-bit gangster."

"It wasn't the most flattering photo."

He managed to laugh. "Have you *ever* seen a flattering wanted poster?"

She leaned back beside him, against the wall. "We've got to get out of this city, Victor."

"Amend that. *You've* got to get out."

"What's that supposed to mean?"

"The police aren't looking for you. So *you* take that bus to Palo Alto. I'll put you in touch with some old friends. They'll see you make it somewhere safe."

"No."

"Cathy, they've probably got my mug posted in every airport and car rental agency in town! We've spent almost all our money for those bus tickets. I say you use them!"

"I'm not leaving you."

"You don't have a choice."

"Yes I do. I choose to stick to you like glue. Because you're the only one I feel safe with. The only one I can count on!"

"I can move faster on my own. Without you slowing me down." He looked off, toward the street. "Hell, I don't even *want* you around."

"I don't believe that."

"Why should I care what you believe?"

"Look at me! Look at me and say that!" She grabbed

his arm, willing him to face her. "Say you don't want me around!"

He started to speak, to repeat the lie. She knew then that it *was* a lie; she could see it in his eyes. And she saw something else in that gaze, something that took her breath away.

He said, "I don't—I won't have you—"

She just stood there, looking up at him, waiting for the truth to come.

What she didn't expect was the kiss. She never remembered how it happened. She only knew that all at once his arms were around her and she was being swept up into some warm and safe and wonderful place. It started as an embrace more of desperation than passion, a coming together of two terrified people. But the instant their lips met, it became something much more. This went beyond fear, beyond need. This was a souls' joining, one that wouldn't be broken, even after this embrace was over, even if they never touched again.

When at last they drew apart and stared at each other, the taste of him was still fresh on her lips.

"You see?" she whispered. "I was right. You do want me around. You do."

He smiled and touched her cheek. "I'm not a very good liar."

"And I'm not leaving you. You need me. You can't show your face, but I can! I can buy bus tickets, run errands—"

"What I really need," he sighed, "is a new face." He glanced out at the street. "Since there's no plastic surgeon handy, I suggest we hoof it over to the BART station. It'll be crowded at this hour. We might make it to the East Bay—"

"God, I'm such an *idiot!*" she groaned. "A new face is exactly what you need!" She turned toward the street. "Come on. There isn't much time…"

"Cathy?" He followed her up the alley. They both paused, scanning the street for policemen. There were none in sight. "Where are we going?" he whispered.

"To find a phone booth."

"Oh. And who are we calling?"

She turned and the look she gave him was distinctly pained. "Someone we both know and love."

Jack was packing his suitcase when the phone rang. He considered not answering it, but something about the sound, an urgency that could only have been imagined, made him pick up the receiver. He was instantly sorry he had.

"Jack?"

He sighed. "Tell me I'm hearing things."

"Jack, I'm going to talk fast because your phone might be tapped—"

"You don't say."

"I need my kit. The whole shebang. And some cash. I swear I'll pay it all back. Get it for me right now. Then drop it off where we shot the last scene of *Cretinoid.* You know the spot."

"Cathy, you wait a minute! I'm in trouble enough as it is!"

"One hour. That's all I can wait."

"It's rush hour! I can't—"

"It's the last favor I'll ask of you." There was a pause. Then, softly, she added, "Please."

He let out a breath. "This is the absolute last time, right?"

"One hour, Jack. I'll be waiting."

Jack hung up and stared at his suitcase. It was only half packed, but it would have to do. He sure as hell wasn't coming back *here* tonight.

He closed the suitcase and carried it out to the Jaguar. As he drove away it suddenly occurred to him that he'd forgotten to cancel his date with Lulu tonight.

No time now, he thought. I've got more important things on my mind—like getting out of town.

Lulu would be mad as a hornet, but he'd make it up to her. Maybe a pair of diamond ear studs. Yeah, that would do the trick.

Good old Lulu, so easy to please. Now there was a woman he could understand.

The corner of Fifth and Mission was a hunker-down, chew-the-fat sort of gathering place for the street folk. At five forty-five it was even busier than usual. Rumor had it the soup kitchen down the block was fixing to serve beef Bourguignonne, which, as those who re-membered better days and better meals could tell you, was made with red wine. No one passed up the chance for a taste of the grape, even if every drop of alcohol was simmered clean out of it. And so they stood around on the corner, talking of other meals they'd had, of the weather, of the long lines at the unemployment office.

No one noticed the two wretched souls huddled in the doorway of the pawnshop.

Lucky for us, thought Cathy, burying herself in the folds of the raincoat. The sad truth was, they were both beginning to fit right into this crowd. Just a moment earlier she'd caught sight of her own reflection in the pawnshop window and had almost failed to recognize

the disheveled image staring back. *Has it been that long
since I've combed my hair? That long since I've had a
meal or a decent night's sleep?*

Victor looked no better. A torn shirt and two days'
worth of stubble on his jaw only emphasized that unmistakable look of exhaustion. He could walk into that soup
kitchen down the block and no one would look twice.

*He's going to look a hell of a lot worse when I get
through with him,* she thought with a grim sense of
humor.

If Jack ever showed up with the kit.

"It's 6:05," Victor muttered. "He's had an hour."

"Give him time."

"We're running out of time."

"We can still make the bus." She peered up the street,
as though by force of will she could conjure up her ex-
husband. But only a city bus barreled into view. *Come
on, Jack, come on! Don't let me down this time...*

"Will ya lookit that!" came a low growl, followed by
general murmurs of admiration from the crowd.

"Hey, pretty boy!" someone called as the group gathered on the corner to stare. "What'd you have to push
to get yerself wheels like that?"

Through the gathering of men, Cathy spied the bright
gleam of chrome and burgundy. "Get away from my
car!" demanded a querulous voice. "I just had her
waxed!"

"Looks like Pretty Boy got hisself lost. Turned down
the wrong damn street, did ya?"

Cathy leaped to her feet. "He's here!"

She and Victor pushed through the crowd to find
Jack standing guard over the Jaguar's gleaming finish.

"Don't—don't touch her!" he snapped as one man ran

a grimy finger across the hood. "Why can't you people go find yourselves a job or something?"

"A job?" someone yelled. "What's that?"

"Jack!" called Cathy.

Jack let out a sigh of relief when he spotted her. "This is the last favor. The absolute *last* favor—"

"Where is it?" she asked.

Jack walked around to the trunk, where he slapped away another hand as it stroked the Jaguar's burgundy flank. "It's right here. The whole kit and kaboodle." He swung out the makeup case and handed it over. "Delivered as promised. Now I gotta run."

"Where are you going?" she called.

"I don't know." He climbed back into the car. "Somewhere. Anywhere!"

"Sounds like we're headed in the same direction."

"God, I hope not." He started the engine and revved it up a few times.

Someone yelled, "So long, Pretty Boy!"

Jack gazed out dryly at Cathy. "You know, you really should do something about the company you keep. Ciao, sweetcakes."

The Jaguar lurched away. With a screech of tires, it spun around the corner and vanished into traffic.

Cathy turned and saw that every eye was watching her. Automatically, Victor moved close beside her, one tired and hungry man facing a tired and hungry crowd.

Someone called out, "So who's the jerk in the Jag?"

"My ex-husband," said Cathy.

"Doin' a lot better than you are, honey."

"No kidding." She held up the makeup case and managed a careless laugh. "I ask the creep for my clothes, he throws me a change of underwear."

"Babe, now ain't that just the way it works?"

Already, the men were wandering away, regrouping in doorways, or over by the corner newsstands. The Jaguar was gone, and so was their interest.

Only one man stood before Cathy and Victor, and the look he gave them was distinctly sympathetic. "That's all he left you, huh? Him with that nice, fancy car?" He turned to leave, then glanced back at them. "Say, you two need a place to stay or somethin'? I got a lot of friends. And I hate to see a lady out in the cold."

"Thanks for the offer," said Victor, taking Cathy's hand. "But we've got a bus to catch."

The man nodded and shuffled away, a kind but unfortunate soul whom the streets had not robbed of decency.

"We have a half hour to get on that bus," said Victor, hurrying Cathy along. "Better get to work."

They were headed up the street, toward the cover of an alley, when Cathy suddenly halted. "Victor—"

"What's the matter?"

"Look." She pointed at the newsstand, her hand shaking.

Beneath the plastic cover was the afternoon edition of the *San Francisco Examiner*. The headline read: "Two Victims, Same Name. Police Probe Coincidence." Beside it was a photo of a young blond woman. The caption was hidden by the fold, but Cathy didn't need to read it. She could already guess the woman's name.

"Two of them," she whispered. "Victor, you were right…"

"All the more reason for us to get out of town." He pulled on her arm. "Hurry."

She let him lead her away. But even as they headed

down the street, even as they left the newsstand behind them, she carried that image in her mind: the photograph of a blond woman, the second victim.

The second Catherine Weaver.

Patrolman O'Hanley was a helpful soul. Unlike too many of his colleagues, O'Hanley had joined the force out of a true desire to serve and protect. The "Boy Scout" was what the other men called him behind his back. The epithet both annoyed and pleased him. It told him he didn't fit in with the rough-and-tumble gang on the force. It also told him he was above it all, above the petty bribe-taking and backbiting and maneuverings for promotion. He wasn't out to glorify the badge on his chest. What he wanted was the chance to pat a kid on the head, rescue an old granny from a mugging.

That's why he found this particular assignment so frustrating. All this standing around in the bus depot, watching for a man some witness *might* have spotted a few hours ago. O'Hanley hadn't noticed any such character. He'd eyeballed every person who'd walked in the door. A sorry lot, most of them. Not surprising since, these days, anyone with the cash to spare took a plane. By the looks of these folks, none of 'em could spare much more than pennies. Take that pair over there, huddled together in the waiting area. A father and daughter, he figured, and both of 'em down on their luck. The daughter was bundled up in an old raincoat, the collar pulled up to reveal only a mop of windblown hair. The father was an even sorrier sight, gaunt-faced, white-whiskered, about as old as Methuselah. Still, there was a remnant of pride in the old codger—O'Hanley could see it in the way the man held himself, stiff and straight.

Must've been an impressive fellow in his younger years since he was still well over six feet tall.

The public speaker announced final boarding for number fourteen to Palo Alto.

The old man and his daughter rose to their feet.

O'Hanley watched with concern as the pair shuffled across the terminal toward the departure gate. The woman was carrying only one small case, but it appeared to be a heavy one. And she already had her hands full, trying to guide the old man in the right direction. But they were making progress, and O'Hanley figured they'd make it to the bus okay.

That is, until the kid ran into them.

He was about six, the kind of kid no mother wants to admit she produced, the kind of kid who gives all six-year-olds a bad name. For the last half hour the boy had been tearing around the terminal, scattering ashtray sand, tipping over suitcases, banging locker doors. Now he was running. Only this kid was doing it *backward.*

O'Hanley saw it coming. The old man and his daughter were crossing slowly toward the departure gate. The kid was scuttling toward them. Intersecting paths, inevitable collision. The kid slammed into the woman's knees; the case flew out of her grasp. She stumbled against her companion. O'Hanley, paralyzed, expected the codger to keel over. To his surprise, the old man simply caught the woman in his arms and handily set her back on her feet.

By now O'Hanley was hurrying to their aid. He got to the woman just as she'd regained her footing. "You folks okay?" he asked.

The woman reacted as though he'd slapped her. She stared up at him with the eyes of a terrified animal. "What?" she said.

"Are you okay? Looked to me like he hit you pretty hard."

She nodded.

"How 'bout you, Gramps?"

The woman glanced at her companion. It seemed to O'Hanley that there was a lot being said in that glance, a lot he wasn't privy to.

"We're both fine," the woman said quickly. "Come on, Pop. We'll miss our bus."

"Can I give you a hand with him?"

"That's mighty kind of you, officer, but we'll do fine." The woman smiled at O'Hanley. Something about that smile wasn't right. As he watched the pair shuffle off toward bus number fourteen, O'Hanley kept trying to figure it out. Kept trying to put his finger on what was wrong with that pair of travelers.

He turned away and almost tripped over the fallen case. The woman had forgotten it. He snatched it up and started to run for the bus. Too late; the number fourteen to Palo Alto was already pulling away. O'Hanley stood helplessly on the curb, watching the taillights vanish around the corner.

Oh, well.

He turned in the makeup case at Lost and Found. Then he stationed himself once again at the entrance. Seven o'clock already and still no sighting of the suspect Victor Holland.

O'Hanley sighed. What a waste of a policeman's time.

Five minutes out of San Francisco, aboard the number fourteen bus, the old man turned to the woman in the raincoat and said, "This beard is killing me."

Laughing, Cathy reached up and gave the fake whiskers a tug. "It did the trick, didn't it?"

"No kidding. We practically got a police escort to the getaway bus." He scratched furiously at his chin. "Geez, how do those actors stand this stuff, anyway? The itch is driving me up a wall."

"Want me to take it off?"

"Better not. Not till we get to Palo Alto."

Another hour, she thought. She sat back and gazed out at the highway gliding past the bus window. "Then what?" she asked softly.

"I'll knock on a few doors. See if I can dig up an old friend or two. It's been a long time, but I think there are still a few in town."

"You used to live there?"

"Years ago. Back when I was in college."

"Oh." She sat up straight. "A *Stanford* man."

"Why do you make it sound just a tad disreputable?"

"I rooted for the Bears, myself."

"I'm consorting with the arch enemy?"

Giggling, she burrowed against his chest and inhaled the warm, familiar scent of his body. "It seems like another lifetime. Berkeley and blue jeans."

"Football. Wild parties."

"Wild parties?" she asked. "You?"

"Well, *rumors* of wild parties."

"Frisbee. Classes on the lawn…"

"Innocence," he said softly.

They both fell silent.

"Victor?" she asked. "What if your friends aren't there any longer? Or what if they won't take us in?"

"One step at a time. That's how we have to take it. Otherwise it'll all seem too overwhelming."

"It already does."

He squeezed her tightly against him. "Hey, we're

doing okay. We made it out of the city. In fact, we waltzed out right under the nose of a cop. I'd call that pretty damn impressive."

Cathy couldn't help grinning at the memory of the earnest young Patrolman O'Hanley. "All policemen should be so helpful."

"Or blind," Victor snorted. "I can't believe he called me *Gramps*."

"When I set out to change a face, I do it right."

"Apparently."

She looped her arm through his and pressed a kiss to one scowling, bewhiskered cheek. "Can I tell you a secret?"

"What's that?"

"I'm crazy about older men."

The scowl melted away, slowly reformed into a dubious smile. "How much older are we talking about?"

She kissed him again, this time full on the lips. "Much older."

"Hm. Maybe these whiskers aren't so bad, after all." He took her face in his hands. This time he was the one kissing her, long and deeply, with no thought of where they were or where they were going. Cathy felt herself sliding back against the seat, into a space that was inescapable and infinitely safe.

Someone behind them hooted: "Way to go, Gramps!"

Reluctantly, they pulled apart. Through the flickering shadows of the bus, Cathy could see the twinkle in Victor's eyes, the gleam of a wry smile.

She smiled back and whispered, "Way to go, Gramps."

The posters with Victor Holland's face were plastered all over the bus station.

Polowski couldn't help a snort of irritation as he

gazed at that unflattering visage of what he knew in his gut was an innocent man. A damn witchhunt, that's what this'd turned into. If Holland wasn't already scared enough, this public stalking would surely send him diving for cover, beyond the reach of those who could help him. Polowski only hoped it'd also be beyond the reach of those with less benign intentions.

With all these posters staring him in the face, Holland would've been a fool to stroll through this bus depot. Still, Polowski had an instinct about these things, a sense of how people behaved when they were desperate. If he were in Holland's shoes, a killer on his trail and a woman companion to worry about, he knew what *he'd* do—get the hell out of San Francisco. A plane was unlikely. According to Jack Zuckerman, Holland was operating on a thin wallet. A credit card would've been out of the question. That also knocked out a rental car. What was left? It was either hitchhike or take the bus.

Polowski was betting on the bus.

His last piece of info supported that hunch. The tap on Zuckerman's phone had picked up a call from Cathy Weaver. She'd arranged some sort of drop-off at a site Polowski couldn't identify at first. He'd spent a frustrating hour asking around the office, trying to locate someone who'd not only seen Zuckerman's forgettable film, *Cretinoid,* but could also pinpoint where the last scene was filmed. The Mission District, some movie nut file clerk had finally told him. Yeah, she was sure of it. The monster came up through the manhole cover right at the corner of Fifth and Mission and slurped down a derelict or two just before the hero smashed him with a crated piano. Polowski hadn't stayed to hear the rest; he'd made a run for his car.

By that time, it was too late. Holland and the woman were gone, and Zuckerman had vanished. Polowski found himself cruising down Mission, his doors locked, his windows rolled up, wondering when the local police were going to clean up the damn streets.

That's when he remembered the bus depot was only a few blocks away.

Now, standing among the tired and slack-jawed travelers at the bus station, he was beginning to think he'd wasted his time. All those wanted posters staring him in the face. And there was a cop standing over by the coffee machine, taking furtive sips from a foam cup.

Polowski strolled over to the cop. "FBI," he said, flashing his badge.

The cop—he was scarcely more than a boy—instantly straightened. "Patrolman O'Hanley, sir."

"Seeing much action?"

"Uh—you mean today?"

"Yeah. Here."

"No, sir." O'Hanley sighed. "Pretty much a bust. I mean, I could be out on patrol. Instead they got me hanging around here eyeballing faces."

"Surveillance?"

"Yes, sir." He nodded at the poster of Holland. "That guy. Everyone's hot to find him. They say he's a spy."

"Do they, now?" Polowski took a lazy glance around the room. "Seen anyone around here who looks like him?"

"Not a one. I been watching every minute."

Polowski didn't doubt it. O'Hanley was the kind of

kid who, if you asked him to, would scrub the Captain's boots with a toothbrush. He'd do a good job of it, too.

Obviously Holland hadn't come through here. Polowski turned to leave. Then another thought came to mind, and he turned back to O'Hanley. "The suspect may be traveling with a woman," he said. He pulled out a photo of Cathy Weaver, one Jack Zuckerman had been persuaded to donate to the FBI. "Have you seen her come through here?"

O'Hanley frowned. "Gee. She sure does look like... Naw. That can't be her."

"Who?"

"Well, there was this woman in here 'bout an hour ago. Kind of a down and outer. Some little brat ran smack into her. I sort've brushed her off and sent her on her way. She looked a lot like this gal, only in a lot worse shape."

"Was she traveling alone?"

"She had an old guy with her. Her pop, I think."

Suddenly Polowski was all ears. That instinct again—it was telling him something. "What did this old man look like?"

"Real old. Maybe seventy. Had this bushy beard, lot of white hair."

"How tall?"

"Pretty tall. Over six feet..." O'Hanley's voice trailed off as his gaze focused on the wanted poster. Victor Holland was six foot three. O'Hanley's face went white. "Oh, God..."

"Was it him?"

"I—I can't be sure—"

"Come on, come on!"

"I just don't know... Wait. The woman, she dropped a makeup case! I turned it in at that window there—"

It took only a flash of an FBI badge for the clerk in Lost and Found to hand over the case. The instant Polowski opened the thing, he knew he'd hit pay dirt. It was filled with theatrical makeup supplies. Stenciled inside the lid was: Property of Jack Zuckerman Productions.

He slammed the lid shut. "Where did they go?" he snapped at O'Hanley.

"They—uh, they boarded a bus right over there. That gate. Around seven o'clock."

Polowski glanced up at the departure schedule. At seven o'clock, the number fourteen had departed for Palo Alto.

It took him ten minutes to get hold of the Palo Alto depot manager, another five minutes to convince the man this wasn't just another Prince-Albert-in-the-can phone call.

"The number fourteen from San Francisco?" came the answer. "Arrived twenty minutes ago."

"What about the passengers?" pressed Polowski. "You see any of 'em still around?"

The manager only laughed. "Hey, man. If you had a choice, would *you* hang around a stinking bus station?"

Muttering an oath, Polowski hung up.

"Sir?" It was O'Hanley. He looked sick. "I messed up, didn't I? I let him walk right past me. I can't believe—"

"Forget it."

"But—"

Polowski headed for the exit. "You're just a rookie," he called over his shoulder. "Chalk it up to experience."

"Should I call this in?"
"I'll take care of it. I'm headed there, anyway."
"Where?"
Polowski shoved open the station door. "Palo Alto."

Chapter 8

The front door was answered by an elderly oriental woman whose command of English was limited.

"Mrs. Lum? Remember me? Victor Holland. I used to know your son."

"Yes, yes!"

"Is he here?"

"Yes." Her gaze shifted to Cathy now, as though the woman didn't want her second visitor to feel left out of the conversation.

"I need to see him," said Victor. "Is Milo here?"

"Milo?" At last here was a word she seemed to know. She turned and called out loudly in Chinese.

Somewhere a door squealed open and footsteps stamped up the stairs. A fortyish oriental man in blue jeans and chambray shirt came to the front door. He was a dumpling of a fellow, and he brought with him the vague odor of chemicals, something sharp and acidic. He was wiping his hands on a rag.

"What can I do for you?" he asked.

Victor grinned. "Milo Lum! Are you still skulking around in your mother's basement?"

"Excuse me?" Milo inquired politely. "Am I supposed to know you, sir?"

"Don't recognize an old horn player from the Out of Tuners?"

Milo stared in disbelief. "Gershwin? That can't be *you?*"

"Yeah, I know," Victor said with a laugh. "The years haven't been kind."

"I didn't want to say anything, but…"

"I won't take it personally. Since—" Victor peeled off his false beard "—the face isn't all mine."

Milo gazed down at the lump of fake whispers, hanging like a dead animal in Victor's grasp. Then he stared up at Victor's jaw, still blotchy with spirit gum. "This is some kind of joke on old Milo, right?" He stuck his head out the door, glancing past Victor at the sidewalk. "And the other guys are hiding out there somewhere, waiting to yell *surprise!* Aren't they? Some big practical joke."

"I wish it were a joke," said Victor.

Milo instantly caught the undertone of urgency in Victor's voice. He looked at Cathy, then back at Victor. Nodding, he stepped aside. "Come in, Gersh. Sounds like I have some catching up to do."

Over a late supper of duck noodle soup and jasmine tea, Milo heard the story. He said little; he seemed more intent on slurping down the last of his noodles. Only when the ever-smiling Mrs. Lum had bowed good-night and creaked off to bed did Milo offer his comment.

"When you get in trouble, man, you sure as hell do it right."

"Astute as always, Milo," sighed Victor.

"Too bad we can't say the same for the cops," Milo snorted. "If they'd just bothered to ask around, they would've learned you're harmless. Far as I know, you're guilty of only one serious crime."

Cathy looked up, startled. "What crime?"

"Assaulting the ears of victims unlucky enough to hear his saxophone."

"This from a piccolo player who practises with earplugs," observed Victor.

"That's to drown out extraneous noise."

"Yeah. Mainly your own."

Cathy grinned. "I'm beginning to understand why you called yourselves the Out of Tuners."

"Just some healthy self-deprecating humor," said Milo. "Something we needed after we failed to make the Stanford band." Milo rose, shoving away from the kitchen table. "Well, come on. Let's see what's on that mysterious roll of film."

He led them along the hall and down a rickety set of steps to the basement. The chemical tang of the air, the row of trays lined up on a stainless-steel countertop and the slow drip, drip of water from the faucet told Cathy she was standing in an enormous darkroom. Tacked on the walls was a jumble of photos. Faces, mostly, apparently snapped around the world. Here and there she spotted a newsworthy shot: soldiers storming an airport, protestors unfurling a banner.

"Is this your job, Milo?" she asked.

"I wish," said Milo, agitating the developing canister. "No, I just work in the ol' family business."

"Which is?"

"Shoes. Italian, Brazilian, leather, alligator, you name it, we import it." He cocked his head at the photos. "That's how I get my exotic faces. Shoe-buying trips. I'm an expert on the female arch."

"For that," said Victor, "he spent four years at Stanford?"

"Why not? Good a place as any to study the fine feet of the fair sex." A timer rang. Milo poured out the developer, removed the roll of film, and hung it up to dry. "Actually," he said, squinting at the negatives, "it was my dad's dying request. He wanted a son with a Stanford degree. I wanted four years of nonstop partying. We both got our wishes." He paused and gazed off wistfully at his photos. "Too bad I can't say the same of the years since then."

"What do you mean?" asked Cathy.

"I mean the partying's long since over. Gotta earn those profits, keep up those sales. Never thought life'd come down to the bottom line. Whatever happened to all that rabble-rousing potential, hey, Gersh? We sort of lost it along the way. All of us, Bach and Ollie and Roger. The Out of Tuners finally stepped into line. Now we're all marching to the beat of the same boring drummer." He sighed and glanced at Victor. "You make out anything on those negatives?"

Victor shook his head. "We need prints."

Milo flipped off the lights, leaving only the red glow of the darkroom lamp. "Coming up."

As Milo laid out the photographic paper, Victor asked, "What happened to the other guys? They still around?"

Milo flipped the exposure switch. "Roger's VP at

some multinational bank in Tokyo. Into silk suits and ties, the whole nine yards. Bach's got an electronics firm in San José."

"And Ollie?"

"What can I say about Ollie?" Milo slipped the first print into the bath. "He's still lurking around in that lab over at Stanford Med. I doubt he ever sees the light of day. I figure he's got some secret chamber in the basement where he keeps his assistant Igor chained to the wall."

"This guy I have to meet," said Cathy.

"Oh, he'd love you." Victor laughed and gave her arm a squeeze. "Seeing as he's probably forgotten what the female of the species looks like."

Milo slid the print into the next tray. "Yeah, Ollie's the one who never changed. Still the night owl. Still plays a mean clarinet." He glanced at Victor. "How's the sax, Gersh? You keeping it up?"

"Haven't played in months."

"Lucky neighbors."

"How did you ever get that name?" asked Cathy. "Gersh?"

"Because," said Milo, wielding tongs as he transferred another batch of prints between trays, "he's a firm believer in the power of George Gershwin to win a lady's heart. 'Someone to Watch Over Me,' wasn't that the tune that made Lily say…" Milo's voice suddenly faded. He looked at his friend with regret.

"You're right," said Victor quietly. "That was the tune. And Lily said yes."

Milo shook his head. "Sorry. Guess I still have a hard time remembering she's gone."

"Well, she is," said Victor, his voice matter-of-fact.

Cathy knew there was pain buried in the undertones. But he hid it well. "And right now," Victor said, "we've got other things to think about."

"Yeah." Milo, chastened, turned his attention back to the prints he'd just developed. He fished them out and clipped the first few sheets on the line to dry. "Okay, Gersh. Tell us what's on this roll that's worth killing for."

Milo switched on the lights.

Victor stood in silence for a moment, frowning at the first five dripping prints. To Cathy, the data was meaningless, only a set of numbers and codes, recorded in an almost illegible hand.

"Well," grunted Milo. "That sure tells me a lot."

Victor's gaze shifted quickly from one page to the next. He paused at the fifth photo, where a column ran down the length of the page. It contained a series of twenty-seven entries, each one a date followed by the same three letters: EXP.

"Victor?" asked Cathy. "What does it mean?"

He turned to them. It was the look in his eyes that worried her. The stillness. Quietly he said, "We need to call Ollie."

"You mean tonight?" asked Milo. "Why?"

"This isn't just some experiment in test tubes and petri dishes. They've gone beyond that, to clinical trials." Victor pointed to the last page. "These are monkeys. Each one was infected with a new virus. A manmade virus. And in every case the results were the same."

"You mean this?" Milo pointed to the last column. "EXP?"

"It stands for expired," said Victor. "They all died."

* * *

Sam Polowski sat on a bench in the Palo Alto bus terminal and wondered: If I wanted to disappear, where would I go next? He watched a dozen or so passengers straggle off to board the 210 from San José, noting they were by and large the Birkenstock and backpack set. Probably Stanford students heading off for Christmas break. He wondered why it was that students who could afford such a pricey university couldn't seem to scrape up enough to buy a decent pair of jeans. Or even a decent haircut, for that matter.

At last Polowski rose and automatically dusted off his coat, a habit he'd picked up from his early years of hanging around the seamier side of town. Even if the grime wasn't actually visible, he'd always *felt* it was there, coating any surface he happened to brush against, ready to cling to him like wet paint.

He made one phone call—to Dafoe's answering machine, to tell him Victor Holland had moved on to Palo Alto. It was, after all, his responsibility to keep his supervisor informed. He was glad he only had to talk to a recording and not to the man himself.

He left the bus station and strolled down the street, heading Lord knew where, in search of a spark, a hunch. It was a nice-enough neighborhood, a nice-enough town. Palo Alto had its old professors' houses, its bookshops and coffee houses where university types, the ones with the beards and wire-rim glasses, liked to sit and argue the meaning of Proust and Brecht and Goethe. Polowski remembered his own university days, when, after being subjected to an hour of such crap from the students at the next table, he had finally stormed over to them and yelled, "Maybe Brecht meant it that way, maybe not. But can you guys answer this? *What the hell difference does it make?*"

This did not, needless to say, enhance his reputation as a serious scholar.

Now, as he paced along the street, no doubt in the footsteps of more serious philosophers, Polowski turned over in his head the question of Victor Holland. More specifically the question of where such a man, in his desperation, would hide. He stalked past the lit windows, the glow of TVs, the cars spilling from garages. Where in this warren of suburbia was the man hiding?

Holland was a scientist, a musician, a man of few but lasting friendships. He had a Ph.D. from MIT, a B.S. from Stanford. The university was right up the road. The man must know his way around here. Maybe he still had friends in the neighborhood, people who'd take him in, keep his secrets.

Polowski decided to take another look at Holland's file. Somewhere in the Viratek records, there had to be some employment reference, some recommendation from a Stanford contact. A friend Holland might turn to.

Sooner or later, he would have to turn to *someone.*

It was after midnight when Dafoe and his wife returned home. He was in an excellent mood, his head pleasantly abuzz with champagne, his ears still ringing with the heart-wrenching aria from *Samson and Delilah.* Opera was a passion for him, a brilliant staging of courage and conflict and *amore,* a vision of life so much grander than the petty little world in which he found himself. It launched him to a plane of such thrilling intensity that even his own wife took on exciting new aspects. He watched her peel off her coat and kick off her shoes. Forty pounds overweight, hair streaked with silver, yet she had her attractions. *It's been three weeks. Surely she'll let me tonight...*

But his wife ignored his amorous looks and wandered off to the kitchen. A moment later, the rumble of the automatic dishwasher announced another of her fits of housecleaning.

In frustration, Dafoe turned and stabbed the blinking button on his answering machine. The message from Polowski completely destroyed any amorous intentions he had left.

"...Reason to believe Holland is in, or has just left, the Palo Alto area. Following leads. Will keep you informed..."

Polowski, you half-wit. Is following orders so damn difficult?

It was 3:00 a.m. Washington time. An ungodly hour, but he made the phone call.

The voice that answered was raspy with sleep. "Tyrone here."

"Cowboy, this is Dafoe. Sorry to wake you."

The voice became instantly alert, all sleep shaken from it. "What's up?"

"New lead on Holland. I don't know the particulars, but he's headed south, to Palo Alto. May still be there."

"The university?"

"It is the Stanford area."

"That may be a very big help."

"Anything for an old buddy. I'll keep you posted."

"One thing, Dafoe."

"Yeah?"

"I can't have any interference. Pull all your people out. We'll take it from here."

Dafoe paused. "I might…have a problem."

"A problem?" The voice, though quiet, took on a razor's edge.

"It's, uh, one of my men. Sort of a wild card. Sam Polowski. He's got this Holland case under his skin, wants to go after him."

"There's such a thing as a direct order."

"At the moment, Polowski's unreachable. He's in Palo Alto, digging around in God knows what."

"Loose cannons. I don't like them."

"I'll pull him back as soon as I can."

"Do that. And keep it quiet. It's a matter of utmost security."

After Dafoe hung up, his gaze shifted automatically to the photo on the mantelpiece. It was a '68 snapshot of him and the Cowboy: two young marines, both of them grinning, their rifles slung over their shoulders as they stood ankle-deep in a rice paddy. It was a crazy time, when one's very life depended on the loyalty of buddies. When Semper Fi applied not only to the corps in general but to each other in particular. Matt Tyrone was a hero then, and he was a hero now. Dafoe stared at that smiling face in the photo, disturbed by the threads of envy that had woven into his admiration for the man. Though Dafoe had much to be proud of—a solid eighteen years in the FBI, maybe even a shot at assistant director somewhere in his stars, he couldn't match the heady climb of Matt Tyrone in the NSA. Though Dafoe wasn't clear as to exactly what position the Cowboy held in the NSA, he had heard that Tyrone regularly attended cabinet meetings, that he held the trust of the president, that he dealt in secrets and shadows and security. He was the sort of man the country needed, a man for whom patriotism was more than mere flag-waving and rhetoric; it was a way of life. Matt Tyrone would do more than die for his country; he'd live for it.

Dafoe couldn't let such a man, such a friend, down.

He dialed Sam Polowski's home phone and left a message on the recorder.

This is a direct order. You are to withdraw from the Holland case immediately. Until further notice you are on suspension.

He was tempted to add, *by special request from my friends in Washington,* but thought better of it. No room for vanity here. The Cowboy had said national security was at stake.

Dafoe had no doubt it truly was. He'd gotten the word from Matt Tyrone. And Matt Tyrone's authority came direct from the President himself.

"This does not look good. This does not look good at all."

Ollie Wozniak squinted through his wire-rim glasses at the twenty-four photographs strewn across Milo's dining table. He held one up for a closer look. Through the bottle-glass lens, one pale blue eye stared out, enormous. One only saw Ollie's eyes; everything else, hollow cheeks, pencil lips and baby-fine hair, seemed to recede into the background pallor. He shook his head and picked up another photo.

"You're right, of course," he said. "Some of these I can't interpret. I'd like to study 'em later. But these here are definitely raw mortality data. Rhesus monkeys, I suspect." He paused and added quietly, "I hope."

"Surely they wouldn't use people for this sort of thing," said Cathy.

"Not officially." Ollie put down the photo and looked at her. "But it's been done."

"Maybe in Nazi Germany."

"Here, too," said Victor.

"What?" Cathy looked at him in disbelief.

"Army studies in germ warfare. They released colonies of Serratia Marcescens over San Francisco and waited to see how far the organism spread. Infections popped up in a number of Bay Area hospitals. Some of the cases were fatal."

"I can't believe it," murmured Cathy.

"The damage was unintentional, of course. But people died just the same."

"Don't forget Tuskegee," said Ollie. "People died in those experiments, too. And then there was that case in New York. Mentally retarded kids in a state hospital who were deliberately exposed to hepatitis. No one died there, but the ethics were just as shaky. So it's been done. Sometimes in the name of humanity."

"Sometimes not," said Victor.

Ollie nodded. "As in this particular case."

"What exactly are we talking about here?" asked Cathy, nodding at the photos. "Is this medical research? Or weapons development?"

"Both." Ollie pointed to one of the photos on the table. "By all appearances, Viratek's engaged in biological weapons research. They've dubbed it Project Cerberus. From what I can tell, the organism they're working on is an RNA virus, extremely virulent, highly contagious, producing over eighty-percent mortality in its lab animal hosts. This photo here—" he tapped one of the pages "—shows the organism produces vesicular skin lesions on the infected subjects."

"Vesicular?"

"Blisterlike. That could be one route of transmission, the fluid in those lesions." He sifted through the pile and pulled out another page. "This shows the time course of the illness. The viral counts, periods of infectiousness. In almost every case the course is the same. The subject's exposed here." He pointed to Day One on the time graph. "Minor signs of illness here at Day Seven. Full-blown pox on Day Twelve. And here—" he tapped the graph at Day Fourteen "—the deaths begin. The time varies, but the result's the same. They all die."

"You used the word *pox*," said Cathy.

Ollie turned to her, his eyes like blue glass. "Because that's what it is."

"You mean like chickenpox?"

"I wish it was. Then it wouldn't be so deadly. Almost everyone gets exposed to chickenpox as a kid, so most of us are immune. But this one's a different story."

"Is it a new virus?" asked Milo.

"Yes and no." He reached for an electron micrograph. "When I saw this I thought there was something weirdly familiar about all this. The appearance of the organism, the skin lesions, the course of illness. The whole damn picture. It reminded me of something I haven't read about in decades. Something I never dreamed I'd see again."

"You're saying it's an old virus?" said Milo.

"Ancient. But they've made some modifications. Made it more infectious. And deadlier. Which turns this into a real humdinger of a weapon, considering the millions of folks it's already killed."

"*Millions?*" Cathy stared at him. "What are we talking about?"

"A killer we've known for centuries. Smallpox."

"That's impossible!" said Cathy. "From what I've read, we conquered smallpox. It's supposed to be extinct."

"It was," said Victor. "For all practical purposes. Worldwide vaccination wiped it out. Smallpox hasn't been reported in decades. I'm not even sure they still make the vaccine. Ollie?"

"Not available. No need for it since the virus has vanished."

"So where did *this* virus come from?" asked Cathy.

Ollie shrugged. "Probably someone's closet."

"Come on."

"I'm serious. After smallpox was eradicated, a few samples of the virus were kept alive in government labs, just in case someone needed it for future research. It's the scientific skeleton in the closet, so to speak. I'd assume those labs are top security. Because if any of the virus got out, there could be a major epidemic." He looked at the stack of photos. "Looks like security's already been breached. Someone obviously got hold of the virus."

"Or had it handed to them," said Victor. "Courtesy of the U.S. government."

"I find that incredible, Gersh," said Ollie. "This is a powderkeg experiment you're talking about. No committee would approve this sort of project."

"Right. That's why I think this is a maverick operation. It's easy to come up with a scenario. Bunch of hardliners cooking this up over at NSA. Or joint chiefs of staff. Or even the Oval Office. Someone says: 'World politics have changed. We can't get away with nuking the enemy. We need a new weapons option, one that'll work well against a Third World army. Let's find one.' And some guy in that room, some red, white and blue robot, will take that as the go-ahead. International law be damned."

"And since it's unofficial," said Cathy, "it'd be completely deniable."

"Right. The administration could claim it knew nothing."

"Sounds like Iran-Contra all over again."

"With one big difference," said Ollie. "When Iran-Contra fell apart, all you had were a few ruined political careers. If Project Cerberus goes awry, what you'll have is a few million dead people."

"But Ollie," said Milo. "I got vaccinated for smallpox when I was a kid. Doesn't that mean I'm safe?"

"Probably. Assuming the virus hasn't been altered too much. In fact, everyone over 35 is probably okay. But remember, there's a whole generation after us that never got the vaccine. Young adults and kids. By the time you could manufacture enough vaccine for them all, we'd have a raging epidemic."

"I'm beginning to see the logic of this weapon," said Victor. "In any war, who makes up the bulk of combat soldiers? Young adults."

Ollie nodded. "They'd be hit bad. As would the kids."

"A whole generation," Cathy murmured. "And only the old would be spared." She glanced at Victor and saw, mirrored in his eyes, the horror she felt.

"They chose an appropriate name," said Milo.

Ollie frowned. "What?"

"Cerberus. The three-headed dog of Hades." Milo looked up, visibly shaken. "Guardian of the dead."

* * *

It wasn't until Cathy was fast asleep and Milo had retired upstairs that Victor finally broached the subject to Ollie. It had troubled him all evening, had shadowed his every moment since they'd arrived at Milo's house. He couldn't look at Cathy, couldn't listen to the sound of her voice or inhale the scent of her hair without thinking of the terrible possibilities. And in the deepest hours of night, when it seemed all the world was asleep except for him and Ollie, he made the decision.

"I need to ask you a favor," he said.

Ollie gazed at him across the dining table, steam wafting up from his fourth cup of coffee. "What sort of favor?"

"It has to do with Cathy."

Ollie's gaze shifted to the woman lying asleep on the living room floor. She looked very small, very defenseless, curled up beneath the comforter. Ollie said, "She's a nice woman, Gersh."

"I know."

"There hasn't really been anyone since Lily. Has there?"

Victor shook his head. "I guess I haven't felt ready for it. There were always other things to think about…"

Ollie smiled. "There are always excuses. I should know. People keep telling me there's a glut of unattached female baby boomers. I haven't noticed."

"And I never bothered to notice." Victor looked at Cathy. "Until now."

"What're you gonna do with her, Gersh?"

"That's what I need you for. I'm not the safest guy to hang around with these days. A woman could get hurt."

Ollie laughed. "Hell, a *guy* could get hurt."

"I feel responsible for her. And if something happened to her, I'm not sure I could ever..." He let out a long sigh and rubbed his bloodshot eyes. "Anyway, I think it's best if she leaves."

"For where?"

"She has an ex-husband. He'll be working down in Mexico for a few months. I think she'd be pretty safe."

"You're sending her to her ex-husband?"

"I've met him. He's a jerk, but at least she won't be alone down there."

"Does Cathy agree to this?"

"I didn't ask her."

"Maybe you should."

"I'm not giving her a choice."

"What if she wants the choice?"

"I'm not in the mood to take any crap, Okay? I'm doing this for her own good."

Ollie took off his glasses and cleaned them on the tablecloth. "Excuse me for saying this, Gersh, but if it was me, I'd want her nearby, where I could sort of keep an eye on her."

"You mean where I can watch her get killed?" Victor shook his head. "Lily was enough. I won't go through it with Cathy."

Ollie thought it over for a moment, then he nodded. "What do you want me to do?"

"Tomorrow I want you to take her to the airport. Buy her a ticket to Mexico. Let her use your name. Mrs. Wozniak. Make sure she gets safely off the ground. I'll pay you back when I can."

"What if she won't get on the plane? Do I just shove her aboard?"

"Do whatever it takes, Ollie. I'm counting on you."

Ollie sighed. "I guess I can do it. I'll call in sick tomorrow. That'll free up my day." He looked at Victor. "I just hope you know what you're doing."

So do I, thought Victor.

Ollie rose to his feet and tucked the envelope with the photos under his arm. "I'll get back to you in the morning. After I show these last two photos to Bach. Maybe he can identify what those grids are."

"If it's anything electronic, Bach'll figure it out."

Together they walked to the door. There they paused and regarded each other, two old friends who'd grown a little grayer and, Victor hoped, a little wiser.

"Somehow it'll all work out," said Ollie. "Remember. The system's there to be beaten."

"Sounds like the old Stanford radical again."

"It's been a long time." Grinning, Ollie gave Victor a clap on the back. "But we're still not too old to raise a little hell, hey, Gersh? See you in the morning."

Victor waved as Ollie walked away into the darkness. Then he closed the door and turned off all the lights.

In the living room he sat beside Cathy and watched her sleep. The glow of a streetlight spilled in through the window onto her tumbled hair. *Ordinary,* she had called herself. Perhaps, if she'd been a stranger he'd merely passed on the street, he might have thought so, too. A chance meeting on a rainy highway in Garberville had made it impossible for him to ever consider this woman ordinary. In her gentleness, her kindness, she was very much like Lily.

In other ways, she was very different.

Though he'd cared about his wife, though they'd never stopped being good friends, he'd found Lily strangely passionless, a pristine, spiritual being trapped by human flesh. Lily had never been comfortable with her own body. She'd undress in the dark, make love—the rare times they did—in the dark. And then, the illness had robbed her of what little desire she had left.

Gazing at Cathy, he couldn't help wondering what passions might lie harbored in her still form.

He cut short the speculation. What did it matter now? Tomorrow, he'd send her away. *Get rid of her,* he thought brutally. It was necessary. He couldn't think straight while she was around. He couldn't stay focused on the business at hand: exposing Viratek. Jerry Martinique had counted on him. Thousands of potential victims counted on him. He was a scientist, a man who prided himself on logic. His attraction to this particular woman was, in the grand scheme of things, clearly unimportant.

That was what the scientist in him said.

That problem finally settled, he decided to get some rest while he could. He kicked off his shoes and stretched out beside her to sleep. The comforter was large enough—they could share it. He climbed beneath it and lay for a moment, not touching her, almost afraid to share her warmth.

She whimpered in her sleep and turned toward him, her silky hair tumbling against his face.

This was more than he could resist. Sighing, he wrapped his arms around her and felt her curl up against his chest. It was their last night together. They might as well spend it keeping each other warm.

That was how he fell asleep, with Cathy in his arms.

Only once during the night did he awaken. He had been dreaming of Lily. They were walking together, in a garden of pure white flowers. She said absolutely nothing. She simply looked at him with profound sadness, as if to say, *Here I am, Victor. I've come back to you. Why doesn't that make you happy?* He couldn't answer her. So he simply took her in his arms and held her.

He'd awakened to find he was holding Cathy, instead.

Joy instantly flooded his heart, warmed the darkest corners of his soul. It took him by surprise, that burst of happiness; it also made him feel guilty. But there it was. And the joy was all too short-lived. He remembered that today she'd be going away.

Cathy, Cathy. What a complication you've become.

He turned on his side, away from her, mentally building a wall between them.

He concentrated on the dream, trying to remember what had happened. He and Lily had been walking. He tried to picture Lily's face, her brown eyes, her curly black hair. It was the face of the woman he'd been married to for ten years, a face he should know well.

But the only face he saw when he closed his eyes was that of Catherine Weaver.

It took Nicholas Savitch only two hours to pack his bags and drive down to Palo Alto. The word from Matt Tyrone was that Holland had slipped south to the Stanford area, perhaps to seek out old friends. Holland was, after all, a Stanford man. Maybe not the red-and-white rah-rah Cardinals type, but a Stanford man nonetheless. These old school ties could run deep. It was only a guess on Savitch's part; he'd never gone beyond high school. His education consisted of what a hungry and ambitious boy could pick up on Chicago's south side. Mainly a keen, almost uncanny knack for crawling into another man's head, for sensing what a particular man would think and do in a given situation. Call it advanced street psychology. Without spending a day in college, Savitch had earned his degree.

Now he was putting it to use.

The *finder,* they called him. He liked that name. He grinned as he drove, his leather-gloved hands expertly handling the wheel. Nicholas Savitch, diviner of human souls, the hunter who could ferret a man out of deepest hiding.

In most cases it was a simple matter of logic. Even while on the run, most people conformed to old patterns. It was the fear that did it. It made them seek out their old comforts, cling to their usual habits. In a strange town, the familiar was precious, even if it was only the sight of those ubiquitous golden arches.

Like every other fugitive, Victor Holland would seek the familiar.

Savitch turned his car onto Palm Drive and pulled up in front of the Stanford Arch. The campus was silent; it was 2:00 a.m. Savitch sat for a moment, regarding the silent buildings, Holland's alma mater. Here, in his former stomping grounds, Holland would turn to old friends, revisit old haunts. Savitch had already done his homework. He carried, in his briefcase, a list of names he'd culled from the man's file. In the morning he'd start in on those names, knock on neighbors' doors, flash his government ID, ask about new faces in the neighborhood.

The only possible complication was Sam Polowski. By last report, the FBI agent was also in town, also on Holland's trail. Polowski was a dogged operator. It'd be messy business, taking out a Bureau man. But then, Polowski was only a cog, the way the Weaver woman was only a cog, in a much bigger wheel.

Neither of them would be missed.

Chapter 9

In the cold, clear hours before dawn, Cathy woke up shaking, still trapped in the threads of a nightmare. She had been walking in a world of concrete and shadow, where doorways gaped and silhouettes huddled on street corners. She drifted among them, one among the faceless, taking refuge in obscurity, instinctively avoiding the light. No one pursued her; no attacker lunged from the alleys. The real terror lay in the unending maze of concrete, the hard echoes of the streets, the frantic search for a safe place.

And the certainty that she would never find it.

For a moment she lay in the darkness, curled up beneath a down comforter on Milo's living room floor. She barely remembered having crawled under the covers; it must have been sometime after three when she'd fallen asleep. The last she remembered, Ollie and Victor were still huddled in the dining room, discussing the photographs. Now there was only silence. The dining room, like the rest of the house, lay in shadow.

She turned on her back, and her shoulder thumped against something warm and solid. Victor. He stirred, murmuring something she couldn't understand.

"Are you awake?" she whispered.

He turned toward her and in his drowsiness enfolded her in his arms. She knew it was only instinct that drew him to her, the yearning of one warm body for another. Or perhaps it was the memory of his wife sleeping beside him, in his mind always there, always waiting to be held. For the moment, she let him cling to the dream. *While he's still half asleep, let him believe I'm Lily,* she thought. *What harm can there be? He needs the memory. And I need the comfort.*

She burrowed into his arms, into the safe spot that once had belonged to another. She took it without regard for the consequences, willing to be swept up into the fantasy of being, for this moment, the one woman in the world he loved. How good it felt, how protected and cared for. From the soap-and-sweat smell of his chest to the coarse fabric of his shirt, it was sanctuary. He was breathing warmly into her hair now, whispering words she knew were for another, pressing kisses to the top of her head. Then he trapped her face in his hands and pressed his lips to hers in a kiss so undeniably needy it ignited within her a hunger of her own. Her response was instinctive and filled with all the yearning of a woman too long a stranger to love.

She met his kiss with one just as deep, just as needy.

At once she was lost, whirled away into some grand and glorious vortex. He stroked down her face, her neck. His hands moved to the buttons of her blouse. She arched against him, her breasts suddenly aching to be touched. It had been so long, so long.

She didn't know how the blouse fell open. She knew only that one moment his fingers were skimming the fabric, and the next moment, they were cupping her flesh. It was that unexpected contact of skin on forbidden skin, the magic torment of his fingers caressing her nipple, that made any last resistance fall away. How many chances were left to them? How many nights together? She longed for so many more, an eternity, but this might be all they had. She welcomed it, welcomed him, with all the passion of a woman granted one last taste of love.

With a knowing touch, she slid her hands down his shirt, undoing buttons, stroking her way through the dense hair of his chest, to the top of his trousers. There she paused, feeling his startled intake of breath, knowing that he too was past retreat.

Together they fumbled at buttons and zippers, both of them suddenly feverish to be free. It all fell away in a tumult of cotton and lace. And when the last scrap of clothing was shed, when nothing came between them but the velvet darkness, she reached up and pulled him to her, on her.

It was a joyful filling, as if, in that first deep thrust within her, he also reached some long-empty hollow in her soul.

"Please," she murmured, her voice breaking into a whimper.

He fell instantly still. "Cathy?" he asked, his hands anxiously cupping her face. "What—"

"Please. Don't stop…"

His soft laughter was all the reassurance she needed. "I have no intention of stopping," he whispered. "None whatsoever…"

And he didn't stop. Not until he had taken her with him all the way, higher and further than any man ever could, to a place beyond thought or reason. Only when release came, wave flooding upon wave, did she know how very high and far they had climbed.

A sweet exhaustion claimed them.

Outside, in the grayness of dawn, a bird sang. Inside, the silence was broken only by the sound of their breathing.

She sighed into the warmth of his shoulder. "Thank you."

He touched her face. "For what?"

"For making me feel…wanted again."

"Oh, Cathy."

"It's been such a long time. Jack and I, we—we stopped making love way before the divorce. It was me, actually. I couldn't bear having him…" She swallowed. "When you don't love someone anymore, when they don't love you, it's hard to let yourself be…touched."

He brushed his fingers down her cheek. "Is it still hard? Being touched?"

"Not by you. Being touched by you is like…being touched the very first time."

By the window's pale light she saw him smile. "I hope your very first time wasn't too awful."

Now she smiled. "I don't remember it very well. It was such a frantic, ridiculous thing on the floor of a college dorm room."

He reached out and patted the carpet. "I see you've come a long way."

"Haven't I?" she laughed. "But floors can be terribly romantic places."

"Goodness. A carpet connoisseur. How do dorm room and living room floors compare?"

"I couldn't tell you. It's been such a long time since I was eighteen." She paused, hovering on the edge of baring the truth. "In fact," she admitted, "it's been a long time since I've been with anyone."

Softly he said, "It's been a long time for both of us."

She let that revelation hang for a moment in the semi-darkness. "Not—not since Lily?" she finally asked.

"No." A single word, yet it revealed so much. The three years of loyalty to a dead woman. The grief, the loneliness. How she wanted to fill that womanless chasm for him! To be his savior, and he, hers. Could she make him forget? No, not forget; she couldn't expect him ever to forget Lily. But she wanted a space in his heart for herself, a very large space designed for a lifetime. A space to which no other woman, dead or alive, could ever lay claim.

"She must have been a very special woman," she said.

He ran a strand of her hair through his fingers. "She was very wise, very aware. And she was kind. That's something I don't always find in a person."

She's still part of you, isn't she? She's still the one you love.

"It's the same sort of kindness I find in you," he said.

His fingers had slid to her face and were now stroking her cheek. She closed her eyes, savoring his touch, his warmth. "You hardly know me," she whispered.

"But I do. That night, after the accident, I survived

purely on the sound of your voice. And the touch of your hand. I'd know them both, anywhere."

She opened her eyes and gazed at him. "Would you really?"

He pressed his lips to her forehead. "Even in my sleep."

"But I'm not Lily. I could never be Lily."

"That's true. You can't be. No one can."

"I can't replace what you lost."

"What makes you think that's what I want? Some sort of replacement? She was my wife. And yes, I loved her." By the way he said it, his answer invited no exploration.

She didn't try.

From somewhere in the house came the jingle of a telephone. After two rings it stopped. Faintly they heard Milo's voice murmuring upstairs.

Cathy sat up and reached automatically for her clothes. She dressed in silence, her back turned to Victor. A new modesty had sprung up between them, the shyness of strangers.

"Cathy," he said. "People do move on."

"I know."

"You've gotten over Jack."

She laughed, a small, tired sound. "No woman ever really gets over Jack Zuckerman. Yes, I'm over the worst of it. But every time a woman falls in love, really falls in love, it takes something out of her. Something that can never be put back."

"It also gives her something."

"That depends on who you fall in love with, doesn't it?"

Footsteps thumped down the stairs, creaked across the dining room. A wide-awake Milo stood in the doorway, his uncombed hair standing out like a brush. "Hey, you two!" he hissed. "Get up! Hurry."

Cathy rose to her feet in alarm. "What is it?"

"That was Ollie on the phone. He called to say some guy's in the area, asking questions about you. He's already been down to Bach's neighborhood."

"What?" Now Victor was on his feet and hurriedly stuffing his legs into his trousers.

"Ollie figures the guy'll be knocking around here next. Guess they know who your friends are."

"Who was asking the questions?"

"Claimed he was FBI."

"Polowski," muttered Victor, pulling his shirt on. "Has to be."

"You know him?"

"The same guy who set me up. The guy who's been tailing us ever since."

"How did he know we're here?" said Cathy. "No one could've followed us—"

"No one had to. They have my profile. They know I have friends here." Victor glanced at Milo. "Sorry, buddy. Hope this doesn't get you into trouble."

Milo's laugh was distinctly tense. "Hey, I didn't do nothin' wrong. Just harbored a felon." The bravado suddenly melted away. He asked, "Exactly what kind of trouble should I expect?"

"Questions," said Victor, quickly buttoning his shirt. "Lots of 'em. Maybe they'll even take a look around. Just keep cool, tell 'em you haven't heard from me. Think you can do it?"

"Sure. But I don't know about Ma—"

"Your ma's no problem. Just tell her to stick to

Chinese." Victor grabbed the envelope of photos and glanced at Cathy. "Ready?"

"Let's get out of here. Please."

"Back door," Milo suggested.

They followed him through the kitchen. A glance told them the way was clear. As he opened the door, Milo added, "I almost forgot. Ollie wants to see you this afternoon. Something about those photos."

"Where?"

"The lake. Behind the boathouse. You know the place."

They stepped out into the chill dampness of morning. Fog-borne silence hung in the air. *Will we ever stop running?* thought Cathy. *Will we never stop listening for footsteps?*

Victor clapped his friend on the shoulder. "Thanks, Milo. I owe you a big one."

"And one of these days I plan to collect!" Milo hissed as they slipped away.

Victor held up his hand in farewell. "See you around."

"Yeah," Milo muttered into the mist. "Let's hope not in jail."

The Chinese man was lying. Though the man betrayed nothing in his voice, no hesitation, no guilty waver, still Savitch knew this Mr. Milo Lum was hiding something. His eyes betrayed him.

He was seated on the living room couch, across from Savitch. Off to the side sat Mrs. Lum in an easy chair, smiling uncomprehendingly. Savitch might be able to use the old biddy; for now, it was the son who held his interest.

"I can't see why you'd be after him," said Milo. "Victor's as clean as they come. At least, he was when I knew him. But that was a long time ago."

"How far back?" asked Savitch politely.

"Oh, years. Yeah. Haven't seen him since. No, sir."

Savitch raised an eyebrow. Milo shifted on the couch, shuffled his feet, glanced pointlessly around the room.

"You and your mother live here alone?" Savitch asked.

"Since my dad died."

"No tenants? No one else lives here?"

"No. Why?"

"There were reports of a man fitting Holland's description in the neighborhood."

"Believe me, if Victor was wanted by the police, he wouldn't hang around here. You think I'd let a murder suspect in the house? With just me and my old ma?"

Savitch glanced at Mrs. Lum, who merely smiled. The old woman had sharp, all-seeing eyes. A survivor's eyes.

It was time for Savitch to confirm his hunch. "Excuse me," he said, rising to his feet. "I had a long drive from the city. May I use your restroom?"

"Uh, sure. Down that hall."

Savitch headed into the bathroom and closed the door. Within seconds he'd spotted the evidence he was looking for. It was lying on the tiled floor: a long strand of brown hair. Very silky, very fine.

Catherine Weaver's shade.

It was all the proof he needed to proceed. He reached under his jacket for the shoulder holster and pulled out the semiautomatic. Then he gave his crisp white shirt a regretful pat. Messy business, interrogation. He would have to watch the bloodstains.

He stepped out into the hall, casually holding his pistol at his side. He'd go for the old woman first. Hold the barrel to her head, threaten to pull the trigger. There was an uncommonly strong bond between this mother and son. They would protect each other at all costs.

Savitch was halfway down the hall when the doorbell rang. He halted. The front door was opened and a new voice said, "Mr. Milo Lum?"

"And who the hell are you?" came Milo's weary reply.

"The name's Sam Polowski. FBI."

Every muscle in Savitch's body snapped taut. No choice now; he had to take the man out.

He raised his pistol. Soundlessly, he made his way down the hall toward the living room.

"*Another* one?" came Milo's peevish voice. "Look, one of your guys is already here—"

"What?"

"Yeah, he's back in the—"

Savitch stepped out and was swinging his pistol toward the front doorway when Mrs. Lum shrieked.

Milo froze. Polowski didn't. He rolled sideways just as the bullet thudded into the door frame, splintering wood.

By the time Savitch got off a second shot, Polowski was crawling somewhere behind the couch and the bullet slammed uselessly into the stuffing. That was it for chances—Polowski was armed.

Savitch decided it was time to vanish.

He turned and darted back up the hall, into a far bedroom. It was the mother's room; it smelled of incense

and old-lady perfume. The window slid open easily.
Savitch kicked out the screen, scrambled over the sill
and sank heel-deep into the muddy flower bed. Cursing, he slogged away, trailing clumps of mud across
the lawn.

He heard, faintly, "Halt! FBI!" but continued running.

He nursed his rage all the way back to the car.

Milo stared in bewilderment at the trampled pansies.
"What the hell was that all about?" he demanded. "Is
this some sort of FBI practical joke?"

Sam Polowski didn't answer; he was too busy tracking the footprints across the grass. They led to the sidewalk, then faded into the road's pebbly asphalt.

"Hey!" yelled Milo. "What's going on?"

Polowski turned. "I didn't really see him. What did
he look like?"

Milo shrugged. "I dunno. Efrem Zimbalist–type."

"Meaning?"

"Tall, clean-cut, great build. Typical FBI."

There was a silence as Milo regarded Polowski's sagging belly.

"Well," amended Milo, "maybe not *typical*..."

"What about his face?"

"Lemme think. Brown hair? Maybe brown eyes?"

"You're not sure."

"You know how it is. All you white guys look alike
to me."

An eruption of rapid Chinese made them both turn.
Mrs. Lum had followed them out onto the lawn and was
jabbering and gesticulating.

"What's she saying?" asked Polowski.

"She says the man was about six foot one, had straight dark brown hair parted on the left, brown eyes, almost black, a high forehead, a narrow nose and thin lips, and a small tattoo on his inside left wrist."

"Uh—is that all?"

"The tattoo read PJX."

Polowski shook his head in amazement. "Is she always this observant?"

"She can't exactly converse in English. So she does a lot of watching."

"Obviously." Polowski took out a pen and began to jot the information in a notebook.

"So who was this guy?" prodded Milo.

"Not FBI."

"How do I know *you're* FBI."

"Do I look like it?"

"No."

"Only proves my point."

"What?"

"If I wanted to pretend I was an agent, wouldn't I at least try to *look* like one? Whereas, if I *am* one, I wouldn't bother to try and look like one."

"Oh."

"Now." Polowski slid the notebook in his pocket. "You're still going to insist you haven't seen, or heard from, Victor Holland?"

Milo straightened. "That's right."

"And you don't know how to get in touch with him?"

"I have no idea."

"That's too bad. Because I could be the one to save his life. I've already saved yours."

Milo said nothing.

"Just why the hell do you think that guy was here? To pay a social visit? No, he was after information." Polowski paused and added, ominously, "And believe me, he would've gotten it."

Milo shook his head. "I'm confused."

"So am I. That's why I need Holland. He has the answers. But I need him alive. That means I need to find him before the other guy does. Tell me where he is."

Polowski and Milo looked at each other long and hard.

"I don't know," said Milo. "I don't know what to do."

Mrs. Lum was chattering again. She pointed to Polowski and nodded.

"Now what's she saying?" asked Polowski.

"She says you have big ears."

"For that, I can look in the mirror."

"What she means is, the size of your ears indicates sagacity."

"Come again?"

"You're a smart dude. She thinks I should listen to you."

Polowski turned and grinned at Mrs. Lum. "Your mother is a great judge of character." He looked back at Milo. "I wouldn't want anything to happen to her. Or you. You both have to get out of town."

Milo nodded. "On that particular point, we both agree." He turned toward the house.

"What about Holland?" called Polowski. "Will you help me find him?"

Milo took his mother by the arm and guided her across the lawn. Without even a backward look he said, "I'm thinking about it."

* * *

"It was those two photos. I just couldn't figure them out," said Ollie.

They were standing on the boathouse pier, overlooking the bed of Lake Lagunita. The lake was dry now, as it was every winter, drained to a reedy marsh until spring. They were alone, the three of them, sharing the lake with only an occasional duck. In the spring, this would be an idyllic spot, the water lapping the banks, lovers drifting in rowboats, here and there a poet lolling under the trees. But today, under black clouds, with a cold mist rising from the reeds, it was a place of utter desolation.

"I knew they weren't biological data," said Ollie. "I kept thinking they looked like some sort of electrical grid. So this morning, right after I left Milo's, I took 'em over to Bach's, down in San José. Caught him at breakfast."

"Bach?" asked Cathy.

"Another member of the Out of Tuners. Great bassoon player. Started an electronics firm a few years back and now he's working with the big boys. Anyway, the first thing he says as I walk in the door is, 'Hey, did the FBI get to you yet?' And I said, 'What?' and he says, 'They just called. For some reason they're looking for Gershwin. They'll probably get around to you next.' And that's when I knew I had to get you two out of Milo's house, stat."

"So what did he say about those photos?"

"Oh, yeah." Ollie reached into his briefcase and pulled out the photos. "Okay. This one here, it's a circuit diagram. An electronic alarm system. Very sophisticated, very secure. Designed to be breached by use of a keypad code, punched in at this point here. Probably at an entryway. You seen anything like it at Viratek?"

Victor nodded. "Building C-2. Where Jerry worked. The keypad's in the hall, right by the Special Projects door."

"Ever been inside that door?"

"No. Only those with top clearance can get through. Like Jerry."

"Then we'll have to visualize what comes next. Going by the diagram, there's another security point here, probably another keypad. Right inside the first door, they've stationed a camera system."

"You mean like a bank camera?" asked Cathy.

"Similar. Only I'd guess this one's being monitored twenty-four hours a day."

"They went first class, didn't they?" said Victor. "Two secured doors, plus inspection by a guard. Not to mention the guard at the outside gate."

"Don't forget the laser lattice."

"What?"

"This inner room here." Ollie pointed to the diagram's core. "Laser beams, directed at various angles. They'll detect movement of just about anything bigger than a rat."

"How do the lasers get switched off?"

"Has to be done by the security guard. The controls are on his panel."

"You can tell all this from the diagram?" asked Cathy. "I'm impressed."

"No problem." Ollie grinned. "Bach's firm designs security systems."

Victor shook his head. "This looks impossible. We can't get through all that."

Cathy frowned at him. "Wait a minute. What are you talking about? You aren't considering going into that building, are you?"

"We discussed it last night," said Victor. "It may be the only way—"

"Are you crazy? Viratek's out to kill us and you want to break *in?*"

"It's the proof we need," said Ollie. "You try going to the newspapers or the Justice Department and they'll demand evidence. You can bet Viratek's going to deny everything. Even if someone does launch an investigation, all Viratek has to do is toss the virus and, *poof!* your evidence is gone. No one can prove a thing."

"You have photos—"

"Sure. A few pages of animal data. The virus is never identified. And all that evidence could've been fabricated by, say, some disgruntled ex-employee."

"So what *is* proof? What do you need, another dead body? Victor's, for instance?"

"What we need is the virus—a virus that's supposed to be extinct. Just a single vial and the case against them is nailed shut."

"Just a single vial. Right." Cathy shook her head. "I don't know what I'm worried about. No one can get through those doors. Not without the keypad codes."

"Ah, but those we have!" Ollie flipped to the second photo. "The mysterious numbers. See, they finally make sense. Two sets of seven digits. Not phone numbers at all! Jerry was pointing the way through Viratek's top security."

"What about the lasers?" she pointed out, her agitation growing. They couldn't be serious! Surely they could see the futility of this mission. She didn't care if her fear showed; she had to be their voice of reason. "And then there's the guards," she said. "Two of them. Do you have a way past them? Or did Jerry also leave you the formula for invisibility?"

Ollie glanced uneasily at Victor. "Uh, maybe I should let you two discuss this first. Before we make any other plans."

"I thought I was part of all this," said Cathy. "Part of every decision. I guess I was wrong."

Neither man said a thing. Their silence only fueled Cathy's anger. She thought: *So you left me out of this. You didn't respect my opinion enough to ask me what I think, what I want.*

Without a word she turned and walked away.

Moments later, Victor caught up with her. She was standing on the dirt path, hugging herself against the cold. She heard his approach, sensed his uncertainty, his struggle to find the right words. For a moment he simply stood beside her, not speaking.

"I think we should run," she said. She gazed over the dry lake bed and shivered. The wind that swept across the reeds was raw and biting; it sliced right through her sweater. "I want to get away," she said. "I want to go somewhere warm. Some place where the sun's shining, where I can lie on a beach and not worry about who's watching me from the bushes…" Suddenly reminded of the terrible possibilities, she turned and glanced at the oaks hulking behind them. She saw only the fluttering of dead leaves.

"I agree with you," said Victor quietly.

"You do?" She turned to him, relieved. "Let's go, Victor! Let's leave now. Forget this crazy idea. We can catch the next bus south—"

"This very afternoon. You'll be on your way."

"*I* will?" She stared at him, at first not willing to accept what she'd heard. Then the meaning of his words sank in. "You're not coming."

Slowly he shook his head. "I can't."

"You mean you won't."

"Don't you see?" He took her by the shoulders, as though to shake some sense into her. "We're backed into a corner. Unless we do something—I do something—we'll always be running."

"Then let's *run!*" She reached for him, her fingers clutching at his windbreaker. She wanted to scream at him, to tear away his cool mask of reason and get to the raw emotions beneath. They had to be there, buried deep in that logical brain of his. "We could go to Mexico," she said. "I know a place on the coast—in Baja. A little hotel near the beach. We could stay there a few months, wait until things are safer—"

"It'll never be safer."

"Yes, it will! They'll forget about us—"

"You're not thinking straight."

"I am. I'm thinking I want to stay alive."

"And that's exactly why I have to do this." He took her face in his hands, trapping it so she could look nowhere but at him. No longer was he the lover, the friend—his voice now held the cold, steady note of authority and she hated the sound of it. "I'm trying to keep you alive," he said. "With a future ahead of you. And the only way I can do that is to blow this thing wide open so the world knows about it. I owe it to you. And I owe it to Jerry."

She wanted to argue with him, to plead with him to

go with her, but she knew it was useless. What he said was true. Running would only be a temporary solution, one that would give them a few sweet months of safety, but a temporary one just the same.

"I'm sorry, Cathy," he said softly. "I can't think of any other way—"

"—But to get rid of me," she finished for him.

He released her. She stepped back, and the sudden gulf between them left her aching. She couldn't bear to look at him, knowing that the pain she felt wouldn't be reflected in his eyes. "So how does it work?" she said dully. "Do I leave tonight? Will it be plane, train or automobile?"

"Ollie will drive you to the airport. I've asked him to buy you the ticket under his name—Mrs. Wozniak. He'll have to be the one to see you off. We thought it'd be safer if I didn't come along to the airport."

"Of course."

"That'll get you to Mexico. Ollie'll give you enough cash to keep you going for a while. Enough to get you anywhere you want to go from there. Baja. Acapulco. Or just hang around with Jack if you think that's best."

"Jack." She turned away, unwilling to show her tears. "Right."

"Cathy." She felt his hand on her shoulder, as though he wanted to turn her toward him, to pull her back one last time into his arms. She refused to move.

Footsteps approached. They both glanced around to see Ollie, standing a few feet away. "Ready to go?" he asked.

There was a long silence. Then Victor nodded. "She's ready."

"Uh, look," Ollie mumbled, suddenly aware that he'd stepped in at a bad time. "My car's over by the boathouse. If you want, I can, uh, wait for you there…"

Cathy furiously dashed away her tears. "No," she said with sudden determination. "I'm coming."

Victor stood watching her, his gaze veiled by some cool, impenetrable mist.

"Goodbye, Victor," she said.

He didn't answer. He just kept looking at her through that terrible mist.

"If I—if I don't see you again…" She stopped, struggling to be just as brave, just as invulnerable. "Take care of yourself," she finished. Then she turned and followed Ollie down the path.

Through the car window, she glimpsed Victor, still standing on the lake path, his hands jammed in his pockets, his shoulders hunched against the wind. He didn't wave goodbye; he merely watched them drive away.

It was an image she'd carry with her forever, that last, fading view of the man she loved. The man who'd sent her away.

As Ollie turned the car onto the road, she sat stiff and silent, her fists balled in her lap, the pain in her throat so terrible she could scarcely breathe. Now he was behind them. She couldn't see him, but she knew he was still standing there, as unmoving as the oaks that surrounded him. *I love you,* she thought. *And I will never see you again.*

She turned to look out. He was a distant figure now, almost lost among the trees. In a gesture of farewell, she reached up and gently touched the window.

The glass was cold.

* * *

"I have to stop off at the lab," said Ollie, turning into the hospital parking lot. "I just remembered I left the checkbook in my desk. Can't get you a plane ticket without it."

Cathy nodded dully. She was still in a state of shock, still trying to accept the fact that she was now on her own. That Victor had sent her away.

Ollie pulled into a stall marked Reserved, Wozniak. "This'll only take a sec."

"Shall I come in with you?"

"You'd better wait in the car. I work with a very nosy bunch. They see me with a woman and they want to know everything. Not that there's ever anything to know." He climbed out and shut the door. "Be right back."

Cathy watched him stride away and vanish into a side entrance. She had to smile at the thought of Ollie Wozniak squiring around a woman—any woman. Unless it was someone with a Ph.D. who could sit through his scientific monologues.

A minute passed.

Outside, a bird screeched. Cathy glanced out at the trees lining the hospital driveway and spotted the jay, perched among the lower branches. Nothing else moved, not even the leaves.

She leaned back and closed her eyes.

Too little sleep, too much running, had taken its toll. Exhaustion settled over her, so profound she thought she would never again be able to move her limbs. *A beach,* she thought. *Warm sand. Waves washing at my feet...*

The jay's cry cut off in mid-screech. Only vaguely did Cathy register the sudden silence. Then, even through her half sleep, she sensed the shadowing of the window, like a cloud passing before the sun.

She opened her eyes. A face was staring at her through the glass.

Panic sent her lunging for the lock button. Before she could jam it down, the door was wrenched open. A badge was thrust up to her face.

"FBI!" the man barked. "Out of the car, please."

Slowly Cathy emerged, to stand weak-kneed against the door. *Ollie,* she thought, her gaze darting toward the hospital entrance. *Where are you?* If he appeared, she had to be ready to bolt, to flee across the parking lot and into the woods. She doubted the man with the badge would be able to keep up; his stubby legs and thick waist didn't go along with a star athlete.

But he must have a gun. If I bolt, would he shoot me in the back?

"Don't even think about it, Miss Weaver," the man said. He took her arm and gave her a nudge toward the hospital entrance. "Go on. Inside."

"But—"

"Dr. Wozniak's waiting for us in the lab."

Waiting didn't exactly describe Ollie's predicament. Bound and trussed would have been a better description. She found Ollie bent over double in his office, handcuffed to the foot of his desk, while three of his lab colleagues stood by gaping in amazement.

"Back to work, folks," said the agent as he herded the onlookers out of the office. "Just a routine matter." He shut the door and locked it. Then he turned to Cathy and Ollie. "I have to find Victor Holland," he said. "And I have to find him fast."

"Man," Ollie muttered into his chest. "This guy sounds like a broken record."

"Who are you?" demanded Cathy.

"The name's Sam Polowski. I work out of the San Francisco office." He pulled out his badge and slapped it on the desk. "Take a closer look if you want. It's official."

"Uh, excuse me?" called Ollie. "Could I maybe, possibly, get into a more comfortable position?"

Polowski ignored him. His attention was focused on Cathy. "I don't think I need to spell it out for you, Miss Weaver. Holland's in trouble."

"And you're one of his biggest problems," she retorted.

"That's where you're wrong." Polowski moved closer, his gaze unflinching, his voice absolutely steady. "I'm one of his hopes. Maybe his only hope."

"You're trying to kill him."

"Not me. Someone else, someone who's going to succeed. Unless I can stop it."

She shook her head. "I'm not stupid! I know about you. What you've been trying to—"

"Not me. The other guy." He reached for the telephone on the desk. "Here," he said, holding the receiver out to her. "Call Milo Lum. Ask him what happened at his house this morning. Maybe he'll convince you I'm on your side."

Cathy stared at the man, wondering what sort of game he was playing. Wondering why she was falling for it. *Because I want so much to believe him.*

"He's alone out there," said Polowski. "One man trying to buck the U.S. government. He's new to the game. Sooner or later he's going to slip, do something stupid.

And that'll be it." He dialed the phone for her and again held out the receiver. "Go on. Talk to Lum."

She heard the phone ring three times, followed by Milo's answer "Hello? Hello?"

Slowly she took the receiver. "Milo?"

"Is that you? Cathy? God, I was hoping you'd call—"

"Listen, Milo. I need to ask you something. It's about a man named Polowski."

"I've met him."

"You *have?*" She looked up and saw Polowski nodding.

"Lucky for me," said Milo. "The guy's got the charm of an old shoe but he saved my life. I don't know what Gersh was talking about. Is Gersh around? I have to—"

"Thanks, Milo," she murmured. "Thanks a lot." She hung up.

Polowski was still looking at her.

"Okay," she said. "I want your side of it. From the beginning."

"You gonna help me out?"

"I haven't decided." She crossed her arms. "Convince me."

Polowski nodded. "That's just what I plan to do."

Chapter 10

For Victor it was a long and miserable afternoon. After leaving the lake, he wandered around the campus for a while, ending up at last in the main quad. There in the courtyard, standing among the buildings of sandstone and red tile, Victor struggled to keep his mind on the business at hand: exposing Viratek. But his thoughts kept shifting back to Cathy, to that look she'd given him, full of hurt abandonment.

As if I'd betrayed her.

If she could just see the good sense in his actions. He was a scientist, a man whose life and work was ruled by logic. Sending her away was the logical thing to do. The authorities were closing in, the noose was growing ever tighter. He could accept the danger to himself. After all, he'd chosen to take on Jerry's battle, to see this through to the end.

What he hadn't chosen was to put Cathy in danger. *Now she's out of the mess and on her way to a safe place. One less thing to worry about. Time to put her out of my mind.*

As if I could.

He stared up at one of the courtyard's Romanesque arches and reminded himself, once again, of the wisdom of his actions. Still, the uneasiness remained. Where was she? Was she safe? She'd been gone only an hour and he missed her already.

He gave a shrug, as though by that gesture he could somehow cast off the fears. Still they remained, constant and gnawing. He found a place under the eaves and huddled on the steps to wait for Ollie's return.

At dusk he was still waiting. By the last feeble light of day, he paced the stone courtyard. He counted and recounted the number of hours it should've taken Ollie to drive to San José Airport and return. He added in traffic time, red lights, ticket-counter delays. Surely three hours was enough. Cathy had to be on a plane by now, jetting for warmer climes.

Where was Ollie?

At the sound of the first footstep, he spun around. For a moment he couldn't believe what he was seeing, couldn't understand how she could be standing there, silhouetted beneath the sandstone archway. "Cathy?" he said in amazement.

She stepped out, into the courtyard. "Victor," she said softly. She started toward him, slowly at first, and then, in a jubilant burst of flight, ran toward his waiting arms. He swept her up, swung her around, kissed her hair, her face. He didn't understand why she was here but he rejoiced that she was.

"I don't know if I've done the right thing," she murmured. "I hope to God I have."

"Why did you come back?"

"I wasn't sure—I'm still not sure—"

"Cathy, what are you doing here?"

"You can't fight this alone! And he can help you—"

"Who can?"

From out of the twilight came another voice, gruff and startling. "*I* can."

At once Victor stiffened. His gaze shifted back to the arch behind Cathy. A man emerged and walked slowly toward him. Not a tall man, he had the sort of body that, in a weight-loss ad, would've been labeled Before. He came up to Victor and planted himself squarely on the courtyard stones.

"Hello, Holland," he said. "I'm glad we've finally met. The name is Sam Polowski."

Victor turned and looked in disbelief at Cathy. "Why?" he asked in quiet fury. "Just tell me that. *Why?*"

She reacted as though he'd delivered a physical blow. Tentatively she reached for his arm; he pulled away from her at once.

"He wants to help," she said, her voice wretched with pain. "*Listen* to him!"

"I'm not sure there's any point to listening. Not now." He felt his whole body go slack in defeat. He didn't understand it, would never understand it. It was over, the running, the scraping along on fear and hope. All because Cathy had betrayed him. He turned matter-of-factly to Polowski. "I take it I'm under arrest," he said.

"Hardly," said Polowski, nodding toward the archway. "Seeing as he's got my gun."

"What?"

"Hey, Gersh! Over here!" Ollie yelled. "See, I got him covered!"

Polowski winced. "Geez, do ya have to wave the damn thing?"

"Sorry," said Ollie.

"Now, does that convince you, Holland?" asked Polowski. "You think I'd hand my piece over to an idiot like him if I didn't want to talk to you?"

"He's telling the truth," insisted Cathy. "He gave the gun to Ollie. He was willing to take the risk, just to meet you face-to-face."

"Bad move, Polowski," said Victor bitterly. "I'm wanted for murder, remember? Industrial espionage? How do you know I won't just blow you away?"

"'Cause I know you're innocent."

"That makes a difference, does it?"

"It does to me."

"Why?"

"You're caught up in something big, Holland. Something that's going to eat you up alive. Something that's got my supervisor doing backflips to keep me off the case. I don't like being pulled off a case. It hurts my delicate ego."

The two men gazed at each other through the gathering darkness, each sizing up the other.

At last Victor nodded. He looked at Cathy, a quiet plea for forgiveness, for not believing in her. When at last she came into his arms, he felt the world had suddenly gone right again.

He heard a deliberate clearing of a throat. Turning, he saw Polowski hold out his hand. Victor took it in a handshake that could very well be his doom—or his salvation.

"You've led me on a long, hard chase," said Polowski. "I think it's time we worked together."

"Basically," said Ollie, "what we have here is just your simple, everyday mission impossible."

They were assembled in Polowski's hotel room, a five-member team that Milo had just dubbed the "Older, Crazier Out of Tuners," or Old COOTS for short. On the table in the center of the room lay potato chips, beer and the photos detailing Viratek's security system. There was also a map of the Viratek compound, forty acres of buildings and wooded grounds, all of it surrounded by an electrified fence. They had been studying the photos for an hour now, and the job that lay before them looked hopeless.

"No easy way in," said Ollie, shaking his head. "Even if those keypad codes are still valid, you're faced with the human element of recognition. Two guards, two positions. No way they're gonna let you pass."

"There has to be a way," said Polowski. "Come on, Holland. You're the egghead. Use that creative brain of yours."

Cathy looked at Victor. While the others had tossed ideas back and forth, he had said very little. *And he's the one with the most at stake—his life,* she thought. It took incredible courage—or foolhardiness—even to consider such a desperate move. Yet here he was, calmly scanning the map as though he were planning nothing more dangerous than a Sunday drive.

He must have felt her gaze, for he slung his arm around her and tugged her close. Now that they were reunited, she savored every moment they shared, committed to memory every look, every caress. Soon he could be wrenched away from her. Even now he was making plans to enter what looked like a death trap.

He pressed a kiss to the top of her head. Then, reluctantly, he turned his attention back to the map.

"The electronics I'm not worried about," he said. "It's the human element. The guards."

Milo cocked his head toward Polowski. "I still say ol' J. Edgar here should get a warrant and raid the place."

"Right," snorted Polowski. "By the time that order gets through the judge and Dafoe and your aunt Minnie's cousin, Viratek'll have that lab turned into a baby-milk factory. No, we need to get in on our own. Without anyone getting word of it." He looked at Ollie. "And you're sure this is the only evidence we'll need?"

Ollie nodded. "One vial should do it. Then we take it to a reputable lab, have them confirm it's smallpox, and your case is airtight."

"They'll have no way around it?"

"None. The virus is officially extinct. Any company caught playing with a live sample is, ipso facto, dead meat."

"I like that," said Polowski. "That ipso facto stuff. No fancy Viratek attorney can argue that one away."

"But first you gotta get hold of a vial," said Ollie. "And from where I'm standing, it looks impossible. Unless we're willing to try armed robbery."

For one frightening moment, Polowski actually seemed to give that thought serious consideration. "Naw," he conceded. "Wouldn't go over well in court."

"Besides which," said Ollie, "I refuse to shoot another human being. It's against my principles."

"Mine, too," said Milo.

"But theft," said Ollie, "that's acceptable."

Polowski looked at Victor. "A group with high moral standards."

Victor grinned. "Holdovers from the sixties."

"Sounds like we're back to the first option," said Cathy. "We have to steal the virus." She focused on the map of the compound, noting the electrified fence that circled the entire complex. The main road led straight to the front gate. Except for an unpaved fire road, labeled *not maintained,* no other approaches were apparent.

"All right," she said. "Assume you do get through the front gate. You still have to get past two locked doors, two separate guards and a laser grid. Come on."

"The doors are no problem," said Victor. "It's the two guards."

"Maybe a diversion?" suggested Milo. "How about we set a fire?"

"And bring in the town fire department?" said Victor. "Not a good idea. Besides, I've dealt with this night guard at the front gate. I know him. And he goes strictly by the book. Never leaves the booth. At the first hint of anything suspicious, he'll hit the alarm button."

"Maybe Milo could whip up a fake security pass," said Ollie. "You know, the way he used to fix us up with those fake drivers' licenses."

"He falsified IDs?" said Polowski.

"Hey, I just changed the age to twenty-one!" protested Milo.

"Made great passports, too," said Ollie. "I had one from the kingdom of Booga Booga. It got me right past the customs official in Athens."

"Yeah?" Polowski looked impressed. "So what about it, Holland? Would it work?"

"Not a chance. The guard has a master list of top-security employees. If he doesn't know the face, he'll do a double check."

"But he does let some people through automatically?"

"Sure. The bigwigs. The ones he recognizes on—" Victor suddenly paused and turned to stare at Cathy "—on sight. Lord. It just might work."

Cathy took one look at his face and immediately read his mind. "No," she said. "It's not that easy! I need to see the subject! I need molds of his face. Detailed photos from every angle—"

"But you *could* do it. You do it all the time."

"On film it works! But this is face-to-face!"

"It's at night, through a car window. Or through a video camera. If you could just make me pass for one of the execs—"

"What are you talking about?" demanded Polowski.

"Cathy's a makeup artist. You know, horror films, special effects."

"This is different!" Cathy said. The difference being it was Victor's life on the line. No, he couldn't ask her to do this. If anything went wrong, she would be responsible. Having his death on her conscience would be more than she could live with.

She shook her head, praying he'd read the deadly earnestness in her gaze. "There's too much at stake," she insisted. "It's not as simple as—as filming *Slimelords!*"

"You did *Slimelords?*" asked Milo. "Terrific flick!"

"Besides," said Cathy, "it's not that easy, copying a face. I have to cast a mold, to get the features just right. For that I need a model."

"You mean the real guy?" asked Polowski.

"Right. The real guy. And I hardly think you're going

to get some Viratek executive to sit down and let me slap plaster all over his face."

There was a long silence.

"That does present a problem," said Milo.

"Not necessarily."

They all turned and looked at Ollie.

"What are you thinking?" asked Victor.

"About this guy who works with me once in a while. Down in the lab…" Ollie looked up, and the grin on his face was distinctly smug. "He's a veterinarian."

The events of the past few weeks had weighed heavily on Archibald Black, so heavily, in fact, that he found it difficult to carry on with those everyday tasks of life. Just driving to and from his office at Viratek was an ordeal. And then, to sit down at his desk and face his secretary and pretend that nothing, absolutely nothing, was wrong—that was almost more than he could manage. He was a scientist, not an actor.

Not a criminal.

But that's what they would call him, if the experiments in C wing ever came to light. His instinct was to shut the lab down, to destroy the contents of those incubators. But Matthew Tyrone insisted the work continue. They were so close to completion. After all, Defense had underwritten the project, and Defense expected a product. This matter of Victor Holland was only a minor glitch, soon to be solved. The thing to do was carry on.

Easy for Tyrone to say, thought Black. *Tyrone had no conscience to bother him.*

These thoughts had plagued him all day. Now, as Black packed up his briefcase, he felt desperate to flee forever this teak-and-leather office, to take refuge in some safe and anonymous job. It was with a sigh of relief that he walked out the door.

It was dark when he pulled into his gravel driveway. The house, a saltbox of cedar and glass tucked among the trees, looked cold and empty and in need of a woman. Perhaps he should call his neighbor Muriel. She always seemed to appreciate an impromptu dinner together. Her snappy wit and green Jell-O salad almost made up for the fact she was 75. What a shame his generation didn't produce many Muriels.

He stepped out of his car and started up the path to the front door. Halfway there, he heard a soft *whht!* and almost simultaneously, a sharp pain stung his neck. Reflexively he slapped at it; something came away in his hands. In wonderment, he stared down at the dart, trying to understand where it had come from and how such a thing had managed to lodge in his neck. But he found he couldn't think straight. And then he found he was having trouble seeing, that the night had suddenly darkened to a dense blackness, that his legs were being sucked into some sort of quagmire. His briefcase slipped from his grasp and thudded to the ground.

I'm dying, he thought. And then, *Will anyone find me here?*

It was his last conscious thought before he collapsed onto the leaf-strewn path.

"Is he dead?"

Ollie bent forward and listened for Archibald Black's breathing. "He's definitely alive. But out cold." He looked up at Polowski and Victor. "Okay, let's move it. He'll be out for only an hour or so."

Victor grabbed the legs, Ollie and Polowski, the

arms. Together they carried the unconscious man a few dozen yards through the woods, toward the clearing where the van was parked.

"You—you sure we got an hour?" gasped Polowski.

"Plus or minus," said Ollie. "The tranquilizer's designed for large animals, so the dose was only an estimate. And this guy's heavier than I expected." Ollie was panting now. "Hey, Polowski, he's slipping. Pull your weight, will ya?"

"I am! I think his right arm's heavier than his left."

The van's side door was already open for them. They rolled Black inside and slid the door closed. A bright light suddenly glared, but the unconscious man didn't even twitch.

Cathy knelt down at his side and critically examined the man's face.

"Can you do it?" asked Victor.

"Oh, I can do it," she said. "The question is, will you pass for him?" She glanced up and down the man's length, then back at Victor. "Looks about your size and build. We'll have to darken your hair, give you a widow's peak. I think you'll pass." She turned and glanced at Milo, who was already poised with his camera. "Take your photos. A few shots from every angle. I need lots of hair detail."

As Milo's strobe flashed again and again, Cathy donned gloves and an apron. She pointed to a sheet. "Drape him for me," she directed. "Everything but his face. I don't want him to wake up with plaster all over his clothes."

"Assuming he wakes up at all," said Milo, frowning down at Black's inert form.

"Oh, he'll wake up," said Ollie. "Right where we

found him. And if we do the job right, Mr. Archibald Black will never know what hit him."

It was the rain that awakened him. The cold droplets pelted his face and dribbled into his open mouth. Groaning, Black turned over and felt gravel bite into his shoulder. Even in his groggy state it occurred to him that this did not make sense. Slowly he took stock of all the things that were not as they should be: the rain falling from the ceiling, the gravel in his bed, the fact he was still wearing his shoes...

At last he managed to shake himself fully awake. He found to his puzzlement that he was sitting in his driveway, and that his briefcase was lying right beside him. By now the rain had swelled to a downpour—he had to get out of the storm. Half crawling, half walking, Black managed to make it up the porch steps and into the house.

An hour later, huddled in his kitchen, a cup of coffee in hand, he tried to piece together what had happened. He remembered parking his car. He'd taken out his briefcase and apparently had managed to make it halfway up the path. And then...what?

A vague ache worried its way into his awareness. He rubbed his neck. That's when he remembered something strange had happened, just before he blacked out. Something associated with that ache in his neck.

He went to a mirror and looked. There it was, a small puncture in the skin. An absurd thought popped into his head: *Vampires*. Right. *Damn it, Archibald. You are a scientist. Come up with a rational explanation.*

He went to the laundry hamper and fished out his damp shirt. To his alarm he spotted a droplet of blood on the lapel. Then he saw what had caused it: a common, everyday tailor's pin. It was still lodged in the collar, no doubt left there by the dry cleaners. There was his rational explanation. He'd been pricked by a collar pin and the pain had sent him into a faint.

In disgust, he threw the shirt down. First thing in the morning, he was going to complain to the Tidy Girl cleaners and demand they do his suit for free.

Vampires, indeed.

"Even with bad lighting, you'll be lucky if you pass," said Cathy.

She stood back and gave Victor a long, critical look. Slowly she walked around him, eyeing the newly darkened hair, the resculpted face, the new eye color. It was as close as she could make it, but it wasn't good enough. It would never be good enough, not when Victor's life was at stake.

"I think he's the spitting image," said Polowski. "What's the problem now?"

"The problem is, I suddenly realize it's a crazy idea. I say we call it off."

"You've been working on him all afternoon. You got it right down to the damn freckles on his nose. What else can you improve on?"

"I don't know. I just don't feel *good* about this!"

There was a silence as she confronted the four men. Ollie shook his head. "Women's intuition. That's a dangerous thing to disregard."

"Well, here's *my* intuition," said Polowski. "I think it'll work. And I think it's our best option. Our chance to nail the case."

Cathy turned to Victor. "You're the one who'll get

hurt. It's your decision." What she really wanted to say was, *Please. Don't do it. Stay with me. Stay alive and safe and mine.* But she knew, looking into his eyes, that he'd already made his decision, and no matter how much she might wish for it, he would never really be hers.

"Cathy," he said. "It'll work. You have to believe that."

"The only thing I believe," she said, "is that you're going to get killed. And I don't want to be around to watch it."

Without another word, she turned and walked out the door.

Outside, in the parking lot of the Rockabye Motel, she stood in the darkness and hugged herself. She heard the door shut, and then his footsteps moved toward her across the blacktop.

"You don't have to stay," he said. "There's still that beach in Mexico. You could fly there tonight, be out of this mess."

"Do you want me to go?"

A pause, then, "Yes."

She shrugged, a poor attempt at nonchalance. "All right. I suppose it all makes perfect sense. I've done my part."

"You saved my life. At the very least, I owe you a measure of safety."

She turned to him. "Is that what weighs most on your mind, Victor? The fact that you *owe* me?"

"What weighs most on my mind is that you might get caught in the crossfire. I'm prepared to walk through those doors at Viratek. I'm prepared to do a lot of stupid things. But I'm not prepared to watch you get hurt. Does that make any sense?" He pulled her against him, into a place that felt infinitely warm and safe. "Cathy, Cathy. I'm not crazy. I don't want to die. But I don't see any way around this…"

She pressed her face against his chest, felt his heartbeat, so steady, so regular. She was afraid to think of that heart not beating, of those arms no longer alive to hold her. He was brave enough to go through with this crazy scheme; couldn't she somehow dredge up the same courage? She thought, *I've come this far with you. How could I dream of walking away? Now that I know I love you?*

The motel door opened, and light arced across the parking lot. "Gersh?" said Ollie. "It's getting late. If we want to go ahead, we'll have to leave now."

Victor was still looking at her. "Well?" he said. "Do you want Ollie to take you to the airport?"

"No." She squared her shoulders. "I'm coming with you."

"Are you sure that's what you want to do?"

"I'm never sure of anything these days. But on this I've decided. I'll stick it out." She managed a smile. "Besides, you might need me on the set. In case your face falls off."

"I need you for a hell of a lot more than that."

"Gersh?"

Victor reached out for Cathy's hand. She let him take it. "We're coming," he said. "Both of us."

"I'm approaching the front gate. One guard in the booth. No one else around. Copy?"

"Loud and clear," said Polowski.

"Okay. Here I go. Wish me luck."

"We'll be tuned in. Break a leg." Polowski clicked

off the microphone and glanced at the others. "Well, folks, he's on his way."

To what? Cathy wondered. She glanced around at the other faces. There were four of them huddled in the van. They'd parked a half mile from Viratek's front gate. Close enough to hear Victor's transmissions, but too far away to do him much good. With the microphone link, they could mark his progress.

They could also mark his death.

In silence, they waited for the first hurdle.

"Evening," said Victor, pulling up at the gate.

The guard peered out through the booth window. He was in his twenties, cap on straight, collar button fastened. This was Pete Zahn, Mr. By-the-book Extraordinaire. If anyone was to cut the operation short, it would be this man. Victor made a brave attempt at a smile and prayed his mask wouldn't crack. It seemed an eternity, that exchange of looks. Then, to Victor's relief, the man smiled back.

"Working late, Dr. Black?"

"Forgot something at the lab."

"Must be important, huh? To make a special trip at midnight."

"These government contracts. Gotta be done on time."

"Yeah." The guard waved him through. "Have a nice night."

Heart pounding, Victor pulled through the gate. Only when he'd rounded the curve into the empty parking lot did he manage a sigh of relief. "First base," he said into the microphone. "Come on, guys. Talk to me."

"We're here," came the response. It was Polowski.

"I'm heading into the building—can't be sure the signal will get through those walls. So if you don't hear from me—"

"We'll be listening."

"I've got a message for Cathy. Put her on."

There was a pause, then he heard, "I'm here, Victor."

"I just wanted to tell you this. I'm coming back. I promise. Copy?"

He wasn't sure if it was just the signal's waiver, but he thought he heard the beginning of tears in her reply. "I copy."

"I'm going in now. Don't leave without me."

It took Pete Zahn only a minute to look up Archibald Black's license plate number. He kept a Rolodex in the booth, though he seldom referred to it as he had a good memory for numbers. He knew every executive's license by heart. It was his own little mind game, a test of his cleverness. And the plate on Dr. Black's car just didn't seem right.

He found the file card. The auto matched up okay: a gray 1991 Lincoln sedan. And he was fairly certain that *was* Dr. Black sitting in the driver's seat. But the license number was all wrong.

He sat back and thought about it for a while, trying to come up with all the possible explanations. That Black was simply driving a different auto. That Black was playing a joke on him, testing him.

That it hadn't been Archibald Black, at all.

Pete reached for the telephone. The way to find out was to call Black's home. It was after midnight, but it had to be done. If Black didn't answer the phone, then that must be him in the Lincoln. And if he *did* answer, then something was terribly wrong and Black would want to know about it.

Two rings. That's all it took before a groggy voice answered, "Hello?"

"This is Pete Zahn, night man at Viratek. Is this— is this Dr. Black?"

"Yes."

"Dr. *Archibald* Black?"

"Look, it's late! What is it?"

"I don't know how to tell you this, Dr. Black, but…" Pete cleared his throat. "Your double just drove through the gate…"

"I'm through the front door. Heading up the hall to the security wing. In case anyone's listening." Victor didn't expect a reply, and he heard none. The building was a concrete monstrosity, designed to last forever. He doubted a radio signal would make it through these walls. Though he'd been on his own from the moment he'd entered the front gate, at least he'd had the comfort of knowing his friends were listening in on the progress. Now he was truly alone.

He moved at a casual pace to the locked door marked Authorized Personnel Only. A camera hung from the ceiling, its lens pointed straight at him. He pointedly ignored it and turned his attention to the security keypad mounted on the wall. The numbers Jerry had given him had gotten him through the front door; would the second combination get him through this one? His hands were sweating as he punched in the seven digits. He felt a dart of panic as a beep sounded and a message flashed on the screen: *Incorrect security code. Access denied.*

He could feel the sweat building up beneath the

mask. Were the numbers wrong? Had he simply transposed two digits? He knew someone was watching him through the camera, wondering why he was taking so long. He took a deep breath and tried again. This time, he entered the digits slowly, deliberately. He braced himself for the warning beep. To his relief, it didn't go off.

Instead, a new message appeared. *Security code accepted. Please enter.*

He stepped through, into the next room.

Third hurdle, he thought in relief as the door closed behind him. Now for the home run.

Another camera, mounted in a corner, was pointed at him. Acutely conscious of that lens, he made his way across the room to the inner lab door. He turned the knob and a warning bell sounded.

Now what? he thought. Only then did he notice the red light glowing over the door, and the warning *Laser grid activated.* He needed a key to shut it off. He saw no other way to deactivate it, no way to get past it, into the room beyond.

It was time for desperate measures, time for a little chutzpah. He patted his pockets, then turned and faced the camera. "Hello?" He waved.

A voice answered over an intercom. "Is there a problem, Dr. Black?"

"Yes. I can't seem to find my keys. I must have left them at home…"

"I can cut the lasers from here."

"Thanks. Gee, I don't know how this happened."

"No problem."

At once the red warning light shut off. Cautiously

Victor tried the door; it swung open. He gave the camera a goodbye wave and entered the last room.

Inside, to his relief, there were no cameras anywhere— at least, none that he could spot. A bit of breathing space, he thought. He moved into the lab and took a quick survey of his surroundings. What he saw was a mind-numbing display of space-age equipment—not just the expected centrifuges and microscopes, but instruments he'd never seen before, all of them brand-new and gleaming. He headed through the decontamination chamber, past the laminar flow unit, and went straight to the incubators. He opened the door.

Glass vials tinkled in their compartments. He took one out. Pink fluid glistened within. The label read Lot #341. Active.

This must be it, he thought. This was what Ollie had told him to look for. Here was the stuff of nightmares, the grim reaper distilled to sub-microscopic elements.

He removed two vials, fitted them into a specially padded cigarette case, and slipped it into his pocket. *Mission accomplished,* he thought in triumph as he headed back through the lab. All that lay before him was a casual stroll back to his car. Then the champagne…

He was halfway across the room when the alarm bell went off.

He froze, the harsh ring echoing in his ears.

"Dr. Black?" said the guard's voice over some hidden intercom. "Please don't leave. Stay right where you are."

Victor spun around wildly, trying to locate the speaker. "What's going on?"

"I've just been asked to detain you. If you'll hold on, I'll find out what—"

Victor didn't wait to hear the reason—he bolted for

the door. Even as he reached it, he heard the whine of the lasers powering on, felt something slash his arm. He shoved through the first door, dashed across the anteroom and out the security door, into the hallway.

Everywhere, alarms were going off. The whole damn building had turned into an echo chamber of ringing bells. His gaze shot right, to the front entrance. No, not that way—the guard was stationed there.

He sprinted left, toward what he hoped was a fire exit. Somewhere behind him a voice yelled, "Halt!" He ignored it and kept running. At the end of the hall he slammed against the opening bar and found himself in a stairwell. No exit, only steps leading up and down. He wasn't about to be trapped like a rat in the basement. He headed up the stairs.

One flight into his climb, he heard the stairwell door slam open on the first floor. Again a voice commanded, "Halt or I'll shoot!"

A bluff, he thought.

A pistol shot exploded, echoing up the concrete stairwell.

Not a bluff. With new desperation, he pushed through the landing door, into the second-floor hallway. A line of closed doors stretched before him. Which one, which one? There was no time to think. He ducked into the third room and softly shut the door behind him.

In the semidarkness, he spotted the gleam of stainless steel and glass beakers. Another lab. Only this one had a large window, now shimmering with moonlight, looming over the far countertop.

From down the hall came the slam of a door being kicked open and the guard's shouted command: "Freeze!"

He was down to one last escape route. Victor grabbed a chair, raised it over his head, and flung it at the window. The glass shattered, raining moonlight-silvered shards into the darkness below. He scarcely bothered to look before he leapt. Bracing himself for the impact, he jumped from the window and landed in a tangle of shrubbery.

"Halt!" came a shout from above.

That was enough to jar Victor back to his feet. He sprinted off across a lawn, into the cover of trees. Glancing back, he saw no pursuing shadow. The guard wasn't about to risk his neck leaping out any window.

Got to make it out the gate...

Victor circled around the building, burrowing his way through bushes and trees to a stand of oaks. From there he could view the front gate, way off in the distance. What he saw made his heart sink.

Floodlights illuminated the entrance, glaring down on the four security cars blocking the driveway. Now a panel truck pulled up. The driver went around to the back and opened the doors. At his command two German shepherds leaped out and danced around, barking at his feet.

Victor backed away, stumbling deeper into the grove of oaks. *No way out,* he thought, glancing behind him at the fence, topped with coils of barbed wire. Already, the dogs' barking was moving closer. *Unless I can sprout wings and fly, I'm a dead man...*

Chapter 11

"Something's wrong!" Cathy cried as the first security car drove past.

Polowski touched her arm. "Easy. It could be just a routine patrol."

"No. Look!" Through the trees, they spotted three more cars, all roaring down the road at top speed toward Viratek.

Ollie muttered a surprisingly coarse oath and reached for the microphone.

"Wait!" Polowski grabbed his hand. "We can't risk a transmission. Let him contact us first."

"If he's in trouble—"

"Then he already knows it. Give him a chance to make it out on his own."

"What if he's trapped?" said Cathy. "Are we just going to sit here?"

"We don't have a choice. Not if they've blockaded the front gate—"

"We *do* have a choice!" said Cathy, scrambling forward into the driver's seat.

"What the hell are you doing?" demanded Polowski.

"Giving him a fighting chance. If we don't—"

They all fell instantly silent as a transmission suddenly hissed over the receiver. "Looks like I got myself in a bind, guys. Don't see a way out. You copy?"

Ollie snatched up the microphone. "Copy, Gersh. What's your situation?"

"Bad."

"Specify."

"Front gate's blocked and lit up like a football field. Big time alarms going off. They just brought in the dogs—"

"Can you get over the fence?"

"Negative. It's electrified. Low voltage, but more than I can handle. You guys better hit the road without me."

Polowski grabbed the microphone and barked, "Did you get the stuff?"

Cathy turned and snapped: "Forget that! Ask him where he is. *Ask him!*"

"Holland?" said Polowski. "Where are you?"

"At the northeast perimeter. Fence goes all the way around. Look, get moving. I'll manage—"

"Tell him to head for the east fence!" Cathy said. "Near the midpoint!"

"What?"

"Just tell him!"

"Go to the east fence," Polowski said into the microphone. "Midpoint."

"I copy."

Polowski looked up at Cathy in puzzlement. "What the hell are you thinking of?"

"This is a getaway car, right?" she muttered as she turned on the engine. "I say we put it to its intended use!" She threw the van into gear and spun it around, onto the road.

"Hey, you're going the wrong way!" yelled Milo.

"No, I'm not. There's a fire road, just off to the left somewhere. There it is." She made a sharp turn, onto what was little more than a dirt track. They bounced along, crashing through tree branches and shrubs, a ride so violently spine-shaking it was all they could do to hang on.

"How did you find this *wonderful* road?" Polowski managed to ask.

"It was on the map. I saw it when we were studying the plans for Viratek."

"Is this a scenic route? Or does it go somewhere?"

"The east fence. Used to be the construction entrance for the compound. I'm hoping it's still clear enough to get through…"

"And then what happens?"

Ollie sighed. "Don't ask."

Cathy steered around a bush that had sprung up in her path and ran head-on into a sapling. Her passengers tumbled to the floor. "Sorry," she muttered. Reversing gear, she spun them back on the road. "It should be just ahead…"

A barrier of chain link suddenly loomed before them. Instantly she cut the lights. Through the darkness, they could hear dogs barking, moving in. Where was he?

Then they saw him, flitting through the moonlight.

He was running. Somewhere off to the side, a man shouted and gunfire spat the ground.

"Brace yourselves!" yelled Cathy. She snapped on her seatbelt and gripped the steering wheel. Then she stepped on the gas.

The van jerked forward like a bronco, barreled through the underbrush, and slammed into the fence. The chain link sagged; electrical sparks hissed in the night. Cathy threw the gears into reverse, backed up, and hit the gas again.

The fence toppled; barbed wire scraped across the windshield.

"We're through!" said Ollie. He yanked open the sliding door and yelled: "Come on, Gersh! Come on!"

The running figure zigzagged across the grass. All around him, gunfire exploded. He made a last flying leap across the coil of barbed wire and stumbled.

"Come on, Gersh!"

Gunfire spattered the van.

Victor struggled back to his feet. They heard the rip of clothing, then he was reaching up to them, being dragged inside, to safety.

The door slammed shut. Cathy backed up, wheeled the van around and slammed on the gas pedal.

They leaped forward, bouncing through the bushes and across ruts. Another round of bullets pinged the van. Cathy was oblivious to it. She focused only on getting them back to the main road. The sound of gunfire receded. At last the trees gave way to a familiar band of blacktop. She turned left and gunned the engine, anxious to put as many miles as possible between them and Viratek.

Off in the distance, a siren wailed.

"We got company!" said Polowski.

"Which way now?" Cathy cried. Viratek lay behind them; the sirens were approaching from ahead.

"I don't know! Just get the hell out of here!"

As yet her view of the police cars was blocked by trees, but she could hear the sirens moving rapidly closer. *Will they let us pass? Or will they pull us over?*

Almost too late she spotted a clearing, off to the side. On sudden impulse she veered off the pavement, and the van bounced onto a stubbly field.

"Don't tell me," groaned Polowski. "Another fire road?"

"Shut up!" she snapped and steered straight for a clump of bushes. With a quick turn of the wheel, she circled behind the shrubbery and cut her lights.

It was just in time. Seconds later, two patrol cars, lights flashing, sped right past the concealing bushes. She sat frozen, listening as the sirens faded in the distance. Then, in the darkness, she heard Milo say softly, "Her name is Bond. Jane Bond."

Half laughing, half crying, Cathy turned as Victor scrambled beside her, onto the front seat. At once she was in his arms, her tears wetting his shirt, her sobs muffled in the depths of his embrace. He kissed her damp cheeks, her mouth. The touch of his lips stilled her tremors.

From the back came the sound of a throat being cleared. "Uh, Gersh?" inquired Ollie politely. "Don't you think we ought to get moving?"

Victor's mouth was still pressed against Cathy's. Reluctantly he broke contact but his gaze never left her face. "Sure," he murmured, just before he pulled her back for another kiss. "But would somebody else mind driving…?"

"Here's where things get dangerous," said Polowski. He was at the wheel now, as they headed south toward San Francisco. Cathy and Victor sat in front with Polowski; in the back of the van, Milo and Ollie lay curled up asleep like two exhausted puppies. From the radio came the soft strains of a country western song. The dials glowed a vivid green in the darkness.

"We've finally got the evidence," said Polowski. "All we need to hang 'em. They'll be desperate. Ready to try anything. From here on out, folks, it's going to be a game of cat and mouse."

As if it wasn't already, thought Cathy as she huddled closer to Victor. She longed for a chance to be alone with him. There had been no time for tearful reunions, no time for any confessions of love. They'd spent the last two hours on a harrowing journey down backroads, always avoiding the police. By now the break-in at Viratek would have been reported to the authorities. The state police would be on the lookout for a van with frontal damage.

Polowski was right. Things were only getting more dangerous.

"Soon as we hit the city," said Polowski, "we'll get those vials off to separate labs. Independent confirmation. That should wipe any doubts away. You know names we can trust, Holland?"

"Fellow alum back in New Haven. Runs the hospital lab. I can trust him."

"Yale? Great. That'll have clout."

"Ollie has a pal at UCSF. They'll take care of the second vial."

"And when those reports get back, I know a certain journalist who loves to have a little birdie chirp in his ear." Polowski gave the steering wheel a satisfied slap. "Viratek, you are dead meat."

"You enjoy this, don't you?" said Cathy.

"Workin' the right side of the law? I say it's good for the soul. It keeps your mind sharp and your feet on their toes. It helps you stay young."

"Or die young," said Cathy.

Polowski laughed. "Women. They just never understand the game."

"I don't understand it, at all."

"I bet Holland here does. He just had the adrenaline high of his life. Didn't you?"

Victor didn't answer. He was gazing ahead at the blacktop stretching before their headlights.

"Well, wasn't it a high?" asked Polowski. "To claw your way to hell and back again? To know you made it through on nothing much more than your wits?"

"No," said Victor quietly. "Because it's not over yet."

Polowski's grin faded. He turned his attention back to the road. "Almost," he said. "It's almost over."

They passed a sign: San Francisco: 12 Miles.

Four in the morning. The stars were mere pinpricks in a sky washed out by streetlights. In a North Beach doughnut shop, five weary souls had gathered around steaming coffee and cheese Danish. Only one other table was occupied, by a man with bloodshot eyes and shaking hands. The girl behind the counter sat with her nose buried in a paperback. Behind her, the coffee machine hissed out a fresh brew.

"To the Old Coots," said Milo, raising his cup. "Still the best ensemble around."

They all raised their cups. "To the Old Coots!"

"And to our newest and fairest member," said Milo. "The beautiful—the intrepid—"

"Oh, *please,*" said Cathy.

Victor wrapped his arm around her shoulder. "Relax and be honored. Not everyone gets into this highly selective group."

"The only requirement," said Ollie, "is that you have to play a musical instrument badly."

"But I don't play anything."

"No problem." Ollie fished out a piece of waxed paper from the pile of Danishes and wrapped it around his pocket comb. "Kazoo."

"Fitting," said Milo. "Since that was Lily's instrument."

"Oh." She took the comb. Lily's instrument. It always came back to *her,* the ghost who would forever be there. Suddenly the air of celebration was gone, as though swept away by the cold wind of dawn. She glanced at Victor. He was looking out the window, at the garishly lit streets. *What are you thinking? Are you wishing she was here? That it wasn't me being presented this silly kazoo, but her?*

She put the comb to her lips and hummed an appropriately out-of-tune version of "Yankee Doodle." Everyone laughed and clapped, even Victor. But when the applause was over, she saw the sad and weary look in his eyes. Quietly she set the kazoo down on the table.

Outside, a delivery truck roared past. It was 5:00 a.m.; the city was stirring.

"Well, folks," said Polowski, slapping down a dollar tip. "We got a hotshot reporter to roust outta bed. And then you and I—" he looked at Victor "—have a few deliveries to make. When's United leave for New Haven?"

"At ten-fifteen," said Victor.

"Okay. I'll buy you the plane tickets. In the meantime, you see if you can't grow yourself a new mustache or something." Polowski glanced at Cathy. "You're going with him, right?"

"No," she said, looking at Victor.

She was hoping for a reaction, any reaction. What she saw was a look of relief. And, strangely, resignation.

He didn't try to change her mind. He simply asked, "Where will you be going?"

She shrugged. "Maybe I should stick to our original plan. You know, head south. Hang out with Jack for a while. What do you think?"

It was his chance to stop her. His chance to say, *No, I want you around. I won't let you leave, not now, not ever.* If he really loved her, that's exactly what he would say.

Her heart sank when he simply nodded and said, "I think it's a good idea."

She blinked back the tears before anyone could see them. With an indifferent smile she looked at Ollie. "So I guess I'll need a ride. When are you and Milo heading home?"

"Right now, I guess," said Ollie, looking bewildered. "Seeing as our job's pretty much done."

"Can I hitch along? I'll catch the bus at Palo Alto."

"No problem. In fact, you can sit in the honored front seat."

"Long as you don't let her behind the wheel," grumbled Milo. "I want a nice, quiet drive home if you don't mind."

Polowski rose to his feet. "Then we're all set. Everyone's got a place to go. Let's do it."

Outside, on a street rumbling with early-morning traffic, with their friends standing only a few yards away, Cathy and Victor said their goodbyes. It wasn't the place for sentimental farewells. Perhaps that was all for the best. At least she could leave with some trace of dignity. At least she could avoid hearing, from his lips, the brutal truth. She would simply walk away and hold on to the fantasy that he loved her. That in their brief time together she'd managed to work her way, just a little, into his heart.

"You'll be all right?" he asked.

"I'll be fine. And you?"

"I'll manage." He thrust his hands in his pockets and looked off at a bus idling near the corner. "I'll miss you," he said. "But I know it doesn't make sense for us to be together. Not under the circumstances."

I would stay with you, she thought. *Under any circumstances. If I only knew you wanted me.*

"Anyway," he said with a sigh, "I'll let you know when things are safe again. When you can come home."

"And then?"

"And then we'll take it from there," he said softly.

They kissed, a clumsy, polite kiss, all the more hurried because they knew their friends were watching. There was no passion here, only the cool, dry lips of a man saying goodbye. As they pulled apart, she saw his face blur away through the tears.

"Take care of yourself, Victor," she said. Then, shoulders squared, she turned and walked toward Ollie and Milo.

"Is that it?" asked Ollie.

"That's it." Brusquely she rubbed her hand across her eyes. "I'm ready to go."

"Tell me about Lily," she said.

The first light of dawn was already streaking the sky as they drove past the boxy row homes of Pacifica, past the cliffs where sea waves crashed and gulls swooped and dove.

Ollie, his gaze on the road, asked, "What do you want to know?"

"What kind of woman was she?"

"She was a nice person," said Ollie. "And brainy. Though she never went out of her way to impress people, she was probably the smartest one of all of us. Definitely brighter than Milo."

"And a lot better-looking than Ollie," piped a voice from the backseat.

"A real kind, real decent woman. When she and Gersh got married, I remember thinking, 'he's got himself a saint.'" He glanced at Cathy, suddenly noticing her silence. "Of course," he added quickly, "not every man *wants* a saint. I know I'd be happier with a lady who can be a little goofy." He flashed Cathy a grin. "Someone who might, say, crash a van through an electrified fence, just for kicks."

It was a sweet thing to say, a comment designed to lift her spirits. It couldn't take the edge off her pain.

She settled back and watched dawn lighten the sky. How she needed to get away! She thought about Mexico, about warm water and hot sand and the tang of fresh fish and lime. She would throw herself into working on that new film. Of course, Jack would be on the set, Jack with his latest sweetie pie in tow, but she could handle that now. Jack would never be able to hurt her again. She was beyond that now, beyond being hurt by any man.

The drive to Milo's house seemed endless.

When at last they pulled up in the driveway, the dawn had already blossomed into a bright, cold morning. Milo climbed out and stood blinking in the sunshine.

"So, guys," he said through the car window. "Guess here's where we go our separate ways." He looked at Cathy. "Mexico, right?"

She nodded. "Puerto Vallarta. What about you?"

"I'm gonna catch up with Ma in Florida. Maybe get a load of Disney World. Wanna come, Ollie?"

"Some other time. I'm going to go get some sleep."

"Don't know what you're missing. Well, it's been some adventure. I'm almost sorry it's over." Milo turned and headed up the walk to his house. On the front porch he waved and yelled, "See you around!" Then he vanished through the front door.

Ollie laughed. "Milo and his ma, together? Disney World'll never be the same." He reached for the ignition. "Next stop, the bus station. I've got just enough gas to get us there and—"

He didn't get a chance to turn the key.

A gun barrel was thrust in the open car window. It came to rest squarely against Ollie's temple.

"Get out, Dr. Wozniak," said a voice.

Ollie's reply came out in a bare croak. "What—what do you want?"

"Do it now." The click of the hammer being cocked was all the coaxing Ollie needed.

"Okay, okay! I'm getting out!" Ollie scrambled out and backed away, his hands raised in surrender.

Cathy, too, started to climb out, but the gunman snapped, "Not you! You stay inside."

"Look," said Ollie. "You can have the damn car! You don't need her—"

"But I do. Tell Mr. Holland I'll be in contact. Regarding Ms. Weaver's future." He went around and opened the passenger door. "You, into the driver's seat!" he commanded her.

"No. Please—"

The gun barrel dug into her neck. "Need I ask again?"

Trembling, she moved behind the wheel. Her knee brushed the car keys, still dangling from the ignition. The man slid in beside her. Though the gun barrel was still thrust against her neck, it was the man's eyes she focused on. They were black, fathomless. If any spark of humanity lurked in those depths, she couldn't see it.

"Start the engine," he said.

"Where—where are we going?"

"For a drive. Somewhere scenic."

Her thoughts were racing, seeking some means of escape, but she came up with nothing. That gun was insurmountable.

She turned on the ignition.

"Hey!" yelled Ollie, grabbing at the door. "You can't do this!"

Cathy screamed, "Ollie, no!"

The gunman had already shifted his aim out the window.

"Let her go!" yelled Ollie. "Let her—"

The gun went off.

Ollie staggered backward, his face a mask of astonishment.

Cathy lunged at the gunman. Pure animal rage, fueled by the instinct to survive, sent her clawing first for his eyes. At the last split second he flinched away. Her nails scraped down his cheek, drawing blood. Before he could shift his aim, she grabbed his wrist, wrenching desperately for control of the gun. He held fast. Not with all her strength could she keep the gun at bay, keep the barrel from turning toward her.

It was the last image she registered: that black hole, slowly turning until it was pointed straight at her face.

Something lashed at her from the side. Pain exploded in her head, shattering the world into a thousand slivers of light.

They faded, one by one, into darkness.

Chapter 12

"Victor's here," said Milo.

It seemed to take Ollie forever to register their presence. Victor fought the urge to shake him to consciousness, to drag the words out of his friend's throat. He was forced to wait, the silence broken only by the hiss of oxygen, the gurgle of the suction tube. At last Ollie stirred and squinted through pain-glazed eyes at the three men standing beside his bed. "Gersh. I didn't—couldn't—" He stopped, exhausted by the effort just to talk.

"Easy, Ollie," said Milo. "Take it slow."

"Tried to stop him. Had a gun…" Ollie paused, gathering the strength to continue.

Victor listened fearfully for the next terrible words to come out. He was still in a state of disbelief, still hoping that what Milo had told him was one giant mistake, that Cathy was, at this very moment, on a bus somewhere to safety. Only two hours ago he'd been ready to board a plane for New Haven. Then he'd been handed a message at the United gate. It was addressed to passenger Sam Polowski, the name on his ticket. It had consisted of only three words: *Call Milo immediately.*

Passenger "Sam Polowski" never did board the plane.

Two hours, he thought in anguish. What have they done to her in those two long hours?

"This man—what did he look like?" asked Polowski.

"Didn't see him very well. Dark hair. Face sort of… thin."

"Tall? Short?"

"Tall."

"He drove off in your car?"

Ollie nodded.

"What about Cathy?" Victor blurted out, his control shattered. "He—didn't hurt her? She's all right?"

There was a pause that, to Victor, seemed like an eternity in hell. Ollie's gaze settled mournfully on Victor. "I don't know."

It was the best Victor could hope for. *I don't know.* It left open the possibility that she was still alive.

Suddenly agitated, he began to pace the floor. "I know what he wants," he said. "I know what I have to give him—"

"You can't be serious," said Polowski. "That's our evidence! You can't just hand it over—"

"That's exactly what I'm going to do."

"You don't even know how to contact him!"

"He'll contact *me.*" He spun around and looked at Milo. "He must've been watching your house all this time. Waiting for one of us to turn up. That's where he'll call."

"If he calls," said Polowski.

"He will." Victor touched his jacket pocket, where the two vials from Viratek still rested. "I have what he wants. He has what I want. I think we're both ready to make a trade."

The sun, glaring and relentless, was shining in her eyes. She tried to escape it, tried to close her lids tighter, to stop those rays from piercing through to her brain, but the light followed her.

"Wake up. *Wake up!*"

Icy water slapped her face. Cathy gasped awake, coughing, rivulets of water trickling from her hair. She struggled to make out the face hovering above her. At first all she saw was a dark oval against the blinding circle of light. Then the man moved away and she saw eyes like black agate, a slash of a mouth. A scream formed in her throat, to be instantly frozen by the cold barrel of a gun against her cheek.

"Not a sound," he said. "Got that?"

In silent terror she nodded.

"Good." The gun slid away from her cheek and was tucked under his jacket. "Sit up."

She obeyed. Instantly the room began to spin. She sat clutching her aching head, the fear temporarily over-shadowed by waves of pain and nausea. The spell lasted for only a few moments. Then, as the nausea faded, she became aware of a second man in the room, a large, broad-shouldered man she'd never before seen. He sat off in a corner, saying nothing, but watching her every move. The room itself was small and windowless. She couldn't tell if it was day or night. The only furniture was a chair, a card table and the cot she was sitting on.

The floor was a bare slab of concrete. *We're in a basement,* she thought. She heard no other sounds, either outside or in the building. Were they still in Palo Alto? Or were they a hundred miles away?

The man in the chair crossed his arms and smiled. Under different circumstances, she might have considered that smile a charming one. Now it struck her as frighteningly inhuman. "She seems awake enough," he said. "Why don't you proceed, Mr. Savitch?"

The man called Savitch loomed over her. "Where is he?"

"Who?" she said.

Her answer was met by a ringing slap to her cheek. She sprawled backwards on the cot.

"Try again," he said, dragging her back up to a sitting position. "Where is Victor Holland?"

"I don't know."

"You were with him."

"We—we split up."

"Why?"

She touched her mouth. The sight of blood on her fingers shocked her temporarily into silence.

"Why?"

"He—" She bowed her head. Softly she said, "He didn't want me around."

Savitch let out a snort. "Got tired of you pretty quick, did he?"

"Yes," she whispered. "I guess he did."

"I don't know why."

She shuddered as the man ran his finger down her cheek, her throat. He stopped at the top button of her blouse. *No,* she thought. *Not that.*

To her relief, the man in the chair suddenly cut in. "This is getting us nowhere."

Savitch turned to the other man. "You have another suggestion, Mr. Tyrone?"

"Yes. Let's try using her in a different way." Fearfully Cathy watched as Tyrone moved to the card table and opened a satchel. "Since we can't go to him," he said, "we'll have Holland come to us." He turned and smiled at her. "With your help, of course."

She stared at the cellular telephone he was holding. "I told you. I don't know where he is."

"I'm sure one of his friends will track him down."

"He's not stupid. He wouldn't come for me—"

"You're right. He's not stupid." Tyrone began to punch in a phone number. "But he's a man of conscience. And that's a flaw that's every bit as fatal." He paused, then said into the telephone, "Hello? Mr. Milo Lum? I want you to pass this message to Victor Holland for me. Tell him I have something of his. Something that won't be around much longer…"

"It's him!" hissed Milo. "He wants to make a deal."

Victor shot to his feet. "Let me talk to him—"

"Wait!" Polowski grabbed his arm. "We have to take this slow. Think about what we're—"

Victor pulled his arm free and snatched the receiver from Milo. "This is Holland," he barked into the phone. "Where is she?"

The voice on the other end paused, a silence designed to emphasize just who held the upper hand. "She's with me. She's alive."

"How do I know that?"

"You'll have to take my word for it."

"Word, hell! I want proof!"

Again there was a silence. Then, through the crackle of the line, came another voice, so tremulous, so afraid, it almost broke his heart. "Victor, it's me."

"Cathy?" He almost shouted with relief. "Cathy, are you all right?"

"I'm...fine."

"Where are you?"

"I don't know—I think—" She stopped. The silence was agonizing. "I can't be sure."

"He hasn't hurt you?"

A pause. "No."

She's not telling me the truth, he thought. *He's done something to her...*

"Cathy, I promise. You'll be all right. I swear to you I'll—"

"Let's talk business." The man was back on the line.

Victor gripped the receiver in fury. "If you hurt her, if you just touch her, I swear I'll—"

"You're hardly in a position to bargain."

Victor felt a hand grasp his arm. He turned and met Polowski's gaze. *Keep your head* was the message he saw. *Go along with him. Make a bargain. It's the only way to buy time.*

Nodding, Victor fought to regain control. When he spoke again, his voice was calm. "Okay. You want the vials, they're yours."

"Not good enough."

"Then I'll throw myself into the bargain. A trade. Is that acceptable?"

"Acceptable. You and the vials in exchange for her life."

An anguished cry of *"No!"* pierced the dialogue. It was Cathy, somewhere in the background, shouting, "Don't, Victor! They're going to—"

Through the receiver, Victor heard the thud of a blow, followed by soft moans of pain. All his control shattered. He was screaming now, cursing, begging, anything to make the man stop hurting her. The words ran together, making no sense. He couldn't see straight, couldn't think straight.

Again, Polowski took his arm, gave it a shake. Victor, breathing hard, stared at him through a gaze blurred by tears. Polowski's eyes advised: *Make the deal. Go on.*

Victor swallowed and closed his eyes. *Give me strength,* he thought. He managed to ask, "When do we make the exchange?"

"Tonight. At 2:00 a.m."

"Where?"

"East Palo Alto. The old Saracen Theater."

"But it's closed. It's been closed for—"

"It'll be open. Just you, Holland. I spot anyone else and the first bullet has her name on it. Clear?"

"I want a guarantee! I want to know she'll be—"

He was answered by silence. And then, seconds later, he heard a dial tone.

Slowly he hung up.

"Well? What's the deal?" demanded Polowski.

"At 2:00 a.m. Saracen Theater."

"Half an hour. That barely gives us time to set up a—"

"I'm going alone."

Milo and Polowski stared at him. "Like hell," said Polowski.

Victor grabbed his jacket from out of the closet. He gave the pocket a quick pat; the cigarette case was right where he'd left it. He turned and reached for the door.

"But, Gersh!" said Milo. "He's gonna kill you!"

Victor paused in the doorway. "Probably," he said softly. "But it's Cathy's only chance. And it's a chance I have to take."

"He won't come," said Cathy.

"Shut up," Matt Tyrone snapped and shoved her forward.

As they moved down the glass-strewn alley behind the Saracen Theater, Cathy frantically searched her mind for some way to sabotage this fatal meeting. It *would* be fatal, not just for Victor, but for her, as well. The two men now escorting her through the darkness had no intention of letting her live. The best she could hope for was that Victor would survive. She had to do what she could to better his chances.

"He's already got his evidence," she said. "You think he'd give that up just for me?"

Tyrone glanced at Savitch. "What if she's right?"

"Holland's coming," said Savitch. "I know how he thinks. He's not going to leave the little woman behind." Savitch gave Cathy's cheek a deceptively gentle caress. "Not when he knows exactly what we'll do to her."

Cathy flinched away, repelled by his touch. *What if he really doesn't come?* she thought. *What if he does the sensible thing and leaves me to die?*

She wouldn't blame him.

Tyrone gave her a push up the steps and into the building. "Inside. Move."

"I can't see," she protested, feeling her way along a pitch-black passage. She stumbled over boxes, brushed past what felt like heavy drapes. "It's too dark—"

"Then let there be light," said a new voice.

The lights suddenly sprang on, so bright she was temporarily blinded. She raised her hand to shield her eyes. Through the glare she could make out a third man, looming before her. Beyond him, the floor seemed to drop away into a vast blackness.

They were standing on a theater stage. It was obvious no performer had trod these boards in years. Ragged curtains hung like cobwebs from the rafters. Panels of an old set, the ivy-hung battlements of a medieval castle, still leaned at a crazy tilt against the back wall, framed by a pair of mops.

Tyrone said, "Any problems, Dafoe?"

"None," said the new man. "I've reconned the building. One door at the front, one backstage. The emergency side doors are padlocked. If we block both exits, he's trapped."

"I see the FBI deserves its fine reputation."

Dafoe grinned and dipped his head. "I knew the Cowboy would want the very best."

"Okay, Ms. Weaver." Tyrone shoved Cathy forward, toward a chair placed directly under the spotlight. "Let's put you right where he can see you. Center stage."

It was Savitch who tied her to the chair. He knew exactly what he was doing. She had no hope of working her hands free from such tight, professional knots.

He stepped back, satisfied with his job. "She's not

going anywhere," he said. Then, as an afterthought, he ripped off a strip of cloth tape and slapped it over her mouth. "So we don't have any surprises," he said.

Tyrone glanced at his watch. "Zero minus fifteen. Positions, gentlemen."

The three men slipped away into the shadows, leaving Cathy alone on the empty stage. The spotlight beating down on her face was hot as the midday sun. Already she could feel beads of sweat forming on her forehead. Though she couldn't see them, by their voices she could guess the positions of the three men. Tyrone was close by. Savitch was at the back of the theater, near the building's front entrance. And the man named Dafoe had stationed himself somewhere above, in one of the box seats. Three different lines of fire. No route of escape.

Victor, don't be a fool, she thought. *Stay away...*

And if he doesn't come? She couldn't bear to consider that possibility, either, for it meant he was abandoning her. It meant he didn't care enough even to make the effort to save her.

She closed her eyes against the spotlight, against the tears. *I love you. I could take anything, even this, if I only knew you loved me.*

Her hands were numb from the ropes. She tried to wriggle the bonds looser, but only succeeded in rubbing her wrists raw. She fought to remain calm, but with every minute that passed, her heart seemed to pound harder. A drop of sweat trickled down her temple.

Somewhere in the shadows ahead, a door squealed open and closed. Footsteps approached, their pace slow and deliberate. She strained to see against the spotlight's glare, but could make out only the hint of shadow moving through shadow.

The stage floorboards creaked behind her as Tyrone strolled out from the wings. "Stop right where you are, Mr. Holland," he said.

Chapter 13

Another spotlight suddenly sprang on, catching Victor in its glare. He stood halfway up the aisle, a lone figure trapped in a circle of brilliance.

You came for me! she thought. *I knew, somehow I knew, that you would...*

If only she could shout to him, warn him about the other two men. But the tape had been applied so tightly that the only sound she could produce was a whimper.

"Let her go," said Victor.

"You have something we want first."

"I said, *let her go!*"

"You're hardly in a position to bargain." Tyrone strolled out of the wings, onto the stage. Cathy flinched as the icy barrel of a gun pressed against her temple. "Let's see it, Holland," said Tyrone.

"Untie her first."

"I could shoot you both and be done with it."

"Is this what it's come to?" yelled Victor. "Federal dollars for the murder of civilians?"

"It's all a matter of cost and benefit. A few civilians may have to die now. But if this country goes to war, think of all the millions of Americans who'll be saved!"

"I'm thinking of the Americans you've already killed."

"Necessary deaths. But you don't understand that. You've never seen a fellow soldier die, have you, Holland? You don't know what a helpless feeling it is, to watch good boys from good American towns get cut to pieces. With this weapon, they won't have to. It'll be the enemy dying, not us."

"Who gave you the authority?"

"I gave myself the authority."

"And who the hell are *you?*"

"A patriot, Mr. Holland! I do the jobs no one else in the Administration'll touch. Someone says, 'Too bad our weapons don't have a higher kill ratio.' That's my cue to get one developed. They don't even have to ask me. They can claim total ignorance."

"So you're the fall guy."

Tyrone shrugged. "It's part of being a good soldier. The willingness to fall on one's sword. But I'm not ready to do that yet."

Cathy tensed as Tyrone clicked back the gun hammer. The barrel was still poised against her skull.

"As you can see," said Tyrone, "the cards aren't exactly stacked in her favor."

"On the other hand," Victor said calmly, "how do you know I've brought the vials? What if they're stashed somewhere, a publicity time bomb ticking away? Kill her now and you'll never find out."

Deadlock. Tyrone lowered the pistol. He and Victor faced each other for a moment. Then Tyrone reached into his pocket, and Cathy heard the click of a switchblade. "This round goes to you, Holland," he said as he cut the bindings. The sudden rush of circulation back into Cathy's hands was almost painful. Tyrone ripped the tape off her mouth and yanked her out of the chair. "She's all yours!"

Cathy scrambled off the stage. On unsteady legs, she moved up the aisle, toward the circle of the spotlight, toward Victor. He pulled her into his arms. Only by the thud of his racing heart did she know how close he was to panic.

"Your turn, Holland," called Tyrone.

"Go," Victor whispered to her. "Get out of here."

"Victor, he has two other men—"

"Let's have it!" yelled Tyrone.

Victor hesitated. Then he reached into his jacket and pulled out a cigarette case. "They'll be watching me," he whispered. "You move for the door. Go on. *Do it.*"

She stood paralyzed by indecision. She couldn't leave him to die. And she knew the other two gunmen were somewhere in the darkness, watching their every move.

"She stays where she is!" said Tyrone. "Come on, Holland. The vials!"

Victor took a step further, then another.

"No further!" commanded Tyrone.

Victor halted. "You want it, don't you?"

"Put it down on the floor."

Slowly Victor set the cigarette case down by his feet.

"Now slide it to me."

Victor gave the case a shove. It skimmed down the aisle and came to a rest in the orchestra pit.

Tyrone dropped from the stage.

Victor began to back away. Taking Cathy's hand, he edged her slowly up the aisle, toward the exit.

As if on cue, the click of pistol hammers being snapped back echoed through the theater. Reflexively, Victor spun around, trying to sight the other gunmen. It was impossible to see anything clearly against the glare of the spotlight.

"You're not leaving yet," said Tyrone, reaching down for the case. Gingerly he removed the lid. In silence he stared at the contents.

This is it, thought Cathy. *He has no reason to keep us alive, now that he has what he wants...*

Tyrone's head shot up. "Double cross," he said. Then, in a roar, *"Double cross! Kill them!"*

His voice was still reverberating through the far reaches of the theater when, all at once, the lights went out. Blackness fell, so impenetrable that Cathy had to reach out to get her bearings.

That's when Victor pulled her sideways, down a row of theater seats.

"Stop them!" screamed Tyrone in the darkness.

Gunfire seemed to erupt from everywhere at once. As Cathy and Victor scurried on hands and knees along the floor, they could hear bullets thudding into the velvet-backed seats. The gunfire quickly became random, a blind spraying of the theater.

"Hold your fire!" yelled Tyrone. "Listen for them!"

The gunfire stopped. Cathy and Victor froze in the darkness, afraid to give away their position. Except for the pounding of her own pulse, Cathy heard absolute silence. *We're trapped. We make a single move and they'll know where we are.*

Scarcely daring to breathe, she reached back and pulled off her shoe. With a mighty heave, she threw it blindly across the theater. The clatter of the shoe's landing instantly drew a new round of gunfire. In the din of ricocheting bullets, Victor and Cathy scurried along the remainder of the row and emerged in the side aisle.

Again, the gunfire stopped.

"No way out, Holland!" yelled Tyrone. "Both doors are covered! It's just a matter of time…"

Somewhere above, in a theater balcony, a light suddenly flickered on. It was Dafoe, holding aloft a cigarette lighter. As the flame leapt brightly, casting its terrible light against the shadows, Victor shoved Cathy to the floor behind a seat.

"I know they're here!" shouted Tyrone. "See 'em, Dafoe?"

As Dafoe moved the flame, the shadows shifted, revealing new forms, new secrets. "I'll spot 'em any second. Wait. I think I see—"

Dafoe suddenly jerked sideways as a shot rang out. The flame's light danced crazily on his face as he wobbled for a moment on the edge of the balcony. He reached out for the railing, but the rotten wood gave way under his weight. He pitched forward, his body tumbling into a row of seats.

"Dafoe!" screamed Tyrone. "Who the hell—"

A tongue of flame suddenly slithered up from the floor. Dafoe's lighter had set fire to the drapes! The flames spread quickly, dancing their way along the heavy velvet fabric, toward the rafters. As the first flames touched wood, the fire whooshed into a roar.

By the light of the inferno, all was revealed: Victor and Cathy, cowering in the aisle. Savitch, standing near the entrance, semiautomatic at the ready. And onstage, Tyrone, his expression demonic in the fire's glow.

"They're yours, Savitch!" ordered Tyrone.

Savitch aimed. This time there was no place for them to hide, no shadows to scurry off to. Cathy felt Victor's arm encircle her in a last protective embrace.

The gun's explosion made them both flinch. Another shot; still she felt no pain. She glanced at Victor. He was staring at her, as though unable to believe they were both alive.

They looked up to see Savitch, his shirt stained in a spreading abstract of blood, drop to his knees.

"Now's your chance!" yelled a voice. *"Move, Holland!"*

They whirled around to see a familiar figure silhouetted against the flames. Somehow, Sam Polowski had magically appeared from behind the drapes. Now he pivoted, pistol clutched in both hands, and aimed at Tyrone.

He never got a chance to squeeze off the shot.

Tyrone fired first. The bullet knocked Polowski backward and sent him sprawling against the smoldering velvet seats.

"Get out of here!" barked Victor, giving Cathy a push toward the exit. "I'm going back for him—"

"Victor, you can't!"

But he was on his way. Through the swirling smoke she could see him moving at a half crouch between rows of seats. *He needs help. And time's running out...*

Already the air was so hot it seemed to sear its way into her throat. Coughing, she dropped to the floor and took in a few breaths of relatively smoke-free air. She still had time to escape. All she had to do was crawl up the aisle and out the theater door. Every instinct told her to flee now, while she had the chance.

Instead, she turned from the exit and followed Victor into the maelstrom.

She could just make out his figure, scrambling before a solid wall of fire. She raised her arm to shield her face against the heat. Squinting into the smoke, she crawled forward, moving ever closer to the flames. "Victor!" she screamed.

She was answered only by the fire's roar, and by a sound even more ominous: the creak of wood. She glanced up. To her horror she saw that the rafters were sagging and on the verge of collapse.

Panicked, she scurried blindly forward, toward where she'd last spotted Victor. He was no longer visible. In his place was a whirlwind of smoke and flame. Had he already escaped? Was she alone, trapped in this blazing tinderbox?

Something slapped against her cheek. She stared, at first uncomprehending, at the human hand dangling before her face. Slowly she followed it up, along the bloodied arm, to the lifeless eyes of Dafoe. Her cry of terror seemed to funnel into the fiery cyclone.

"Cathy?"

She turned at the sound of Victor's shout. That's when she saw him, crouching in the aisle just a few feet away. He had Polowski under the arms and was struggling to drag him toward the exit. But the heat and smoke had taken its toll; he was on the verge of collapse.

"The roof's about to fall!" she screamed.

"Get out!"

"Not without you!" She scrambled forward and grabbed Polowski's feet. Together they hauled their burden up the aisle, across carpet that was already alight with sparks. Step by step they neared the top of the aisle. Only a few yards to go!

"I've got him," gasped Victor. "Go—open the door—"

She rose to a half crouch and turned.

Matt Tyrone stood before her.

"Victor!" she sobbed.

Victor, his face a mask of soot and sweat, turned to meet Tyrone's gaze. Neither man said a word. They both knew the game had been played out. Now the time had come to finish it.

Tyrone raised his gun.

Just as he did, they heard the loud crack of splintering wood. Tyrone glanced up as one of the rafters sagged, spilling a shower of burning tinder.

That brief distraction was all the time Cathy needed. In an act of sheer desperation she lunged at Tyrone's legs, knocking him backward. The gun flew from his grasp and slid off beneath a row of seats.

At once Tyrone was back on his feet. He aimed a savage kick at her. The blow hit her in the ribs, an impact so agonizing she hadn't the breath to cry out. She simply sprawled in the aisle, stunned and utterly helpless to ward off any other blows.

Through the darkness gathering before her eyes, she saw two figures struggling. Victor and Tyrone. Framed against a sea of fire, they grappled for each other's throats. Tyrone threw a punch; Victor staggered back a few paces. Tyrone charged him like a bull. At the last instant Victor sidestepped him and Tyrone met only empty air. He stumbled and sprawled forward, onto the smoldering carpet. Enraged, he rose to his knees, ready to charge again.

The crack of collapsing timber made him glance skyward.

He was still staring up in astonishment as the beam crashed down on his head.

Cathy tried to cry out Victor's name but no sound escaped. The smoke had left her throat too parched and swollen. She struggled to her knees. Polowski was lying beside her, groaning. Flames were everywhere, shooting up from the floor, clambering up the last untouched drapes.

Then she saw him, stumbling toward her through that vision of hellfire. He grabbed her arm and shoved her toward the exit.

Somehow, they managed to tumble out the door, dragging Polowski behind them. Coughing, choking, they pulled him across the street to the far sidewalk. There they collapsed.

The night sky suddenly lit up as an explosion ripped through the theater. The roof collapsed, sending up a whoosh of flames so brilliant they seemed to reach to the very heavens. Victor threw his body over Cathy's as the windows in the building above shattered, raining splinters onto the sidewalk.

For a moment there was only the sound of the flames, crackling across the street. Then, somewhere in the distance, a siren wailed.

Polowski stirred and groaned.

"Sam!" Victor turned his attention to the wounded man. "How you doing, buddy?"

"Got…got one helluva stitch in my side…"

"You'll be fine." Victor flashed him a tense grin. "Listen! Hear those sirens? Help's on the way."

"Yeah." Polowski, eyes narrowed in pain, stared up at the flame-washed sky.

"Thanks, Sam," said Victor softly.

"Had to. You...too damn stupid to listen..."

"We got her back, didn't we?"

Polowski's gaze shifted to Cathy. "We—we did okay."

Victor rubbed a hand across his smudged and weary face. "But we're back to square one. I've lost the evidence—"

"Milo..."

"It's all in there." Victor stared across at the flames now engulfing the old theater.

"Milo has it," whispered Sam.

"What?"

"You weren't looking. Gave it to Milo."

Victor sat back in bewilderment. "You mean you *took* them? You took the vials?"

Polowski nodded.

"You—you stupid son of a—"

"Victor!" said Cathy.

"He stole my bargaining chip!"

"He saved our lives!"

Victor stared down at Polowski.

Polowski returned a pained grin. "Dame's got a head on her shoulders," he murmured. "Listen to her."

The sirens, which had risen to a scream, suddenly cut off. Men's shouts at once sliced through the hiss and roar of the flames. A burly fireman loped over from the truck and knelt beside Polowski.

"What've we got here?"

"Gunshot wound," said Victor. "And a wise-ass patient."

The fireman nodded. "No problem, sir. We can handle both."

By the time they'd loaded Polowski into an ambulance, the Saracen Theater had been reduced to little more than a dying bonfire. Victor and Cathy watched the taillights of the ambulance vanish, heard the fading wail of the siren, the hiss of water on the flames.

He turned to her. Without a word he pulled her into his arms and held her long and hard, two silent figures framed against a sea of smoldering flames and chaos. They were both so weary neither knew which was holding the other up. Yet even through her exhaustion, Cathy felt the magic of that moment. It was eerily beautiful, that last sputtering glow, the reflections dancing off the nearby buildings. Beautiful and frightening and final.

"You came for me," she murmured. "Oh, Victor, I was so afraid you wouldn't…"

"Cathy, you knew I would!"

"I *didn't* know. You had your evidence. You could have left me—"

"No, I couldn't." He buried a kiss in her singed hair. "Thank God I wasn't already on that plane. They'd have had you, and I'd have been two thousand miles away."

Footsteps crunched toward them across the glass-littered pavement. "Excuse me," a voice said. "Are you Victor Holland?"

They turned to see a man in a rumpled parka, a camera slung over his shoulder, watching them.

"Who are you?" asked Victor.

The man held out his hand. "Jay Wallace. *San Francisco Chronicle*. Sam Polowski called me, said there'd be some fireworks in case I wanted to check it out." He gazed at the last remains of the Saracen Theater and shook his head. "Looks like I got here a little too late."

"Wait. *Sam* called you? When?"

"Maybe two hours ago. If he wasn't my ex-brother-in-law, I'd a hung up on him. For days he's been dropping hints he had a story to spill. Never followed through, not once. I almost didn't come tonight. You know, it's a helluva long drive down here from the city."

"He told you about me?"

"He said you had a story to tell."

"Don't we all?"

"Some stories are better than others." The reporter glanced around, searching. "So where is Sam, anyway? Or didn't the Bozo show up?"

"That Bozo," said Victor, his voice tight with anger, "is a goddamn hero. Stick *that* in your article."

More footsteps approached. This time it was two police officers. Cathy felt Victor's muscles go taut as he turned to face them.

The senior officer spoke. "We've just been informed that a gunshot victim was taken to the ER. And that you were found on the scene."

Victor nodded. His look of tension suddenly gave way to one of overwhelming exhaustion. And resignation. He said, quietly, "I was present. And if you search that building, you'll find three more bodies."

"Three?" The two cops glanced at each other.

"Musta been some fireworks," muttered the reporter.

The senior officer said, "Maybe you'd better give us your name, sir."

"My name..." Victor looked at Cathy. She read the message in those weary eyes: *We've reached the end.*

I have to tell them. Now they'll take me away from you, and God knows when we'll see each other again...

She felt his hand tighten around hers. She held on, knowing with every second that passed that he would soon be wrenched from her grasp.

His gaze still focused on her face, he said, "My name is Victor Holland."

"Holland... Victor Holland?" said the officer. "Isn't that..."

And still Victor was looking at her. Until they'd clapped on the handcuffs, until he'd been pulled away, toward a waiting squad car, his gaze was locked on her.

She was left anchorless, shivering among the dying embers.

"Ma'am, you'll have to come with us."

She looked up, dazed, at the policeman. "What?"

"Hey, she doesn't have to!" cut in Jay Wallace. "You haven't charged her with anything!"

"Shut up, Wallace."

"I've had the court beat. I know her rights!"

Quietly Cathy said, "It doesn't matter. I'll come with you, officer."

"Wait!" said Wallace. "I wanna talk to you first! I got just a few questions—"

"She can talk to you later," snapped the policeman, taking Cathy by the arm. "*After* she talks to us."

The policemen were polite, even kind. Perhaps it was her docile acceptance of the situation, perhaps they could sense she was operating on her last meager reserves of strength. She answered all their questions. She let them examine the rope burns on her wrists. She told them about Ollie and Sarah and the other Catherine Weavers. And the whole time, as she sat in that room in the Palo Alto police station, she kept hoping she'd catch a glimpse of Victor. She knew he had to be close by. Were they, at that very moment, asking him these same questions?

At dawn, they released her.

Jay Wallace was waiting outside near the front steps. "I have to talk to you," he said as she walked out.

"Please. Not now. I'm tired…"

"Just a few questions."

"I can't. I need to—to—" She stopped. And there, standing on that cold and empty street, she burst into tears. "I don't know what to do," she sobbed. "I don't know how to help him. How to reach him."

"You mean Holland? They've already taken him to San Francisco."

"What?" She raised her startled gaze to Wallace.

"An hour ago. The big boys from the Justice Department came down as an escort. I hear tell they're flying him straight to Washington. First-class treatment all the way."

She shook her head in bewilderment. "Then he's all right—he's not under arrest—"

"Hell, lady," said Wallace, laughing. "The man is now a genuine hero."

A hero. But she didn't care what they called him, as long as he was safe.

She took a deep breath of bitingly chill air. "Do you have a car, Mr. Wallace?" she asked.

"It's parked right around the corner."

"Then you can give me a ride."

"Where to?"

"To…" She paused, wondering where to go, where Victor would look for her. Of course. Milo's. "To a friend's house," she said. "I want to be there when Victor calls."

Wallace pointed the way to the car. "I hope it's a long drive," he said. "I got a lot of gaps to fill in before this story goes to press."

Victor didn't call.

For four days she sat waiting near the phone, expecting to hear his voice. For four days, Milo and his mother brought her tea and cookies, smiles and sympathy. On the fifth day, when she still hadn't heard from him, those terrible doubts began to haunt her. She remembered that day by the lake bed, when he'd tried to send her away with Ollie. She thought of all the words he could have said, but never had. True, he'd come back for her. He'd knowingly walked straight into a trap at the Saracen Theater. But wouldn't he have done that for any of his friends? That was the kind of man he was. She'd saved his life once. He remembered his debts, and he paid them back. It had to do with honor.

It might have nothing to do with love.

She stopped waiting by the phone. She returned to her flat in San Francisco, cleaned up the glass, had the windows replaced, the walls replastered. She took long walks and paid frequent visits to Ollie and Polowski in the hospital. Anything to stay away from that silent telephone.

She got a call from Jack. "We're shooting next week," he whined. "And the monster's in terrible shape. All this humidity! Its face keeps melting into green goo. Get down here and do something about it, will you?"

She told him she'd think about it.

A week later she decided. Work was what she needed.

Green goo and cranky actors—it was better than waiting for a call that would never come.

She reserved a one-way flight from San José to Puerto Vallarta. Then she packed, throwing in her entire wardrobe. A long stay, that's what she planned, a long vacation.

But before she left, she would drive down to Palo Alto. She had promised to pay Sam Polowski one last visit.

Chapter 14

(AP) Washington.

Administration spokesman Richard Jung-kuntz repeated today that neither the President nor any of his staff had any knowledge of biological weapons research being conducted at Viratek Industries in California. Viratek's Project Cerberus, which involved development of genetically altered viruses, was clearly in violation of international law. Recent evidence, gathered by reporter Jay Wallace of the San Francisco Chronicle, has revealed that the project received funds directly authorized by the late Matthew Tyrone, a senior aide to the Secretary of Defense.

In today's Justice Department hearings, delayed four hours because of heavy snowstorms, Viratek president Archibald Black testified for the first time, promising to reveal, to the best of his knowledge, the direct links between the Administration and Project Cerberus. Yesterday's testimony, by former Viratek employee Dr. Victor Holland, has already outlined a disturbing tale of deception, cover-ups and possibly murder.

The Attorney General's office continues to resist demands by Congressman Leo D. Fanelli that a special prosecutor be appointed...

Cathy put down the newspaper and smiled across the hospital solarium at her three friends. "Well, guys. Aren't you lucky to be here in sunny California and not freezing your you-know-whats off in Washington."

"Are you kidding?" groused Polowski. "I'd give anything to be in on those hearings right now. Instead of hooked up to all these—these *doohickeys*." He gave his intravenous line a tug, clanging a bottle against the pole.

"Patience, Sam," said Milo. "You'll get to Washington."

"Ha! Holland's already told 'em the good stuff. By the time they get around to hearing my testimony, it'll be back-page news."

"I don't think so," said Cathy. "I think it'll be front-page news for a long time to come." She turned and looked out the window at the sunshine glistening on the grass. *A long time to come.* That's how long it would be before she'd see Victor again. If ever. Three weeks had already passed since she'd last laid eyes on him. Via Jay Wallace in Washington, she'd heard that it was like a shark-feeding whenever Victor appeared in public, mobs of reporters and federal attorneys and Justice Department officials. No one could get near him.

Not even me, she thought.

It had been a comfort, having these three new friends to talk to. Ollie had bounced back quickly and was discharged—or kicked out, as Milo put it—a mere eight days after being shot. Polowski had had a rougher time of it. Post-operative infections, plus a bad case of smoke inhalation, had prolonged his stay to the point that every day was another trial of frustration for him. He wanted out. He wanted back on the beat.

He wanted a real, honest-to-God cheeseburger and a cigarette.

One more week, the doctors said.

At least there's an end to his waiting in sight, Cathy thought. *I don't know when I'll see or hear from Victor again.*

The silence was to be expected, Polowski had told her. Sequestration of witnesses. Protective custody. The Justice Department wanted an airtight case, and for that it would keep its star witness incommunicado. For the rest of them, depositions had been sufficient. Cathy had given her testimony two weeks before. Afterward, they'd told her she was free to leave town any time she wished.

Now she had a plane ticket to Mexico in her purse.

She was through with waiting for telephone calls, through with wondering whether he loved her or missed her. She'd been through this before with Jack, the doubts, the fears, the slow but inevitable realization that something was wrong. She knew enough not to be hurt again, not this way.

At least, out of all this pain, I've discovered three

new friends. Ollie and Polowski and Milo, the most unlikely trio on the face of the earth.

"Look, Sam," said Milo, reaching into his backpack.
"We brought ya something."

"No more hula-girl boxer shorts, okay? Caught hell
from the nurses for that one."

"Naw. It's something for your lungs. To remind you
to breathe deep."

"Cigarettes?" Polowski asked hopefully.

Milo grinned and held up his gift. "A kazoo!"

"I really needed one."

"You really do need it," said Ollie, opening up his
clarinet case. "Seeing as we brought our instruments
today and we weren't about to leave you out of this
particular gig."

"You're not serious."

"What better place to perform?" said Milo, giving his
piccolo a quick and loving rubdown. "All these sick, de-
pressed patients lying around, in need of a bit of cheer-
ing up. Some good music."

"Some peace and quiet!" Polowski turned pleading
eyes to Cathy. "They're not serious."

She looked him in the eye and took out her kazoo.
"Dead serious."

"Okay, guys," said Ollie. "Hit it!"

Never before had the world heard such a rendering
of "California, Here I Come!" And, if the world was
lucky, never again. By the time they'd played the last
note, nurses and patients had spilled into the solarium
to check on the source of that terrible screeching.

"Mr. Polowski!" said the head nurse. "If your visitors can't behave—"

"You'll throw 'em out?" asked Polowski hopefully.

"No need," said Ollie. "We're packing up the pipes. By the way, folks, we're available for private parties, birthdays, cocktail hours. Just get in touch with our business manager—" at this, Milo smiled and waved "—to set up your own special performance."

Polowski groaned, "I want to go back to bed."

"Not yet," said the nurse. "You need the extra stimulation." Then, with a sly wink at Ollie, she turned and whisked out of the room.

"Well," said Cathy. "I think I've done my part to cheer you up. Now it's time I hit the road."

Polowski looked at her in astonishment. "You're leaving me with these lunatics?"

"Have to. I have a plane to catch."

"Where you going?"

"Mexico. Jack called to say they're shooting already. So I thought I'd get on down there and whip up a few monsters."

"What about Victor?"

"What about him?"

"I thought—that is—" Polowski looked at Ollie and Milo. Both men merely shrugged. "He's going to miss you."

"I don't think so." She turned once again to gaze out the window. Below, in the walkway, an old woman sat in a wheelchair, her wan face turned gratefully to the sun. Soon Cathy would be enjoying that very sunshine, somewhere on a Mexican beach.

By their silence, she knew the three men didn't know what to say. After all, Victor was their friend, as well. They couldn't defend or condemn him. Neither could she. She simply loved him, in ways that made her decision to leave all the more right. She'd been in love before, she knew that the very worst thing a woman can sense in a man is indifference.

She didn't want to be around to see it in Victor's eyes.

Gathering up her purse, she said, "Guys, I guess this is it."

Ollie shook his head. "I really wish you'd hang around. He'll be back any day. Besides, you can't break up our great little quartet."

"Sam can take my place on the kazoo."

"No way," said Polowski.

She planted a kiss on his balding head. "Get better. The country needs you."

Polowski sighed. "I'm glad somebody does."

"I'll write you from Mexico!" She slung her purse over her shoulder and turned. One step was all she managed before she halted in astonishment.

Victor was standing in the doorway, a suitcase in hand. He cocked his head. "What's this about Mexico?"

She couldn't answer. She just kept staring at him, thinking how unfair it was that the man she was trying so hard to escape should look so heartbreakingly wonderful.

"You got back just in time," said Ollie. "She's leaving."

"What?" Victor dropped his suitcase and stared at her in dismay. Only then did she notice his wrinkled clothes, the day-old growth of beard shadowing his face. The toe of a sock poked out from a corner of the closed suitcase.

"You can't be leaving," he said.

She cleared her throat. "It was unexpected. Jack needs me."

"Did something happen? Is there some emergency?"

"No, it's just that they're filming and, oh, things are a royal mess on the set…" She glanced at her watch, a gesture designed to speed her escape. "Look, I'll miss my plane. I promise I'll give you a call when I get to—"

"You're not his only makeup artist."

"No, but—"

"He can do the movie without you."

"Yes, but—"

"Do you *want* to leave? Is that it?"

She didn't answer. She could only look at him mutely, the anguish showing plainly in her eyes.

Gently, firmly, he took her hand. "Excuse us, guys," he said to the others. "The lady and I are going for a walk."

Outside, leaves blew across the brown winter lawn. They walked beneath a row of oak trees, through patches of sun and shadow. Suddenly he stopped and pulled her around to face him.

"Tell me now," he said. "What gave you this crazy idea of leaving?"

She looked down. "I didn't think it made much difference to you."

"Wouldn't make a *difference?* Cathy, I was climbing the walls! Thinking of ways to get out of that hotel room and back to you! You have no idea how I worried. I wondered if you were safe—if this whole crazy mess was really over. The lawyers wouldn't let me call out, not until the hearings were finished. I did manage to sneak out and call Milo's house. No one answered."

"We were probably here, visiting Sam."

"And I was going crazy. They had me answering the same damn questions over and over again. And all I could think of was how much I missed you." He shook his head. "First chance I got, I flew the coop. And got snowed in for hours in Chicago. But I made it. I'm here. Just in time, it seems." Gently he took her by the shoulders. "Now. Tell me. Are you still flying off to Jack?"

"I'm not leaving for Jack. I'm leaving for *myself*. Because I know this won't work."

"Cathy, after what we've been through together, we can make *anything* work."

"Not—not this."

Slowly he let his hands drop, but his gaze remained on her face. "That night we made love," he said softly. "That didn't tell you something?"

"But it wasn't *me* you were making love to! You were thinking of Lily—"

"Lily?" He shook his head in bewilderment. "Where does she come in?"

"You loved her so much—"

"And you loved Jack once. Remember?"

"I fell out of love. You never did. No matter how much I try, I'll never measure up to her. I won't be smart enough or kind enough—"

"Cathy, stop."

"I won't be *her*."

"I don't want you to be her! I want the woman who'll hang off fire escapes with me and—and drag me off the side of the road. I want the woman who saved my life. The woman who calls herself average. The woman who doesn't know just how extraordinary she really is." He took her face in his hands and tilted it up to his. "Yes, Lily was a wonderful woman. She was wise and kind and caring. But she wasn't you. And she and I— we weren't the perfect couple. I used to think it was my fault, that if I were just a better lover—"

"You're a wonderful lover, Victor."

"No. Don't you see, it's *you*. You bring it out in me. All the want and need." He pulled her face close to his and his voice dropped to a whisper. "When you and I made love that night, it was like the very first time for me. No, it was even better. Because I loved you."

"And I loved you," she whispered.

He pulled her into his arms and kissed her, his fingers burrowing deep into her hair. "Cathy, Cathy," he murmured. "We've been so busy trying to stay alive we haven't had time to say all the things we should have…"

His arms suddenly stiffened as a startling round of applause erupted above them. They looked up. Three grinning faces peered down at them from a hospital balcony.

"Hit it, boys!" yelled Ollie.

A clarinet, piccolo and kazoo screeched into concert. The melody was doubtful. Still, Cathy thought she recognized the familiar strains of George Gershwin. "Someone to Watch Over Me."

Victor groaned. "I say we try this again, but with a different band. And no audience."

She laughed. "Mexico?"

"Definitely." He grabbed her hand and pulled her toward a taxi idling at the curb.

"But, Victor!" she protested. "What about our luggage? All my clothes—"

He cut her off with another kiss, one that left her dizzy and breathless and starved for more.

"Forget the luggage," she whispered. "Forget everything. Let's just go…"

They climbed into the taxi. That's when the band on the hospital balcony abruptly switched to a new melody, one Cathy didn't at first recognize. Then, out of the muddy strains, the kazoo screeched out a solo that, for a few notes, was perfectly in tune. They were playing *Tannhäuser*. Wedding music!

"What the hell's that terrible noise?" asked the taxi driver.

"Music," said Victor, grinning down at Cathy. "The most beautiful music in the world."

She fell into his arms, and he held her there.

The taxi pulled away from the curb. But even as they drove away, even as they left the hospital far behind them, they thought they could hear it in the distance: the sound of Sam Polowski's kazoo, playing one last fading note of farewell.

* * * * *

USA TODAY bestselling author **Rita Herron** wrote her first book when she was twelve but didn't think real people grew up to be writers. Now she writes so she doesn't have to get a real job. A former kindergarten teacher and workshop leader, she traded storytelling to kids for writing romance, and now she writes romantic comedies and romantic suspense. Rita lives in Georgia with her family. She loves to hear from readers, so please visit her website, ritaherron.com.

Books by Rita Herron

Harlequin Intrigue

A Badge of Honor Mystery

Mysterious Abduction
Left to Die
Protective Order
Suspicious Circumstances

The Heroes of Horseshoe Creek

Lock, Stock and McCullen
McCullen's Secret Son
Roping Ray McCullen
Warrior Son
The Missing McCullen
The Last McCullen

Cold Case at Camden Crossing
Cold Case at Carlton's Canyon
Cold Case at Cobra Creek
Cold Case in Cherokee Crossing

Visit the Author Profile page at
Harlequin.com for more titles.

THE MISSING
TWIN

Rita Herron

To Mother
for all the love she gave her own twins...

Chapter 1

Fear clogged five-year-old Sara Andrews's throat. She could see her twin sister running from the old wooden house, stumbling down the porch steps, crying as she raced toward the woods.

"Help me," Cissy cried. "He's gonna hurt Mommy!"

The wind whistled, shaking the trees. Leaves swirled and rained down. A dog howled in the distance.

Then thunder boomed.

No, not thunder.

It was the big, hulking man storming down the steps. "Cissy!" the monster bellowed. "Come back here."

He slapped at the branches with his beefy fists, moving so fast he was nearly on top of her. Then he lunged for her.

Cissy screamed and darted to the right, running, running, running into the darkness....

The monster reached a pawlike hand toward her and snatched her jacket. Cissy screamed again, stumbled and fell to the ground. But her jacket slid off in the man's hands, and he cursed.

Sweat slid down Sara's temple. Her heart was pounding so loud she could hear it beating in her ears. "Get up," Sara whispered. "Get up and run, Cissy."

As if Cissy heard her, she took a deep breath, grabbed a fistful of dirt and hurled it at the man.

The dust sprayed his eyes and he cursed, then swung one fist toward Cissy. Cissy dodged the blow, pushed herself to her hands and knees and stood. Tree branches cracked. The wind screeched.

The monster roared and dove for her.

"No!" Sara cried. "Run, Cissy, run."

Tears streamed down her sister's cheeks as Cissy tried to run, but the monster yanked her by the hair and dragged her back toward the house.

"Help me!" Cissy cried. "Please, help me!"

"No!" Sara screamed. "Let her go...."

Madelyn Andrews raced toward her daughter's bedroom, her lungs tightening at the sound of her daughter's terrified sobs. Outside, the wind roared off the mountain and sleet pelted the window, reminding her that a late winter storm raged around the small town of Sanctuary, North Carolina.

Shivering with the cold, she threw open the door, flipped on the sunflower lamp Sara had begged for and crossed the distance to her little girl's bed. Sara was thrashing around, tangled in the bright green comforter, sobbing and shaking.

"No, don't hurt her, don't hurt Cissy..."

Madelyn's heart broke, worry throbbing inside her as she eased herself onto the mattress and gently shook Sara.

"Honey, wake up. It's just a nightmare," she whispered. Although Sara would insist that it was real.

Sara sobbed harder, swinging out her hands as if fighting off an invisible monster, and Madelyn pulled her into her arms. Tears blurred her own eyes as she rocked her back and forth. "Shh, honey, Mommy's here. It's all right."

"Gonna hurt Mommy…" Sara wailed. "Help Cissy. We have to help Cissy!"

"Shh, baby." Madelyn stroked Sara's fine, blond hair. "No one is going to hurt Mommy. I'm right here."

Sara jerked her eyes open, her pupils distorted, her lower lip quivering. For a moment, she stared at Madelyn as if she didn't recognize her.

"But Cissy's mommy is hurt," Sara said in a shaky voice. "The bad man chased Cissy into the woods and he catched her, and…"

"It was a dream." Madelyn cupped Sara's face between her hands, imploring her to believe her. "A really bad dream, sweetheart, but it was just a nightmare."

"No," Sara choked out. "It was real. Cissy's in trouble and we gots to help her or he's gonna hurt her…"

"Oh, honey," Madelyn said softly.

Sara gulped. "It *was* real, Mommy. I saw Cissy." Tears rolled down her face. "And she saw me. She begged me to help her. I tolded her to get up and run, but he caught her and dragged her back to the house…."

Shaken by the horror in Sara's voice, Madelyn took a deep breath, desperately trying to calm the anxiety bleeding through her.

She dried Sara's tears with her fingers. "Sara, I told you that we lost Cissy a long time ago."

"No," Sara said with a firm shake of her head. "She lives with that other mommy. But if we don't helps her, that mean man's gonna kill 'em both."

Madelyn hugged Sara to her, lost in turmoil.

Something was very wrong with her little girl. She'd been having these nightmares for the past two months, ever since they'd moved back to Sanctuary, and nothing Madelyn had done or said had helped. Not her long talks with her about Cissy, Sara's twin who they'd lost at birth, or the therapists Madelyn had consulted for assistance.

"Please, Mommy," Sara cried. "We gots to do something."

A tear slid down Madelyn's cheek. The day the twins had been born was the happiest and saddest day of her life. She'd gotten Sara but lost her sister.

She'd heard that twins had a special connection, but why was Sara still dreaming that Cissy had survived?

Knowing neither she nor Sara would sleep well the rest of the night, she carried Sara to her bed, then snuggled beside her. Sara lay on her side, sniffling for another hour, then finally drifted into an exhausted sleep.

Madelyn's heart wrenched, and she lay and watched her daughter, unable to sleep. Just as dawn streaked the sky, her telephone jangled. Who could be calling at this hour? She checked the caller ID. Her mother.

She grabbed the handset, then slid from the bed, walked to the window and connected the call.

"Mom? What's wrong? Are you all right?"

"Yes, honey, I'm fine. Have you seen the news?"

"No, why? What's going on?"

"A big story aired about a doctor in Sanctuary who stole babies and sold them. His name was Dr. Emery. Isn't that the doctor who delivered the twins?"

"Yes. Oh, my god. What else did the story say?"

"This lady named Nina Nash thought her baby died in that big hospital fire eight years ago but discovered her child was alive. She hired these detectives at an agency called Guardian Angel Investigations there in Sanctuary. These men are all dedicated to finding missing children and they found her little girl."

A cold chill swept up Madelyn's spine. She glanced back at the bed where Sara was sleeping.

Dear God.

Was it possible that Cissy could have survived?

Caleb Walker entered the offices of GAI, his neck knotted with nerves. He hadn't liked the sound of his boss's voice when he called. The urgency had him postponing his visit to the cemetery to visit his wife's grave this morning, and that pissed him off. He'd wanted to go by first thing, to pay his respects, leave Mara's flowers, talk to her and beg her forgiveness one more time....

Gage's voice rose from his office, breaking into his thoughts, and Caleb forced himself to focus. There would be time for seeing Mara later. Time to drown his sorrows and guilt.

He climbed the steps to Gage's office, his mind racing. Had another child gone missing?

Or was there another case related to Sanctuary Hospital? Ever since the news had broken about the recovery of Nina Nash's daughter and Dr. Emery's arrest for selling babies, the phones had gone crazy.

People from all over were demanding to know if

their adoptions were legal. GAI had been plagued by crank calls, as well, two from distraught women whose accusations of baby kidnapping had turned out to be false. The women had been so desperate for a child they'd tried to use the illegal adoptions to claim one for themselves.

Caleb twisted the hand-carved arrowhead around his neck to calm himself as he knocked on his boss's office door.

"Come in."

Caleb opened the door and Gage stood.

"I'm glad you're here," Gage said without preamble. "We have a new client. One I'd like for you to handle."

Caleb narrowed his eyes. "Why me?"

Gage's eyes darkened. "You'll know after you meet her and her five-year-old daughter, Sara. Sara insists she sees her twin in her nightmares, that her sister is in trouble."

"I don't understand," Caleb said. "Sounds like a child having bad dreams, not a missing person case."

"It gets even more interesting." Gage flicked his gaze to the conference room across the hall. "The mother claims the twin died at birth, but Sara insists she's alive."

Damn. Gage requested him because of his so-called sixth sense. He wished to hell he'd never divulged that detail.

But Gage had caught him in a weak moment.

Gage motioned for him to follow. "Come on, they're waiting."

Caleb rolled his hands into fists, then forced himself to flex them again, struggling to control his emotions. Emotions had no place in business. And business was his life now.

The moment Caleb entered the conference room, he spotted the woman sitting in a wing chair cradling the little girl in her lap. Gage had purposely designed the room with cozy seating nooks to put clients at ease.

But nothing about this woman appeared to be at ease.

Her slender body radiated with tension, her eyes looked haunted, her expression wary.

Yet he was also struck by her startling beauty. Copper-colored hair draped her shoulders and flowed like silk around a heart-shaped face. Big, green eyes gazed at him as if she desperately needed a friend, and freckles dotted her fair skin, making her look young and vulnerable. Her outfit was simple, too, not meant to be enticing—long denim skirt, peasant blouse—yet the soft colors made her look utterly feminine.

And downright earthy.

Earthy in his book meant sexy. Lethal combinations to a man who had been celibate for the past three years.

Dammit. He hadn't been attracted to another woman since Mara. He sure as hell didn't want to be attracted to a client. Not one with a kid who claimed to see her dead sister.

Then his gaze fell to the little blonde munchkin, and his lungs tightened. She looked tiny and frail and terrified and so lost that his protective instincts kicked in.

"Ms. Andrews," Gage began. "This is Caleb Walker. He's one of our agents at GAI. I'd like for him to hear your story."

The woman squared her shoulders as if anticipating a confrontation. She expected skepticism.

"You can call me Madelyn," she said in a husky voice that sounded as if it was laced with whiskey.

Gage claimed the love seat, leaving the other wing

chair nearest Madelyn for him. Caleb lowered himself into it, aware his size might intimidate the little girl.

"What's your name?" he asked in a gentle tone.

Eyes that mirrored her mother's stared up at him as if she was trying to decide if he was friend or foe. Smart kid. She should be wary of strangers.

He smiled slowly, trying to ease her discomfort. But his senses prickled, suggesting she was special in some way. That she possessed a sixth sense herself.

Not that he would wish that on anyone, especially a kid.

"Let's see," he said, a smile quirking his mouth. "Are you Little Miss Sunshine?"

A tiny smile lit her eyes, and she relaxed slightly and loosened her grip on her blanket. "No, silly. I'm Sara."

"Hi, Sara," he said gruffly. "That's a pretty name."

"Thank you," she said, her tone sounding grown up for such a little bitty thing. "It's my Gran's middle name."

"Okay, Sara. Tell me what's going on so I can help you."

Madelyn stroked her daughter's hair. "Sara's been having nightmares for the past two months, ever since we moved back to town."

"Where are you from?" Caleb asked, probing for background information.

Madelyn hugged Sara closer. "We moved to Charlotte four years ago to be near my mom, but Sara was born in Sanctuary. Recently my mother suffered a stroke, and I found a nursing facility here that she liked, so I bought the craft shop in town, and we packed up and moved back."

"I see," Caleb said. Had the move triggered these

nightmares? "Sara, did you have dreams of your sister when you lived in Charlotte?"

Sara nodded and twirled a strand of hair around her finger. "We talked and sang songs and told secrets."

Caleb narrowed his eyes. "What kinds of secrets?"

Sara pursed her mouth. "They're not secrets if I tell."

Hmm. She was loyal to her sister. But those secrets might be important.

"She has dreamed about her twin all her life," Madelyn confirmed. "But lately those dreams have been disturbing."

Sara piped up. "Her name is Cissy, and she looks just like me."

Caleb nodded, aware that she used the present tense. "Sara and Cissy. How old are you?"

"Five," Sara said and held up five fingers. "Cissy's five, too."

He smiled again. "You're identical twins?"

She swung her feet. "Yep, 'cept I gots a birthmark on my right arm and hers is on the other side." She pointed to a small, pale, crescent-moon shape on her forearm.

Caleb folded his hands. He needed to keep Sara talking. "Tell me what happens in your dreams, Sara."

Terror darkened the little girl's face. "Cissy is scared and she's screamin' and she runned into the woods."

Damn. He understood about nightmares, how real and haunting they could seem. "Who is she running from?" Caleb asked.

"From a big, mean man. He screamed at her mommy," Sara said with conviction. "Cissy says he's gonna kill them."

Caleb intentionally lowered his voice. "Can you see his face? Does she call him by name?"

Sara chewed on her thumb for a moment as if trying to picture the man in her mind. "No, I can't see him." Her voice rose with anxiety. "But I saw Cissy running and crying."

Caleb clenched his hands, listening, hating the terror in the little girl's voice. The last thing he wanted to do was traumatize a troubled child by doubting her or confirming her fears. And she was genuinely afraid and believed what she was telling him.

His sixth sense kicked in. This little girl was…different. Did she truly have a psychic connection to her twin?

Other questions bombarded him: If her sister was dead, was Sara seeing and conversing with her spirit? Was Sara a medium? If so, why was she seeing images of Cissy at the same age as herself instead of the infant she'd been when she died? Was Cissy's growth a figment of Sara's imagination?

Another theory rattled through his head. Or could Sara be experiencing premonitions? Could Cissy's spirit be trying to warn Sara that Sara was in danger from some future attacker?

"You're a brave girl," Caleb said, then patted Sara's arm. "And if you see anything else—the man's face, or the mommy's—I want you to tell me. Okay?"

Sara bobbed her little head up and down, although she looked wrung out now, as if relaying her nightmare had drained her. Or maybe she was worried that describing the terrifying ordeal might make it come true.

He lifted his gaze to Madelyn. "Can we talk alone?"

Her wary gaze flew to his. "I don't like to leave Sara by herself."

Gage retrieved a pad of paper and some crayons and

gestured to the coffee table. "It's okay, Madelyn. I have a little girl, too. Her name is Ruby and she likes to draw when she comes to the office." He stooped down and handed the crayons to Sara. "Would you like to use Ruby's crayons to draw a picture of Cissy while Caleb talks to your mother?"

Sara studied him for a long moment, then nodded. Madelyn reluctantly stood and settled Sara on the floor in front of the coffee table. Caleb gestured to the door, and she led the way out into the hallway.

The moment he closed the door, she whirled on him, arms crossed. "Listen, Mr. Walker, I know you probably think that Sara is disturbed, and believe me, I've taken her to shrinks, consulted with specialists, tried to talk to her myself, but these nightmares keep reoccurring, and there has to be a reason."

Caleb shifted. "Did these doctors make a diagnosis?"

Madelyn sighed, her expression strained. "Oh, yes, lots of them. The first doctor suggested Sara was seeing herself, that the twin was a mirror image. Doctor Number Two implied that she was terrified because she had no father, then suggested she made up the bizarre connection with Cissy to get attention. His colleague indicated Sara might be bipolar and wanted to put her in a special twin study, run a mountain of tests and analyze her brain." She blew out a breath, sending her bangs fluttering. "The last one suggested she was schizophrenic and advised me to let him prescribe drugs."

Caleb frowned. "Did you try medication?"

"No," Madelyn said emphatically. "She's only five years old." She paced across the hall, her hands knotting in the folds of her skirt. "I really hoped that I could handle it, that if I carried Sara to see Cissy's grave she'd accept that her sister is gone."

"What happened at the cemetery?" Caleb asked. "Did she see Cissy?"

Madelyn cleared her throat. "She insisted that Cissy wasn't buried in the grave. That it was empty."

Tears filled Madelyn's eyes, making Caleb's gut clench.

"But I know she is," Madelyn said in a haunted whisper. "Because I buried her myself."

Chapter 2

Sara's words haunted Madelyn as Caleb coaxed her into his office.

"Cissy's not dead, Mommy. She gots another mommy, and she likes to play dolls and read stories just like me." Then Sara had started to cry. *"But her mommy's in trouble and this mean man's gonna hurt her and Cissy."*

Only she *had* buried Cissy five years ago.

Caleb propped himself against the desk edge while she sank onto a chair.

"If you're so sure Sara is wrong, why did you come to GAI?" Caleb asked.

Madelyn desperately tried to decipher the intensity in his deep brown eyes. The man scared the hell out of her.

He was huge, broad-shouldered, muscular, dark-skinned, with shoulder-length thick, black hair, and had the gruffest voice she'd ever heard. His Native American roots ran deep and infused him with a quiet strength that radiated from his every pore but also made him appear dangerous, like a warrior from the past.

Yet he had been gentle with Sara and obviously the head of GAI trusted him.

"My mother phoned. She heard a news story about GAI uncovering some illegal adoptions associated with Dr. Emery, babies he delivered at Sanctuary Hospital."

"You delivered the twins there?"

"Yes."

"What about the father?" Caleb asked.

Madelyn chewed her bottom lip. "He left us when Sara started calling her dead sister's name. I haven't seen him or heard from him since."

Caleb frowned. "He doesn't send child support?"

"I didn't want it," Madelyn said. "Not that he would have come through. He was having financial problems back then, his business failing."

Caleb sighed. "I'm sorry. Tell me about the delivery."

Grief welled inside Madelyn. "The night I went into labor, I had a car accident," Madelyn began. "I was going to the store when a car sideswiped me. I lost control and careened into a ditch." She knotted her hands. "My water broke and I went into labor."

Caleb narrowed his eyes. "What happened to the driver?"

Anger surged through Madelyn at the reminder. "He left the scene."

Caleb's big body tensed. "He didn't stop to see if you were okay or call an ambulance?"

"No." Madelyn rubbed her hands up and down her arms. "And the police never caught him." Not that they'd looked very hard. And she hadn't seen the vehicle so she hadn't been able to give them a description of it or the driver.

Caleb's expression darkened. "So the accident triggered your labor?"

Madelyn nodded.

"Were you injured anywhere else?"

She shrugged. "Some bruises and contusions. I lost consciousness and the doctor said I was hemorrhaging, so he did an emergency C-section and took the babies."

Caleb's jaw clenched. "You weren't awake during the delivery?"

"No," Madelyn said, fidgeting.

"But you held the babies when you regained consciousness?"

"I was out for a couple of hours. When I came to, I got to hold Sara for a minute. She'd been in ICU, being monitored." Madelyn ran a hand through her hair. "But Cissy... No, I never held her. Dr. Emery said...she was deformed, stillborn, that it was better that I not remember her that way."

Caleb arched a thick, black brow. "So you never actually saw your other baby?"

"No..." Emotions welled in her throat. She tried to steel herself against them, but memories of that night crashed around her. The fear, the disorientation, the joy, the loss... "I...was so distraught, so grief-stricken that the doctor sedated me." She wiped at a tear slipping down her cheek. "Besides I... I believed Dr. Emery. Then there was Sara, and she was so beautiful and tiny, and I was so glad she'd survived. And she needed me...."

Caleb's silence made her rethink that night, and questions nagged at her. If she hadn't seen Cissy, maybe she hadn't died or been deformed at all.

"Did the medical examiner perform an autopsy on the baby?" Caleb asked.

"No." Tears burned the backs of her eyelids. "I... didn't want it. Didn't want to put her through it."

Although maybe she should have insisted. Then she'd have proof that her baby hadn't survived, and she'd know exactly what had been wrong with her.

Sara's insistence that she saw Cissy in her visions taunted her. If Dr. Emery had lied to other people, perhaps he'd lied to her. "We have to talk to Dr. Emery and force him to tell me the truth about Cissy."

"I'm afraid that's impossible," Caleb said quietly. "Dr. Emery hanged himself the day after he was arrested."

A desolate feeling engulfed Madelyn. "If he's dead, how will we ever learn the truth?"

Caleb's intense gaze settled on her. "Trust me. We'll find the truth."

"Then you'll investigate?"

"Yes." He gestured toward the conference room and pushed open the door to where Sara was drawing.

The childlike sketch showed Sara and her twin sister displaying their birthmarks. A second picture revealed a greenhouse full of sunflowers, and a tire swing hanging from a big tree in the yard.

Sara had also drawn an ugly, hairy, monsterlike man with jagged teeth and pawlike hands. "That's the meanie gonna hurt Cissy and her mommy," Sara said.

She turned her big, green eyes toward Caleb. "Will you stop him, Mister?"

Anxiety knotted Caleb's shoulders. How could he say no to this innocent little girl? She seemed so terrified....

But if he promised to save her sister and this woman and failed, he wouldn't be able to live with himself. Not after failing Mara and his own son.

Hell, he was getting way ahead of himself. First, he had to determine if Cissy Andrews was actually alive.

The fact that Sara truly believed that she was real was obvious. But he couldn't dismiss the shrinks' theories, either. Not yet.

Gage glanced at the sketch, then at him as if silently asking his opinion.

He gave him a noncommittal look. "We need access to Emery's records."

"Afraid that's not going to happen," Gage said. "He destroyed them before he killed himself."

Damn. So they had no records, and he couldn't push a dead man for answers. His visions didn't work that way.

"What about the lawyer who handled the adoptions?" Caleb asked. "Wasn't his name Mansfield?"

"Yeah. The sheriff brought him in for questioning. He's facing charges, but his case is still pending, so he was released on bail."

"Then we look at his records," Caleb said.

"D.A. already confiscated them," Gage said. "And she's not sharing. Not with privacy issues and the legal and moral rights regarding adoptions."

Caleb stewed over that problem. They didn't work for the cops or have to follow the rules. If he knew where those records were, he'd find a way to search them.

But talking to Mansfield would be faster.

First, there was something else that had to be done. Something that would be painful for Madelyn. But a task that was necessary in order to verify whether or not that grave held a baby.

"Madelyn," he said in a voice low enough not to reach Sara's ears. "We need to exhume the casket you buried."

Grief flickered in her eyes as she glanced at Sara who was madly coloring another picture of her and Cissy. This time they were holding hands, dancing in the middle of a sea of sunflowers.

"All right," Madelyn said firmly. "If it'll help us learn the truth, then let's do it as soon as possible."

Madelyn pictured the Lost Angels section at Sanctuary Gardens where they'd held Cissy's memorial service in her mind and nausea flooded her. Still, with the questions Caleb had raised, Sara's nightmares, and the revelations about Dr. Emery, she wouldn't rest until she knew if Cissy was really buried in that grave.

Compassion darkened Caleb's eyes. "Okay. We'll get the ball rolling."

Madelyn nodded, gripping her emotions with a firm hand. For so long she had accepted that Cissy was dead that it was hard for her to wrap her mind around the fact that she might have survived. That she might be living somewhere with another family. That a physician would actually deceive his patients and sell their babies.

But the doctor's arrest was proof of the possibility, creating doubts, and she had to investigate or she would always wonder.

Sara ran to her, waving her drawing, her ponytail bobbing. "Look, Mommy, Cissy's gonna be so happy when we brings her home with us. She loves sunflowers. They're all around her."

"The sunflowers are beautiful," Madelyn said, her heart aching as worry knotted her insides. Was it true that twins were only half of a whole? What if they didn't find out Cissy was alive and bring her home? How would Sara take the news?

Would she be able to move on and finally be happy?

Sara tugged at Madelyn's hand. "We gots to hurry, Mommy."

Madelyn stroked Sara's hair away from her forehead. "Sweetheart, that's why we're here. Caleb—Mr. Walker—is going to investigate and find out why you're seeing these scary things."

Sara angled her face toward Caleb. "Thank you for 'vestigatin', Mister."

Madelyn smiled in spite of her turmoil because, after all, Sara was a charmer. Caleb knelt and extended his hand to Sara, and Madelyn couldn't help but notice how strong and calloused and tanned his fingers were, how masculine.

"I promise I'll do whatever I can to help you, Sara."

An odd look crossed Sara's face, then she took Caleb's hand and turned it over in her own small one and studied his palm as if she could see inside the man through his fingers. Madelyn noted the breadth of his palm against Sara's tiny one and thought that Sara might be frightened of him, but she seemed to immediately trust him.

In fact, neither one spoke for a moment. They simply stared at each other, silent, assessing, as if sharing some private moment.

"You gots an Indian name?" Sara asked in a whisper.

Caleb nodded. "Firewalker."

Sara's eyes widened. "You walks on fire? Does it hurt?"

Caleb shook his head then pressed a hand to his chest. "No. Not if you hone in on your inner strength and power. On peace and faith."

Sara smiled. "I gots faith that you're gonna find Cissy."

A pained look crossed Caleb's face. "I will do my best, Sara," he said gruffly.

Madelyn's heart melted. Sara had not only missed her twin sister, but she'd missed having a father, as well. And she had been so caught up in raising her little girl, on being a single mother, surviving the loss of her husband and Cissy and making ends meet, that Madelyn hadn't once considered a personal relationship with a man.

Or finding a father for Sara.

She didn't need a man, she'd decided long ago. Sara had her, and she would be enough.

Only she wasn't enough. And now she needed this detective's help.

Her breath fluttered as he swung his gaze up to her. His dark eyes sparkled with questions, yet she also sensed that she could trust him.

She hoped to hell that was true.

Sara dropped his hand and skipped to the door.

"Caleb, you'll let me know what you find." She didn't know if she could bear to be at the exhumation.

He nodded, then extended his hand to her this time. Wariness filled Madelyn, but she slid her hand into his. An odd sensation rippled through her at the feel of his rough, leathery skin against her own. It had been so long since she'd touched a man that her belly fluttered with awareness.

She pulled away immediately. She couldn't afford to indulge in a romantic flirtation. Finding out the truth about Cissy and ending these nightmares for Sara was all that mattered.

As soon as Madelyn left, Caleb set the wheels in motion for the exhumation.

"Sheriff Gray said he expects this won't be the last request for one," Gage said. "Damn Dr. Emery."

"Damn him for killing himself," Caleb said. "He should have to face every patient he deceived and make things right." Although there was no restitution, nothing that could make up for the loss of a child.

"The sheriff said workers will be meeting at the cemetery early in the morning for the exhumation. They want to make sure it's as private as possible," Gage said.

Caleb nodded. "I'll meet them there."

Yanking on his rawhide jacket, he headed outside. Time to pay his respects to Mara.

Wind battered his Jeep as he plowed across the mountain toward the Native American burial grounds. As he parked and climbed out, the sounds of ancient war drums and echoes of fallen friends bombarded him. Stones and wooden markers etched with family names stood in honor of loved ones, while handmade Native American beads and baskets decorated others, holding treasures.

Gripping a bouquet of lilies in one hand, he crossed the graveyard, grateful he'd managed to bring Mara here where her own parents were also buried. He paused at their markers, then stopped in front of Mara's, his heart heavy as he placed the flowers on her grave.

Today would have been Mara's twenty-eighth birthday. If she had lived.

And his son, if he'd been born, would have been two.

That hollowness he'd lived with since Mara's murder gnawed at him, and he traced a finger over Mara's name. His throat tightened as an image of what his son might have looked like materialized in his mind.

A toddler with chubby cheeks, thick, black hair, dark skin, and brown eyes like Mara's. His son would have been walking and climbing onto everything now.

But his little boy had never had a chance…

The icy cold of the winter wind seeped through him, adding to the chill he'd felt for the past three years. Three years of living alone. Of wondering why Mara and his unborn child had been taken instead of him.

Three years of living with the guilt.

Gritting his teeth, he stood, the vision of his son disappearing in the foggy haze. But Mara waited, an ethereal beauty in her traditional white wedding dress.

Although each day he sensed her fading. That her soul was preparing to move on. That she was waiting on something…something she needed from him…

For him to let her go? He wasn't sure that was possible. The guilt alone kept him coming back, kept him praying, kept him…prisoner.

Why couldn't it have been him instead of her?

Sara's insistence that her sister was still alive echoed in his mind. He understood the draw Sara felt, the difficulty in letting a loved one go. Did Sara suffer from survivor guilt as he did?

The sound of a flute echoed in the wind, and he

closed his eyes, remembering their marriage ceremony. The traditional Love Flute playing, the fire ceremony with the golden glow illuminating Mara's beautiful face, the Rite of Seven Steps, the moment the traditional blue blanket had been removed from around them and the white one enfolded them, signifying their new ways of happiness and peace.

Yet that happiness and peace had been shattered a month later with bullets that had been meant for him. Mara had been struck instead and died in his place.

Hell. A fat lot of good his vision or gift, whatever the hell it was, had done him.

He hadn't foreseen Mara's death or he might have been able to stop it.

"What should I do, Mara? I don't want this gift, and I sure as hell don't want that little girl to have it."

But he had felt something kinetic pass between them when he'd touched Sara's tiny hand. He'd seen the dark images in her mind. Felt the violence she felt.

And he'd witnessed a little girl identical to Sara running for her life, disappearing into the dark woods just as Sara had described....

What if Sara was right? What if her sister was alive and in trouble?

"I know I failed you," Caleb said in a pained voice. "I just pray I do not fail this little girl."

Madelyn's big, green eyes and frail smile flashed in his head, and a twinge of guilt assaulted him. He had also experienced a faint flicker of awareness when he'd touched Madelyn, a current of desire he hadn't felt since Mara.

But that was wrong. Mara had been his wife. He owed her his dedication. His life.

The wind suddenly whipped through the trees, hissing as it tossed dry leaves to the ground and sent them swirling across the cemetery. The scent of wilted roses filled the air, the sound of broken limbs snapping mingled with the echoes of the dead.

He waited, hoped, prayed he would hear Mara's voice one more time, but a bleak silence followed.

He turned and hurried back to his Jeep, started the engine and peeled from the parking lot. Tomorrow was the exhumation. It wouldn't be easy for Madelyn.

But nothing personal could or would happen between them.

Not ever.

Nightmares of Mara and his son tormented Caleb all night. He woke drenched in sweat. No wonder he had connected with Madelyn and her daughter.

He and Madelyn had both lost a child.

A five-mile run and shower, then he grabbed a Thermos of coffee and jumped in his Jeep. But dread filled him as he drove across the mountain to Sanctuary Gardens. The sheriff's car was parked in the cemetery parking lot, a crew of men a few feet away preparing to exhume the body.

Anxiety needled him as he swerved in beside the patrol car, jammed his hands in the pockets of his jacket and strode toward the sheriff.

Sheriff Gray extended his hand. "You must be Caleb Walker?"

Caleb nodded. "Thanks for arranging this so quickly. You have the paperwork in order?"

Gray indicated the envelope in his hand. "Signature from Madelyn Andrews giving us permission. The license. And—" he gestured toward a tall, white-haired man with glasses wearing a lab coat "—Environmental Health Officer present, as required by law."

Caleb glanced at the E.H. Officer as he met up with the men designated to dig the grave. The transport service with the second coffin arrived and the driver stepped out, then crossed the graveyard to speak to the sheriff while two men from the funeral home erected a tent around the grave for privacy and to show respect for the grave while the exhumation took place.

Sheriff Gray introduced him to the medical examiner, Dr. Hal Rollo, who seemed pensive as he waited to do his job.

Caleb had witnessed a couple of exhumations before, but none for a child.

The thought made his stomach knot.

"You really believe there's truth to the woman's story?" Sheriff Gray asked. "I heard her kid is the one stirring things up, that she claims she sees her dead twin."

So much for keeping that part of the story under wraps to avoid skepticism. "I guess we'll know soon enough."

He followed Gray over to the Lost Angels corner of the cemetery, noting the wrought-iron gate protecting the resting place for the little souls. Ivory doves were perched above a bubbling fountain, and a statue of Jesus, hands folded in prayer as he looked toward the heavens, sat at the head of the plots as if guarding the angels below. Bright flowers, toy trucks, teddy bears, dolls and various other toys had been left as if to keep the children company, marking birthdays and holidays.

His throat tightened at the sight. Two rows back, he spotted the marker for Cissy Andrews.

The plot had been well maintained, her marker adorned with plastic sunflowers. A small photo of Madelyn and Sara also sat at the head as if to reassure Cissy she wasn't forgotten or alone.

Drawn to the spot, he walked over and knelt beside it, his vision blurring as he studied Cissy's name and birth date. Sometimes touching objects, items of clothing, people triggered his visions.

His hands shook as he reached out to press them over the small grave. Behind him the other men's voices faded to a distant hum. He hesitated, a sliver of apprehension needling him. He might see nothing.

Or he might see the child's small body in the ground.

Sucking in a sharp breath, he told himself he had to do this.

Reality slipped away and the wind screamed through the trees as he laid his hand on the mound.

Chapter 3

Madelyn's emotions pinged back and forth as she drove Sara to her mother's home. She had already called her assistant at the craft shop and asked her to cover for her for a few days. She needed time to see this through, and Sara needed her.

She so did not want to see Cissy's grave upturned. Or her body desecrated.

But she'd trusted Dr. Emery and the hospital staff, virtual strangers, with her daughter before, because of her vulnerable emotional state, and she refused to do that now.

She had to know for sure if Cissy was buried and, if not, where she was.

The images Sara had painted tormented her.

Please dear God, if she did survive, let her be okay.

She glanced at Sara who gripped her blanket in

one hand, a bouquet of sunflowers in her other for her grandmother. Sara never visited without a bouquet, and she always insisted they were from her and Cissy, not just her. Why was Sara obsessed with sunflowers?

Could her daughter possibly have some kind of psychic ability? Madelyn had never actually believed in anything supernatural, but what if she was wrong?

Perspiration trickled down the back of her neck, and she gripped the steering wheel tighter, mentally giving herself a pep talk as she had over the years.

She could do this. She was strong.

She had Sara, and no matter what happened, nothing was going to change that.

"Mommy, I liked Mr. Firewalker."

Madelyn smiled, ignoring the tickle in her belly that the mere mention of the man's name evoked. "I think he liked you, too, sweet pea." She tousled Sara's hair, well aware that Sara didn't always make friends easily. Some of the children in preschool shied away when she boasted about a sister they couldn't see. "After all, how could he not? You're adorable and smart and have that gorgeous smile."

Sara beamed a gap-toothed grin, and Madelyn steered the station wagon into the driveway at the assisted living facility, Sanctuary Seniors, and parked in front of her mother's unit. A few months ago, her mother had suffered a stroke and was partially paralyzed on one side, leaving her confined to a wheelchair. But her mind was quick and seeing Sara always lifted her spirits.

Sara bounded out of the car clutching the flowers in one hand, raced up to the door and banged on the front. "Gran, guess who's here," she sang. "We gots a surprise for you!"

A second later, Liz Cummings, one of the health care workers, greeted Sara with a big hug.

By the time Madelyn made it inside, Sara was already perched on her mother's lap in the wheelchair, talking in an animated voice about the big, dark-skinned Indian who could walk on fire, and Liz was putting the flowers in a vase on the window ledge so her mother could enjoy them.

Sara's mother arched a brow as Madelyn entered. "So is this young man handsome, dear?"

Madelyn blushed. Her mother never ceased to play matchmaker. So far, Madelyn had managed to avoid a real date with the men her mother had thrown in front of her.

"He's big, so biggg, Gran." Sara threw up her hands indicating that he was gigantic, and Madelyn bit back a laugh. "And he's gonna find Cissy. He promised."

Madelyn's smile faded. She hated to give Sara false hopes and then have her be even more devastated if things fell through. "Honey, he's investigating, but we can't be sure what we'll find."

"He will find her," Sara insisted stubbornly. "He said he would and he can walk on fire so he can do anything."

Madelyn's mother, Cora, stroked Sara's hair. "I'm sure he'll do his best, pumpkin. Now, why don't we have a tea party while your mommy does her errands? Liz brought us some cookies, but they look pretty bare to me."

Sara clapped her hands. "We can decorate them, Gran! We'll make 'em look like sunflowers for Cissy!"

"That sounds like a fabulous idea," her mother said.

"Come on," Liz said. "Help me put out the icing and sprinkles so we can make those cookies pretty."

Sara skipped to the kitchen with Liz but worry knitted Madelyn's brow.

"She'll be all right." Her mother wheeled her chair over and clasped Madelyn's hand. "And so will you."

Madelyn soaked in her mother's smile. She loved her and Sara more than she could say. "I don't know what I'd do without you, Mom. Sara and I...we both need you."

Her mother barked a laugh. "Well, I'm not going anywhere, sugar. Now you go and do what you need to do. I'll take care of Sara while you look for Cissy." She tilted her head toward the sunflowers. "I think Sara is right. Cissy loves sunflowers."

Madelyn's stomach twisted. Apparently her mother trusted Sara's visions.

They exchanged concerned looks. But her mother refrained from commenting further on Sara's recent sunflower obsession. They'd both hoped it would play itself out, but now Madelyn wondered if the sunflowers might be some kind of clue to her other daughter.

Pasting on a brave face, she hugged her mother. "I'll call. You two have fun."

"We always do," her mother said with a beaming smile.

Madelyn's throat thickened, and she nodded, afraid if she spoke, the dam holding back her emotions would break, and she'd fall on the floor in a puddle and start sobbing. Once she started, she might not be able to stop.

The morning sun sliced through the bare trees as she jogged to the minivan, then drove around the mountain. Early morning shadows flickered across the dark asphalt as the sun fought through the storm clouds gathering above. She slowed as she spotted the cemetery, dread flooding her at the sight of the sheriff's car and the hearse.

The day of the funeral threatened to replay through Madelyn's head, but she hit the pause button in her brain and zapped it on hold. She refused to relive that day again now with all these men watching.

Swallowing back nerves, she parked and walked to the top of the hill overlooking the Lost Angels corner where the sheriff and three other men stood conferring. Where was Caleb?

Inhaling a breath to fortify her courage, she stumbled down the hill and through the iron gate. Sheriff Gray gave her a concerned look, but she rushed past them, then looked into the tent protecting the site.

Caleb *was* there, kneeling with his hand on Cissy's grave. His dark skin had drained of color, and an odd mixture of grief and pain marred his face.

What was he doing? Could he see inside the grave?

Caleb's world shimmered out of control as he felt a vision coming on. Darkness pulled at him, dragging him into an endless tunnel, a pit of silence that stretched below the ground, desolate, screaming with secrets…

"Caleb?"

The sound of a woman's voice jerked him free of the spell.

"What are you doing?"

Twisting his head sideways, he spotted Madelyn staring at him, her arms crossed, her expression troubled.

He stood abruptly, taking a step back, confused by what he'd seen. By what he hadn't seen. He needed more time, dammit. And he wasn't ready to share his gift just yet. "Nothing. Just thinking about the case." He crooked a thumb toward the sheriff. "Are you ready?"

"Yes." Sheriff Gray gestured toward the E.H. Officer. "Madelyn, this is Oliver Gordon, the Environmental Health Officer. He'll oversee the exhumation."

Madelyn nodded in greeting, obviously struggling with the reality of the task to come and its ramifications.

Gordon cleared his throat. "For health reasons, I have to ask everyone to wait a safe distance away. We must respect this grave as well as the surrounding ones."

"Of course." Madelyn folded her arms around her waist as if to hold herself together while the funeral home employees approached with shovels. The distress on her face made Caleb's protective instincts surge. He wished he could spare her this ordeal, but this exhumation was vital to whether or not they moved forward with an investigation.

Amanda Peterson, GAI's resident forensic anthropologist, climbed from a sporty gray sedan at the top of the hill and walked toward them.

Caleb gestured to Madelyn. "Come on, let's take a walk."

Her face paled, but she didn't argue. Instead, she allowed him to guide her up the hill. Fine tremors rippled through her body as she stopped beneath a giant oak. Caleb rubbed a hand along her neck, hoping to calm her.

Amanda approached them, her expression sympathetic. "You must be Madelyn Andrews." She extended her hand. "I'm Amanda Peterson. I work with Caleb and Gage at GAI."

"It's nice to meet you," Madelyn said. "I didn't realize another agent would be present."

Caleb's gut pinched. "Amanda is a forensics anthropologist. We thought she might be helpful today."

Madelyn's eyes widened as the implications registered.

"She's going to oversee the medical examiner's work," Caleb continued, "just so we can verify the findings. In light of Dr. Emery's lies, we can't be too careful."

Amanda tugged her all-weather coat around her. "I'm sorry, Madelyn. I know this is difficult."

"Yes, well, thank you for being here. If I'd had my wits about me five years ago, I would have demanded to see my child before I buried her."

"Don't blame yourself," Amanda said, her voice and smile genuinely understanding. "You were a victim. And we're going to find out just how much of one today."

Amanda's pep talk seemed to give Madelyn strength, because she offered her a tiny smile.

Amanda nudged his arm as she headed down the hill as if silently ordering him to stay with Madelyn. Hell, she didn't have to tell him that Madelyn was vulnerable.

But getting too close to her was dangerous for him.

"You didn't answer me earlier, Caleb," Madelyn said. "What were you doing at Cissy's grave?" Suspicion flared in her eyes. "Do you have some kind of psychic ability that you didn't mention? Is that why you believed Sara? Could you see inside the grave?"

Irritated that she'd caught him when he'd had no intention of revealing his personal visions, he hesitated. Telling her meant opening himself up to scrutiny.

His grandfather's image flashed in his mind. White Feather, a shaman, a man with strong faith and belief in the Cherokee customs, in the healing power of herbs and the earth. And in the healing power of love.

He'd also believed in Caleb, in his visions, because his grandfather simply believed that he was special.

But if he had been so damn special, why hadn't he foreseen the shooter that horrible day?

"Caleb, I'm not going to judge. I saw you with Sara, the look on your face. She trusted you and her trust doesn't come easily." Madelyn laid her palm against his cheek, stirring primal instincts and needs that had lain dormant too long. "Just tell me the truth," she said softly.

His gaze met hers, and something sweet and frightening and sensual rippled between them, a connection he'd never felt, not even with Mara.

Because he had never shared the truth about himself with her. He had tried to be a man she'd approve of. A hard worker, a provider. They'd married because they both wanted to raise a family without the stigma of a mixed race.

But this sensual connection, this drive to be near Madelyn, was foreign and disturbing and heated his blood.

Arousing him.

Arousal and lust had no place in an investigation.

Self-loathing filled him. They were at a graveyard, for God's sake. And Madelyn was inquiring about his gift and how it might impact this case. Not because she was remotely interested in him personally.

"Sometimes I sense things," he said quietly, watching her for a reaction. "It's not an ability I can control or call upon at will. It just…happens."

Her expression softened. "That's the reason you believed Sara? You sensed something when you shook her hand?"

"Yes, I believe that Sara is special," he said by way of an answer. He jammed his hands in his pockets, ignoring the whistle of the wind bringing cries of the dead from the graves. He had to focus on one case here and that was the Andrews child. The other lost spirits would have to find another medium to hear their pleas.

Madelyn shivered and rubbed her hands up and down her arms. Leaves fluttered down from the trees, scattering amongst the markers, adding bold reds, yellows, and oranges to the brittle, brown grass.

Madelyn cleared her throat as if summoning courage. "What did you see when you touched the grave?"

His former vision flashed back. But he wasn't certain it was a vision at all. A world of darkness spun around him, that long empty pit clawing at him.

Madelyn clutched his arm. "Caleb, tell me the truth. Please."

"I didn't see anything," he said gruffly. "It was just dark and... I felt an emptiness. I...can't explain it. Sometimes my senses, my visions aren't correct. Sometimes they don't even make sense."

The heartbeat of silence while Madelyn stared at him felt like an eternity. "Just don't lie to me," she said. "I may seem like a fragile woman to you, but I can handle whatever happens."

Caleb's hearing suddenly seemed more acute. He could hear the scene behind him, the voices of the sheriff and funeral workers. Twigs snapped in the wind, leaves rustled, the shovel crunched dry dirt....

"How long has Sara had these nightmares about Cissy?" he asked.

Madelyn sighed, the weary sound of a worried mother. "I told you, the past two months, ever since we moved back to Sanctuary."

"But you said she talked about her twin before?"

Madelyn nodded. "At eighteen months, she started acting as if she was playing with her. Even now, when she has tea parties, she sets a place for Cissy. When she colors, she draws Cissy and those sunflowers. When she plays on the seesaw, Cissy is always on the other end."

Her voice broke, and she pressed a hand to her mouth to regain control, then forged ahead as if she needed to share her story. "When she was a baby, she'd lay on her side and giggle and reach out as if someone was there."

Caleb's mind raced to paranormal research he'd done. "Parapsychologists believe that children can see ghosts when they're babies. They have a connection then, but once their innocence is lost and society trains them, they no longer believe, so the spirits don't appear to them anymore."

Madelyn chewed her bottom lip. "I read that, too. But Sara never lost that ability. In fact, her connection only seemed to grow stronger. Last year she started insisting that Cissy was alive, telling me stories about things she did, places she went. That's when I got really worried."

Caleb heard the pain in her voice. "When you consulted the shrinks?"

"Yes." The wind swept Madelyn's hair into her face, and she tucked it back with her fingers. "Sara seems so certain that her dreams are real, that her sister is alive, that I started to believe her." Her shoulders fell. "Maybe because I really wanted to so badly."

"That's understandable." Caleb ached to touch her,

to soothe the torment in her voice, but the only way to help Madelyn was to uncover the truth.

If Sara was right, then her sister had been kidnapped and adopted by another family, she might be in danger.... And if she was wrong, Sara's visions might be ESP—or she might have some form of mental illness.

Or she might be communing with a dead girl....

A noise down the hill jarred him, and he jerked his head toward the gravesite. Sheriff Gray had stepped outside the tent and was motioning for him.

"Walker, we're ready," Gray shouted.

Madelyn's legs buckled, and he caught her around the waist. "Sit down on that bench by the fountain. Let me see what they found."

Too weak to argue, she nodded and allowed him to guide her to the bench. His heart climbed into his throat as he left her small form hunched inside her coat, shivering on that cold, stone slab.

But he squared his shoulders, determined to end the questions in her mind. It was the only way she and her daughter could find closure and move on.

Clenching his jaw, he raced down the hill and stepped inside the tent beside Amanda. The mood was somber, reverent, racked with tension and dread.

Slowly the E.H. Officer opened the casket.

Caleb braced himself but shock still ripped through him.

The casket was empty.

Madelyn twisted her hands together, willing herself to remain calm as she waited. But every second that ticked by felt like someone was pulling out her fingernails one by one. The sound of a car motor drew her gaze back to the parking lot, and she saw an elderly man exit a sedan and hobble toward a grave near the church. Probably his wife's.

Poor man. How long had they been married before he'd lost her?

She'd thought she and Tim would grow old together, not that he would abandon her and Sara when they needed him most.

Bitterness threatened but she tamped it down. She'd long ago vowed not to indulge herself in that emotion for fear Sara would pick up on it.

She never wanted her daughter to know the truth about her father.

Voices carried in the wind, and she spotted Caleb walking toward her. Her lungs squeezed for air at his bleak expression. A bird chirped from a tree nearby, and leaves fluttered down into the fountain. One landed on the wings of the angel, another at her feet.

She gripped her hands together, waiting, watching for the small casket to appear.

"Madelyn," he said in a gruff voice. "I'm sorry."

She lunged to her feet. "What's wrong?" Her voice cracked, and for the first time, she realized that she'd actually held out hope that Sara might be right. That Cissy was alive.

Suddenly oblivious to her surroundings, she vaulted down the hill, stumbling blindly. Whatever he had seen, she had to know.

"Madelyn, wait!"

Her boots pounded the ground as she ran down the hill. All she could think of was seeing that tiny casket, knowing whether her daughter was in there…

Her pulse pounded, sweat slid down her temple, and

she stumbled over a loose rock and felt herself flailing to remain on two feet.

Caleb caught her arm and righted her, then helped her to the tent. Her heart pounded as she stepped beneath the tarp.

Dear God…

She gaped at Caleb. "I don't understand," she whispered.

A muscle ticked in Caleb's jaw. "Someone lied to you, Madelyn. Dr. Emery, the funeral director maybe. But you didn't bury your daughter five years ago. You buried an empty casket."

Anger, shock and betrayal slammed into her along with a million questions. But the one fact that she latched onto was the one she wanted to believe more than anything.

The casket was empty because Sara was right.

Cissy was alive.

Cissy ran and hid behind the door between the den and the kitchen clutching her dolly to her chest. They were screaming again. They'd been at it for a long time now.

"How could you do this?" her mama shouted. "Why?"

"Because you wanted a kid, you were grieving over losing Doug."

"I know, but you lied to me."

"Just keep your mouth shut!" the big man yelled.

Cissy peered around the corner and saw her mama reach for the phone. "It's not right," her mama cried. "What you've done… It's not right. No wonder Cissy has bad dreams."

"That kid is crazy. She always has been." He grabbed

her mama's shoulders and shook her. "Listen to me. You call, you'll lose her, and I'll go to jail. You wouldn't do that to your own family, would you?"

"But Cissy has a right to know the truth," her mama argued. "And I won't go to jail because I'll tell the truth."

"The truth. Hell, you don't even know the truth, you stupid bitch." He slapped her mother across the face. "You're up to your damn eyeballs in this. The kid is evidence, and we can't leave evidence behind."

"What are you talking about?" Cissy's mama looked terrified as she leaned against the sink.

Terror streaked through Cissy, and she backed into the hallway, but she tripped over a pair of work boots and yelped. He heard the noise and swung around. His face was red, his nostrils wide. His eyes bulged like a madman's.

He was going to kill her.

"Damn kid," he mumbled then turned and stomped toward Cissy, his big footsteps pounding the floor like a giant's.

"No, I won't let you hurt my baby." Her mama grabbed his arm to stop him, but he swung his arm back with such force that he slung her to the floor. Her mama hit her head on the table with a whack and blood spurted and ran down her face.

Cissy bit back a scream. Tears blurred her vision.

His growl dragged her from her stupor though, and she turned and darted out the back door. The porch door slammed behind her. His loud bellow followed.

"Get back here, kid. Come on, we'll play a little game."

He didn't want to play games, Cissy thought, as she

barreled down the steps. He'd hurt her mama and now he was gonna hurt her.

She had to get away.

She dashed down the steps as quick as she could and ran toward the greenhouse and the sunflowers. It was the only place she'd be safe.

Sweat streamed down her face, and she heaved for a breath as she shoved open the heavy door and sneaked inside. She tucked her doll beneath her arm, then pushed with all her might to shut the door, pulling the metal latch. Then she ducked between the rows of sunflowers, weaving her way until she was hidden deep within the rows.

Crouching as low as she could, she hugged her dolly to her, closed her eyes and felt the tears flow.

"Please, Sara, help me," she whispered. "I don't know how much longer I can hide."

The door rattled as he shook it. "Get out here right now, kid!"

Cissy rocked herself back and forth and rolled into a tiny ball. She could see her sister in her mind. She wasn't crazy like the big meanie said.

"Sara, please come and get me," she whispered. "I'm scared. I don't wanna die."

Chapter 4

Caleb contemplated the implications of the empty grave. He wished like hell Dr. Emery was alive to explain how he could have deceived Madelyn. She was a new mother, had been in labor, suffering from an accident, and he had lied to her about one of her babies. The enormity of that cruelty boggled his mind.

"I can't believe it…" Madelyn murmured. "After all these years of thinking Cissy was gone…of visiting her grave…"

A mixture of grief, shock, rage and desolation spread across her face, and he couldn't resist. He slid an arm around her to support her, wanting to offer comfort. She surprised him by bowing her head and resting it against his chest.

"She could be alive," Madelyn whispered in a tormented voice. "All this time, she could have been out there, alone, hurting, wondering why her mother didn't want her."

Caleb hated to remind her of Dr. Emery's crimes and the other possibilities, but it was inevitable. And she had asked him to be honest.

"Or he could have given her to another family, Madelyn. A couple who wanted a baby and had no idea that Emery was stealing children from unsuspecting mothers." He paused. "A couple who loved her."

Her silent words echoed in his head even though she didn't speak them. *But she should have been with her mother and her twin.*

Madelyn furrowed her brows. "Except that's not what Sara saw."

He shrugged. "It still could be possible."

Pain flashed in her eyes again. "But if Sara was right about Cissy being alive, then maybe she's right about Cissy being in trouble now." She clutched his arms. "Caleb, we have to find her. Sara says she's in danger and so is her m—the woman who adopted her. We have to hurry."

The E.H. Officer, Sheriff Gray, the men from the funeral home and the medical examiner all filed from the tent.

"What the hell is going on?" one of the funeral workers muttered.

"The fact that there is no body proves Dr. Emery lied to Madelyn," Caleb said, "and that her baby might have been adopted just as little Peyton Nash was."

"But I thought that was an isolated incident," the medical examiner said, "that it was personal. The girlfriend of the baby's father and his mother kidnapped that little girl and arranged the adoption."

"Emery was guilty of more than that," Sheriff Gray said. "According to the files from the former sheriff, he had a problem with single mothers and liked money."

"But I wasn't single at the time," Madelyn pointed out.

Caleb considered that. "Maybe not. But you had two babies, and he was in the business. He probably figured he could take one, and you still had the other baby, so you wouldn't question him."

Madelyn clenched her jaw. "And he was right. But I haven't been okay and neither has Sara."

Questions ticked through Caleb's mind. "Madelyn's baby did not have an autopsy. Did you know Dr. Emery at the time, Dr. Rollo?"

Dr. Rollo wrinkled his brow. "No, I only came on last year. But I'm surprised the M.E. at the time didn't request one."

"Where is he now?" Madelyn asked.

"He died last year," Dr. Rollo said. "Had an embolism."

Dammit. Dr. Emery was dead and so was the former medical examiner. "I want to talk to that lawyer, now."

Caleb firmly set his jaw. Jameson Stanford Mansfield. According to Gage, Mansfield was a sleaze.

If he knew anything about Madelyn's missing child, he'd find out. No matter what it took.

Madelyn phoned her mother while Caleb studied the grave site and casket. He was examining the site to verify that it hadn't been disturbed by anyone prior to them.

"Yes, Mom, it was empty," she said softly.

"Oh, my God. So little Sara's visions are real?"

Madelyn's chest ached. How many times had her

daughter tried to convince her that Cissy was alive, yet she hadn't believed her? "Yes. Maybe. Poor Sara, I should have listened to her before. She kept insisting Cissy wasn't in that cemetery."

Her mother's breath wheezed out. "You know your grandmother had visions."

"What?" This was the first she'd ever heard of it. "Why didn't you ever tell me, Mother?"

A labored sigh echoed back. "Because she didn't like to talk about them, said people thought she was odd because of them." Another wheezed breath. "All this time I hoped…prayed… Sara didn't have them. Although at the same time, I hoped she did."

Madelyn didn't know what to make of that. "How is Sara now?"

"She's okay at the moment, but she became agitated earlier."

"What happened?"

"She and I were drawing. She drew more sunflowers except this time Cissy was hiding in the midst of them."

A cold wave of fear washed over Madelyn. "I planned to go with Caleb to confront the lawyer who arranged adoptions with Dr. Emery, but I can come and pick her up right now."

"No, she's settled down now, honey, and she and Liz are decorating the cookies. Take your time. The sooner you find Cissy, the sooner these disturbing images and nightmares will end for Sara."

"Are you sure you're feeling up to it, Mom? You've had a difficult year."

"Oh, honey," her mother said. "Sara keeps me young. Besides, just knowing Cissy might be out there is enough to make me work harder to free myself of this wheelchair."

Tears threatened to surface. It would be a miracle if her mother walked again. And another one if she found Cissy and brought her home.

Both seemed light-years away and impossible.

She closed her eyes and sighed, hating that Sara was suffering. And what about Cissy? What was happening to her?

"Sara's calling me to help with the sprinkles." Her mother lowered her voice. "Be careful, honey. When Nina Nash tried to find her child, someone tried to kill her. And if Sara is right about a man threatening her and her adopted mother, going after them could be dangerous."

Chills skated up Madelyn's spine, but she shook off the fear. Nothing was going to stop her now. "I'll be fine, Mom. I'm with Caleb."

"Ahh, yes. That handsome Native American."

"Mother…"

"It's all right to lean on someone, Madelyn. Tim did a number on you, but not every man is a scumbag like him."

Her mother hung up and Madelyn shivered, then opened her eyes and looked across the graveyard. The small town was supposed to be a great place to raise a family, a haven for her and Sara.

But recently the revelations about the hospital fire eight years ago and now babies being sold made her wonder what other secrets lay in the town.

Did someone in Sanctuary know where her daughter was?

* * *

"Sheriff, we're going to pay a visit to Mansfield," Caleb said.

Sheriff Gray shrugged. "Good luck. But don't expect a confession from the bastard. He's pleading innocence and lawyered-up."

"Maybe he'll talk to me," Madelyn said.

Gray studied her for a long moment. "It's worth a shot. But Mansfield is shrewd and devious. He also uses his money and his daddy's name to get his way."

"His money and name don't mean crap to me," Caleb muttered, already contemplating ways to force the man to spill the truth if Madelyn's pleas didn't work.

"But what about his records?" Caleb asked. "Is there any way we can look at those?"

Gray shook his head. "District attorney subpoenaed them. You can talk to her, but I doubt she'll share with the case pending. That and adoptions being sealed and the rights of the adopted parents being a priority makes these types of situations almost impossible."

Exactly what Gage had already told him.

Caleb ground his teeth. Then again, he didn't work for the cops or play by their rules. Wasn't that one advantage Gage had pointed out when he'd recruited him for GAI?

Madelyn glanced toward the empty casket. "What are you going to do with that coffin?"

"It appears to be clean." The medical examiner squinted through the sun. "But I'd like a crime unit to process it. All right with you?"

Madelyn nodded.

Caleb placed his hand at the small of her back. "Let's

go, Madelyn. I want to pay a surprise visit to Mansfield."

Determination settled on Madelyn's face. "Me, too. If he knows where Cissy is, he'd better tell us."

Caleb rubbed her back. If he didn't, court would be the least of Mansfield's problems.

Caleb walked her to her car, and they agreed to meet back at GAI headquarters. A few minutes later, Caleb led the way inside the agency to Gage's office.

"Amanda filled me in when she called." Gage frowned. "So Emery's adoption ring was bigger than just the Nash case."

"It appears that way," Caleb said.

"I'll talk to Sheila English, the D.A., and see if she'll give us any leads," Gage said. "I also phoned a buddy of mine at the Bureau. I'll let you know if he has any helpful information."

Caleb shifted on the balls of his feet. "Thanks. Since kidnapping is a federal case, we might need him."

Gage punched his intercom button and requested Benjamin Camp and Derrick McKinney come to his office. Five minutes later, Ben Camp, the computer expert, stood with them, arms crossed and solemn as Caleb caught him up on the case. Derrick listened silently as well, his hands jammed in his pockets.

"The sheriff said Mansfield's records have been subpoenaed. It's going to be hell getting access to them," Caleb said.

Ben shrugged, a mischievous smile tugging at his mouth. "I'll see what I can do."

Derrick cleared his throat. "Madelyn, my wife, Brianna, has connections with several adoption agencies and the local orphanage. I'll have her put out some feelers."

"Thank you." Madelyn offered him a tentative smile. "I really appreciate all of your help."

Ben gestured toward Caleb. "Can I see you for a minute? My office."

Caleb nodded. "Wait for me outside, Madelyn."

She gave him a questioning look but did as he said. Caleb followed Ben to his office, curious. He'd heard Ben had been in trouble with the law before, that his expertise had landed him in jail. But he didn't give a damn. "What is it? Did you find something already?"

Ben shook his head, reached inside his desk and slid a small device into Caleb's hand. "It's a bug. Plant it in Mansfield's office."

It was illegal and inadmissible in court, but that was the advantage in working with a private agency. They'd get information any way they could get it.

Caleb tucked the bug in his pocket. "Thanks, Camp. Oh, and see what you can dig up on Madelyn's ex. Tim Andrews."

"You think he's involved?"

Caleb shrugged. "Who knows? But the jerk left when Sara started calling her dead sister's name. That makes him suspect in my book."

"Sounds like a real winner," Ben muttered. "I'll get on it right away and keep you posted."

Caleb hurried outside and found Madelyn tapping her foot by his Jeep. "What was that about?"

Caleb shrugged and opened the Jeep door. "Just business."

Madelyn caught his arm. "Please, Caleb, tell me the

truth. Do you know something about Cissy you're not telling me?"

Caleb covered her hand with his. "No, just speaking to Ben about research."

Her eyes flickered with unease, then trust, making his insides knot. God help him. He didn't want to disappoint her.

Her fingers curled beneath his, her skin soft, her hand small in his. The urge to hold her seized him.

Sensations zinged through him, heating his blood. His mouth watered for hers.

Suddenly the wind whipped her hair around her face, and a drop of rain pinged on the sidewalk. Madelyn clamped her teeth over her bottom lip as she glanced at the mountains.

The fear that stretched across her face jerked him out of his lust-driven stupor, reminding him that a little girl might be out there somewhere in danger.

No time for play. They had work to do.

"Let's go meet Mansfield, Madelyn. Maybe we can convince him to talk and get some answers."

Madelyn clenched her hands in her lap, missing the sweet comfort of her hand cradled inside Caleb's. For a brief moment, she'd felt a frisson of sensual heat rippling between them. But it must have been her imagination.

Caleb was a professional and had only been offering support in a trying time. She could not become dependant on him.

As he drove to Mansfield's office, images of Cissy flashed through her head. Where had she been all these years? Who was raising her? What kind of life had she had? Did she live in North Carolina? Near Sanctuary?

Was she loved?

Did she know that she had a twin or that she was adopted? What had her family told her?

Anger boiled inside her, as well, as picture after picture of Sara and Cissy together surfaced. All the years they could have been together, played together, shared toys and secrets and laughter.

And to think, Sara would have gone without nightmares these past two months.

And if Sara was connected to Cissy, did the connection work both ways? Was Cissy calling out to Sara for help?

Or could Sara be wrong? Only seeing what she wanted to see; that Cissy wanted to be with them because Sara missed her?

She swallowed back tears. No. She would not doubt Sara again.

"Madelyn, if you want me to drive you home first, I can do this alone," Caleb offered as he pulled in front of the lawyer's office and parked. The building was an older, Georgian-style house that had been renovated into an office, but it looked well maintained. She'd heard that Mansfield had family money, and that he used it to throw his weight around.

But she wasn't afraid of the man. And if he'd earned any part of that money by selling babies, *her* baby, she'd make sure he rotted in jail.

"No." She interjected steel into her voice. "I want to see this man's face when we confront him."

Caleb's gaze locked with hers. "Good. I think he should have to face the people he wronged."

She reached for the door handle and climbed out, then followed Caleb up the steps to the office. Traffic crawled by the downtown area, the sound of tires skating over slushy, wet leaves echoing behind them.

Caleb entered without knocking and she followed him inside. A chunky bottled-blonde with a miniscule skirt and cleavage to spare beamed a smile up at Caleb.

"Hi, Mister, how can we help you?"

"We need to see Mansfield," Caleb said, ignoring her flirtatious smile. "It's urgent."

"Is this a legal matter?"

"I'd rather speak to Mansfield about it in private." Caleb strode toward the door. "Don't bother to get up. We'll let ourselves in."

The woman's expression morphed from solicitous to concerned in a nanosecond, and she rushed toward the lawyer's door, tottering on three-inch heels. But Caleb was already stalking in. Taking his cue, Madelyn elbowed her way past the receptionist.

"What the hell?" A balding man jumped to his feet behind a massive, cherry desk and glared at them. "Brenda, what's going on? I told you no one gets through."

"Don't blame her," Caleb said in a tone that brooked no argument. "No one, especially your receptionist, could stop us from being here, Mansfield."

Mansfield reached for his phone, his scalp reddening. "I'm calling the police."

Their gazes locked in challenge. "Put down the phone," Caleb ordered.

Madelyn barely resisted the urge to pummel the man with her fists. "Tell me what you did with my daughter, Mr. Mansfield."

Mansfield's eyes widened in shock. "I don't know who you are or what you're talking about." He slanted a panicked look toward the doorway where his receptionist still stood. "Get my lawyer here now!"

Madelyn wasn't backing down. Instead, she leaned forward, planted her fists on his desk and gave him an icy look. "Don't pretend innocence, Mr. Mansfield. Just tell me who you sold my little girl to, because I want her back."

Chapter 5

Caleb narrowed his eyes, scrutinizing Mansfield, as panic etched lines across the lawyer's face. The creep was hiding something. He wasn't as innocent as he and his damn lawyer wanted everyone to believe.

"Tell me," Madelyn said sharply. "Where is my daughter?"

Mansfield shot his receptionist another frantic look indicating for her to hurry and make the phone call.

"You can call your lawyer," Caleb said sharply. "But we're not going away. We know you handled arrangements for Nina Nash's daughter's illegal adoption, and now we suspect that Mrs. Andrews's child was also abducted at birth."

"Like I said, I have no idea what you're talking about." Mansfield ran a shaky hand over his sweating forehead. "I don't even know who you are, Mrs.

Andrews, much less anything about your child. And I don't recall seeing anything about a child abduction in the area regarding a baby named Andrews."

"That's because Dr. Emery lied and told me my little girl died at birth." Anger tinged Madelyn's voice. "He said she was deformed and it was better that I not see her."

Mansfield's nostrils flared. "Again, I have no knowledge of improprieties regarding you or your child. If Dr. Emery deceived you, then he did so without my knowledge."

Caleb cleared his throat. "Oh, come on, Mansfield. The D.A. has your files. She's going to fry your ass and you know it. So why not cooperate and help rectify the damage you did years ago by helping us find Madelyn's baby?" He hesitated, then continued, hoping to drive his point home. "Maybe the D.A. will even cut you a deal for your assistance."

"I did not sell babies!" Mansfield bellowed. "I'm an upstanding member of this town. Do you know who my father is?"

"I don't care if your old man owns all of the southern states combined," Caleb snapped. "All I care about is finding the child that was stolen from Madelyn Andrews."

Madelyn inched forward. "How could you and Dr. Emery allow me to believe that my little girl died? You all let me have a memorial service for her, watch that tiny casket be buried."

"I'm sorry for your loss," Mansfield said, desperately striving to turn on the charm. "But just because Nina Nash's baby was kidnapped—a kidnapping I swear I had no knowledge of—that doesn't mean your baby was, too."

"Mr. Mansfield, Dr. Emery delivered Mrs. Andrews's twins five years ago, and as she said, told her one of them died. But we just exhumed that casket and there is no baby inside."

Shock flared across Mansfield's face. "Even if he deceived her, you have no evidence that I had any part in it."

"You can check your files to see if you handled the baby's adoption," Caleb said.

"I don't have to check my files," Mansfield blurted. "I remember names and I did not arrange an adoption for any baby named Andrews."

"Her first name was Cissy," Madelyn said.

"As I said, I wasn't involved."

Caleb felt like choking the man. "You're lying and we're going to prove it."

Brenda tottered back in with a faint knock at the open door. "Excuse me. Mr. Mansfield, your father and lawyer are on their way."

"Thanks, Brenda." Mansfield swung his head toward Madelyn, slightly calmer now he knew the cavalry was near.

"Please," Madelyn said in a pained voice. "I think my little girl is in danger. You can help us save her."

"I told you I don't know what you're talking about. All I did was handle paperwork for a few adoptions, but they were all legitimate."

"The Nash baby's wasn't," Caleb pointed out.

Mansfield's eyes bulged. "I was a victim the same as that mother! Now Emery killed himself, everyone wants to use me as a scapegoat!"

Caleb grunted sarcastically. "You are anything but a victim, Mansfield. You got paid well for your silence and now you're lying to cover your ass."

Anger reddened Mansfield's face. "You have no right to talk to me like that."

"Then prove you're telling the truth by showing me your records," Caleb pushed.

A vein throbbed in Mansfield's neck. "Even if I wanted to let you see them, I couldn't. There are confidentiality laws. I could lose my license as well as trust from clients and future clients."

"When I get through with you, you won't have any clients," Caleb growled.

A tense second passed as Mansfield fidgeted and glanced at the door, obviously searching for help.

"Please," Madelyn said softly. "I'm begging you. Cissy is in danger. Who adopted her?"

His face twisted with unease. "Any adoptions I arranged were between willing parties. Trust me, the adoptive parents were desperate for babies."

"So desperate they didn't care where the child came from or if he or she was stolen," Caleb said bitterly. "Or how much money they had to pay to get the baby."

Mansfield's long-winded sigh punctuated the air. Footsteps clattered behind them, a door slammed, and another man's voice boomed as the man cleared the front office and stepped into the doorway.

"I'm Mansfield's lawyer, Leo Holbrook," a young man in an expensive, black suit said with authority. "What's going on here?"

"These people are harassing me," Mansfield said, his look flying to his father, an astute, gray-haired man with ice cubes for eyes, who appeared beside Holbrook.

"Mrs. Andrews just discovered that the baby she thought died five years ago may be alive," Caleb explained. "We thought Mr. Mansfield would do the right thing and help us determine what happened to her child."

"Mr. Mansfield knows nothing of this," Mansfield, Sr., said with a snarl. "Now get out before I sue you both for harassment."

Madelyn lifted her chin. "You don't frighten me, Mr. Mansfield. My daughter is alive, and she may be in danger. And I will do anything to find her." She stabbed a finger in his chest punctuating her point. "And nothing you or any of your lawyers do or say will stop me."

A small grin tugged at Caleb's face, admiration stirring in his gut as Madelyn squared her shoulders and brushed past the men leaving them stunned by her boldness.

Madelyn stormed out to Caleb's Jeep, furious and frustrated. "Well, that was a bust."

"Maybe. Maybe not."

"How can you say that? His lawyer and father are hovering around him like guard dogs. We'll never convince him to talk."

Caleb coaxed her into the Jeep, then settled inside the driver's seat. "Shh, Madelyn. There are other ways of finding out what someone is up to."

She crossed her arms. "How? He's not about to admit anything. He's too worried about his precious career and money."

"True," Caleb said gruffly. "But trust me, Madelyn. I will do everything I can to discover the truth, to find

Cissy." He took her hand in his and stroked it, and Madelyn felt like whimpering.

How long had it been since anyone except her mother had soothed her? She was the one who always comforted Sara.

But completely trust him?

She didn't know if she was capable of giving her complete trust to anyone. Not after the twins' father, the man who had vowed to love, honor and cherish her, the man she'd believed would love his children no matter what, had walked out on them.

She eased her hand from Caleb's, but her gaze remained fixed on his dark brown eyes. Eyes that could swallow a woman. Seduce her. Make her want to believe anything he said.

Dangerous eyes. Sexy eyes.

Eyes laden with promises.

Ones she didn't intend to fall prey to.

She wrestled her emotions into control. "What do we do now?"

Caleb drummed his fingers in thought. "Who assisted Dr. Emery in your delivery?"

Madelyn massaged her temple. She had relived that night so many times. Had berated herself for driving. Had blamed herself. If only she'd waited on Tim to go to the store, if she'd stayed home, if she hadn't been so hysterical when Dr. Emery had relayed the devastating news about Cissy...

The list of recriminations was endless.

"Madelyn?" Caleb asked.

"I'm sorry." She banished the guilt to that faraway corner in her mind in order to survive. After all, she had Sara, and Sara needed her. "I was unconscious," she said. "But there had to be some hospital staff on duty. Nurses. Assistants."

"Do you remember anyone specifically who talked to you about Cissy afterward? Anyone else who saw Cissy?"

Chills skated along Madelyn's spine. If Cissy had been born normal, if Dr. Emery had whisked her away to sell her, then someone else had to know. "My God. Dr. Emery had to have a helper."

Caleb arched a brow. "I'm going to ask Gage to track down the doctor who signed off on your baby's release to the funeral home. Which funeral home did you use?"

Madelyn frowned. "The one in Sanctuary. You think the director at the funeral home knew?"

"It's possible," Caleb said. "Think about the staff that night, the nurses. Anyone stand out?"

A shudder coursed through her. "I was so traumatized, it's a blur," she whispered. Images of faces, white coats, a man with glasses…a woman, heavy, short, curly brown hair, a gap between her front teeth…spun in and out of her head. "Come to think of it, there was a nurse, an older, heavyset woman who tried to console me the next day. Her name was Nadine."

Caleb sped up. "Let's find Nadine and stop by the hospital. Maybe another employee remembers something."

Madelyn nodded, hope desperately budding to life in her chest. But if Nadine knew something, why hadn't she come forward sooner?

Caleb punched in Ben's number. "It's Caleb. Have you found anything on those files?"

"Still working on it, but I'm getting close."

"How about Mansfield?"

"When you left, he and his father had words. His old man is irate that he's scandalizing the family name."

Caleb grunted his distaste. "Not that he was involved in the phony adoptions, just that he got caught."

"Right." Ben made a sound of disgust. "Old Man Mansfield wants the case tied up and fast."

"Did Mansfield admit that he knew Emery kidnapped the Nash baby without the mother's permission?"

"No outright confession. His lawyer shut him up fast the moment he mentioned Emery."

Damn. "How about financials?"

"That gets interesting. Mansfield made sizeable deposits over the past few years in both his personal and business accounts, some corresponding with the Nash baby's disappearance and Madelyn's daughter's, as well as a boatload more. According to the D.A., Mansfield admitted to professionally handling adoptions, but he insists he thought they were legit." Ben heaved a sigh. "I suppose it's possible that Emery passed on forged papers to Mansfield without his knowledge."

"Possible but unlikely," Caleb muttered.

"All the defense needs is to create reasonable doubt," Ben said darkly.

True. "But we're going to nail him." Caleb glanced at Madelyn, his chest clenching. "Will you have Amanda find out who signed the baby's release to the funeral home, and see if the same people are still running the business? If the director or one of his employees knew the coffin was empty, maybe we can force them to talk."

"Copy that," Ben said. "Maybe Mansfield will make a mistake, too, and we can catch him."

Caleb had started driving toward the hospital but had a second thought. "Listen, Ben, can you access Sanctuary's hospital records and find out if a nurse named Nadine currently works there? She was on duty the night Madelyn gave birth." He gave him the date and year. "I'd like a list of any staff working the E.R. or delivery as well, especially if they have a record."

"You don't ask much, do you?" Ben said sarcastically.

Caleb chuckled. "I have a feeling you can handle it, Camp."

This time Ben laughed. "I'll try to work my magic. Hang on and I'll search for the nurse."

"We should talk to the hospital director," Caleb said, thinking out loud.

"Doubt that will do you any good," Ben muttered. "He's denied any involvement in Emery's wrongdoings, and his lawyer has hired personal guards to protect him. The hospital is facing multiple charges in both criminal and civil court, and he's received threats and hate mail from anonymous sources."

Damn. Caleb heard the sound of keys clicking on the computer.

"Okay, I found Nadine. Last name is Cotter. She left the hospital and works for a private home health care service." Ben paused. "Looks like she resigned a couple of months after the Andrews's twins were delivered."

Suspicious. "Do you have a home address?"

"One second." More keys clicked, then Ben came back. "Cotter lives at Widow's Peak just north of here." He recited the address. "And Caleb, I found something else."

"What?"

"Her bank records." Ben whistled. "Looks like Nadine came into some money about five years ago."

"How much?"

"Ten thousand," Ben said. "Could have been a payoff."

Caleb grunted. Ten thousand for her silence. For a baby's life.

Disgusting.

But that bribe had allowed Emery to go free so he could rob more women of their children and profit from it.

"We're on our way to Nadine's house," Caleb said. "With Emery dead, maybe the threat of jail will convince her to talk."

The sun was starting to set as Caleb and Madelyn drove up to Widow's Peak. Nadine Cotter lived at the top of a ridge surrounded by the Blue Ridge Mountains, miles from town or neighbors. Had Nadine turned into some kind of hermit, or was she hiding out from someone?

Madelyn studied the scenery. She liked her privacy, but she couldn't imagine living so far out that she wouldn't have contact with friends or neighbors. It was dangerous, too—black bears, coyotes and foxes roamed these mountains.

"What did your friend at GAI say?" Madelyn asked.

"Ben's still investigating."

"Did he have information about Nadine?"

A muscle ticked in Caleb's jaw.

"Tell me," Madelyn insisted. "I hired you for the truth, not to protect me from it."

His eyes darkened with concern and she realized the truth must be ugly.

"Caleb, please," she said, then touched his hand, immediately feeling a jolt connecting them.

His fingers tightened around the steering wheel. "Nadine deposited ten thousand dollars a few days after you gave birth."

Madelyn gritted her teeth, blinking back tears as she turned to stare out the window. Ten thousand lousy dollars? Was that what her baby had been worth to the woman?

The winter chill suffused her, the brittle bare branches and brown leaves mirroring how empty and dead she felt inside. "I don't understand how a woman could do that to another woman," she said, haunted by the memory of crying in Nadine's arms. "For God's sake. She consoled me, she saw how grief-stricken I was."

"You'd be surprised at what people will do for money. Especially if they're desperate." He lowered his voice to a soothing pitch. "Maybe she had a good reason, Madelyn."

Bitterness shot through Madelyn. "There is no reason good enough to lie to a mother about her child or to steal her baby from her arms."

"I agree," Caleb said gently.

His compassion made her throat close, and she fought against breaking down. She had to remain strong, see this through, for her and for Sara.

And for Cissy. Especially for Cissy.

Gravel spewed from Caleb's Jeep as he sped up the drive. A faded yellow house with white shutters sat at the top of the hill surrounded by oaks and hickory trees. A cheap, metal carport had been erected beside the house to shelter the car, a rusted dark green sedan that looked as if it needed painting. A bird feeder that had seen better days was littered with dry leaves and twigs, its base tilting as if the ground was sucking it into the earth.

Caleb cut the engine and turned to her. "Do you want to wait here while I see if she's home?"

"No way," Madelyn said as she reached for the door handle. "I'm going to make her look me in the eye and tell me the truth."

Caleb clenched his jaw. "All right. But follow my lead."

Anxious to confront Nadine, Madelyn strode up the driveway to the porch, Caleb on her heels. Adrenaline surged through her as she knocked on the door. This woman might know where her other daughter was.

Then she could find her and bring her home. Sara's nightmares would end, and the twins would be together as they should have been all along.

There was no answer, so she knocked again while Caleb scanned the front yard. Several long seconds passed, her heart beating like a drum while she waited. But again silence.

Caleb frowned, then reached for the doorknob and turned it. Instead of being locked, the door screeched open. Surprised, Madelyn started to step inside, but Caleb caught her arm.

"Wait, let me go first."

An acrid odor permeated the air as she entered the foyer. The ticktock of an ancient grandfather clock punctuated the eerie silence. Caleb paused again, listening. "Something's wrong."

Madelyn's heart beat faster.

"Go back to the Jeep," he murmured.

"No, I'm staying with you." Madelyn latched onto his arm and trailed him as he peered into the connecting living room and kitchen. The room was dusty, filled with magazines and outdated furniture, and dirty dishes were stacked in the sink, flies swarming.

Desk drawers stood open as if they'd been ransacked, the contents spilling out.

Had someone broken in? If so, what were they looking for? And where was Nadine?

A rumbling sounded from the furnace, old pipes groaning, and wind whistled through the eaves as Caleb moved to the staircase. He placed a palm on the rail, and his big body went still.

The sound of water pinging onto the floor echoed from above, and the screech of a cat followed, shrill and nerve-racking.

Caleb inched up the stairs, and Madelyn stayed tucked close behind him until they reached the landing. A master bedroom sat to the right, the source of the water coming from somewhere beyond. A connecting bathroom?

Caleb halted, throwing out a hand to stop her, and she noticed the disarray in the bedroom. Clothes tossed from the dresser drawers, underwear dangling, cotton panties and bras dumped on a flowered chair in the corner. A jewelry cabinet plundered through, costume jewelry scattered across the carpet as if the intruder had been searching for something valuable, then had been furious when he hadn't found a treasure chest.

Judging from the outside of the house and the furniture, why would a burglar have thought Nadine had valuables?

The metallic scent of blood suddenly assaulted Madelyn, the foul odors of death swirling around her in a rush. Water dripped and pinged against the floor, then she spotted blood, a river of it streaking the worn, white linoleum in the bathroom.

"Dear God." Caleb spun around, gripped her arms and tried to shield her from the sight with his body.

But Madelyn was frozen in horror, her gaze riveted to the floor where Nadine lay, her eyes staring blankly into space, her neck slashed, naked except for the towel wrapped around her.

A towel drenched in blood.

Chapter 6

Caleb silently murmured a Cherokee prayer at the sight of the dead woman. She'd been brutally assaulted and left naked lying in her own blood. Whoever had killed her was not only a cold-blooded killer, but he had no respect for women…or human life itself.

Madelyn gasped in horror, and he instinctively yanked her into his arms and backed her away from the bedroom into the hallway. He'd known something was wrong when he'd entered, had felt the violence in the house.

"Oh, my God," Madelyn whispered. "Nadine…she's been murdered."

"Don't touch anything, Madelyn."

Madelyn nodded, trembling. "I can't believe this. The poor woman. Who would do such a horrible thing?"

Caleb stilled, listening, his mind already ticking

away possibilities. Judging from the signs of rigor and the bloodstains, Nadine had probably been dead for hours, maybe even a day or two.

"Why would someone come all the way out here to rob Nadine?" Madelyn frowned at the mess. "What were they looking for?"

Caleb's thoughts fast-tracked into detective mode. If the perp was a drug addict or homeless person, they might be looking for cash or anything to sell.

But the pervading presence of evil simmered in the tension-laden air. "This doesn't look like a burglary gone bad," Caleb said. "The degree of violence, the lack of hesitation wounds, the force and depth of the slice on the woman's throat indicates intent." And the timing definitely added to his suspicions. If Nadine had information about Cissy's abduction, someone could have killed her to keep her quiet.

Madelyn's pallor turned a dismal gray as the implications sank in. "You think it has to do with me? With us looking for her?" Hysteria tinged her voice. "How would anyone know we were coming here?"

"I don't know," Caleb said, ushering her down the stairs. Unless the killer learned Madelyn had hired a detective. It was a small town, and word had probably spread that they'd been asking questions. And if the exhumation itself had been leaked, the killer/abductor would realize they knew the grave was empty.

"Mansfield knew we were working together. He might have guessed our intentions and warned whoever else was involved," Caleb finally answered.

"So either Mansfield or another accomplice is trying to shut people up," Madelyn said, her tone tinged with disbelief.

"Right." The thought made fury rail through him. The conniving, lying bastard.

And even if Mansfield hadn't killed the woman himself, he could have hired cronies. A man like him—or his father—wouldn't bloody his own hands.

However, he might murder to protect himself from prison.

He coaxed Madelyn into the living room, scanning the outside of the house through the windows as he punched in Ben's number.

"GAI. Camp speaking."

"It's Walker. We're at Nadine Cotter's. She's dead." Caleb paced by the window, checking outside again as Madelyn sank into a chair. He could see the wheels turning in her head. She was probably thinking about Nadine, that she'd lost her chance to find out whatever information the woman possessed.

"What happened?" Ben asked.

"Someone slashed her throat. I need you to call the local sheriff and get him out here with a crime unit. But give me a few minutes. I'd like to look around first." Although if whoever had broken in was hunting for evidence Nadine had hidden about the adoptions, they might have already found it.

Still, he had to search himself.

"You got it," Ben said.

"And keep an ear out for Mansfield," Caleb added. "If he was behind this woman's murder, maybe he'll spill his guts and we can catch him."

The image of Nadine's dead body was imprinted in Madelyn's brain. She had seen news reports of murders before but never anyone close and personal. All that blood…

And with Nadine gone, how would Madelyn know if she'd been involved in her daughter's disappearance?

What if she never found Cissy?

Accepting Cissy's death had been difficult enough, but she couldn't rest now, not knowing she was alive and possibly in danger.

Caleb disconnected the call, then shifted. "I'm going to my car for gloves, then I'll search the house before the police arrive."

Madelyn shifted. "What are you looking for?"

Caleb shrugged. "Evidence that Nadine knew about the adoptions. Maybe someone sent her a threatening note. Or she could have kept a journal or date book."

Madelyn's gaze swung across the kitchen to the adjoining living room. The killer might have ransacked the house to cover his tracks.

Which meant that the killer was aware that Nadine knew about Emery's illicit dealings. But who?

The back door from the kitchen stood slightly ajar, and Caleb walked over and studied it. "The lock's been jimmied," Caleb said. "This is how the killer got in."

Madelyn pulled herself together and removed her own gloves from her jacket pocket. Nadine's body needed to be tended to. Her family notified.

Guilt assaulted her for searching her private space.

But if Nadine had known about Cissy and kept silent all these years, then Madelyn shouldn't feel guilty.

Caleb clenched her arms. "Madelyn, let me do this. I don't want you involved."

Hysterical laughter bubbled in her throat. "I am involved, Caleb. If we both search, we can finish faster, then the police can come."

He stared at her for a heartbeat, then nodded in concession. "All right. But let me get some latex gloves for both of us. I'll take the upstairs and you check the kitchen and living room."

Madelyn's heart raced as he hurried outside to the Jeep. Seconds later, he returned and they both donned the gloves. "Put everything back like you found it," Caleb added. "We don't want to interfere with the investigation, just see if there's anything that can help us nail Mansfield or lead us to Cissy."

Madelyn agreed, then started with the kitchen desk and drawers while Caleb disappeared up the stairs. She found shopping receipts, coupons, thank-you notes from several patients' families, paycheck stubs from the medical service where Nadine was employed and insurance statements along with bills that hadn't been paid.

Frustrated when the kitchen turned up nothing, she moved to the den and examined the coffee table, the drawers in the end tables and the coat closet. Nothing there, either.

Footsteps sounded, and Caleb descended the steps, his expression solemn. "Did you find anything?"

"No. How about you?"

He shook his head. "If she had a journal or received threats, the killer must have taken the evidence." His gaze fell to the fireplace, and he strode over and squatted down.

Using the fire poker, he dug through the ashes, unearthing the charred remains of a leather-bound book.

Madelyn's pulse pounded. "Is it salvageable?"

Caleb lifted it to study the contents, but the pages disintegrated into ashes, scattering onto the hearth. A siren wailed in the distance, and Madelyn wanted to scream.

They had been too late for the evidence and too late for Nadine.

What were they going to do now?

Caleb pocketed his and Madelyn's gloves, then he and Madelyn stepped onto the front porch to meet the sheriff.

Sheriff Gray stepped from the squad car; a deputy emerged from the passenger side.

Sheriff Gray crooked his head toward the deputy. "This is Deputy Stone Alexander."

Caleb extended his hand. "Caleb Walker, GAI. This is Madelyn Andrews, my client."

"The sheriff filled me in about the exhumation," Deputy Stone said.

"What are you doing here?" Gray asked. "You found a body?"

Caleb nodded. "Mrs. Andrews and I drove out to talk to Nadine Cotter, the woman who lives here, about Mrs. Andrews's missing child."

"I remembered her from the hospital," Madelyn said. "She was on duty the night I delivered the twins."

"I see." Sheriff Gray made a sound in his throat. "Go upstairs, Alexander. Check out the scene. I'll be right up."

Deputy Alexander nodded and climbed the stairs, then Gray turned back to them. "So you broke into the house and found her dead?"

Madelyn started to speak, but Caleb cleared his

throat, piping up first. The last thing he wanted was for Madelyn to implicate herself with a motive. "No. We knocked several times but when there was no answer, I tried the door. It swung open, and I noticed that the place was in disarray then smelled blood, so I came in to see if Nadine was all right."

Sheriff Gray gave them both a long, assessing stare.

"It looks like she might have been dead for a while," Caleb said before the sheriff could ask more questions. "Someone slashed her throat."

"Did either of you touch anything?"

Caleb shook his head. "No. But Madelyn was in shock, so I brought her downstairs to sit down."

The sheriff gave them another curious look as if he was trying to decide whether or not to believe them, then moved toward the front door. "Wait outside until the crime van arrives." He glared at Caleb. "You will wait, won't you?"

"Of course," Caleb said. "I'm a professional, Sheriff. All we want are answers."

The next two hours dragged by as the medical examiner arrived, and the sheriff and crime unit examined the scene.

"You were right," Dr. Rollo said after he'd completed his initial exam. "I'd put time of death sometime during the night or early this morning. Rigor's already setting in."

"My bet is on Mansfield," Caleb said. "He was pretty upset when we questioned him."

The sheriff cocked his head sideways. "You think he killed Miss Cotter to cover himself."

Caleb shrugged. "What better way to silence her than murder?"

* * *

Madelyn wrestled with guilt as Caleb drove her to pick up her car at GAI.

"I'm going to phone Ben and see if he's made any headway hacking into that list."

"It's late. I need to pick up Sara." Madelyn jiggled her keys. "My mom adores her, but she needs her rest."

Caleb nodded. "I'll let you know if Ben finds anything."

The weight of the day washed over Madelyn. Cissy was alive.

But Nadine, her only lead, was dead. Murdered.

Perhaps because someone didn't want her to find Cissy.

Caleb squeezed her shoulder, and Madelyn had the insane urge to lean into him. To ask him to hold her and make her forget the image of Nadine's blood splattered all over the bathroom floor.

"Madelyn, it's not your fault, you know," Caleb said gruffly.

She jerked her gaze to his. "Isn't it?"

"No," Caleb said matter-of-factly. "If Nadine was killed because of her involvement in Cissy's disappearance, she was guilty of conspiracy and should have come forward."

"Maybe." Madelyn ached inside. "But what if Emery or Mansfield, or whoever else was involved, coerced her into cooperating? Maybe they threatened her family or her. Then she was a victim, too."

"That's possible. But she could have turned to the police or someone else for help," Caleb suggested.

Madelyn's mind worked. "Maybe she'd decided to come forward."

"That's possible," Caleb agreed.

But they might never know. The secrets Nadine had hidden would be buried with her in her grave.

And what about Cissy? Did her adopted parents know she'd been stolen from her real mother? Was she in danger?

Would she ever find her now?

Her shoulders sagging from the stress of the day, she climbed in her minivan and started for her mom's. Caleb watched as she backed from the drive, and once again, she had the crazy urge to stop and ask him to go home with her. To hold her hand tonight.

To stay with her and help her forget.

But Madelyn had a daughter to think of. She had no time to think about herself.

One man had hurt her terribly and abandoned her and their child. She wouldn't give another man the chance to break her heart.

Swinging the van around, she sped toward Sanctuary's seniors home, pushing thoughts of Caleb from her mind. He was a detective. A man she'd hired to help her.

That was all he would ever be.

The quiet of the small town reminded her that Sanctuary was supposed to be safe, but Madelyn felt the darkness smothering her like a storm cloud ready to unleash more misery on her soul.

The ten-minute drive passed in a blur, and she parked and rushed in to get Sara.

"We've had a great day." Her mother patted Sara where she lay curled on the sofa with her blanket asleep.

Madelyn hugged her mother. "Thanks for letting her stay so long."

"You don't have to thank me, honey. We're family."

The corners of her eyes crinkled with worry. "Poor child was so exhausted she conked out about a half hour ago."

"She didn't sleep well last night," Madelyn admitted.

Madelyn's mother clutched her hand. "Did you make any progress?"

Madelyn flinched. "The lawyer who handled the adoptions won't talk. And we went to see one of the nurses who was on staff the night I delivered, but she had been murdered."

"Oh, my God, that's horrible." Madelyn's mother squared her shoulders. "But you can't give up, honey. You will find Cissy and bring her home where she belongs."

The tears were threatening, but Madelyn blinked them back. "You're always so strong, Mom, so positive." She hugged her hard. "Thank you for giving me courage."

Her mother held her for a long moment, massaging her back like she had when Madelyn was little, and emotions nearly overwhelmed her. Three generations—her mother, her, Sara and Cissy—were all bound together in love and loyalty.

They all needed answers and closure to move on.

"I love you, Madelyn," her mother whispered. "But I won't be around forever. I want you to find someone, a good man for you, a father for the girls."

"Mom, hush, don't even talk like that." In spite of her best efforts, a tear slipped down Madelyn's cheek. "Sara and I love you with all our hearts. *You* are all we need. And one day soon I'll bring Sara and Cissy here to see you, and you're going to take a walk with us and everything will be all right again."

Her mother laughed softly. "Yes, darling, that is the picture I see, too."

Madelyn clung to her for a moment, then realized she needed to let her mother rest. So she blinked back her tears, kissed her mother on the cheek, then released her and scooped a sleepy Sara into her arms and carried her to the car.

Sara roused for a moment. "Mommy?"

"Yes, precious, I'm here." Madelyn kissed Sara's cheek then buckled her in and drove them home.

Her house seemed unusually quiet and lonely, she thought, as she carried Sara up the stairs and tucked her into the white twin bed.

Then haunted by the memory of Nadine's blood and too anxious to sleep, she descended the steps to make a cup of tea. Or maybe she'd break down and have a glass of wine.

But the phone trilled as she hit the bottom step. Thinking it might be her mother or her nurse, or Caleb, she rushed over and yanked up the handset. "Hello."

"Stop nosing around," a low, coarse voice growled. "Or you'll lose Daughter Number Two this time."

Chapter 7

Caleb rapped his knuckles on the glass windows of Camp's office door, mentally stewing over the fact that Nadine, their closest lead, had been murdered.

The bastard who'd slashed her throat had wanted to keep her quiet. Which meant he was scared.

Ben motioned him in, then leaned back in his chair. Caleb sensed he was wired and wondered what he'd discovered. "Sheriff met you at the Cotter house," Ben said.

Caleb nodded. "Forensics is processing the place now. I doubt they find anything though. Killer ransacked the house to make it look like a robbery. I found a journal that had been burned in the fireplace."

Ben chewed the inside of his cheek. "You must be on the right track."

Yeah, but not fast enough. "Can you examine Nadine Cotter's phone records?" Caleb asked. "Maybe the

killer has had contact with her the past few weeks…
or months."

Ben began digging through computer printouts on
his desk. He was like a mad scientist, scattered, but
brilliant at his job. Even better, he covered his tracks
so the cops and feds couldn't trace him.

"Madelyn said there were late bills in Nadine's
kitchen," Caleb continued. "Maybe she went back for
more blackmail money."

"And the killer got nervous and ended it."

Caleb's cell phone vibrated on his hip, and he reached
for it to check the number just as Ben pushed the papers toward him.

"Here's a preliminary list of people who used Mansfield's services for adoptions."

"There were ten names I've found so far. Six babies
were boys, so I ruled those out. Three couples lived in
North Carolina. The fourth couple moved to Tennessee,
although they've fallen off the radar. I'll keep searching for an address."

Caleb's phone vibrated again, and he punched the
connect key. "Madelyn?"

"Caleb, I… A man just called and threatened me."

Caleb rushed down the stairs and outside. "What
did he say?"

Madelyn's shaky breath echoed back.

"Madelyn? Is someone there?"

"No… At least not now." She sighed shakily. "But
I'm scared, Caleb. He said if I didn't stop nosing around,
that I'd lose D… Daughter Number Two."

Son of a bitch!

Caleb jumped in his Jeep. "Lock all the doors, Madelyn. I'll be right there."

* * *

You'll lose Daughter Number Two this time. Daughter Number Two... Daughter Number Two...

The taunting voice echoed over and over in Madelyn's head.

No! She ran to the kitchen and checked the lock on the back door, then raced from room to room checking the windows. Her heart pounded as she slipped into Sara's room and stood by her bed watching her sleep, soaking in the fact that for now she was safe and alive and in her own bed.

She clenched and unclenched her fists. No one would hurt Sara. They would have to kill her first.

She needed a gun. Some way to defend them. She'd ask Caleb to suggest the best place for her to buy one in the morning. There was no way she'd let anyone hurt Sara.

You'll lose Daughter Number Two this time...

Whoever this man was, he knew what had happened to Cissy.

Did he know where she was now?

Frantic, she raced back down the steps, grabbed the phone and checked the caller log for a number, but the display screen showed *Unknown.*

Coward. He was a coward who stole children and threatened mothers and didn't even leave his name.

She'd kill him if she ever found him. Kill him if he hurt Cissy....

A car engine sounded, rumbling as it beat a path up her drive. The wind howled off the mountain, whipping at the roof of the wooden house. Clenching the phone in one hand, she dashed to the window, flipped on the porch light and peered out.

Car lights fanned the front porch, then a Jeep screeched to a stop. Her breath puffed out in relief, and she started to run to the door but caution made her wait until she saw Caleb emerge from the SUV. His big body looked ominous in the moonlight, his long hair falling loose and brushing his collar, his expression dark as he scanned the yard and perimeter in search of a predator.

The threatening call taunted her again, and she flew to the door and swung it open. Caleb climbed the porch steps in three quick strides, his strong jaw snapped taut as he met her gaze.

"Are you all right?"

She shook her head no, then fell into his arms.

Caleb wrapped his arms around Madelyn and held her tight. His heart had nearly pounded out of his chest on the way over. He kept imagining that someone had been outside Madelyn's house, lurking in the bushes, waiting to attack.

Waiting to slash her throat just as he had Nadine Cotter's.

And then little Sara... Was this killer so evil that he would hurt a child?

Madelyn clung to him, and he stroked her back, rocking her gently. She felt so tiny in his arms, so fragile, and she had been through so much today already that he had to make her feel safe. "It's all right, Madelyn. I won't let him hurt you or Sara."

Even as he made the promise, recriminations screamed in his head. He'd vowed to protect Mara, too, but he had lost her and his unborn son.

He couldn't fail this woman and her child, too.

"I can't believe this is happening," Madelyn said,

then stared up at him, her big eyes swimming in shock. "I want a gun, Caleb," she said, that fierceness back in her tone. "I need protection for me and Sara."

Mixed feelings warred in Caleb's head. "Madelyn, I know you're scared, but I'm not sure a gun is the answer. Not with a child in the house."

"But you carry a weapon," she argued. "And I can't leave us vulnerable. I have to take action."

"You took action," he said in a soothing tone. "You hired me, and I promise to protect you and Sara and find the person who kidnapped Cissy."

"But you won't always be around," Madelyn said. "One day we'll be alone, and I need to know that I can keep my girls safe. They need to know it, too. They shouldn't have to grow up afraid all the time."

That picture disturbed Caleb, as well. He wanted to promise Madelyn he would be around forever, but that would be a lie. When the case ended, she'd move on with her life. Find some man worthy to be her husband and a father to her girls.

He admired Madelyn's gutsy attitude. But considering shooting someone and actually following through were two different things. Too many times an intruder managed to wrestle the person's gun away and turn it against him.

Tormented by the desperation in her voice though, he spoke softly. "Listen, when there's time to teach you how to use a weapon safely, I'll teach you myself. It would probably be a good idea for you to take some self-defense classes, too. But for now, trust me."

He hoped to hell he wasn't asking for blind trust that he couldn't deliver.

Fear darkened her eyes, but he sensed he was getting through. "I guess I'm just panicking," she said in a hoarse whisper. "That man…the threat… His voice sounded so ominous."

"Which means we're on the right track and he's scared," Caleb said. A strand of hair fell across her cheek and he brushed it back. "It means Nadine's death must be related to our investigation, that she was hiding something."

"But she died and now we'll never find out what she knew," Madelyn said, her voice warbling.

"Not necessarily," Caleb said. "Ben is examining her phone records, so if the killer has been communicating with her, we can track him down. He's also cross-checking her calls with yours to see if there's a common number." He paused, arching a brow. "And if you'll agree, I'll have him place a trace on your phone so if this bastard calls back, we might be able to track his location."

Hope flickered in her eyes. "Of course you can trace my calls," she said. "Anything to protect Sara."

"Good." Caleb forced himself to release her. He liked the feel of her close to him too damn much. This was a case, and that was all it could be. He couldn't become attached to her or her child.

"Ben gave me a list of couples who used Mansfield to handle their adoptions," Caleb said. "There are four names we need to check out. They may not have Cissy, but it's a place to start."

Excitement lit her face. "Oh, my God, Mansfield disclosed his list?"

"Not exactly." Caleb shot her a warning look not to probe, then led her to the kitchen table and handed her the printout. "Study these names and see if any of them sound familiar."

She frowned as she read the names. "No one rings a bell. You think the person who adopted Cissy was someone I knew?" she asked in an incredulous tone.

"I don't know," Caleb said honestly. "The adoptive parents could have been innocent, unaware that Cissy was kidnapped."

Anxiety replaced the hope in her expression. "That's true, but Cissy is my little girl. And if Sara says she's in trouble, I believe her." She jutted up her chin. "If you don't, Caleb, I need to find someone who does."

Caleb wanted to deny that he believed Sara's gift, but how could he when he was cursed with his own sixth sense? When he knew gifts like theirs couldn't be trusted, but they sure as hell couldn't be ignored, either?

Because if Sara was right about a man threatening Cissy and her mother, and this killer was panicked enough to kill Nadine to silence her, he might kill Cissy and her mother to cover his tracks.

"Should I call someone else?" Madelyn asked.

Caleb shook his head. "No. I promised I'd find out what happened to your daughter, and I will. But there is something I need to ask you."

Madelyn stared at him warily. "What?"

"Is there anyone you can think of who would have wanted to hurt you years ago?"

Madelyn frowned. "No. Not that I know of."

"Did your family support the pregnancy and your marriage?"

"Yes."

"Tell me about them."

"My father walked out on us before I was born," Madelyn said matter-of-factly. "So my mother was hesitant about me marrying Tim, but she supported my decision and was ecstatic about the twins."

"How about Tim? Did he want children?"

"We hadn't exactly planned on children so soon, but he acted happy about the pregnancy."

"What does he do for a living?"

"I'm not sure what he's doing now. When we were married, Tim was a salesman for a hardware store."

"He traveled a lot?"

"All the time." Despair threatened again. "He felt horrible for not being home the night I had the accident."

"Where was he?"

"Raleigh, on business, but he rushed to the hospital as soon as he received word."

"How did he react over losing the baby?"

Madelyn massaged her temple, remembering those first shocked, grief-stricken days.

"Madelyn?"

"He was understandably upset," she said shakily. "Riddled with guilt. I think that's what eventually caused the rift between us. He couldn't get past the guilt." Her voice dropped. "Neither could I."

"It wasn't your fault," Caleb said gruffly.

Other people had assured Madelyn of the same thing, but guilt wasn't rational. She was the mother; she was supposed to protect her child at all costs.

"Tim abandoned you and Sara when you needed him most." Caleb's tone reeked of disgust.

Madelyn had long ago tried to let go of the anger. If she'd allowed it to fester, it would have clouded every moment of her day and affected Sara. And she'd vowed to be a good mother to the little baby who'd survived.

"We were no good to each other back then," Madelyn said. "I suppose it was my fault, too. I was so obsessed with being a mother and grieving that I had no time for him."

Caleb muttered a curse. "Don't blame yourself or defend the creep. Any man who leaves his wife and child is not worthy of having a family."

His words soothed the ache building in her chest from the troubling memories.

"I'm going to phone Ben in the morning to start that trace and check your phone records. You'd better get some sleep."

Their fingers brushed as she handed him the printout, and a tingle shot through her, the warmth of knowing that he'd come to her rescue tonight creating an intimacy in the small kitchen.

An intimacy she hadn't shared with anyone in ages. One she didn't dare dwell on now.

"Thank you for staying," she said quietly. "I'll leave a pillow and blanket on the sofa."

"Thanks," Caleb said. "We'll start fresh in the morning."

His gaze locked with hers, emotions flickering in its depth. The air felt charged, electric. Sensual. Filled with the kind of tension that made her pulse pound and her breasts feel heavy.

But she stifled her feelings. If Cissy was in danger, they had to hurry.

* * *

Cissy heard her mommy's scream, jumped out of bed and ran down the hall. The kitchen door was open, the big man hovering over her mommy.

No...

Her mommy had told the big man to leave them alone, but he'd come back.

Now he had her by the throat. Something shiny glinted in the dim light. Cissy stared at it, terrified. It was big and sharp and jagged...

A knife!

No, no, no! She wanted to scream, but the sound died in her throat. She had to do something. Help her mommy.

Think, Cissy, think.

Help, Sara, help!

The man jerked her mother around like a rag doll and flung her against the kitchen sink. Her mother pushed against him, but he slapped her in the face so hard her mother's legs buckled.

She hated the meanie. Her mommy said he was her uncle, but he'd never been nice to her. And he was always yelling at her mommy.

She had to stop him!

Cissy ran to her room to get the bat she'd gotten for her birthday. But she stumbled and tripped in the hall. Her knees hit the cold wood, her hands clawing for something to hold on to.

A cry pierced the air behind her, and she choked on a scream herself. The man was hurting her mama. She had to get help.

But it was dark and spooky and tears burned her eyes as she crawled to her room. She swept her hand along the floor behind the doorway searching for it, but the bat was gone.

No, no, no! Where was it?

Choking back another sob, she slid on her belly and felt beneath the bed. Her fingers closed around the bat's end, and she grabbed it and ran toward the kitchen.

But another loud scream pierced the air just as she made it to the door.

"Run, Cissy!" her mother shouted.

The shiny metal thing flickered in the light. The monster swung it up and jabbed it straight into her mommy's throat.

Her mommy screamed again. Her throat gurgled. Her head fell back.

Then all Cissy saw was red....

Chapter 8

Sara's terrified scream cut through Madelyn like a knife, and she jerked from sleep, jumped from bed and raced across the hall. Another nightmare?

Or could the man who'd threatened her have sneaked in?

Caleb's boots pounded up the steps, and he reached out his arm to push her behind him, then scanned the dark room.

A ribbon of sunlight peeked through the blinds, and Madelyn searched the room, as well. Nothing.

Except Sara was thrashing in the sheets again, sobs racking her body.

"It's clear," he said, then stepped aside for her to enter.

Her heart in her throat, Madelyn rushed toward her daughter.

"No, no, no..." Sara cried. "Run, Cissy, run!" Sara

twisted back and forth, tangling the sheets around her. Tears flowed down her little face. "Go the other way. Hurry! He's gonna get you!"

Madelyn gently shook Sara. "Honey, wake up. You're dreaming again."

Another scream pierced the air, and Sara's body convulsed with fear. "Run, Cissy!"

"Sara," Madelyn said more firmly. "Please wake up. You're safe, honey."

But Sara beat her fists at Madelyn's chest, lost in the throes of the nightmare. Madelyn hugged her daughter, swaying her back and forth. "Shh, honey, Mommy's here. I won't let anyone hurt you."

The lamp flickered on, casting a faint glow across the room, and she glanced at Caleb, tears blurring her eyes. Her little girl was in agony and Madelyn felt helpless.

Caleb inched toward her, his big body filling the room with his presence as he placed a comforting hand on her shoulder.

"Cissy, hide..." Sara whimpered. "No, mister, please, don't hurt her!"

Madelyn's throat ached. She wanted to scream that it wasn't fair for Sara to be plagued with these nightmares. Why hadn't God given her this second sight instead of little Sara? "Honey, wake up and talk to Mommy."

Slowly Sara stirred from the dream, her body trembling. A terrified, glazed look clouded her eyes.

"Sara, look, it's Mommy. And Caleb is here, too." Madelyn cradled Sara, rocking her again. "You're safe in your room and no one is going to hurt you."

Shock and fear etched itself on Sara's small face. "But Mommy... He killed Cissy's mama... He had a

knife...then it was red...so red...red everywhere..."
Sara's voice cracked. "And now he's got Cissy, and
he's gonna kill her, too."

Caleb clenched his jaw at the fear in the child's voice.

Madelyn's teary-eyed look sent a wave of unexpected
feelings over him. More than anything, he wanted to
help her and Sara.

Maybe somehow it would make up for failing his
own family.

He knelt by the bed and pulled one of Sara's tiny
hands in his. Suddenly the images from Sara's mind
filled his own. A dark crimson stain bled across the
floor. The knife glinted in the dark, the jagged blade
carving a hole in the woman's throat. Then splatters of
red spurted from her neck and dripped down her body.

Blood. It was everywhere.

His heart thrummed. He squeezed Sara's hand, hoping to deepen the connection. "Tell me what you see,
Sara."

Sara made a strangled sound and clutched his hand
tighter. Once again the images in her mind appeared
in his as if a camera was showing him live feed. The
red grew brighter, stronger, filling up the space in her
mind. Then sounds and scents flooded him as if she
was reliving the gruesome murder.

*A loud scream pierced the air. A woman's. The sound
of a struggle. A glass breaking. A man's grunt. Another
scream from the woman, shrill with pain. The metallic scent of blood assaulted him along with the other
acrid odors of death.*

A little girl's gasp followed, low, scared. Shocked.
What else?

He tried to hone in on everything in the room, but he could only see through Sara's eyes. And at the moment, Sara was in shock over the sight of the blood.

"Sara, I know it's dark and it's red. Really red." He lowered his voice to a soothing pitch. "But try to drag your eyes away from the red. Look around the room, at the man and tell us what else you saw."

Madelyn's fingernails dug into his arm, disapproving, desperate. "Caleb stop. She needs to forget about it, not remember."

Caleb met Madelyn's agonized gaze. "If what she's seeing is real, the only way to make the nightmares end is to find Cissy and save her."

Surprise flickered in Madelyn's eyes as if she'd just realized that he believed Sara when no one else did. Then turmoil, because if Sara was right, her sister was in terrible danger.

That meant they had to encourage her to talk.

"Sara, baby," Madelyn said softly. "It's important. Where is Cissy? Is she with her mommy?"

Sara shook her head. "I don't know. I can't see her anymore."

"What happened when she saw the red?" Caleb asked. "Where was she?"

"In the hall by the kitchen."

"Now look up past the red, past the floor. Do you see the man?"

Sara nodded, a tremor making her body shake. "His hand?"

"His hand? What else?"

"A knife," she whispered. "It's shiny and sharp and the red… It's dripping from the end…."

Caleb silently cursed. So the image he'd seen in his

mind was the same as Sara's visions. She'd witnessed the poor woman's murder.

Sucking in a calming breath, he rubbed Sara's hand. Her skin was clammy, her hand jittery. "Look past the knife, Sara. Do you see the man's face?"

Suddenly Sara released a wail, buried her head in her mommy's chest and the connection between her and Caleb was lost. "No," Sara cried. "I don't wants to see him. He's a monster."

"I know, Sara, but you're safe here, and I know you want to help Cissy, don't you?" Caleb said gently.

She gulped. "Yes."

Caleb wiped a tear from her cheek with his thumb. "If we know what this man looks like, we can catch him, honey."

Sara hiccupped on another sob. "He's mean and ugly and gots big hands."

Caleb gave Madelyn a sympathetic look as she soothed her little girl. He hated pushing the child, but any detail she offered might help.

"Sara," he said quietly. "Why don't you rest with your mommy for a while. Then when you feel better, maybe you can draw some pictures of the man. Okay?"

Sara nodded, and clung to her mother, obviously terrified the man might come and hurt them, as well.

If Sara was right and the killer had murdered Cissy's adopted mother, he must be getting rid of everyone who could nail him for the kidnapping.

Which meant he might come after Sara and Madelyn.

Caleb stepped into the hallway then removed his cell phone from the clip on his belt and punched in the number for GAI. They needed to find out if any women with five-year-old daughters had been reported murdered.

Every second counted.

Madelyn's stomach knotted with fear. Cissy might be running from a crazed killer this very second.

She wanted to scream and cry and rail against the injustice. What if they weren't doing enough? What if they didn't find Cissy in time?

Guilt mingled with terror. If only she'd trusted Sara earlier and insisted on exhuming that coffin herself. Then maybe she could have discovered the truth and found Cissy before…

Don't give up. If Sara had a connection with Cissy, Sara would know if it was too late.…

Sara sniffled, her breath choppy. Poor baby.

Madelyn tucked a strand of hair behind Sara's ear. "You are such a courageous little girl, Sara," Madelyn said softly. "I know you're scared and what you saw was awful. But you're brave to tell Caleb and me about it."

Sara clung to her. "I wants to find her, Mommy. To saves her."

"Oh, baby…" Madelyn almost choked herself. "We will find her." God, she prayed she was right. How would Sara survive if they didn't?

How would she?

Feeling helpless, she sagged against the chair. Then Sara reached up and kissed her cheek. "I loves you, Mommy. I don't wants to ever lose you."

Anger suffused Madelyn. Her five-year-old should be contemplating what game to play next, planning tea parties with her friends, thinking about learning to ride her bike without training wheels, and sledding down the big hill during the next snowfall, not about death and murder and monster men attacking her.

"Don't you worry, precious." She kissed away her daughter's tears. "Mommy will always be here with you."

Sara studied her for a long moment, then took a deep breath, pushed away and straightened as if she'd gotten a bolt of courage. "I'm ready to draw that picture now."

Madelyn cradled her daughter's face in her hands. She was so beautiful that her heart ached. "Are you sure? You don't have to do anything you don't want to do."

Sara pursed her lips in a stubborn gesture that Madelyn recognized well.

"Yes, Mommy. I need my crayons and paper."

"All right. Go get them."

Sara scooted off the bed and raced over to her craft table with a determined gleam in her eyes.

"Mommy's going to make coffee while you get started," Madelyn said. "Is that all right?"

Sara nodded, and studied the paper as if trying to decide where to begin. Madelyn didn't want to leave her alone for long, but she hadn't slept well either and needed some caffeine so she hurried down the steps.

Caleb stood at the kitchen window looking out, yet he must have heard her footsteps because he turned around, his phone pressed to his ear. His gaze met hers, his eyes stormy.

Then his gaze raked down her body, over the flannel shirt to her bare legs, and she suddenly felt naked.

As if he was literally touching her with his eyes.

Shivering at the mere thought of his hands on her

bare skin, Madelyn crossed her arms, wishing she'd donned a robe.

Self-recriminations quickly followed. Good heavens, what Caleb thought of her should be the last thing on her mind. Cissy's life depended on them.

Caleb's jaw snapped tight, and he glanced away, speaking low into the phone, and she quickly set the coffee to brew and retrieved a couple of hand-painted mugs from the cabinet.

"Thanks, Gage," Caleb said. "I'll discuss it with Madelyn."

He ended the call, then turned back to her, his professional look tacked into place as if they hadn't shared an intimate moment earlier. "Coffee smells good."

She tapped her fingers on the counter. "Did you sleep?"

"Some. I hope you don't mind," he said, "but I keep a duffel bag with clean clothes in my car. I grabbed a shower down here to clean up."

"That's fine." Lord help her. He looked fresh and sexy with his damp hair brushing his collar.

"Sara all right?"

"She's terrified. But she's drawing that picture now."

Caleb eyes flickered with admiration. "She's a brave little girl, Madelyn."

"I know." Madelyn's throat thickened. "But I don't want her to have to be brave. I want her to be a child, to have fun...."

Caleb moved toward her to comfort her, but Madelyn threw up a warning hand. If he touched her now, if he held her, she might completely fall apart.

Either that or beg him to never leave her.

Neither one would help them find Cissy. And finding her was all that mattered.

She gestured to his phone as he tucked it into his belt. "What are you supposed to discuss with me?"

He sighed. "I'm going to track down those couples on the list today. If you want to go, Gage suggested we drop Sara at his house to play with his little girl, Ruby. His wife Leah loves kids, and it might do Sara good to distract her for a while."

His sensitivity touched her. "That sounds like a good idea." She jerked her head toward the doorway. "I should get back. I hate for her to be alone."

He nodded, then surprised her by brushing her hair back with his hand. "I understand this is difficult, Madelyn, but she's a tough little girl." His gaze darkened, fastening so intently on her face that Madelyn squirmed.

"She's just like her mother," he finished. "She'll be okay."

Madelyn's throat thickened at his praise. If only her husband had seen Sara that way. Instead he'd bought into her psychosis and deserted them.

Unable to reply for fear she'd reveal how much his comment meant to her, she simply nodded, then reached for the coffee mug. But she felt his gaze on her as she poured herself some coffee, added sweetener and turned to go back upstairs.

He filled the other mug, then followed her, making her body tingle with awareness. She should have gotten her robe, shouldn't have looked into his eyes and seen that spark of heat.

But as she walked into Sara's room and spotted the crimson splatters her daughter had drawn, her breath hitched. The dead woman lay on the floor in the middle of the blood, the crude drawing of the killer erasing all thoughts of heat and Caleb's eyes.

Sara's description of the man as being a monster was mirrored in the sketch. Madelyn studied the details—his face was round, and Sara had added stray marks that gave him a wooly look suggesting he had a beard. A long, jagged line ran across the upper right side of his forehead. A scar?

Her heart pounded. For a brief second, the man looked familiar.

Clenching the coffee mug with a white-knuckled grip, she tried to remember if she'd seen him before, but the brief image in her mind faded, and she couldn't put her finger on anything specific.

Then again, Sara's crude drawing might not be accurate at all. Certainly not enough for an ID.

Still, what if she had seen the man? What if he lived around Sanctuary or had been lurking around town? Maybe he'd shopped in her own store?

No… She would have remembered customers…

Her nerves pinged. Dear God. He could have been at the grocery store or the park or even the library.

And if he was watching, he'd know she hadn't called off her search.

They had exhumed the coffin. And now they knew it was empty.

Damn Madelyn. She should have heeded his warning. But he'd watched her house all night, and he had planted a bug on her phone, and the bitch wasn't giving up. She'd called that private investigator the minute he'd hung up.

He balled his hands into fists. She would be sorry for making that call.

Hell, he didn't want to hurt the kid.

But he had to protect himself and his family.

That meant he had to tie up all loose ends.

Dammit, it was her fault the others had to die. Her fault if she lost her little girl this time.

Hunching in his coat, he slunk back to his car and headed toward the funeral home. Five years ago, Howard Zimmerman had needed money just like him. And he'd done his part and kept quiet.

But now?

If the police linked that wimpy funeral director to the kidnapping, he might spill his guts.

Laughter bubbled in his throat. The wimpy moron wouldn't get the chance.

Chapter 9

Caleb was anxious to start tracking down the couples on the list Ben had given him, so he rustled up some eggs and toast while he waited on Madelyn and Sara. He figured they needed time alone, and he hoped Sara could offer some clue through her sketches as to Cissy's location and the identity of the killer.

He had just poured some orange juice for the three of them when they entered the kitchen. Madelyn's look of surprise made his pulse jump.

"You cooked?" she asked.

He shrugged. "Thought we could use something to eat before we get started today."

Sara plopped into a chair, then dug the spoon into the jelly jar and spread a glob on her toast while Madelyn showed him Sara's drawings. He glanced at them but refrained from asking questions until Sara had a chance to eat. Madelyn even managed a few bites herself, although anxiety riddled her every movement.

"Brush your teeth and get dressed, Sara," Madelyn said after handing Sara a napkin. "We're going to drop you off to play with a little girl named Ruby. She's the daughter of one of Caleb's friends."

Sara looked wary. "But I wants to go with you to find Cissy."

Madelyn folded her napkin into a tiny square. "Honey, Caleb and I need to do this alone today."

Caleb wiped jelly off his mouth. "You'll like Ruby, Sara. And I promise to bring your mother back safe and sound."

Reluctantly Sara agreed and lumbered up the steps to dress. Caleb studied the drawings. "Did Sara relay any more details about this man or where her sister might be?"

"Not really." Madelyn sighed, then gestured at the sketch of the man's face. "Just that he had a beard. And the line on his forehead is a scar."

"That's helpful," Caleb said. "Did Cissy ever call the man by name?"

"No. And when I asked her to draw a picture of Cissy's mommy and daddy, she said she'd never seen Cissy's daddy."

Hmm. The sketch indicated the woman had short reddish hair. Brown eyes. And she was slightly plump. Other than that, there was nothing distinctive.

"How about her name?" Caleb asked.

"No." Frustration lined Madelyn's face. "Cissy just calls her Mommy."

Of course.

"Madelyn, when I first talked to Sara, she mentioned

that she and Cissy shared secrets. Can you try to find out what those secrets are?"

Madelyn scraped the scraps into the trash, then began loading the dishwasher. "You think there might have been abuse?"

Caleb shrugged, hating the fear and horror he'd planted in Madelyn's mind. But Sara's comment about secrets had needled him. "I don't know. The girls might have been discussing which boy they liked at preschool. On the other hand, it might be a lead. Maybe there's a special place they visit, or the name of that preschool or a family member that might lead us to their location."

"Right, I hadn't thought of that. I'll talk to Sara."

Caleb's cell phone buzzed. The caller ID showed it was Amanda Peterson, so he excused himself and answered the call while Madelyn went to help Sara dress.

"Caleb, I spoke with the hospital. Dr. Emery claimed Madelyn refused an autopsy. But get this. The medical examiner didn't sign off on the death certificate—Dr. Emery did."

"What about the funeral director?"

"His name is Howard Zimmerman. He's still with the local funeral home," Amanda said. "Do you want me to pay him a visit?"

"No, I'll stop by there then track down the couples on the list Ben gave me." He paused. "Thanks, Amanda. Maybe you could check with Derek's wife and see if her contacts with the adoption agency have a lead. Also, check with the Department of Children and Family Services. Perhaps they've had reports of abuse regarding a little girl named Cissy."

"I'm on it. Oh, and by the way, Caleb, forensics didn't

find anything in that coffin. No skin cells, DNA, no sign
at all that a body had ever been placed inside."

Good news, Caleb thought.

But the images from Sara's nightmare taunted him.
Cissy had survived five years ago.

But her time might be running out now.

Madelyn studied Leah and Gage's home; the sense
that they were a happy, trustworthy family was evident
in the way the couple exchanged loving looks between
themselves and their daughter, Ruby. On the ride over,
Caleb had explained that Gage had adopted Ruby, but
Madelyn would never have guessed that the little girl
wasn't his own daughter.

"We can play dress up in my room." Ruby's eyes
sparkled with excitement as she offered her hand to
Sara. "Mommy gave me a trunk full of prom dresses
and high heels. There's even a princess's tiara!"

Sara smiled, obviously torn between what sounded
like a fun adventure and the search for her sister, but
Madelyn gave her an encouraging pat, and Sara followed Ruby to her room.

"She's adorable," Leah said with a sincere smile.
"Gage explained about her twin. I'm so sorry, Madelyn. We went through a terrible scare with Ruby a
while back. I still wake up in a cold sweat just thinking about it."

"Thank you." Madelyn fidgeted, picking at an invisible piece of lint on her jacket. "I appreciate you watching Sara today."

"No problem." Leah rubbed her swollen abdomen.
"Ruby loves playmates. And Sara needs a friend right
now, too."

Madelyn sighed. "I've tried to do everything I can to protect her, but what if I fail?"

"You won't," Leah assured her. "Gage and Caleb are on your side now. They'll find your other daughter."

But what if she was too late? If Cissy's adopted mother was dead, who was protecting Cissy now?

Madelyn forced the negative thoughts aside. She could not think like that. "When are you due?"

Leah grinned. "Six weeks. We're having a boy this time."

Gage pulled Leah up against him with a proud grin. "Little girls are special, but I have to admit I can't wait to have a son and take him fishing."

Leah poked him. "Hey, Ruby and I like to fish, too."

They laughed and Madelyn's heart clenched. They obviously loved each other dearly and were a happy family. She wanted that for Sara and Cissy.

And for the first time in her life, she wanted it for herself.

Her gaze shot to Caleb, and an image of him holding her, kissing her, looking at her and the twins with love filled her head.

Oblivious, Caleb cleared his throat. "Thanks, Leah. We really need to go. We have several leads to check out."

Madelyn wrung her hands. "I'm not sure what time we'll be back."

"Don't worry. If it's late, Sara can sleep over. Tonight's movie night anyway. We usually make popcorn and spread sleeping bags out on the floor."

Exactly what she'd like to be doing with her daughter.

Madelyn glanced anxiously at Ruby's room. "I hope

Sara won't be a problem. She's been having terrible nightmares."

Leah squeezed her hands. "All the more reason for you to skedaddle and find her sister so those nightmares will end."

Madelyn nodded. That was the best thing she could do for Sara.

Gage walked them out to the car. "I talked to the sheriff," Gage said. "He agreed to inform us about any reported female murders in the state that fit our profile."

Caleb jangled his keys. "Thanks. Although he should expand that to include neighboring states. We have no idea if the couple who adopted Cissy stayed in North Carolina or moved."

"True. I'll talk to him and ask him to widen the search. Ben is also checking."

The details in Sara's sketches nagged at Madelyn. "I don't know if this means anything, but Cissy has been drawing sunflowers. Once, she depicted her sister hiding in a building with sunflowers growing inside."

Caleb quirked his mouth in thought. "Like a hothouse."

Gage's interest perked up. "I'll ask Slade to check on that angle. A specific type of greenhouse might help narrow down the location where the mother lives or works."

Madelyn climbed in the car, knotting her hands in her lap as Caleb drove them to the funeral home. The brick building with its adjoining chapel stirred painful memories of the memorial service she'd held for Cissy. She'd been in shock, grief stricken, and recovering from the C-section.

Yet now she knew her daughter hadn't been dead.

"I can't believe Dr. Emery lied to me and that he persuaded other people to cover for him."

Caleb's strong jaw twitched as he parked. "If Zimmerman was involved, he'll pay."

But justice would not replace the years she'd lost with her child.

She pushed aside the thought and squared her shoulders. She had to be strong. Focus on the future.

Together she and Caleb walked up to the front door of the funeral parlor. The bare flowerbeds mocked her. Ironically it had been the first day of spring when she'd held Cissy's memorial service. The azaleas had glowed with color, the air fragrant with spring. She'd stood in this very spot and wondered how she could possibly bury a child on such a beautiful day.

But she hadn't buried her. She'd buried an empty casket.

Renewed anger fortified her, and she shoved her way through the door. Inside, the scent of cleaning chemicals mingled with the sickening-sweet aroma of roses. The same soft elevator music echoed through the intercom, grating on her nerves.

A quick inventory of the interior, and she noted that the decor hadn't changed, either. Seating areas in grays and burgundy offered conversation areas to mourners, an office to the right served as the headquarters for the director and four viewing rooms flanked the hallway. Though usually at least one of them held a casket and was overflowing with visitors, this morning all four were empty, giving the place an eerie, morbid feel.

Caleb veered toward the office where a young blond man in his early twenties sat doing paperwork. Caleb knocked. "Excuse me, we need to speak to Howard Zimmerman."

The young man stood, fastening his dark suit jacket.

"I'm his son, Roy. Maybe I can help you? Are you here for a consultation about a lost loved one?"

Caleb's gaze cut across the sterile surroundings. "No, we really must speak with Howard. Is he here?"

Roy shifted, obviously curious now. "He's downstairs. I can get him for you if you'll just tell me what this is about."

Madelyn tried lamely to wrestle her emotions under control. But the cloying scents of the roses and memories of grief-filled faces and voices haunted her.

"It's regarding a missing child case." Caleb flashed his GAI identification. "Now lead the way, and we'll follow."

Roy looked uncertain, but Caleb's voice had been commanding, and his size obviously intimidated the young man, so he motioned for them to follow him down a flight of stairs, then a dark hall. The scent of formaldehyde, alcohol, bleach and other chemicals reeked from the end room, obviously meant to mask the stench of death, but failing.

Roy cracked the door and glanced inside, then shook his head. "Not in there. He must be inventorying the coffins."

Nerves gathered along Madelyn's spine, a chilling bleakness filling the air. Then Roy veered to the left and opened a set of double doors. Inside, caskets in various shades of gray, bronze and silver lined the room. Roy flicked on the overhead light making Madelyn blink against the sudden brightness.

Then Roy gasped and staggered backward.

Madelyn peered around him, and bile rose to her throat.

Howard Zimmerman was sprawled inside a pewter

casket, his limbs askew, his chest torn open by a bullet wound, blood soaking the white satin bedding and pillow.

Caleb shoved Madelyn behind him and out the door.

"Dad?" Roy's face turned a pasty white, and he stumbled forward toward the body, but Caleb blocked him.

"No, Roy, don't touch anything. This is a crime scene."

"My father..." Roy doubled over with shock and grief, then started to shake.

Madelyn pulled herself together faster than he would have imagined and gently gripped Roy's arm. "Come on, Roy. Step into the hall and take a deep breath."

Not that the hallway was any less of a reminder of death. The scents of chemicals permeated the floors and walls. The overwhelming feeling of grief and death and lost spirits lingered, their whispers taunting him. Angry spirits. Lost souls. Ones hanging in limbo and desperate for redemption. Others determined to exact revenge for a life cut short.

Then others who simply weren't ready to accept their fate and let go of loved ones.

Was that the reason Mara's spirit hovered by her grave? Was she angry with him? Or was she ready to move on but needed some kind of closure with him?

For a moment, he wondered if that could be the case between Sara and Cissy, if Cissy had already passed. Was her spirit hanging on, needing Sara to find her murderer so she could rest in peace?

No. He had to remain positive.

Sara's images had been reflected in his own mind. He'd heard Cissy's screams and felt her terror as if she was very much alive.

A low, keening sound erupted from Roy, jerking Caleb from his thoughts.

Madelyn helped the undertaker into a chair, and Roy leaned over, his elbows on his knees, gasping for air as if he might faint.

Caleb glanced back at Howard and silently cursed. Dammit, another lead gone.

How had the killer known they were going to question Nadine and Howard? Was there anyone else on his hit list?

Caleb punched the sheriff's number. "Sheriff Gray, this is Caleb Walker. I'm at the funeral home. Howard Zimmerman is dead."

"I'll be right there." Sheriff Gray's breath quickened as if he was hurrying outside. "What happened?"

Caleb explained his suspicions about the exhumation and funeral home. "Howard's son Roy brought us downstairs to speak to his father, but we found his body in one of the caskets."

"Damn," Sheriff Gray muttered. "Seems like everyone connected to Emery and the adoptions is being killed off."

"Yeah, someone is determined not to leave any witnesses behind." Caleb remembered the threat to Madelyn and Sara.

But the bastard would not hurt either one of them. Not unless he killed Caleb first.

He cursed as he watched little Sara Andrews playing with Gage McDermont's kid. The damn P.I. was watching them like a freaking hawk.

He'd never get the kid without getting caught.

Hell. He dropped his head into his hands and groaned. What was he going to do?

Nadine was dead and now Zimmerman was, too.

Two off his list.

And Cissy's mother. Number three. Stupid bitch shouldn't have started asking questions. He'd warned her, but just like Madelyn, she hadn't listened.

What to do with Cissy though… That was the big question.

He studied the P.I. and the kids again, then considered his options. Madelyn loved family more than anything. The fool woman would throw herself in front of a bus to protect her babies.

She had another family member that she worshipped, too.

Her mother.

He'd already researched her. Knew her phone number. Her address. Where she shopped. Who administered her meds at that senior home.

And when the woman was alone.

A grin curled his lips. He knew exactly how to force Madelyn to do as he ordered.

She'd learn the hard way.

He didn't like it, but it had to be.

Bye-bye Mama…

Chapter 10

Although Roy Zimmerman was visibly distraught over his father's murder, Caleb approached him as a suspect. Being upset or even in shock didn't negate the fact that he might have information.

"Roy." Caleb crossed his arms and faced the young man. "We need to talk about your father."

Roy squinted through the bright morning sunlight. Around them trees swayed in the wind and a flock of birds flew above, heading farther south.

"He's dead," Roy said in a high-pitched voice. "Why would someone kill Daddy?"

"That's what I'd like to know," Caleb said. "Maybe we should go into your office."

Roy's brows furrowed in confusion, and he led them back to his office like a kid who needed to be told what to do.

"Are you sure we should question him now?" Madelyn asked in a low voice. "He's in shock."

"If he's hiding something, it's better to catch him before he has time to think about it." And plan a cover-up.

Madelyn's eyes flickered with understanding, and they stepped inside Zimmerman's office. Roy filled a paper cup with water from the dispenser in the corner and slumped down in the desk chair, his hand shaking as he drank.

Madelyn claimed one of the chairs and Caleb settled his bulk in the other one, facing Roy. "Roy, we're investigating a possible kidnapping from five years ago with Mrs. Andrews." Caleb gestured toward Madelyn. "We suspect your father had information that could help us."

Clearly confused, Roy glanced back and forth between them. "Do we have to do this now?"

Caleb sensed the man's rising panic. "The sheriff is on his way, Roy. But this case might be related to your father's murder."

Roy crunched the paper cup and tossed it into the trash. "What are you talking about?"

Caleb forced himself to tread slowly. He didn't want to spook Roy; he wanted to reel him in. "Did you work here with your father five years ago?"

Roy shook his head. "No. I was away at school." Suspicion filled his eyes. "Why? What is this about?"

"Does your dad have financial problems?" Caleb asked instead of answering.

"No." Roy indicated the funeral parlor with a sweep of one narrow hand. "The business has done well."

"How about five years ago? Any problems back then?"

Roy's complexion paled slightly. "No," he stammered, although this time his response had a false ring to it. "Why do you want to know?"

Caleb explained about the twins' birth and the exhumation. "So you see, Roy, someone here, your father probably, buried that empty casket, and we want to know who put him up to it."

Roy shot up from his seat, his eyes twitching. "My father would never do something like that. He was an upstanding citizen. In the Rotary Club. A friend of the mayor."

"We believe he did," Caleb said, standing as well, and bracing himself in case the man turned violent. "It's possible someone paid him to cover up the fact that there was no body."

"No…" Roy shook his head vehemently. "How dare you bad-mouth my father. For God's sake, his body isn't even cold and you're accusing him of a crime!"

"Think about it, Roy," Caleb said sharply. "Your father's murder wasn't random. Someone had a reason, a motive, to murder him. Do you know what it was?"

"I have no idea," Roy's voice cracked with disbelief. "My father is a good man. He wouldn't do anything illegal."

Caleb sighed. "Roy, maybe you are innocent. But we believe your father was murdered to keep him from talking to us."

Roy shook his head in denial. "No, you're wrong."

"Please," Madelyn cut in. "Somebody stole my baby, Roy. And I think she's in danger now. Help us find her."

Roy swallowed hard as his gaze veered toward Madelyn. "I'm sorry but I can't." He swung his hand toward Caleb. "Now, this conversation is over."

"It's not over." Caleb jammed his face into Roy's.

"And it won't be until we find Madelyn's missing child. So if you know anything about it, then step up. Because if you're covering for your father, I'll make sure you're charged with accessory, and your butt will go to jail."

Sirens screeched outside. Roy shouted at Caleb and Madelyn to leave again, so they went outside to meet the sheriff.

Needing some fresh air, Madelyn waited on the park bench as Caleb relayed their conversation with Roy and how they'd discovered Howard's corpse. Then he accompanied the sheriff inside to the crime scene.

She shivered as the cool breeze rustled trees and tossed drying leaves to the ground.

Poor Roy. He was devastated.

And Howard... She had mixed feelings about his death. On a basic human level, it disgusted her that he'd been shot in cold blood. But his murder suggested he had been involved in Cissy's disappearance.

Damn him.

She balled her hands into fists. How could all these people have lied to her? How could they have stolen her child and allowed her to believe her baby was dead? That was beyond cruel....

Caleb strode outside, the sight of him automatically filling her with relief. He looked so big and strong and formidable, that she wanted to melt in his arms and let him make the horrid memory of all that blood fade.

He gave her a concerned look, then slid down beside her and spread his hands on his knees. "They're searching for forensics, but the medical examiner puts Zimmerman's death at around 11:00 p.m."

A shudder coursed through Madelyn. "Then he's been lying there all night?"

"Yes." Caleb wrapped an arm around her. Immediately his warmth seeped through her, warding off the chill from the wind and the memory of seeing Howard's bulging eyes staring up at them in death.

"I can't believe this is happening. Two people murdered," Madelyn whispered.

Caleb cupped her face in his hands. "It must mean that we're on to something, Madelyn. Try to hold on to that fact."

She nodded, then looked into his dark eyes. Compassion, worry and determination flickered in the depths, along with a sensitivity that made her pulse pound.

A sliver of desire sparked, heating her blood and making her yearn to lean into him even more. To place her lips on his and taste his sexy mouth.

But noises intruded, reminding her that a dead man lay inside, quickly obliterating any fantasies of kissing Caleb and having him return that kiss.

"The sheriff sent his deputy to Zimmerman's house with another forensics team. Maybe they'll find a lead for us." Caleb glanced into the woods surrounding the funeral home. "I also called Ben, and he's checking Zimmerman's financials."

"Even if you find something, what good will it do now?" Madelyn asked. "He's dead. He can't tell us where Cissy is."

Caleb rubbed her arms. "A paper trail could lead us to the killer or whoever hired him," Caleb said. "And we want concrete evidence to be able to nail him in court."

"Right." Madelyn wasn't thinking about court. Only finding Cissy. "I should check on Sara."

"Done. Gage is staying with the girls and Leah to make sure Sara is safe."

Madelyn sighed in relief. It had been so long since anyone had taken care of her and Sara that it felt oddly unsettling. Uncomfortable in one regard and blissful in another. But she couldn't allow herself to grow accustomed to it. Still, for now, it was nice. "Thank you, Caleb."

His gaze softened. "I told you I'd protect you and find the truth and I keep my promises."

"I guess I'm not accustomed to men I can count on," she said, then wished she hadn't revealed so much.

He rubbed the back of her neck with his thumb, and a frisson of something sweet and sensual rippled between them. "Not every man is your ex, Madelyn. Some of us care about family and honor, about protecting women and children."

Madelyn desperately wanted to believe him. All the agents at GAI must care about families or they wouldn't have dedicated their careers to finding missing children. "But you don't have a family of your own?"

Intense pain flashed in his eyes so quickly that it sucked the air from Madelyn's lungs. Then a shuttered look fell across his face, and he pulled away as if she'd crossed some invisible line.

"Since the police have the crime scene covered, we should get moving," he said, back to business.

"I'm sorry if I said something wrong, Caleb." Madelyn touched his arm, needing to apologize, to make up for whatever she'd said to upset him, but he launched himself to his feet and slanted her a look that warned her that the conversation was over.

"The first couple on Ben's list lives about an hour

from here." He headed to his Jeep and she raced to catch up with him.

"Their names are Bill and Ava Butterworth." His keys jangled in his hands. "He's an accountant. She's a pharmacist but gave up her job to stay home with the kids."

Madelyn missed the intimacy she'd felt between them. But he was right to keep their relationship focused on the case.

Still, the anguish in his eyes haunted her. Caleb had his own secrets. Secrets he obviously didn't want to share. Secrets that had hurt him deeply.

And for once, instead of thinking about her own pain, she wanted to alleviate his.

Caleb realized he'd been rude by cutting Madelyn off, but he wasn't prepared to discuss the loss of his wife and child, not with her.

Not with anyone.

Guilt plagued him for the momentary spark of attraction he'd felt for her. He could not allow himself to fantasize about holding her or having her. And he sure as hell didn't deserve for her to look at him as if he was a savior when he hadn't been able to save his own family.

But he'd do his best to save hers.

She lapsed into silence as he drove from town onto the highway leading to Hopewell, the small town where Ava and Bill Butterworth lived. Mountains fanned out, the rolling hills and valleys picturesque, although those same ridges and cliffs offered hiding places for those who didn't want to be found.

It was nearly noon by the time they crawled into the town. Signs for winter sales filled shops while people hunched in their coats and hurried from their cars to their destinations, too rushed and cold to stop and chat.

He followed the GPS directions down a small side street that led to an older subdivision, the houses a mixture of wood cottages and brick ranches. Children's bicycles, outdoor play equipment and remnants of a snowman painted it as a family neighborhood.

Caleb parked in front of a gray, well-kept, one-story house with white shutters and sprawling oaks that swept the ground with yards of Spanish moss.

Madelyn twisted her hands. "God, Caleb. What if this couple has Cissy? What do we do?"

His hands tightened around the steering wheel. If Sara was right, they might walk in and find another dead body.

"We'll cross that bridge when we come to it," he replied.

Madelyn gritted her teeth, then opened her car door. He slid from the driver's side, circled the front of the car to her and placed his hand at the small of her back for reassurance as they made their way up the pebbled path to the front door. Caleb's mind ticked over the details of the history Ben had printed out on the couple. From the looks of the Butterworths' financials, their house and the van parked in the drive, the couple appeared to be a normal, middle-class family.

One who wouldn't welcome his questions, even if they hadn't adopted Cissy. Of course, no adopted parent wanted their histories dug up or exposed.

He didn't blame them, especially if they were legitimate and innocent and had been deceived themselves.

But he approached with caution. Who knew what secrets lay behind closed doors?

Madelyn ran her fingers through her hair. "Do we tell them who we are?"

Caleb contemplated that question. Being honest might work in their favor or send people running. Either way, Sara and Cissy were identical twins, so Madelyn would recognize her child if she was here.

"Let's just feel them out," he said. He rang the doorbell and they waited several seconds. The sound of voices echoed from behind the door, then the door opened and a brunette stood in the doorway with a baby on her hip. Behind her, two more children appeared, somewhere between the ages of two and four, then a tow-headed child about five joined them, jelly streaking her mouth.

"Can I help you?" The woman ushered the kids behind her in a protective gesture.

But they tugged and shouted at her. "Mommy, we want cookies."

"When are we going to Nana's?"

"Jamie looked at me."

"I did not."

"He did, too."

Ava rolled her eyes. "Enough, Jacob and Jamie. Hang on a minute."

Caleb cleared his throat and glanced at Madelyn who was intently studying the oldest child.

"My name is Caleb Walker." He presented his identification. "I'm with a private investigative firm called GAI."

She spun around and directed her comment to the oldest child. "Esme, take the others into the kitchen. Hand out the sandwiches. I'll be there in a minute."

Esme gave her mother an obedient smile, then gathered the bickering brood and shooed them toward the kitchen. "Come on, cookies for dessert!"

After they skedaddled away, Ava turned back to them. "I don't know how I can help you."

"I hired him," Madelyn softly cut him off. "Five years ago, I gave birth to twins at Sanctuary Hospital, but Dr. Emery told me one of them died. Recently I learned that wasn't true. I believe he sold my baby to a couple who adopted her, and I'm trying to locate them now."

Panic stretched across Ava's face. "I heard about Dr. Emery's death and the accusations against him, but Esme is not your child." Her throat worked as she swallowed. "We met the young woman who gave birth to her. Her name was Penelope, and we paid her expenses during childbirth. She was only fifteen and was grateful to find us."

"How about your other children?" Caleb asked. "Did you adopt them through Dr. Emery?"

"No." The woman gave a humorless laugh. "A month after we adopted, I learned I was pregnant. Since then, I've been a hotbed of fertility."

Madelyn chewed her bottom lip. "Did you know any of the other couples who adopted?"

"No." Ava clenched the door edge. The sound of the kids escalated. "You really believe this doctor stole your baby?"

Madelyn removed a photo of Sara from her purse. "Yes. This is my little girl Sara. She has a twin named Cissy, the baby Dr. Emery told me had died. But I buried an empty casket."

Ava's shocked gasp rattled in the silence.

"Please, if there's any way you can help us, I'd appreciate it. I think Cissy and her adopted mother are in danger." Madelyn drew a labored breath. "I want to save them both if I can."

A seed of doubt flickered in Ava's eyes. "I'm sorry," she said, her tone sincere. "But I don't know anything about your baby or where she is now."

Then she closed the door in their faces.

"What do you think?" Caleb asked.

"Esme is not Cissy," Madelyn said wearily.

"No, but we scared Ava," Caleb said. "I say we head to the others on the list before Ava has a chance to contact anyone."

Madelyn had a stricken look. "You think she knows where Cissy is?"

"Not necessarily," Caleb said. "But I don't want to take the chance just in case she's hiding something."

Madelyn contemplated Caleb's comment as they drove the forty-five minutes to the next house on the list. This place was much more ritzy, a private estate in the mountains that belonged to a couple named Stacy and James Ingles. Judging from their property and the Mercedes and BMW parked in the three-car garage, they definitely had the money to pay for a child.

And more.

When Stacy Ingles opened the door and greeted them, Caleb quickly explained who they were and Madelyn filled in the rest.

"I'm sorry to hear your story," Stacy said. "But you have a lot of nerve invading our privacy."

"I'm not here to make trouble for you," Madelyn said.

"Mrs. Ingles," Caleb cut in. "Whoever adopted Cissy

needs to know that she was kidnapped, not given up willingly."

"So you're going to tear her family's lives apart," Stacy said. "And that child's. If she's with a loving family, think what that will do to her."

Madelyn's lungs tightened. "If that's the case, we'll work together for whatever is best for Cissy," Madelyn said through gritted teeth.

Her child belonged with her. She had not given her up and she wanted her back. Sara deserved to have her sister.

"However," Caleb said sharply. "We don't think that's the case. We have reason to believe that Cissy and her adopted mother are in danger." He explained about Nadine Cotter's and Howard Zimmerman's murders. "We're trying to save their lives."

Stacy's fingers tightened to a white-knuckled grip around the door edge as she stared at them, obviously struggling for a response. Finally she drew a deep breath. "I don't have your child, Mrs. Andrews." She walked to the table in the foyer, picked up a family photo and brought it back. The moment Madelyn saw it she knew the Ingles hadn't adopted Cissy.

Their child was Asian. "We didn't adopt through Dr. Emery," Stacy said quietly. "He referred us to an international adoption agency when our fertility treatments failed. Sue Li is from China."

Desperation tore at Madelyn's insides. "I'm sorry we bothered you."

Caleb removed a business card and pushed it into Stacy's hand. "If you think of anything that can help, a name, maybe, someone who might have a lead for us, please call me."

Stacy chewed her bottom lip but accepted the business card with a nod.

Frustration filled Madelyn as they headed back to Caleb's Jeep.

"We're not giving up, Madelyn," Caleb said.

But a thick silence fell between them as they drove away. Madelyn stared out the window at the desolate mountains, the sharp cliffs and ridges, the winter wind biting through her bones.

What if Cissy was out there now, running from that madman, lost?

The late afternoon sun was waning as they stopped at a small barbecue restaurant, and Caleb ordered a late lunch for them both. He wolfed down two barbecue sandwiches, but she could barely force herself to eat a bite. Instead the images from Sara's drawings, the images of Nadine and Howard both lying in their own blood, taunted her.

What if Sara was right, and Cissy's adopted mother was dead, too? Would they find Cissy in time?

Nausea flooded her, and she had to force herself not to think as they walked to the car, and Caleb drove into the mountains near Boone.

"Third couple—the Peddersons," Caleb said. "Rayland Pedderson bought a mountain lodge six years ago. Wife helps him run it."

Madelyn glanced around the log cabin resort. It had obviously been designed for hunters, people who wanted to escape to a rustic, more primitive life.

Remembering Sara's sketch of the greenhouse, she glanced to the side in search of another building, but the outbuildings were individual dining halls and clubhouses for guests and special functions.

Caleb climbed out, and Madelyn followed, her legs weak as she mounted the stairs. Rocking chairs lined the front porch with checkerboards arranged strategically throughout, and the sound of the river rushing over rocks echoed from behind the lodge, slivers of sunlight slanting through the pines.

Caleb escorted her inside, the mountain theme continuing with deer, elk heads and fish mounted on the rustic walls. A gun cabinet behind the registration desk was filled with rifles and shotguns and a second cabinet in the corner held various knives.

A grunt indicated someone was behind the counter. Caleb rang the bell, and a mountain of a man suddenly stood.

"Rayland Pedderson?" Caleb called out as they approached.

"That's me." The big, burly man leaned across the registration desk, clawing beefy fingers through his thick beard.

Madelyn's heart pounded. The image Sara had drawn of the monster flashed in her head.

Rayland Pedderson could be their man.

Chapter 11

"Would you two like a room?" Pedderson's gaze skated over Madelyn insinuating he thought their visit was a clandestine love affair.

Caleb flashed his ID. "No, thanks. We're here for information."

All friendliness fled from the man's beefy face. "Oh, hell. You're that damn P.I. and the chick asking questions about Dr. Emery."

"You were expecting us?" Caleb asked, senses alert. "Who told we were coming?"

"Don't matter," Pedderson muttered. "I can't help you."

"Can't or won't?" Caleb asked.

"Can't." Pedderson retrieved a photo from the mantle and showed them a framed five-by-seven of him, a dyed-blonde woman and a chubby, brown-haired girl with dimples. "This is me and Beatrice and little Bea."

"You adopted little Bea," Caleb said. "Through Dr. Emery?"

Pedderson yanked a rifle from below the desk. "Don't you go spreadin' rumors like that. Little Bea is *ours*." He braced the rifle on his shoulder and aimed at Caleb. "Ours, you hear me? And no one is sayin' any different and takin' her away." He gestured toward the door with the moose's head mounted above it. "Now git."

Beside Caleb, Madelyn's breath hitched. "Mr. Pedderson, please help us…"

"*Please* git," Pedderson said with a snarl that showcased tobacco-stained teeth. "And don't come back or meddle in our lives or you'll be sorry."

Caleb held up his hands to indicate they were not a threat, then led Madelyn toward the exit. Outside, she sighed against him.

"He's a nasty man and he does have a beard, but he didn't adopt Cissy."

"No," Caleb agreed. "But he may be hiding something. I'll ask Ben to keep these names on file. GAI is receiving other calls from people who claim to have been duped by Emery. If Pedderson is on the list and illegally adopted Bea, someone needs to know."

Madelyn shivered as they rushed to Caleb's SUV and headed back toward town. "It's getting late. I should pick up Sara."

"We have one more stop," Caleb said. "Don't worry. Leah and Gage are taking care of Sara. I know it's difficult, Madelyn. But trust us to help you."

He didn't know why it was important to him that she did, but he wanted her trust. And he wanted to deliver for her more than anything he'd wanted in a long time.

"All right," she said softly. "At least now I feel like I'm finally doing something, taking action. Hopefully Sara will understand."

"She will, she's a tough little girl." Caleb squeezed her hand. "Cissy must be strong, too, Madelyn. She's reaching out to Sara. We'll find her because of that connection."

Hope filled Madelyn's haunted eyes. Damn her sorry ex-husband. Obviously she wasn't accustomed to accepting help or to people believing Sara, and he was going to do both.

Madelyn licked her lips. "Tell me about this last couple on the list."

He mentally ticked away the few details on the printout. They were, by far, the couple with the least background information, which raised suspicions in itself. "The Smiths. Husband was in the service. Wife was an admin assistant at a lawyer's office."

"Could that lawyer have handled the adoption?"

Caleb shrugged. "It's possible. But there's not much here to go on. The file is slim, which makes me wonder if Smith is an alias." Caleb followed that logic. "Hell, now that I think about it, your accident could have been a set-up. Maybe the driver sideswiped you hoping you'd go into labor, then followed you to the hospital and set the adoption in place with Emery."

Madelyn grew silent as if she'd collapsed within herself, making him desperately want to erase her pain. But they'd both known digging for answers might lead to painful truths. And there was no turning back now.

"If someone orchestrated that attack and took Cissy, he deserves to rot in jail," Madelyn said, her voice strained.

"He will pay," Caleb assured her. Although, hell, he'd like to kill the bastard himself.

Finally Madelyn closed her eyes and dozed while he wound around the mountain and crossed into Tennessee. But even in her sleep, Madelyn didn't relax. She twitched and moaned and a tear trickled down her cheek.

Caleb gently wiped it away with the pad of his thumb, then covered her hand with his. "It's going to be okay, Madelyn. You're not alone now."

Slowly she opened her eyes and looked at him. Her lost look twisted him inside out. Made him want to step up and be the man she needed.

To hold her, forget his own problems and assuage her pain.

The thought terrified him. Yet at the same time, he ached to do it, anyway. To jump in without caution.

"Are we almost there?" she asked in a low voice.

Thank God she was oblivious to his thoughts. Dangerous ones for a man who'd failed one family and didn't deserve to dream about another one.

"Yeah." He swung the SUV up the graveled road, and they bounced over the ruts, spitting dust and rocks as they barreled up the drive to the remote cabin at the top of the ridge. The wind hurled leaves and broken branches from a recent storm across the patchwork drive as he pulled to a stop. Storm clouds gathered above, rumbling and threatening sleet, and the sun disappeared, night descending.

He scanned the property, the clapboard house, the woods beyond. A stray dog barked from the woods somewhere, but there were no cars in sight.

Madelyn leaned forward, surveying the property. "This is where the Smiths live?"

"It's the latest address Ben found." But Caleb sensed Madelyn's train of thought. Any family who'd bought a child would have money. They wouldn't live in a broken-down shack like this.

Unless they were on the run. Maybe they hadn't adopted Cissy at all. Maybe they had stolen her from the hospital, and Emery had covered it up.

And if Pedderson had been warned, someone might have tipped off this couple and they'd disappeared.

Checking his gun to make sure it was still tucked into his pants, he climbed out. But his sixth sense hinted that something was wrong. So far, the body count had been piling up. He hoped to hell he wasn't about to stumble on another corpse.

Especially a woman's. Or worse, a child's. Madelyn's child.

"Caleb?" Madelyn reached for the door handle.

"Wait here, Madelyn."

She dropped her hand to her lap and looked warily around. He locked the car doors and inched forward, senses honed as he scanned left and right.

His pulse pounded as he made his way up to the cabin. The steps to the front stoop squeaked, brittle wood sagging beneath the weight of his boots, and he paused on each step, scanning all directions, braced for an attack.

But when he reached the front, a sense of desolation overwhelmed him. An emptiness. The scent of dust and mold and decay.

Wielding his gun, he peered inside the window to the right and saw no movement inside. Jaw clenched, he pushed open the door and inched inside just to make sure. Cissy had supposedly seen the mother killed in the kitchen.

The wood floor creaked as he crossed the foyer. The living area was small, a faded green sofa and plaid chair left behind, but no other furniture or signs of life. To the right he spotted a small hallway which led to the bedrooms but the kitchen adjoined the living area, separated by swinging doors. He elbowed through them and scanned the room. Worn, yellowed linoleum. Beat up cabinets. The scent of cigarette smoke and stale beer.

Empty otherwise.

Removing a penlight from his pocket, he shined it across the floor in search of blood, but detected none. Just mud stains, dust and spilled beer. Obviously Mrs. Smith wasn't a housekeeper. And there was no sign or hint of bleach used to remove blood.

Instincts sharpened, he strode to the bedrooms, expecting the worst.

But he found no body there, either.

Determined to know if they'd been here, he searched for clues as to the couple's whereabouts—mail, a note left behind, an address of a friend—but barring the metal beds in the rooms, the space had been cleaned out completely.

The Smiths had left without a trace.

The isolated location of this place made Madelyn's skin crawl. Were the couple simply outdoors people, hermits, or were they hiding from someone?

She scanned the deep, dark pockets of the forests. If Cissy lived here and had run from this madman, she could be anywhere, lost in those woods. Alone. Scared.

Maybe hurt.

Wild animals, bears, coyotes, snakes, the elements…
Any one of them could be lethal to a small child. And
if she hadn't escaped…

No, she couldn't allow herself to think the worst.
Couldn't let herself believe that her precious little girl
was in the hands of a killer.

But she might be. Sara had seen the man murder
Cissy's adopted mother.

Caleb stalked down the front steps of the porch, and
she released a pained breath. His chiseled jaw was set
firmly as if he had bad news, making her stomach pitch.

He flung open the car door and settled inside, reaching for his cell phone.

"What did you find?" she asked, anxiety knotting
her shoulders.

He sighed warily. "Good and bad news. No one was
there. No body. But no Cissy, either."

She clung to hope. "Did you see anything? Photos
maybe?"

"No. There was no sign of them, nothing personal.
No clothes, dishes, toys, food." He clasped her hand.
"No blood, either. So if this couple is the one who ad-
opted Cissy, they moved on."

"And if the mother was killed?"

"It didn't happen in this house," Caleb said. "There
was no evidence of blood or indication that someone
had cleaned up after a crime. In fact, the house was
dusty, as though no one has lived here for a while."

Her optimism deflated. She hadn't wanted to find a
dead woman, but she needed to know they were making progress, that they were on the right track.

"Let me phone GAI and check in." Caleb started the engine and headed down the mountain. "Maybe Ben will have some information."

She looked out the window again, the forest growing more ominous as night swallowed the horizon. She tried to wrangle her thoughts out of despair while she listened to Caleb confer with his colleague.

"Looks like this couple left a while back. Smith could be an alias, so see what else you can dig up." He paused. "Any word on Nadine's or Mansfield's phones, or a murder victim fitting our profile?" He made a low sound in his throat. "Okay, we're headed back to Sanctuary. Keep us posted."

"Any news?" Madelyn asked as soon as he ended the call.

"Nadine's phone records indicate she called this address last month shortly after Emery was arrested. Mansfield also made phone calls around the same time."

Madelyn twined her fingers in her lap. "Meaning Nadine and Mansfield both covered for Emery?"

"It looks that way."

Madelyn glanced back at the deserted house. "Where is this couple now?" And did they have Cissy?

Caleb covered her hand with his again. "We're working on it, Madelyn. Hang in there, okay?"

Her throat closed. "I will. I just hope Cissy can."

Madelyn felt herself shutting down, physically and mentally. Caleb lapsed into silence, as well, and seemed to focus on driving. She studied his face wondering about his Native American roots.

Anything to take her mind off the fact that they might not find Cissy in time.

* * *

Caleb stewed over the last few hours, trying to piece together the truth.

"What tribe are you from?" Madelyn asked, interrupting his thoughts. "Cherokee? Apache?"

Caleb whipped his head toward her, surprised at the question. He'd thought prejudices would die with time but still occasionally encountered them. "Does it matter?"

"No, not at all," Madelyn said. "I was just curious. Trying to distract myself from worrying."

At the quiver in her voice, Caleb relaxed his steely grip on the steering wheel. So she was just making conversation. Madelyn didn't have a mean bone in her body.

But she had no idea she'd hit one of his hot buttons. "My mother was white, my father Cherokee," he said, battling bitterness. "But my mother's parents never accepted my father."

"What happened?"

Did he really want to revisit his past? "It's not important," Caleb said.

"You know everything about me, Caleb," Madelyn said softly. "I'd really like to know more about you. I think of you as a friend."

A bead of perspiration trickled down his temple. He itched to touch her but tightened his fingers around the steering wheel instead. A friend? Unfortunately he was starting to want more than that.

Starting to want Madelyn in his arms, in his life.

But friendship was all they could have.

Besides, better the subject of his cultural heritage than Mara. "My mother's parents accused my father of taking advantage of my mother. Eventually they pressured her into giving me up. My red skin embarrassed them."

"That's awful," Madelyn said. "How could your mother have given in to that pressure, though? How could she give up her child?"

Caleb glanced at her, moved that she was incensed over his mother's abandonment. "Her family was prestigious, she was young." Excuses, excuses, excuses. "I don't think she really wanted to be saddled with a child anyway."

"I can't imagine ever feeling like that," Madelyn said. "Children are a blessing and should be treasured."

He chuckled at her vehement tone. She was a barracuda when it came to kids. A trait that stirred his admiration.

He wished his own mother had been as nurturing and protective as Madelyn.

But not all women were as unselfish.

"Where's your father?" Madelyn asked.

"He died about ten years ago. A couple of bikers jumped him in an alley and beat him to death. That's when I decided to be a cop." And the reason he'd decided to marry a Native American. He didn't want his own family to endure the prejudice he'd encountered. Prejudices that had no place in modern times, but nonetheless seeped through like poison.

"He must have been very special for you to honor him that way," Madelyn said.

He simply gave a clipped nod. Let her think what she wanted. Truth was, his old man had been bitter after the way Caleb's mother had treated him, and he'd carried a chip on his shoulder that had attracted trouble.

But he'd said enough. Talking about his family and past wasn't something he intended to dwell on.

His cell phone buzzed, thankfully ending Madelyn's questions. He grabbed the phone from his belt and punched Connect. "Walker here."

"Caleb, it's Gage. I just talked to Ben. Mansfield has disappeared."

"What?"

"Don't worry, I'm with Leah and the girls and they're safe. But Ben said he heard him talking about needing a new passport."

"Under a different name?"

"That's right. Ben tried to trace the call but it was a throwaway cell. I sent Colt Mason over but Mansfield was gone. Looks like he packed up and skipped town."

"Does the sheriff know?"

"Yes. He's already issued an APB on Mansfield, but I wanted to give you a heads-up."

Caleb sighed. Dammit. Mansfield knew they were closing in on him, linking him to Cissy's kidnapping and the sketchy adoptions. And he was probably afraid whoever killed Nadine would come after him, too.

Unless he was more involved than they'd thought. Maybe he was the mastermind behind the adoption ring and he had ordered the hit on Nadine.

Either way, they had to track him down and make him talk.

The lights were turned off at Sanctuary Seniors at ten. Just like little kids, the old folks had a bedtime. The nurses checked in. Made sure the residents took their blood pressure medicines and countless other pills. Helped them to the bathroom if they needed it. Changed their diapers if that was the case. Then tucked them in for the night.

Madelyn's mother, Cora Barker—the old bag—was probably sleeping. Snoring away like some pampered princess in her little garden suite.

Well, her peaceful sleep was about to come to an end.

Pulling the janitor's hat low on his forehead, he leaned the broom against the concrete wall, careful to keep his face averted from the security cameras as he ducked behind the red-tips flanking the back windows of Cora's unit. Using his handy tool kit, he jiggled open a window in seconds and slipped inside.

Just as he'd expected, the place was dark. Silent. It didn't smell of old people like he expected, not like that nursing home where his grandpa had been shoved for the last ten years of his sorry life.

Instead, the kitchen smelled like chocolate chip cookies as if the old broad had been baking. He thought she was in a wheelchair now, half crippled in her body and mind.

Inching past the oven, sure enough, he spotted the batch of cookies and snagged one, then wolfed it down, and grabbed another one and jammed it in his pocket.

Then moving slowly, he scanned the tiny apartment and tiptoed into the living room. The single bedroom was to the right. Inhaling a deep breath, he darted through the doorway as quiet as a mouse.

Cora was curled in bed, her white hair fanned across the pillow like Snow White. He stared at her for a moment, his Grandma Giselle's face flashing in his mind.

Dammit, he couldn't go soft now. The old biddy's own daughter had brought this on herself.

Gritting his teeth, he removed his phone from his pocket and texted Madelyn.

"I warned you to back off."

Then he slowly eased a pillow from the rocking chair beside Cora's bed and pressed it over her face.

Chapter 12

Madelyn's cell phone dinged, indicating she had a text. But the message on the screen made her pulse spike with fear.

I warned you to back off.

"Oh, my God…"

Caleb had just turned onto the main street of Sanctuary. "What's wrong?"

Panic rose in Madelyn's throat as she showed him the text. "What if he has Sara? Oh, God, oh, God, he warned me…" Tears blurred her vision.

"Don't panic. I just talked to Gage." Caleb grabbed his cell phone and punched Gage's number again. "It's Caleb. Is Sara all right?" A pause, then Caleb breathed out. "Good. Madelyn just received another text from the guy who threatened her before."

"Is Sara awake? If she is, let me speak to her," Madelyn pleaded. "Please. I need to hear her voice."

Caleb nodded. "Gage, if Sara is awake, put her on the phone. And watch out in case this guy tries something."

He handed the phone to Madelyn, and she gripped it with a shaky hand, unable to breathe for the few seconds it took for Gage to retrieve her daughter.

"Mommy," Sara said in a sleepy voice.

Relief nearly overwhelmed her. "Sara, baby, are you okay?"

"Yes. We're watching the movie—and Ruby likes to play dress up and paint, and we made Rudolph sandwiches with peanut butter and pretzels and raisins and a cherry for his nose."

Madelyn choked on a sob. Her daughter sounded so happy.

Caleb gently massaged her shoulder, and she took a deep breath.

"Mommy, what's wrong?" Sara asked as if she suddenly sensed Madelyn was upset. "Did you find Cissy?"

Oh, Lord, how was she going to answer Sara?

With the truth. That's all she could do. "Not yet, honey, but we're not giving up. Caleb and I are on our way to pick you up. We'll be there soon."

"'Kay. But Mommy, I likes Ruby so you don't gots to hurry."

Madelyn smiled, her heart finally calming as she heard the joy in her daughter's voice. Sara deserved to have friends and be normal, not plagued with worry or visions of murder.

Her cell phone jangled in her lap, and she checked the Caller ID. Sanctuary Seniors. "Grandma's calling, baby, let me talk to her and I'll see you in a bit."

"'Kay, Mommy. Love you."

"Love you, too." Madelyn clicked on the incoming one.

"Mrs. Andrews, this is security from Sanctuary Seniors. I'm sorry to have to call you this late, but there's been an incident."

Madelyn's blood ran cold. "What do you mean, an incident?"

"It's your mother," he said gruffly. "You should come over here."

"What happened?" Madelyn cried.

Instead of replying though, the phone went dead in her hand. Shuddering with fear, Madelyn gave Caleb a panicked look. The warning, the text…

Sara was safe. But the threat?

This maniac had gone after her mother.…

Madelyn clutched Caleb's arm. "Caleb, go to my mom's complex. Hurry!"

Caleb's stomach roiled at the fear in her eyes. "Madelyn, what's wrong?"

"That was security at Sanctuary Seniors. Something's happened to Mom."

Caleb sped down the street leading to the seniors' community. He remembered the text message, and cold fear clenched his gut. The killer must have been watching. He knew Sara was being guarded, so he'd targeted the only other person in the world Madelyn cared about—her mother.

Frustration burned his gut. Dammit, who was this bastard? How could he be all over the place at once?

Because he wasn't working alone. First Nadine, then Howard and now Madelyn's mother… Someone was cleaning up the past and determined to keep them from finding Cissy.

Headlights glared from an oncoming vehicle, and he blinked his lights as a signal, but the car nearly skimmed his side and raced on.

Cursing, he spun the SUV into the parking lot of the seniors' home and screeched to a halt. But his mind remained on the car that had nearly run them off the road.

That driver could have been the killer leaving the scene.

Madelyn wrenched open the door and vaulted out at a dead run toward her mother's unit. Bright lights from the outside shot across the lawn like golden spikes. Afraid she might be walking into a trap, he dashed after her. If the killer had called instead of security and hadn't been in that car, he might be hiding out, waiting to ambush Madelyn.

"Madelyn, wait." He grabbed her arm. "Let me check first. If your mother was attacked, her attacker might still be here."

"But I have to go to her," she protested, yanking at his arm.

"Stop and think for a second." He massaged her shoulder. "Are you sure the caller was security? Did he give you his name?"

"No…he hung up before I could get it." Her gaze filled with terror as she realized his train of thought. "Oh, God, Caleb, what if he's hurt her?"

His pulse accelerated. He hoped to hell that wasn't the case. "Stay behind me."

Madelyn nodded and trailed him as they slowly walked up the sidewalk. If security had called, they would have phoned the police. But the police were nowhere in sight.

Caleb jiggled the front door and found it locked.

Madelyn dug in her purse. "I have a key." She handed it to him, and he unlocked the door, then threw up a warning hand urging her to pause for a moment.

A thump echoed from the bedroom, then a scream.

Caleb pulled a gun from inside his jacket, then scanned the dark interior, alert and posed in defense mode.

A low cry erupted from the bedroom this time, and Madelyn lunged toward the sound. But he pushed her behind him, and inched through the small living room. The window was open, cold air blowing in, chilling the room. The bedroom sat to the right of the hallway. Slowly they closed the distance to it.

But a board squeaked, and a gunshot zinged toward them. Madelyn screamed, and he shoved her down. "Stay low. I'm going after him."

Cocking his gun, he edged close to the wall and inched to the bedroom doorway. The man was leaning over Madelyn's mother, one hand shoving a pillow over her face while he aimed the gun at him.

Her mother was kicking and fighting, desperately trying to shove him off of her.

Caleb pointed his Glock at the attacker. "Let her go."

The man spun around, the mask over his face hiding his features.

"It's over," Caleb said. "Let her go and drop it."

They stared at each other for a long, tense moment, then suddenly the man released the pillow and vaulted through the window. Madelyn's mother wheezed and coughed, struggling for air.

He raced to her. "Are you all right?"

A sob erupted from her, but she gestured for him to go after the intruder. Madelyn raced to them.

"Call 911," Caleb shouted as he climbed through the window. He visually scanned the shadows for the culprit. Behind him, he heard Madelyn and her mother crying.

"Maddie?"

"I'm here, Mom," Madelyn whispered.

A shot zipped by Caleb's head, and he crouched to his knees taking cover by the corner of the building.

The back of the building was wooded, trees jutting up to the property with the units lined in a row, small yards and gardens separating them. Lights began flickering on in various homes, the residents obviously disturbed by the gunshots. Footsteps pounded to the left, and he headed in that direction.

A large courtyard sat to the left with walkways that wound through a garden and to a small man-made lake nestled by woods.

He spotted a shadow slinking through the maze and jogged toward it. Did the perp have a getaway vehicle stashed on a side road nearby?

A siren wailed in the distance, but Caleb saw the figure move again and followed him toward the wooded area. Then the man suddenly fled into the dense forest.

Squinting in the darkness, Caleb tried to see which direction he went, but the sound of a gun firing forced him to duck behind a tree. The bullet grazed his arm, and he cursed.

A second later, a car engine revved up. He ran after it and fired, but the son of a bitch had disappeared out of sight.

* * *

Madelyn's pulse thrummed with fear. Her mother was hysterical and breathing so hard she thought she might be having a heart attack.

"Mom, you're safe now." Madelyn gripped her mother's arms and forced her mother to look at her. The terror in her eyes was so stark it robbed Madelyn's breath.

"He... Someone was here," she cried. "He shoved a pillow over my face...."

Madelyn hugged her mother close. If they'd been a few minutes later, her mother might not be here.

"I know, Mom. Caleb ran after him." They clung together, both crying for a moment, hanging on to each other for dear life.

Finally when her mother calmed, Madelyn pulled back to examine her. "Does your chest hurt, Mom?"

"No...no, I just couldn't breathe for a minute." She raised a shaky hand to her throat. "Why would some man try to kill me? I'm an old woman, I don't have anything valuable...."

Guilt and anger suffused Madelyn. "I know, Mom. He attacked you to get at me." She swallowed hard and forced out the words. "I received a phone call warning me he'd hurt Sara if I didn't stop nosing around, but we left her with Caleb's friend, so he came after you instead."

Her mother's nails dug into Madelyn's arms. "What? Who threatened Sara?"

"I don't know his name," Madelyn said, shaking with fury. "But he knows I'm looking for Cissy and warned me to stop."

"You are not going to stop," her mother declared emphatically. "You're going to find Cissy and this maniac and put him in jail where he belongs."

"Mrs. Barker!" A loud pounding on the front door followed the shout, and Madelyn ran to the door. A security guard from the complex stood on the threshold, the sheriff on his heels along with an ambulance. "You called 911," the guard said. "What happened?"

Madelyn raked her hair back. "My mother was attacked tonight. The man escaped through the window, but Caleb ran after him."

"Where's your mother?" one of the medics asked.

She gestured toward the bedroom and the medics rushed to check on her. Madelyn crossed her arms in an attempt to hold her emotions at bay.

"Did you see your mother's attacker?" Sheriff Gray asked.

Madelyn shook her head. "Just his shadow, then he fired at me and Caleb."

"He had a gun?"

Madelyn nodded.

"Then we'll get a crime unit here. I also need to question your mother."

"Of course. She's shaken up, but I'm sure she'll talk to you." Madelyn led him to the bedroom but stopped before they entered. "I think this may be the same man who killed Nadine Cotter and Howard Zimmerman. He called me and told me to stop investigating. Caleb and I left Sara with Gage McDermont. Then I got a call from some man claiming to be security saying that someone attacked my mother."

Sheriff Gray muttered something under his breath. "We should have your phone analyzed."

"Caleb already has one of his agents working on it."

Her mother was propped against the pillows now, her pallor slowly returning to normal, a stubborn gleam in her eyes. "I told these gentlemen that I'm fine."

"Her vitals are steady," one of the medics said. "But we can transport her to the hospital for observation overnight if you want."

"That's not necessary," Madelyn's mother said. But she absentmindedly rubbed at her neck, a sign that the ordeal had terrified her. "I'm just angry that that madman escaped."

Madelyn smiled at her mother. She might be partially paralyzed but she had spunk. "Mom, Sheriff Gray needs to ask you about the attack. Are you up to it?"

Her mother nodded. "Yes, of course."

The sheriff crossed the room and took the chair across from Madelyn's mother. "Mrs. Barker, tell me exactly what happened tonight."

Madelyn's mother cleared her throat, her look haunted. But anger flushed her cheeks, as well. A good sign. If she and Sara and Cissy had fight in them, Cora Barker was their inspiration.

"I was sleeping," she began. "Then suddenly the floor squeaked. That sound woke me. When I looked up, a big man was hovering over me. Then he shoved a pillow over my face and tried to smother me."

Sheriff Gray propped his hands on his knees. "Did you see the man's face?"

She fiddled with the sheet edge. "No, he wore a ski mask. One of those that cover your face."

"Did he say anything to you?" Sheriff Gray asked.

Madelyn's mother shook her head no.

"How about anything else distinctive? Did you notice an odor or hear another sound?"

Madelyn's mother closed her eyes for a moment and massaged her temple. When she opened her eyes, a frown marred her face. "Come to think of it, there was a smell. Some kind of oil, maybe cleaning oil or machine oil."

"Gun oil?" Sheriff Gray suggested.

Madelyn stiffened. Rayland Pedderson was a hunter. He had a shotgun that he'd aimed at them. And dozens of trophies on the walls of his lodge.

Had Pedderson attacked her mother?

Caleb cursed as he jogged back to Cora Barker's apartment. Several neighbors peeped from behind curtains, curious about the commotion, but obviously too frightened to step outside. Had one of them witnessed something?

Thankfully the sheriff and a crime unit had arrived.

He stowed his weapon as he met Madelyn on the porch steps. She looked as if she was barely holding herself together. "Caleb, did you catch him?"

The sheriff appeared behind her, eyebrows raised.

"Afraid not." He scrubbed a hand through his hair. "He had a car waiting on the street."

"Did you get a look at him or the vehicle?" the sheriff asked.

Caleb shook his head. "No, it was too dark and far away to see the car. The perp was dressed in all black and wore a ski mask." He turned to Madelyn. "How's your mother?"

"Hanging in there," Madelyn said. "She smelled some kind of oil on her attacker. It made me think of Rayland Pedderson. Could it be gun oil?"

Caleb frowned. "It's possible."

"Who is Pedderson?" Sheriff Gray asked.

Caleb filled him in. "He wasn't very happy to see us," Caleb said. "I'm sure he's hiding something."

"Adopted parents can become defensive when their adoptions are questioned," Sheriff Gray said. "I'm adopted myself so I can't say as I blame them."

"But we're not trying to tear their lives apart," Madelyn said. "We just want to find my daughter."

"You think Pedderson kidnapped your baby?" Sheriff Gray asked.

Madelyn shifted, jamming her hands in her jacket. "No, at least not from the photo of his family. But he might have information about the person who did."

"There's another couple we're looking for," Caleb admitted. "They go by the name Smith. When we tracked down their latest address, the place had been cleaned out. There were no signs indicating where they'd moved, either."

"I guess word has spread about Emery's adoptions being questionable and people are panicking. The adopted parents are afraid they'll lose their children," Sheriff Gray said. "Just raising that question could cause legal problems for the couples, as well as upset their families."

"It is a conundrum," Caleb agreed. "But Madelyn didn't give her daughter away, and if she's in danger, she needs us to save her."

"I'll check out Pedderson," Sheriff Gray agreed. "And this Smith couple. But first a crime unit needs to process your mother's room. Maybe the bullet casings will lead to something." He descended the steps to make the call, leaving the two of them alone on the porch.

Madelyn's gaze fell to Caleb's arm, then a horror-stricken expression crossed her face. "Caleb, you're hurt."

He glanced down at the rip in his shirt. A few drops of blood had seeped through the denim fabric. "It's just a flesh wound," he said shrugging it off.

Madelyn lifted his arm to examine it. Her adrenaline was waning, the worry in her eyes nagging at him. He wanted to wipe away that worry. Find her daughter and place her in Madelyn's arms.

Hell, he wanted to hold her so bad he ached.

She traced her fingers over his injury, leaning close to make sure he hadn't lied, that the bullet wasn't embedded in his arm. Her simple touch sent shards of sensations rippling through him.

He pressed his hand over hers. "It's nothing, I promise," he said, heat thrumming through him. When he'd chased after the shooter, he'd been terrified that the guy might have had an accomplice. That while he was distracted chasing one guy, another one would hurt Madelyn.

"Caleb," Madelyn whispered. "You should have the medics tend to this."

"I told you it's just a scratch. I'll clean it later." Her gaze locked with his, and need and desire heated his blood, hardening his body.

Desperate to touch her, to hold her, he feathered a strand of hair behind her ear. The temptation to kiss her seized him. He wanted to feel her against him, to know she was safe in his arms.

But voices inside interceded, jerking him back to reality, and he stepped away.

"I'm going to call Gage and have him post one of our agents with your mother."

Fear flashed in Madelyn's eyes for a moment, then gratitude. "Yes, please. Then I need to pick up Sara."

"Gage offered for her to spend the night."

"No," Madelyn said. "I need to see her. To have her home with me."

Caleb nodded. He understood that need. He felt the same way about being with her.

And that was crazy.

Madelyn was just a case to him.

But even as he phoned Gage and set up the guard, he knew he was lying to himself. Madelyn was not just a case.

He cared about her, dammit.

And that was dangerous.

Chapter 13

Leaving her mother was difficult for Madelyn. But her mom assured Madelyn she was fine, then insisted that Madelyn be with Sara and continue the investigation.

Gage had sent Colt Mason over to guard her mother. He and Slade Blackburn planned to take shifts. Knowing they were guarding her mother helped alleviate the anxiety knotting Madelyn's shoulders as she and Caleb drove to Gage's.

But too many unanswered questions remained. The attacker was still free. People were dead. Cissy was missing.

Ben Camp had tried to trace the source of that text, but it turned out to be a dead lead. The message had come from a throwaway cell.

The sheriff had canvassed the neighbors to see if anyone had seen or heard anything, but with hearing impairments, poor vision, and the late hour, most of the seniors had only been aware something had happened when the sheriff and ambulance arrived.

Caleb was quiet on the drive, as well. In fact, he'd acted distant ever since she'd touched his arm and examined his wound. The big guy was definitely the silent type. Intense. Focused. Angry.

But she'd sensed his anger was triggered by the brute who had attacked her mother and escaped, not at her. That some part of him wanted her, at least on a primal level.

The same part of her that craved him.

The lights were still on at Gage's house when they arrived, and they hurried to the door together. Gage met them, his expression concerned.

"Are you all right, Madelyn?" Gage asked.

Madelyn nodded. "Thanks for assigning a guard to protect my mother. I don't know what I'd do if I lost her."

"We'll make sure that doesn't happen," Gage assured her.

Madelyn glanced over his shoulder. "Where are the girls?"

"They fell asleep watching a movie." They followed Gage through the foyer, and Madelyn spotted Ruby and Sara sprawled on a big, pink sleeping bag in front of the TV.

Leah looked up from the sofa with a smile. "Sara's an angel," she said softly. "The girls had a great time today."

"Thank you, I'm so grateful to you," Madelyn said, her emotions beginning to unfurl. "I'd be glad to return the favor sometime."

Leah stood, rubbing her lower back, then squeezed Madelyn's hands between hers. "Of course. I think we're all going to be good friends."

Madelyn nearly choked with gratitude. She hadn't realized how much she'd isolated herself since Tim had abandoned her. She'd been afraid of getting close to anyone, including another woman. But she was tired of being afraid. She and Sara both needed friends, a support group, as well as family.

Madelyn knelt to get Sara, but Caleb swooped her into his big arms instead. Sara stirred slightly, then curled against his broad chest, and Madelyn couldn't help but remember the connection her daughter shared with this man. She'd trusted him immediately.

Madelyn was so moved she couldn't speak. Caleb was tough and strong, protective and kind, and looked like an ancient Indian warrior. Yet he held her precious child more gently and with more care than Sara's father ever had.

The thought stayed with her while they drove back to her house.

"Let me check the house before you go inside," Caleb insisted as he pulled into the drive.

Reality made fear return, and she nodded, waiting in the Jeep until Caleb cleared the house. Thankfully, he returned and said it was safe. Then he carried Sara up to bed.

Sara stirred and looked up at her as Madelyn tucked her in bed. "Today was fun, Mommy. I like Ruby. Cissy will, too."

Madelyn dropped a kiss on Sara's cheek. "I love you, baby."

"I love you, too." Then Sara closed her eyes again

and drifted back to sleep. Today had been harrowing. She'd nearly lost her mother.

And she couldn't lose her or Sara. Then she would be all alone.

She said a small prayer that Sara would rest tonight and be spared the nightmares.

But Sara's nightmares were the only real connection they had to her sister. And if Sara didn't dream of Cissy or see her in her sleep, she was terrified of what that meant.

That they were too late. That they'd never find her other daughter.

Caleb couldn't stop thinking about the fear on Madelyn's face when they'd heard her mother scream.

Or the way his body had tingled when Madelyn had touched him.

And then when he'd carried her daughter up the stairs, he'd seen the longing in Madelyn's eyes. She'd shut herself off from friends, from love, from relationships because she'd unselfishly been taking care of her daughter and her mother.

But who had taken care of Madelyn?

No one.

Her husband had deserted her. So had her father.

He would not desert her now.

Desperately trying to distract himself from wanting Madelyn, he studied her house. Homey, cozy furnishings. Comfortable, big club chairs draped with afghans that looked homemade. The fact that she owned a craft and hobby shop showed in the hand-painted folk art, stenciled walls and quilts in the room.

Her footsteps echoed as she descended the steps,

and he jammed his hands in the pockets of his jacket, vying for control when he wanted to pull her into his arms and feel her up against him.

"Is she asleep?"

Madelyn nodded, then went to the corner cabinet and removed a wooden plaque. When she turned back, he saw that it was a nameplate with Cissy's name on it, one similar to the nameplate he'd seen hanging above Sara's bed. Both were painted with flowers in pinks and greens, their names decorated with swirls of color.

"You saved that all these years?" Caleb asked.

She nodded and hugged it to her chest. "I know we need to ask Sara about the secrets, but I couldn't bear to wake her."

"It's been a long day for all of us. We'll talk to her in the morning."

A relieved sigh escaped her, then she glanced at the nameplate again and a tear trickled down her cheek. "Thanks. I'm not sure how much more I could take today."

Her admission did it. He couldn't help himself.

He closed the distance between them in one stride, set the nameplate on the desk and pulled her up against him. "You're not alone, Madelyn," he whispered as she collapsed into his arms. "I'm here. Tonight you and Sara are safe."

"But what about Cissy?" she choked out.

Caleb closed his eyes, praying that Cissy was safe, too. "Remember, she's strong. We'll find her. I promise."

God, take him from this earth if he broke that promise. Madelyn deserved to find her daughter. Sara deserved to have her twin.

And him… He didn't deserve to be holding her or to even entertain ideas of being a family with them, but he'd punished himself for so long that he sent up a second prayer. A prayer that Mara would understand. That she would want him to help Madelyn and her daughters.

That somehow God would give him the strength to perform a miracle and reunite the twins and their mother and catch the man who'd tried to kill Cora.

Madelyn's small body trembled against him, and he forgot about prayers and simply gave in to the need to comfort her. He stroked her back, rubbing circles between her shoulder blades, at the same time breathing in her sweet scent.

She made a soft sound of pleasure, and he savored the sound, nuzzling her hair with his face.

"Caleb, thank you for being here," she whispered.

He didn't want her thanks. He wanted her to want him. To crave him as much as he craved her.

"You don't need to thank me," he said gruffly. "I'm just doing my job."

She suddenly pulled away and dropped her hands, confusion and hurt mingling with the desire darkening her eyes. "I'm sorry, Caleb. You're right. You're just doing your job, and I'm being foolish, falling all over you."

Guilt hit him swift and hard. Desire and something primal and hot, something out of control, snapped inside him. Too many people had hurt Madelyn.

He couldn't allow her to think that he was rejecting her.

"It's not just my job," he said between gritted teeth because admitting his own needs cost him. "I want you, Madelyn. I want to help you, to protect you, to… hold you."

The truth of his words registered in her eyes and made them sparkle with desire and a hunger that mirrored the aching hole clawing at his gut.

Emboldened by that look, he yanked her up against him, angled his head and closed his mouth over hers.

She seemed stunned at first, and he ordered himself to move slowly, not to frighten her with his raging need for her. But it had been so long since he'd held a woman, desired a woman, that emotions and lust and hunger made him run his tongue along her lips, pushing, probing, begging to venture inside.

A low, throaty moan escaped her, and she leaned into him and tunneled her fingers through his hair and parted her lips. Then she whispered his name on a moan and sucked his tongue into her mouth.

The feel of her lips closing around his tongue sent white-hot heat blazing through his body. His bloodstream flooded with sensations, his sex going rock-hard.

She shifted her body against him as if she felt his thick length and ached for it, and he backed her against the wall, running his hands down the sides of her body until one hand cupped her breast and the other pressed her hips forward, planting her sex into the V of his thighs.

"Caleb…" She moaned again, dragged her mouth from his and sucked and nibbled at his neck.

"Madelyn," he whispered against her hair. His body ached for her.

He kneaded her breast, heaving for a breath as she slowly unbuttoned his shirt and dropped kisses along his chest and torso. When her head dipped lower, he cupped her face between his hands, lifted her face and stared into her eyes. "You have to slow down or I'm not going to make it," he said with a wicked grin.

The sensuous look she returned nearly undid him. "I can't help it," Madelyn whispered. "I want you, Caleb. Like I've never wanted a man."

"I want you, too," he admitted. But dammit, he didn't have a condom. It had been so damn long that he had stopped carrying protection.

And he'd never take the chance of impregnating another woman. Not unless they were married and he knew she wanted his child.

His child...her child.

Guilt slammed into him. He couldn't screw up this case because of his own needs for Madelyn.

She deserved better.

"You changed your mind?" Madelyn said, hurt flashing in her eyes.

"No, I want you," he said, his voice gruff with desire. "But I want to do right by you even more."

Madelyn's pulse clamored. Caleb wanted to do right by her.

But right now all she wanted was to have him kiss her again. To have him take her upstairs, strip her clothes and make love to her.

And she was going to have it.

"Please, Caleb," she whispered. "I need you tonight."

Questions filled his eyes. Then a flash of raw, primal need that took her breath away. She didn't know his story, but knew enough to realize that he didn't do this lightly. He was honorable, decent. He kept his promises.

And he was all man. She felt it in the thick, hard

length between her thighs. In the control he maintained. In the heat flaring in his expression.

"Are you sure?" he asked gruffly.

She nodded.

"I don't have protection," he said with a frown.

Madelyn smiled. "I do." She blushed at the surprised look on his face. One of the times her mother had tried to fix her up, she'd given her a gift basket.

His mouth closed over hers again, gentle, then probing, then demanding, and she parted her lips and welcomed him inside. His tongue danced and teased her lips, played a game of tag with her own, then he suddenly swept her in his arms and carried her to her bedroom.

A sliver of moonlight flickered through the sheers illuminating his broad body, and her heart raced as he allowed her to remove his shirt. She ran her hands over his slick, smooth, bronzed chest, then flicked the leather thong from his hair and threaded her fingers through the decadent strands.

His gruff moan spurned her on and she nibbled and kissed and licked his neck and chest, until he grabbed her hands and pushed her back onto the bed. "My turn," he murmured as he began to strip her clothes.

"Condom?"

She gestured toward the decorative basket on her nightstand, and he chuckled. "You were prepared?"

"My mother," she said with a smile.

A sensual almost possessive look flared in his eyes, and he buried his head in her hair for a moment, as if savoring the way she felt in his arms. Madelyn felt a tenderness for him wash over her.

Then he lifted his head and a wicked gleam replaced

that look, the raw, primal need in his eyes sending a buzz of euphoric anticipation through her as he began to peel off her clothes.

Madelyn hadn't been naked for anyone except her ex, and now she had a scar from the C-section. For a moment, she threw her hands down to cover it, but Caleb shook his head and flung her hands by her sides, holding them down as he ravaged her mouth again.

"You're beautiful," he growled. "I want to taste all of you."

Erotic sensations rippled through her as he swept his tongue down her neck, then he teased and nibbled and sucked her nipples into his mouth until she arched and cried out for more. She parted her legs, silently begging for him to fill her, but his tongue found its way down her belly and into her heat, and pure pleasure shot through her.

A million butterflies danced in her stomach as he kissed the insides of her thighs then tilted her hips to taste her.

"Caleb…"

Then she could speak no more. Her body became a minefield of sensations, exploding with each touch and caress, each kiss and lap of his tongue, and when she shouted his name as her orgasm claimed her, he rose above her, kissed her again, then plunged his huge length inside her.

Caleb shifted, allowing Madelyn to adjust to his size. She was so damn small and tight that he was afraid he would hurt her. But stopping now was out of the question. Her pleas for him to take her echoed in his head, the heat in his blood roaring.

Her body quivered around his sex, hugging him, holding him, then she wrapped her legs around him, and any rational thoughts fled. On some basic, male level, he had wanted her from the moment he'd seen her.

And it was destiny that he have her.

Her pain, her sweetness, her strength, her love for her family all made her sexy. And her body... She had the body of a vixen.

Tempting. Delicious. Sensual.

She clawed at his back, and his muscles rippled. She raked her feet down his calves and his sex hardened even more. She suckled his neck, and he rocked inside her, plunging to her core.

Need and desire and emotions he didn't want to name drove him faster, and he built a tempo that had his own climax teetering to the surface. Then she lowered her hands to grip his hips, and pleasure overcame him.

He stroked her inside and out, lifted her legs and sank deeper, so deep he felt another orgasm shivering through her. So deep his own came so swift and hard that he lost all thought and shouted her name as his body unloaded inside her.

Madelyn quivered from the delicious sensations buzzing through her body. She had never been made love to like that, not with such force and need and... emotion.

She stroked his hair back from his forehead as he rolled them to their sides and cradled her against his chest.

She was falling in love with Caleb.

How stupid was she?

For a man, sex was sex. And she had practically

begged Caleb for it. She couldn't become emotional and declare her feelings. She needed him to finish the investigation.

A sound from Sara's room startled her, then Sara's cry rent the air. She was having another nightmare.

Caleb heard it, too, and instantly released her. "You'd better check on her."

Madelyn nodded, her skin still tingling from his touch, her breasts heavy and aching. But she put aside her desires, grabbed a nightshirt from her dresser, yanked it on and rushed to her daughter.

Lost in the throes of another nightmare, Sara thrashed beneath the covers, a low sob ripping from her. "No, don't put me in there. It's dark...."

Madelyn sank down on the bed beside her and shook her gently. "Wake up, sweetie. You're having another bad dream."

Sara cried out again, then opened her eyes. The glazed fear in her expression made Madelyn's stomach knot. "Sara, what did you see, baby?"

Sara stared at her for a heartbeat, the air vibrating with her terror. Behind her, Madelyn heard Caleb step to the door and realized he was watching. Listening. Waiting.

"What did you see?" Madelyn asked gently.

"Cissy," Sara said in a strained voice. "She's scared."

"Why is she scared, honey?"

"The mean man, he gots her and he dragged her away from the sunflowers."

Madelyn's gaze flew to Caleb's, and he slowly walked over to join them. He'd put on his jeans and shirt, although the shirt was half buttoned, reminding her of what they'd been doing. Making her want him again.

Making her feel guilty for indulging in pleasure when her daughters both needed her.

"Where are they now?" Caleb asked.

Sara tightened her fingers around the edge of her comforter. "He put her in the back of his car. But it's dark. She can't see anything."

"The back? You mean the backseat?" Caleb asked.

Sara shook her head. "No, the back where you puts stuff."

"You mean the trunk?" Madelyn said unable to keep the horror from her voice.

Sara bobbed her head up and down. "He slammed the top and closed Cissy in, and it's really dark and she's scared, and she's crying."

Madelyn shook with anger.

"What kind of car is he driving?" Caleb asked. "Can you see what color it is?"

Sara pressed her fist to her mouth. "Black."

"Does it have two doors or are there doors in the back?" Caleb asked.

Sara shrugged. "I don't know. Cissy can't see the doors. It's too dark in the trunk."

Madelyn ached for both of her girls. Apparently Sara saw everything through Cissy's eyes. And she felt her emotions. Her fear.

"Did the man say where he was taking Cissy?" Caleb asked.

Sara shook her head. "No, but the man killed her mama, and now he's taking her away."

Madelyn exchanged a worried look with Caleb. He knelt by Sara's bed. "Sara, you said once that Cissy shared her secrets with you. Can you tell us about those secrets?"

Sara's traumatized gaze flew to Caleb. "You're not supposed to tell each other's secrets."

Madelyn chewed her bottom lip, then gathered Sara's hand in hers. "You're right, honey. But Cissy's in trouble. And if there's something about her secrets that can help us find her, I don't think she'd mind if you told us."

"Your mom is right," Caleb said in a soothing tone.

Sara studied them both for a moment, indecision in her eyes. She was loyal to her twin, but she was terrified for Cissy's life. She clutched her teddy bear under one arm and clung to Madelyn's hand, squeezing it for dear life. "Cissy said no one's supposed to know."

"Know what, Sara?" Caleb asked.

Sara heaved a weary sigh. "That we gots the same daddy."

Cissy rolled into a ball, hugging her blanket to her chest. Tears leaked from her eyes and dripped down her face. Her breath hitched. She'd screamed so much already that her throat hurt and her voice sounded like a frog.

But nobody had heard.

Unless Sara had....

The car bounced over the rough road, tossing her back and forth. It was so dark she couldn't see anything. It smelled awful, too. Dirty and greasy, and she felt a spider crawling up her leg.

She swiped at the spider with her hand and felt along the inside of the trunk for something to help her get out. But her hand hit something sharp. A shovel.

She jerked her hand back.

Her mommy's face flashed in her mind. Her mommy lying on the floor in all that red. The red was blood. Her mommy's blood cause the mean monster man had cut her throat.

The monster man had killed her. And now he'd left her mommy behind.

Where was he taking her now? To her daddy? Back to Sara?

No… He was going to kill her, too. That's why he had that shovel. He was going to kill her, then he would bury her in the ground and no one would ever find her.

And she would never get to be with Sara.

Chapter 14

Madelyn's mind raced as Sara's words sank in.

Cissy knew that she shared a daddy with Sara. Had she actually met her father?

If that was the case, then her ex-husband knew that Cissy had survived. He might have even seen her. He might even know where she was.

Pain knifed through her. No... Tim would not have betrayed her like that. He couldn't be involved in Cissy's disappearance, in her adoption.

He wouldn't have given away one of his own children....

Would he?

"Thank you for sharing with us." Caleb patted Sara's shoulder. "You're a brave little girl and a big help, Sara."

Panic mushroomed inside Madelyn. "Sara, is the mean man who hurt Cissy's mother—is that man Cissy's daddy?"

Sara scrunched her nose. "No... Her mama says it's her uncle. But he don't like Cissy. And he and Cissy's mama was yelling at each other and then...the knife..."

A horror-stricken look filled Sara's eyes again, and Madelyn pulled her into her arms. "It's okay, honey. It's over. We'll find Cissy. I promise."

Caleb stood, indicating his phone, then left the room as if he was on a mission. She laid down beside Sara and comforted her until she finally drifted back to sleep.

Madelyn closed her eyes, too, sleep pulling at her.

They had to find Tim.

And if he'd had any part in Cissy's adoption, she would kill him.

Caleb could barely contain his rage. Had Madelyn's husband sold their daughter?

And what was this about an uncle killing the mother?

He strode to Madelyn's kitchen table, the scent of her still lingering on his skin and tormenting him. Making love with her had been a mistake. He'd thought it would sate him, but now that he'd tasted her, touched her, felt her body join with his, he couldn't shake the need for her.

He checked his watch—too late to call Ben. So he stretched out on the couch and closed his eyes. He dozed for a few hours, but woke with a start, adrenaline pumping through him. He retrieved his duffel bag from his car and hurriedly showered in the downstairs bath, not wanting to disturb Madelyn and Sara.

His mind spinning, he grabbed a pad and began to jot down the leads they had so far as he punched Ben's number.

"Hello. Camp here."

Caleb winced. Ben sounded half asleep.

"Ben, I'm sorry. I know it's early, but I think Madelyn's ex may have had something to do with her daughter's disappearance. Do you have a current address on him?"

"Hang on and let me pull up his file."

Caleb heard computer keys clicking, and continued to make his list, trying to pinpoint a connection. Emery had sold babies. Mansfield had helped arrange the adoptions.

Madelyn had a car accident—or had it been an accident?

Out of the couples who'd adopted through Emery, Pedderson was the most suspicious, and his beard matched Sara's description.

The last couple, the Smiths—probably a phony name—had disappeared, making them jump to the top of his suspect list.

Also, the two people who might have known that Cissy hadn't died had been murdered.

The killer was still at large. He'd sent Madelyn a threatening text and attacked her mother.

And he might not be working alone....

"Last address for Tim Andrews is a small town in the mountains of Tennessee," Ben said, interrupting his thoughts. "555 Trinity Lane, Bear's Landing."

Caleb jotted down the address, then Tim's name and drew a big question mark beside his name. "Anything else?"

Ben cleared his throat. "I ran his financials. Guy's in debt up to his eyeballs. He seems to have a pattern of big deposits, then equally large withdrawals. I'd say investments, but there's no evidence of a portfolio."

Son of a bitch. "Gambling," Caleb suggested.

"Sounds like it to me, too," Ben said.

Caleb glanced at the stairs, grateful Madelyn was still with Sara. "If the guy was in trouble five years ago, maybe he was desperate enough to sell his daughter to pay off his debt."

Ben whistled.

"Sara said something else disturbing. She said the man who killed her mother is her uncle." He paused. "See if any of the mothers or fathers on our list have brothers, then dig up everything you can on them. Maybe one of them has a police record or we'll find another connection."

"That'll take time, but I'm on it."

Caleb spotted one of Sara's sketches on the refrigerator. "Oh, and see if there are any greenhouses that specialize in sunflowers near Bear's Landing."

"Okay, hang on."

"I don't see any commercial greenhouses," Ben said a moment later. "That doesn't mean someone might not own a private one, but there are no wholesale ones in the area."

"It was a long shot," Caleb said, although he wanted to curse.

"Do you want me to ask Gage to send another agent to Andrews's place?"

"No," Caleb said. "I'm heading up there myself." He had a feeling Madelyn would insist on going, as well.

As much as he hated to put her through such an ordeal, they both needed to see her ex's face when they confronted him.

Sunlight shimmered through the blinds in Sara's room, but Madelyn had barely closed her eyes. Each time she did, images of her husband trading their baby for money taunted her.

She had to be wrong. Surely Tim wouldn't do something so horrible....

Madelyn slipped from bed and tiptoed to her room, then showered, closing her eyes and willing the images to fade, but they refused to go away.

She shampooed her hair, rinsed and dried off, then blew it dry and dressed in jeans and a loose sweater. She headed downstairs for coffee, wondering where Caleb was, if he'd slept on her sofa.

Their heated lovemaking the night before flashed back, and she inwardly groaned. That had been wonderful. Then Sara's cry had reminded her of the reason Caleb was there, that he'd be leaving as soon as they found her daughter.

The scent of coffee permeated the air, and Madelyn found Caleb in the kitchen with a mug, his face stony. No remnants of desire. No heated looks.

No good morning kiss or embrace or a hint that they would repeat it.

"Did you sleep?" he asked.

"Some." She poured herself a mug, aching to touch him again, but knowing she shouldn't. She had to put distance between them, couldn't let herself fantasize about a life with Caleb when she was certain the night before had only been sex for him. "You?"

He gave a nod. "I talked to Ben. I have an address for your ex. I'm heading to his place to talk to him."

Madelyn's stomach pitched, but she steeled herself. "Where is he?"

"A small town in the Smokies called Bear's Landing."

"I'm going with you."

Caleb didn't argue. He simply nodded. "I already talked to Gage. Leah and Ruby are expecting Sara."

Madelyn stared down into her coffee, tears threatening. "I'm going to owe her again."

"Leah and Gage are friends who want to help, Madelyn." Caleb placed both hands on her shoulders and massaged them. "So you don't owe anyone anything."

"I owed it to my daughters to protect them." She whirled around, anguish nearly suffocating her. "What if Tim did this, Caleb? What kind of mother am I if I didn't see what their father was capable of?"

"You are a wonderful mother," Caleb said gruffly. "And you trusted your husband. There's no crime in that."

Madelyn choked back a sob. "There is if he sold one of my children."

"We don't know that for sure," Caleb said. "But we are going to find out. Do you want me to get Sara?"

She sucked in a breath. "No, I need to get her dressed. While she has breakfast, I'll fill us some to-go mugs and we can take our coffee with us."

"Good idea. It's a long drive."

A half hour later, they drove to Leah's. "Did you have more bad dreams last night, Sara?" Caleb asked as he parked at Gage's.

She shook her head. "I think Cissy's sleeping."

He prayed the child was right, that her silence didn't mean something worse.

Madelyn walked Sara to the door, and Sara hugged her so tightly, Madelyn feared she wouldn't let her go. As much as she hated leaving Sara, she had to spare her the trauma ahead. Sara hadn't seen Tim in years; she wouldn't even recognize him. She certainly didn't need to watch her mother confront him with her suspicions.

"Come on, Sara," Ruby squealed. "Mommy made playdough for us!"

Sara smiled at Ruby and clasped her hand, then followed her to the kitchen.

Storm clouds gathered as Madelyn and Caleb left Sanctuary and headed toward Tennessee. Caleb concentrated on the road, and she concentrated on not falling apart.

Because with every mile that passed, her sense that Tim had lied to her and done the unspeakable mounted.

Four hours later, Caleb steered the Jeep up the winding road toward Bear's Landing. The sun had battled to make its way through the ominous clouds, the temperature dropping. Wind rattled trees, shaking leaves and sending them skittering to the ground, the shrill whistle of it roaring off the mountain like a siren screeching.

The small town of Bear's Landing was barely a blip on the map, a quaint little place with two stoplights, a couple of tourist shops, a diner and a gas station. A Native American reservation bordered the town with signs offering handmade crafts. Signs for a fishing lodge, waterfalls and camping pointed to a dirt road; another sign indicated a group of log homes built along the creek running along the mountain.

Madelyn gazed out the window, but he sensed she wasn't looking at the scenery, that she was contemplating what her husband might have done.

He spotted a sign for a place called Hog's Valley, then Trinity Lane, and turned left, then followed it along the creek. The graveled road ended at a split-level log house surrounded by natural woods. A deer grazed in the field to the side, the creek rippling behind the property.

Caleb scanned the drive and surrounding property in search of Andrews, his vehicle, even toys indicating that Tim might have actually taken custody of Cissy himself.

A shiny black pickup sat adjacent to the house. But he saw no sign of the man or any evidence of a child.

"This is where Tim lives?" Madelyn asked surprised.

"It's the address Ben gave me."

"Odd. Tim never seemed like the outdoors type." She reached for the door handle. "Then again, I obviously didn't know my husband at all, did I?"

"Some people are masters of deception," he said, hating the self-recriminations in her tone.

Instincts kicking in, Caleb checked his weapon as he exited the Jeep, then took Madelyn's arm. "We have to be careful. If he's on to us, he might be armed and dangerous."

"I wish I had that gun we talked about," Madelyn said. "I'd show him dangerous."

A tiny smile quirked at the corners of Caleb's mouth. He didn't blame her.

They slowly made their way up to the door, the wind beating at the porch rocking chair and sending it swinging back and forth as if a ghost was sitting in it. Dead ferns hung from the rail as if long forgotten, an empty beer can was tipped on its side by a hammock, a newspaper rattled in the breeze.

The paper was an old issue—the front-page story featuring the arrest of Dr. Emery. That event had obviously triggered panic among those involved in the illegal adoptions. Everyone had been scrambling to cover their butts.

And Nadine and Zimmerman were dead because of it.

Madelyn exhaled beside him, and he squeezed her arm, silently offering encouragement. He opened the screen door, then rapped the bear-paw door knocker.

Shadows from the storm clouds darkened the porch, the wind pounding the roof.

Caleb knocked again, then wielded his gun at the ready as he turned the knob. The door was locked so he removed a clip from his pocket and picked the lock.

The door swung open with a screech. He threw up a hand, silently commanding Madelyn to stay behind him.

Slowly he inched inside the house. The rooms were dark, the sound of a clock ticking in the silence. He scanned the foyer, then moved toward the open room spanning the back of the house, a large den with a stone fireplace that adjoined the kitchen. All rustic decor. A plain, beige rug. Brown sofa. Cheap paintings of deer and wildlife. A barrel-shaped lamp had been knocked on the floor, magazines scattered, another wooden chair overturned as if there had been some kind of trouble.

Caleb eased through the room, careful not to touch anything, then spotted a dark reddish-brown stain on the braided rug beneath the oak table.

A stain that looked like blood.

Dammit.

"Stay here, Madelyn. I'm going to check upstairs."

He hoped to hell he found Andrews alive so they could get some answers. Then he could have the pleasure of killing him.

But that blood wasn't a good sign. Tim Andrews might already be dead.

If he was, then who in the hell was behind all the murders?

Madelyn shuddered as she glanced across the room. Something bad had happened here. A fight.

Where was Tim?

Her gaze swept across the overturned chair, the broken lamp, then the bare furnishings, the lack of personal touches, the lack of warmth, and she realized Tim hadn't made a home here.

The cheap watercolors on the walls were probably from a discount store. There were no videos or CD's, no comfortable throw pillows, no sign of the man she'd known.

Except for the one framed photo on the mantle. Sara.

Had he been watching them?

She picked up the photograph, zeroing in on the details. Sara wore a red bathing suit, and she was standing in front of a kiddie pool in the backyard, her hair in pigtails.

Her breath caught.

Except Sara didn't have a red bathing suit. And that yard was not Madelyn's.

Her throat flooded with nausea and happiness and shock.

It wasn't Sara.

This was a picture of Cissy. The little girl she'd lost. The baby her husband had told her had died.

The extent of Tim's betrayal hit her like a fist in the gut. She doubled over, the pain and grief so intense her legs buckled and she collapsed on the floor, hugging the picture to her.

Tim had known where Cissy was all this time and hadn't told her....

Chapter 15

Caleb recognized the signs of a bachelor living in the house. No personal items. No warmth of a woman's touch. Basic black comforter and lack of pictures on the walls upstairs. There was also a desolate, lonely feel to the place as if it had been a self-imposed prison of sorts.

You should have been locked in a damn cell for what you've done, Andrews.

He quickly surveyed the two bedrooms and found them empty, the master bed unmade. But there was no blood or signs of a struggle upstairs.

He glanced around for a computer, hoping to glean information from it, but didn't find one. He dug in the man's dresser drawers searching for notes, a secret file, but came up empty, as well.

Suddenly a heart-wrenching sob echoed from downstairs, then another, and Caleb's heart constricted.

Madelyn.

Forgetting all else but her, he stormed down the steps. When he saw her kneeling on the floor, her anguish seeped into his soul.

Dear God, had she found something? Evidence that Cissy was dead?

Fear clawed at him as he slowly approached her. He stooped down to her level, terrified what that photo might reveal. Gently he stroked her arms, then pulled her to him, rocking her back and forth and rubbing slow circles around her back while she sobbed.

Several tense minutes passed while she purged her emotions, but he waited until her crying subsided before he spoke.

"Madelyn, honey, I'm so sorry," he said gruffly. "Talk to me. Tell me what's wrong."

Dragging in a cleansing breath, she lifted her face and showed him the photo. "It's Cissy," she whispered raggedly. "Not Sara. This is Cissy and it was taken recently."

Which meant that her damn husband had not only known her daughter had survived, but he'd known where she was all along.

His gaze flew toward the blood on the floor. So where was the bastard now?

Madelyn suddenly raced over to the built-in bookcases, flung open the doors and began to search inside.

"What are you doing?" Caleb asked.

"Looking for more pictures, a scrapbook, an address. Something that will give us a clue as to where Cissy and her adopted mother live." She heaved a breath. "Did you find anything upstairs?"

"No. No computer. Nothing about Cissy."

Caleb's phone jangled, so he connected the call.

"Caleb, it's Gage. Have you made it to Andrews's place?"

"Yeah. But he's not here, and I found blood." Caleb released a frustrated sigh, then lowered his voice. "Madelyn also found a photo of Cissy."

"She's alive?"

He angled his body away from Madelyn. "She was in the picture, and it looks as if it was taken recently."

Gage emitted a long-winded sigh. "He deserves to rot for this."

"I agree. Can you have the sheriff issue an APB for Andrews? And send word to the Tennessee authorities, too."

"I'll do it as soon as we hang up."

"Is Sara all right?"

"Yes, but I'm here with Ben, and we're on speakerphone. We may have a lead."

"Thank God. We need one. Did Brianna find something on the adoptions or through DFAS?"

"No, but Ben accessed incoming police reports and there's been a murder not too far from Bear's Landing. Woman with her throat slashed."

Caleb's adrenaline kicked in. "Did she have a child?"

"Yes, a daughter. Police report said they identified the woman as Danielle Smith."

"We were hunting for the Smiths." Caleb clicked his teeth. "What about the child?"

"No sign of her at the house. But I figured you'd want to check it out."

"Definitely." Caleb reached in his pocket for a pen and a notepad, then scribbled down the address. "Now see if you can find out the Smiths' real name. I think the woman's brother may be responsible for her death."

"I'm on it," Ben said. "Let us know what you find at the Smith house."

"Right." Caleb disconnected the call. "Madelyn," he said in a quiet tone.

She whirled around, then flung out her hands. "There's nothing else here. No photo albums. No letters or signs of where she is." She gestured toward the framed photo. "Why would he have that photo and nothing more?"

"I don't know," Caleb said honestly. "There's a lot I don't understand about your ex. Why he left you. How he could have abandoned his children."

Hurt flickered in her eyes. "I can't believe he knew where Cissy was all these years and let me believe she was dead."

Caleb moved toward her, wanting to comfort her, yet they didn't have time. He had a lead and they needed to act upon it. "He'll pay. I promise, Madelyn." He gently took her face and cupped it between his hands. "I know you're hurting, but Gage phoned. There's been a murder, a woman killed, not too far from here. We need to go."

"Oh, God, you think it's Cissy's adopted mother?"

"It's possible." He coaxed her toward the door. "Police said her name is Danielle Smith."

"Did they find a child?"

He shook his head. "No. The woman had a little girl, but she wasn't at the house."

Still there might be evidence confirming that this Smith woman had adopted Cissy. And some lead as to where the killer had taken her.

* * *

Fear and shock settled over Madelyn but she forced her mind to turn itself off. The horrible scenarios bombarding her were too painful to bear.

Caleb raced around the mountain, cutting through side roads and speeding around curves. The short drive felt like hours.

Ten minutes. Tim had lived *ten* damn minutes from their daughter and never told her. He'd watched Cissy grow up.

Had he shared birthdays with her and this woman? Had she called him Daddy?

And what had they told Cissy about her? Did Cissy think she had given her away?

She balled her hands into fists in her lap as they turned up a drive and climbed a hill which leveled off to an acre at the top offering a majestic view of the mountain. Two police cars were parked in front of the house, an ambulance and a black sedan beside them.

A white two-story house sat on the edge of the ridge, but to the left Madelyn spotted a greenhouse.

Her breath quickened. The sunflower greenhouse Sara had seen through Cissy. "This is it, Caleb. This is where Cissy has been living."

Caleb reached for his door handle. "Wait here. I'll talk to the sheriff."

"No way." Madelyn leaped from the Jeep and jogged up the hill to the house, but Caleb caught up with her.

"Remember, Madelyn, this woman has been murdered. The police are going to be suspicious of everyone until they catch the killer, so watch what you say."

Madelyn froze and stared at him, her lungs tightening. "You mean they'll think I killed her?"

"You have motive," he said in a low voice. "But thankfully, I can alibi you. Still, be careful."

Madelyn nodded, swallowing back a protest, then walked with Caleb to the front door. The uniformed officer guarding the entrance narrowed his eyes at them. "Deputy Holbrook," the man said. "Who are you and what are you doing here?"

Caleb flashed his ID. "I'm an investigator with GAI in Sanctuary, North Carolina, and we're looking into a missing child case," he explained. "Sheriff Gray is aware of our investigation and notified us there was a murder here. We believe the victim may be related to our case."

"Did you know the victim?" Deputy Holbrook asked.

"Not personally," Caleb said. "We think she may have adopted Mrs. Andrews's daughter."

The deputy spoke into his mike. "Sheriff, there's a couple here demanding to speak to you."

Voices from the back indicated the police, crime scene techs and probably a medical examiner were consulting, then footsteps sounded and a short, stocky man with wavy, brown hair appeared.

"Sheriff Dwight Haynes," the man said, looking back and forth between the two of them.

"Caleb Walker from GAI in Sanctuary, North Carolina, and this is Madelyn Andrews."

"What are you doing in Tennessee?"

Caleb explained about Cissy's disappearance. "I'm sure you're aware that a doctor at Sanctuary Hospital was arrested for kidnapping and arranging illegal adoptions?"

Sheriff Haynes nodded. "Yeah, I heard about the case."

"Mrs. Andrews was told that her baby died at birth," Caleb continued. "But recently we've uncovered evidence indicating she's alive, and we think your victim adopted her. She also might have been an accomplice in the baby's kidnapping."

The sheriff narrowed his eyes. "What led you to believe that?"

Caleb explained about Nadine Cotter's and Howard Zimmerman's deaths, the connection between phone calls, then the link with Madelyn's ex-husband.

Madelyn stood on tiptoe, struggling to see past the deputy and sheriff to the inside of the foyer. She wanted pictures, proof, anything to confirm that Cissy had actually lived in this house. She was starved to know what her life had been like, if she had friends, if she was…loved.

"Interesting story," the sheriff said. "We'll let you know what we find here."

Caleb refused to be dismissed so easily. "The victim's name was Danielle Smith, correct?"

Sheriff Haynes nodded.

"Smith was the name of one of the adopted couples on the list we're investigating."

"If you'd just let us look around," Madelyn cut in. "Maybe there are pictures of this woman and my daughter that will prove our theory."

"If you lost her when she was born, how would you even know what she looked like?" Haynes asked.

"She was an identical twin," Madelyn said, irritated. "Please, I think she may be in danger. I need to know if she was here."

"This is a crime scene," the sheriff said. "I'm sorry, but I can't allow you inside."

"Listen to me," Madelyn said, desperation tingeing her voice. "My other daughter Sara has a connection with her sister. She saw this woman being murdered."

"You're telling me that your child witnessed Ms. Smith's murder?" Sheriff Haynes asked sharply. "If so, where is she? We need to question her."

Perspiration beaded on Madelyn's neck. "She wasn't here at the time. I told you they have a connection, a psychic, twin connection," Madelyn said, then quickly realized by the skeptical expression on his face that he didn't believe her.

Instead he gave her a dismissive look, then addressed Caleb. "Mr. Walker, I suggest you take your client and leave. I'm investigating a murder, and I don't have time for these games." With that curt statement, he turned around and walked away.

"He has to let us in," Madelyn said, ready to plow her way through.

But Caleb pulled her back from the doorway. She pushed at him, but he gently grabbed her hands and urged her down the stairs. "We'll come back when they're gone, Madelyn. Then we'll search the inside. I promise."

Still Madelyn's heart ached and panic clawed at her as he escorted her to the Jeep. If Sara was right and the killer had put Cissy in the trunk of his car, there was no telling where he was now or what he intended to do with her.

Every second counted.

Sara plunged her paintbrush into the brown paint. Ruby was painting a beautiful sunset in red and yellow and orange.

But Sara's vision blurred, and suddenly she saw Cissy crying.

"Sara, I don't like it here."

"Where are you, Cissy?"

"I don't know. It's dark," she whispered.

Sara gripped the paintbrush tighter. "Tell me, so I can find you."

"He dragged me from the trunk into this old cabin," Cissy whispered. "But I can't move 'cause he tied me in the closet." She sniffled. "But I saw an old well house outside."

Sara's hand began to move, drawing a picture of the old wooden house. She closed her eyes for a minute, then she was in Cissy's mind. She saw the house, the dirty floor, the woods, the old well house.

There were long buildings on the hill beside the house, too. Long and narrow. Three of them. And they smelled like…poop.

Her hand shook as she opened her eyes and began to give them shape on the canvas.

Ruby walked over and looked at her painting. "That's good, Sara. Those must be chicken houses."

Sara added a wooden sign with a rooster etched on it. "It's where the mean man has my sister." She turned and ran to the kitchen. "Miss Leah, Miss Leah."

Leah stooped down and patted her shoulder. "What is it, honey?"

"I gots to call Mommy and Mr. Firewalker and tell them where Cissy is."

Chapter 16

Caleb drove to the small diner in town and ordered a late lunch, hoping the crime unit would finish with the house by the time they were done. Although truthfully it might take hours before they finished processing the place.

He scarfed down two burgers, but Madelyn barely touched her turkey sandwich. Her gaunt face disturbed him. "You should try to eat something to keep up your strength."

"I can't think about food." She traced a drop of water from her tea glass then glanced out the window at the snow that had started to fall. "Just look at the weather. It's getting colder, and the weatherman is predicting a blizzard."

Caleb covered her hand with his, searching for words to console her, but his cell phone buzzed. He checked the caller ID. Gage's home phone.

He quickly punched Connect. "Caleb speaking."

"Caleb, it's Leah. Sara needs to speak to her mother."

"Is everything okay?"

Madelyn tensed across from him, and he squeezed her hand.

"Yes, but she saw Cissy again and she needs to tell you where she is."

A sliver of alarm ran up Caleb's spine. "Put her on the phone."

A second later, Sara's tiny voice echoed over the line. "Mr. Firewalker?"

"Yes, Sara. Miss Leah said that you know where Cissy is."

Madelyn's eyes widened, and she gestured for him to hand her the phone, but he held up a finger silently asking her to wait.

"She's in an old cabin, but he tied her in the closet." Tears laced Sara's voice.

Damn. He forced himself not to react so as not to frighten Madelyn.

"Can you tell me more about the cabin?"

"There's a well house outside." Sara sniffled loudly. "And three chicken houses that smell like poop and a wood sign."

"That's good, Sara," Caleb said. "Anything else?"

"The sign has a picture of a rooster on it."

He frowned. Maybe it was an old chicken farm. Probably an abandoned one.

"Anything else, honey?"

Sara's shaky breath echoed back. "No. Does that help, Mr. Firewalker? Can you find Cissy now?"

"That is a huge help," Caleb assured her. "If you think of anything more, ask Miss Leah to call back."

"'Kay."

"Let me speak to her," Madelyn insisted.

"Sara, I'm going to have your mommy call back on her phone. I need to use mine to call my friends so we can track down those chicken houses."

He said goodbye, then looked up at Madelyn. "Sara described an old house with a well and chicken houses. Maybe Ben can search maps of the area and we can pinpoint a location."

He tossed some cash on the table to pay the bill, punching Ben's number as he strode toward the door. Madelyn hurried after him, dialing Sara.

"I'll start searching now," Ben said after Caleb had caught him up-to-date.

Caleb opened the door and let Madelyn go through, then they rushed through the snow to his Jeep. "Thanks. We're going back to the Smith woman's house to see if we can get inside this time. Maybe we'll find a lead there."

The snow began to thicken as he cranked the Jeep and drove from the diner, the wind howling. Madelyn was talking to Sara in a low voice, praising her for her help.

Unease settled in his gut. With the blizzard threatening and visibility poor, tracking anyone through the mountains was going to be nearly impossible.

But there was a little girl out there missing, a terrified little girl tied in a dark closet somewhere who needed him.

And nothing was going to stop him from finding her.

Madelyn stared at the snowstorm outside as the Jeep ate the miles to the Smith house, her heart thundering. What if this madman left Cissy out there in this cold?

No, she couldn't think like that. They'd come this far. They were going to find her.

Thankfully, the police and crime units had dispersed by the time they reached the house. She assumed the woman's body had been transported to the morgue for an autopsy.

"Where was Danielle Smith's husband?"

Caleb shrugged. "Good question. Maybe we'll find that answer as well as a clue to the killer's identity inside."

Caleb removed latex gloves again and shoved a pair in Madelyn's hands. "We're not supposed to be here, so wear these."

Nerves knotted her stomach as she stared at the yellow crime scene tape and signs warning them not to enter. Caleb motioned for her to follow him around back, and he found a window that wasn't locked. He climbed through it, then rushed and opened the back door for her.

Bile flooded her throat when she spotted the dark crimson stain on the white tile floor. There were also blood splatters on the sink and wall, the smell nauseating.

"Don't think about it," Caleb said matter-of-factly. "We need to hurry, Madelyn. Just look for notes, addresses, something that might tie the Smith woman to the adoptions."

But Madelyn barely heard him. Her gaze was fixed to the refrigerator where a crude child's drawing hung by a magnet. A drawing of twin blonde girls holding hands dancing in the midst of a sea of sunflowers.

A strangled sob caught in her throat, and she raced

over and snatched it. "God, Caleb, look. This is just like Sara's drawing."

Caleb's eyes widened, the realization that Cissy had lived here, that her connection with Sara was real, was undeniable.

Spurred by the sketch, Madelyn's adrenaline kicked in. She needed more, to see pictures of her lost child. To see what she'd been doing, what her life was like.

To see if Tim had been part of it.

Caleb began searching the kitchen desk and she took the drawers, racing from one to the other, hastily pushing through bills and grocery lists and random items. She found other drawings Cissy had made, some depicting herself alone, at the park, some with a woman who must have been Danielle Smith.

But none with her father.

Frantic for more, she rushed into the living area and scanned the room. Photos of Cissy chronicling her growth from infancy to present-day filled the wall. Tears burned Madelyn's throat as she saw the years of her missing daughter's life laid out in front of her. Cissy cradled in a pink blanket shortly after birth. Cissy learning to crawl. Her first step. Playing in the laundry basket. Splashing in a baby pool. Blowing bubbles in the bathtub. Learning to ride a tricycle.

Christmases and birthdays and other holidays—all photographed and honored, all ones she had missed.

The pain threatened to bring her to her knees. But she found something in those photos to hang on to, something to stop her from collapsing with utter grief. The young woman who had adopted Cissy looked at her with such love and adoration that Madelyn's heart swelled with gratitude.

Gratitude and anger.

That should have been her holding Cissy, feeding her, teaching her to ride a trike. Sharing birthdays and holidays and watching her play and grow with her twin.

Had Danielle Smith known she had robbed Cissy's birth mother of those treasured moments? Or had she been innocent? Simply a woman wanting a child and getting caught up in an adoption scheme she knew nothing about?

Caleb's voice jerked her from her emotional tirade. "Did you find anything?"

She gestured toward the photographs unable to speak.

A muscle ticked in Caleb's jaw as he scanned the wall of memories.

"Danielle's husband was killed in Iraq while they were waiting to adopt." Caleb showed her a photo he'd found in the kitchen desk. "Apparently he received an award. Died a hero."

And Danielle—had she died protecting Cissy?

"Madelyn, come on. I found a crude map I think the killer might have dropped. It could lead us to where he took Cissy."

Madelyn choked back the tears and took a deep breath. "Then let's go. Danielle Smith may have loved Cissy, but we're all my little girl has now."

Caleb was on the phone the moment they stepped out the door. "Ben, Gage, I found a map at the Smiths' house." He described the details to them and waited while Ben cross-checked it with the topographical maps online.

"There is an abandoned chicken farm near where

you're describing," Ben said, then gave him the coordinates. "Used to be called Rooster's."

"We're heading there now," Caleb said as he and Madelyn jogged to the Jeep and jumped in.

Caleb ended the call, then tore away from the house, gravel and snow spewing behind his wheels as he careened down the driveway.

"Do you know where this place is?" Madelyn asked.

"I know the general area," Caleb said. "We may have to park and hike in on foot."

Although the storm was growing thicker, the windchill dangerous. And the killer was armed.

Visibility was poor, slowing him down on the road, and tension thrummed in the car as he maneuvered along the mountain road. A half hour later, he found the turnoff. He veered left, then cursed as he spotted a fallen tree blocking the road.

"Dammit. We'll have to go on foot from here."

Madelyn buttoned her coat and yanked on a hat and gloves she retrieved from her pocket. "Then let's go."

Caleb tugged on gloves himself, then climbed out, checked to make sure he had an extra clip for his gun, then took Madelyn's hand and they began to hike. The storm swirled snow and leaves and twigs around them, branches breaking off as the blizzard gained momentum.

Trees swayed with the downfall, the snow so thick that their boots sank in the slush, but they continued to trudge, Caleb using his instincts to follow the road. Madelyn shivered, and he pulled her against him, helping her over stumps and through the thick slush. Animal life scurried for cover and to seek protection while the sun disappeared into the haze of white.

"What if she's out here?" Madelyn shouted over the roar of the wind.

"Sara said she was inside the house." He purposefully omitted the part about her being tied up in the closet fearing that would send Madelyn over the edge. And he needed her to be strong now.

Three miles in, and the storm intensified. Ahead, he spotted a cave and guided Madelyn to it. Maybe she could wait inside.

But a gunshot suddenly rent the air, skating near their heads. Madelyn screamed, and he grabbed her hand and ran toward the cave. Another bullet zinged toward them and Caleb shoved Madelyn down, crouching low as he tried to usher her to safety.

Just as they reached the cave and Madelyn ducked inside, someone jumped Caleb from behind. He felt a hard whack on his head, then struggled with the man, but his attacker slammed the butt of the gun against his head and stars spun in front of Caleb's eyes.

He must have blacked out because when he roused a moment later, he was lying in the snow, blood dripping in his eyes.

And a bearded man was holding a gun to Madelyn's head.

Chapter 17

Sheer terror seized Madelyn as Rayland Pedderson jammed the barrel of his gun into her temple. His fingers tightened around her neck, his grip steely and locking her body against his. The urge to kick and bite and fight him shot through her.

But one wrong move, and she would be dead.

Then her girls would be alone, with no one to love and care for them.

Forcing herself to remain calm took every ounce of restraint she possessed.

When she'd noticed the blood running down Caleb's head, she was terrified he was dead.

And she'd realized she really did love him. Heart-pounding, soul-deep love that could last a lifetime. What if she never got to tell him?

"You bitch, you couldn't leave it alone, could you?" Pedderson growled near her ear.

"No," Madelyn said between gritted teeth. "Cissy is my little girl. Why did you take her?"

"My sister wanted a child and you had two," he hissed. "Your husband thought you'd get over it and be happy with the baby you had."

The pain of Tim's betrayal knifed through her again. "But why did Tim sell our little girl?"

His fingers dug into her throat as he tried to drag her toward the woods. Snow pelted them, the brittle wind biting at her face. "Because the damn fool owed me money for some property he bought. Thought he'd develop it into some condos and make a fortune. But he spent that money gambling and owed me and his bookie. Hell, it was your damn husband who thought up the idea of sideswiping you to make you go into labor."

Madelyn had thought she couldn't be shocked anymore, but the realization that Tim had purposely been a part of her accident made her head reel.

At least Danielle's husband had died with honor. But Tim... "He sold our little girl for cash to pay off gambling debts?" Madelyn cried. "I'm going to kill him."

"Don't worry, I took care of him myself. He panicked in the end and wanted to call you. He even tried to get the girl back."

Tim was dead? She should be relieved, but she felt robbed of the chance to vent her anger and bitterness toward him.

"But Danielle was your sister. How could you kill her?" Madelyn asked, putting the pieces together in her mind.

"Damn idiot woman found out how we got Cissy and wanted to contact you. Said that little girl was psychic or something, that she kept talking about her twin. I warned her if she called you, she'd lose her kid."

Tears blurred Madelyn's eyes, trickling down and freezing on her cheeks. Poor Danielle. She'd obviously loved Cissy, but she'd still planned to do the right thing. Sara and Cissy were right. This man was a monster.

"Where's Cissy?" Madelyn asked. "Please let me have her back, and you can disappear. I don't care. I just want my daughter back."

"You hired a damn P.I.," Pedderson growled. "It's too late to make a deal."

"Please don't hurt Cissy," Madelyn pleaded. "She's just a child."

"I warned you," he mumbled, then a click sounded as he cocked the trigger. He was going to shoot her in cold blood.

A second later, a gunshot echoed, and she felt herself falling.

Falling, falling, falling...

Pedderson collapsed on her, blood soaking her shirt, his weight trapping her.

It took her a moment to realize she hadn't been shot. Pedderson had.

Sobbing with relief, she shoved at his chest, desperate to move him off her.

"Madelyn!" Then suddenly Caleb was there, yanking at Pedderson's beefy body.

"Madelyn, are you hit?"

He dragged the heavy man off her, then shoved his body to the side. Blood pooled from his chest, his eyes were open stark wide, his body limp.

She should feel pity, but she felt nothing for the man except a cold rage. Caleb had shot him straight in the heart.

"Are you hurt?" Caleb raked his hands over her arms and legs and body, searching for injuries.

She shook her head, still in shock, then he hugged her against his chest.

"Dammit. I thought I'd lost you." His voice was hoarse with emotion, his hands soothing. She didn't realize she was crying until he pulled back and wiped her cheeks with his thumbs.

"Tim sold Cissy to him for money," she said, choking on the words. "He sold our baby to pay off gambling debts."

He cradled her face between his hands. "I heard everything. I'm so sorry, Madelyn."

Tears streamed down her face. Snow pelted them. Blood was clotting in Caleb's hair, and she reached up to feel his wound, but he pushed her hand away.

"I'm fine. We have to find Cissy."

Panic threatened to immobilize her. "If she's out here alone, she'll never survive."

Determination hardened Caleb's face. "Sara said she's in a cabin," he said. "We'll follow Pedderson's tracks."

A surge of adrenaline shot through Madelyn, and she pushed to her feet. "Then let's go. We can't waste a minute."

Caleb led Madelyn through the woods, tracking Pedderson, although the snow was making it almost impossible to move quickly or spot his footfalls. But he had the GPS coordinates and an innate sense of direction that guided him along the way.

"Look over there!" Madelyn tugged away from him and ran toward a tree stump. He jogged after her and caught up with her just as she lifted a pink blanket from the ground.

"This is Cissy's," Madelyn cried. "She was holding it in one of the pictures."

"Let me hold the blanket for a moment." Caleb reached for the blanket. "Maybe I can get a vision from it." Madelyn shoved it in his hands, and he closed his eyes and concentrated, but nothing came. Cissy's connection was with her sister, not with him. He needed Sara here, but bringing her out in this storm would be crazy. Choppers would never make it.

They were on their own.

He grabbed Madelyn's hand. "Come on, I think the cabin's close to here." Caleb pointed to the right.

Madelyn tucked the blanket beneath her arm, and they slogged through the snow, running as fast as they could. Wind and snow pummeled them, but they climbed over tree stumps and wove through the woods following the stream until they spotted a small, brown structure nestled on the hill.

"There it is!" Caleb shouted over the howling wind.

Together they ran toward the cabin, heaving for breath as they stumbled to the entrance. Caleb shoved at the door and entered first, still on guard in case Pedderson had had an accomplice.

Madelyn froze, her body going rigid. "Tim, you rotten, lying bastard."

Caleb clenched his jaw at the sight of the man slumped on the floor. Blood soaked his shirt and his body lay at an odd angle.

Caleb kicked at the man's feet to see if he was still alive. Not that he cared. Except he might know where his daughter was.

Andrews groaned and opened his eyes, although they were half-slitted and dull as if he was struggling for air.

"You jerk, how could you sell my baby?" Madelyn dropped to her knees and shook him. "Where's Cissy?"

Caleb scanned the room, found the closet and flung the door open, but Cissy wasn't inside. Dammit!

"Where is she?" Madelyn jerked Tim so hard his head flopped back. "What did you do with our little girl?"

"So sorry," Tim muttered on another groan. "Never meant for this to happen."

"What? You didn't intend to get caught?" Caleb barked.

"Not for Cissy to get hurt," he said in a hoarse whisper. "Tried to get her, stop Pedderson, save her."

Madelyn slapped his jaw. "Did he hurt her? Where is she now?"

Tears choked the man, and he coughed, pressing his hand over his bloody chest. "She ran outside... Thought he was coming back for her... Find her...find her, Mad..."

His voice trailed off and he coughed again.

Caleb removed his gun and crammed it against Tim's temple. "Who else was in on this besides Pedderson and Emery?"

Tim's eyes widened, but he blinked as if he wasn't fazed by the gun. He knew he was going to die anyway.

"Mansfield," Tim croaked. "He handled everything...." He angled his head toward Madelyn. "He hit you with his car, Madelyn. He wanted the money...."

"That picture in your house," Madelyn said. "Have you been seeing Cissy all along?"

Tim shook his head. "No, I followed Danielle one day and saw Cissy. She never knew I took the picture...." Tim wheezed for a breath, his eyes bulged then rolled in his head, and his body went slack.

Caleb knelt and felt his pulse, but Tim had just drawn

his last breath. But at least he'd given them enough to hang Mansfield.

Madelyn was shaking violently, but she pushed to her feet and kicked his leg. "I hope you rot in hell."

Then she whirled around, eyes panicked. "Caleb, Cissy's out there somewhere. We have to find her."

Caleb's phone buzzed, and he connected the call.

"Caleb, I'm with Leah and the girls. Sara is upset. She said Cissy is crying and calling to her."

Sweat beaded on Caleb's neck. "Ask her where Cissy is."

He heard Sara crying in the background, Leah consoling her, Gage talking to her. Then Gage came back. "The chicken house," Gage said. "Cissy thought it was a greenhouse. She was looking for sunflowers, but it's empty and dark and she's hiding there."

"Thanks, Gage. Tell Sara she did great." He snapped the phone closed.

"What?" Madelyn clawed at his arms.

"The chicken house," Caleb said. "Cissy thought it was a greenhouse."

"The sunflowers," Madelyn whispered hoarsely. Then she took off running.

Madelyn dashed outside, her heart racing.

Caleb followed on her heels. Three rotting buildings sat to the right on the hill, the storm swirling snow in a blinding fog as they hurried toward them.

She held her breath as Caleb wrenched open the door to the first one, then stepped inside. It was dark and reeked of chicken feces, but it was empty. They hurried to the second one, the snow pulling at her boots as she waded through the downfall.

Frantic, she shoved tree limbs out of the way to make

a path. The rusty door screeched open, the building dark, the stench of chickens lingering in the air. Dirt and straw snapped as Caleb stepped inside, scanning the interior.

Old tools had been stored inside, a wheelbarrow filled with junk, a lawnmower, bags of feed and gardening supplies.

"Cissy," Madelyn called. "Cissy, we're here to save you, honey."

"Sara sent us," Caleb said. "She wants us to bring you home."

Madelyn inched forward, searching behind supplies while Caleb checked the wheelbarrow.

"Cissy," Madelyn said softly. "I'm Sara's mommy. She told me about the sunflowers. She draws them just like you do."

"I know you're scared, Cissy," Caleb said, walking toward the far end. "But the bad man is gone now. We took care of him and he can't hurt you anymore."

Madelyn thought she detected a movement behind the bags of feed to the right and slowly crept toward it. "Sara wants to play with you, Cissy. She heard you ask her for help, and she wants us to bring you there to see her."

A muffled sound reverberated from the corner behind the feed, and Madelyn's heart raced. But she forced herself to tread slowly, determined not to scare her daughter. Then she rounded the corner and spotted Cissy huddled on the floor with her arms around her knees, her little body trembling.

Tears thickened her throat. Cissy was terrified. She'd witnessed Danielle's murder. Danielle was the only mother she'd known.

And Pedderson had threatened her, stuffed her in his trunk and dragged her away from her home.

"Cissy," Madelyn whispered. "Look at me, sweetheart. I'm Sara's mommy and your birth mommy, too." There would be years to help her understand the truth.

Cissy slowly lifted her little head, her big eyes wide with the horrors of what had happened to her. "You're Sara's mommy?" she asked in a tinny voice.

Madelyn nodded, tears burning her eyes. "Yes. And yours, too. Sara and I got lost from you but that was a mistake. We've been looking for you for a long time, and we want you to come home with us."

Cissy scrunched her button nose, her eyes wary, her lower lip quivering. "I'm scared of the mean man."

Madelyn heard Caleb walk up behind her, his presence offering strength. But he kept his distance, giving them space.

"He's gone now, gone forever. He can't ever hurt you again," Madelyn said in a strained voice. Her heart swelled with love and longing, and she knelt beside Cissy and held out her arms. "Come on, sweetheart. Let's go meet your sister."

Cissy nodded slowly, then lifted her arms, and Madelyn pulled her up against her and hugged her little girl.

She finally had her missing daughter back.

And no one would ever separate them again.

Chapter 18

The next few hours passed in a blur as Caleb contacted the authorities. Tim Andrews's and Rayland Pedderson's bodies were both transported to the morgue. Caleb and Madelyn had given statements to the local sheriff, then Caleb drove Madelyn and Cissy back to Madelyn's.

Gage, Leah and Ruby met them there with Sara.

Caleb's heart clenched as he watched Sara vault from the car. "Cissy!"

Cissy clung to her blanket like a lifeline, but when she spotted Sara, her eyes lit up with a smile and she raced toward her. The girls flew into each other's arms, twirling and swinging each other around as if they'd been waiting for this moment for years.

And they had.

Ecstatic to have both girls safe and reunited, Madelyn's tears flowed freely. She even managed to laugh as she wiped them from her face.

"So Sara was right all along?" Gage asked.

Caleb nodded. "She and her twin have a special connection that saved Cissy's life."

"You saved them," Madelyn said, a look of gratitude warming her face.

He didn't want her gratitude. He wanted her love.

"The authorities caught Mansfield," Gage told them. "Judge revoked his bail, and he'll be going away for a long time."

Caleb sighed. But he'd caused so much damage to so many lives.

Gage and Leah said good-night, then Gage scooped up Ruby and carried her to their car. Caleb watched the happy family, the way Gage protected his pregnant wife, the way he adored his adopted daughter and realized that family was the one thing missing in his life.

The drive back to Sanctuary had been bittersweet. He was happy he'd reunited Madelyn with her daughter, but now the case was over, she no longer needed him.

He needed her though. When he'd seen that man holding the gun to her head, his life had flashed in vivid clarity. He had intended to build a life with Mara and his son.

But that was not to be.

He had been faithful, even loved Mara. Did that mean he couldn't love again?

He did love Madelyn, he realized. He loved her and her girls and he wanted a life with them.

But now was not the time to confess his feelings. Maybe it would never be time. Madelyn needed to be with her daughters, and he didn't have the right to intrude on the family reunion she'd been waiting a lifetime to have.

Besides, he had some things to think through now.

Afraid he would break down and ruin her home-coming with her children by admitting his feelings, he turned and headed back to his car.

Ten minutes later, he found himself standing in front of Mara's grave. Snow littered the grass and tombstone, adding an ethereal touch to the scene as Mara's spirit appeared in front of him, a golden glow shimmering amidst the pristine white.

"I saved them, Mara," he said. "I wish I could have saved you and our son, too."

Suddenly she moved toward him, and he felt a gentle brush of her lips against his cheek. Her image was fading even more, though there was something peaceful and beautiful about her now. "Be happy," she whispered against his ear. "Love the new woman you have found and build a family with them."

He shook himself, certain he had imagined her words, but when he glanced up she was floating away, her hand lifted in a wave, a smile on her face.

She knew he had fallen in love with Madelyn, and she was at peace, moving on into the light.

For a moment, he stood and watched, aching for her and their lost son, aching for Madelyn and her daughters and the life he wanted.

The one he wasn't sure he could have. Or that Madelyn wanted with him.

Madelyn was so excited about having her daughters together and Cissy home that she had barely slept. The only thing that would have made it more perfect was to have Caleb with her. To have him as a part of her family.

But he had his own life.

She woke to the sound of the girls giggling, then they rushed into her room and hopped on her bed. "Good morning, girls," Madelyn said with a beaming smile.

"Morning, Mommy," Sara sang.

Cissy looked a little more hesitant but crawled up and gave her a hug. "Morning."

Madelyn blinked back tears. She had assured Cissy the night before that it was okay that she'd loved her adopted mother, that she could talk about Danielle anytime. She'd also promised they'd take sunflowers to her grave and keep them there year-round.

Then Cissy had told her something disturbing, something she needed to share with Caleb. But first they had to see her mother.

Madelyn winked at the girls. "You know what we need to do today?"

Sara's eyes sparkled. "What?"

"Go see Gran." Madelyn glanced at Cissy, soaking in her features and trying not to let the bitterness over all she'd missed seep into her voice. Cissy was alive and here now. She had to cherish the future, not dwell on the past.

"We gots to get sunflowers for her," Sara said.

Cissy looped her arm through Sara's. "Yep, 'cause sunflowers are the bestest."

An hour later, Madelyn knocked on the door to her mother's unit and found her standing at the door waiting. Her heart overflowed with joy to see her mother standing, then she took a step and more tears flowed.

"Gran, this is Cissy," Sara said proudly.

Madelyn's mother beamed at Cissy and wiped at her own tears as she took the twins by the hands. "We need some girl time," she said and gave Madelyn a pointed look, then gestured toward the kitchen door.

When she glanced up, Caleb was standing in the doorway looking sheepish and wary and more handsome than any man had a right to be.

"Leave the girls with me for a bit, Madelyn. Caleb needs to talk to you."

Madelyn frowned. "I need to talk to him, too."

Her mother grinned. "Go on, then. Sara and I need to show Cissy how we decorate cookies."

"I can help?" Cissy asked.

"Of course." Madelyn's mother pulled her into a hug, and Caleb took Madelyn's hand and led her outside.

He was quiet as he drove, seemingly lost in thought, and her nerves skittered out of control. Then he parked at her house, and remained stony as they went inside.

"Now, what's going on with you, Caleb?" She tossed her jacket on a chair.

He shifted. "You first."

She took a deep breath. "Last night, Cissy talked some about what happened. She said she heard her mommy say something about other missing kids. That's when he killed her."

Caleb frowned. "You mean other phony adoptions?"

"I don't know." Madelyn sighed. "But it makes me wonder if something bigger was going on."

"We'll look into it," Caleb said.

"Is there some problem with my assuming custody of Cissy?"

He closed the distance between them, then gathered her hands in his. "God…no. I'm sorry. I didn't mean to frighten you."

She exhaled in relief. "Then what is it? Why were you at my mother's?"

"I needed to ask her something."

Madelyn frowned in confusion. "I don't understand."

He stroked her arms with his hands. "Just sit down and listen, please."

Madelyn allowed him to guide her to the sofa, then settled on the seat. He joined her, but anxiety lined his face.

"Come on, Caleb. What's going on?"

He sighed wearily, then looked at her, wrestling with his emotions. "You asked me about my family once and I clammed up."

Oh, God, he was married. That was the reason he'd acted so strange. The reason he'd never mentioned the night they'd made love.

She swallowed back the hurt and humiliation. She'd wanted him so badly. "You have a wife?"

He gripped her hands in his. "I had a wife," he said in a gruff voice. "And we were going to have a child, a son, but my wife died."

"Oh, Caleb." Madelyn heard the sorrow and guilt in his voice. "What happened?"

"She was shot by a man who was after me." He paused, gut wrenching. "I should have died instead of them."

No wonder he'd been so tormented when she'd probed into his past. "I'm so sorry."

He shrugged. "It was over three years ago, but I never got over their deaths. I blamed myself."

And he still loved his wife. How could he love Madelyn?

"It wasn't your fault," she said simply. "I'm sure she

knows that. That she'd want you to move on, to have a happy life."

He looked at her with such torment in his expression that she wanted to cradle him to her chest.

"I didn't believe that I deserved to have a family again," he said brokenly. "To have someone love me. To move on."

Anguish for him rippled through her. "But that's not true, Caleb. You're a wonderful man. Strong. Protective. Kind. Loving."

His gaze shot to hers and she smiled. "You are. I saw you with my girls." A blush slowly crept onto her face. "You're also the sexiest, most wonderful man I've ever known. The only man I've desperately wanted in my bed."

Heat flared in his eyes. "I love you, Madelyn. I think I fell in love with you the moment I saw you at GAI that first day."

Shock mingled with joy in her heart. "You did?"

He nodded. "I wanted you then, and I want you now. That's the reason I had to talk to your mother."

She struggled to follow his logic. "I don't understand."

"Since your father is not around, I needed to ask her permission to do this." He lowered himself to one knee, then pulled her hands in his.

Madelyn gaped at him, stunned. "Caleb?"

"Do you love me, Madelyn?"

Good Lord, did she? "Yes. Last night I thought my life was perfect. I had my girls together again, and we were safe. But then you weren't there, and it felt like a piece was missing, that you should have been with us, too."

A slow smile spread on his face, and he reached in his pocket and removed a diamond ring, the simple diamond surrounded by tiny, glittering stones. "Will you marry me, Madelyn, and let me be your husband and the father to your girls?"

Her heart burst with love. "Yes, Caleb. Of course, I'll marry you. I love you with all my heart." She leaned forward, then kissed him tenderly. "And I'd be proud for you to be a father to my girls and to any other little people that come along."

He threw his head back and chuckled, then picked her up and spun her around as he carried her to the bedroom. A second later, they'd stripped and lay curled in each other's arms. His hands and mouth and body loved her in only the way a true friend and lover could do. And when he joined his body with hers, she knew that their union would last forever.

* * * * *

The narrow mountain road ended at the edge of a rock cliff.
It wasn't as if Ford Cardwell had forgotten that. No, when
he saw where he was, he knew it was why he'd taken this
road and why he was going so fast as he approached the
sheer vertical drop to the rocks far below. It would have
been so easy to keep going, to put everything behind him,
to no longer feel pain.

Pine trees blurred past as the pickup roared down the
dirt road to the nothingness ahead. All he could see was
sky and more mountains off in the distance. Welcome back
to Montana. He'd thought coming home would help. He'd
thought he could forget everything and go back to being the
man he'd been.

His heart thundered as he saw the end of the road coming
up quickly. Too quickly. It was now or never.

The words sounded in his ears, his own when he was
young. He saw himself standing in the barn loft looking out
at the long drop to the pile of hay below. Jump or not jump.
It was now or never.

HIEXP0521

He was within yards of the cliff when his cell phone rang. He slammed on his brakes. An impulsive reaction to the ringing in his pocket? Or an instinctive desire to go on living?

The pickup slid to a dust-boiling stop, his front tires just inches from the end of the road. Heart in his throat, he looked out at the plunging drop in front of him.

His heart pounded harder. Just a few more moments—a few more inches—and he wouldn't have been able to stop in time.

His phone rang again. A sign? Or just a coincidence? He put the pickup in Reverse a little too hard and hit the gas pedal. The front tires were so close to the edge that for a moment he thought the tires wouldn't have purchase. Fishtailing backward, the truck spun away from the precipice.

Ford shifted into Park and, hands shaking, pulled out his still-ringing phone. As he did, he had a stray thought. How rare it used to be to get cell phone coverage here in the Gallatin Canyon of all places. Only a few years ago the call wouldn't have gone through.

Without checking to see who was calling, he answered it, his hand shaking as he did. He'd come so close to going over the cliff. Until the call had saved him.

"Hello?" He could hear noises in the background. *"Hello?"* He let out a bitter chuckle. A robocall had saved him at the last moment, he thought, chuckling to himself.

But his laughter died as he heard a bloodcurdling scream coming from his phone.

Don't miss
Trouble in Big Timber *by B.J. Daniels,*
available June 2021 wherever
Harlequin Intrigue books and ebooks are sold.

Harlequin.com

HIEXP0521